Praise for Johanna Bell

'A heartwarming story of women discovering their inner strength . . . I couldn't put it down'

Vicki Beeby, author of *The Ops Room Girls*

'This is a story that needed to be told . . . I love Johanna Bell from the bottom of my heart for giving a voice to the women who first made a way for me and countless others'

Penny Thorpe, bestselling author of *The Quality Street Girls*

'Filled with richly drawn characters that leap from the page, and a plot that's so well researched and well written you will believe you are in the thick of wartime . . . A must-read for all saga fans'

Fiona Ford, author of *Christmas at Liberty's*

'A lovely warm feeling about it and excellently written'

Maureen Lee, RNA award-winning author of *Dancing in the Dark*

'A heartening central message conveyed with verve and empathy that remains relevant to today's readers, both young and old'

Jenny Holmes, author of *The Spitfire Girls*

Johanna Bell is a freelance journalist living in Suffolk with her husband, their daughters and their dog. She developed a passion for learning about the wars after chatting to her granddad about his experiences in World War Two. She is the author of the Bobby Girls series, about the first policewomen in London during World War One, also published by Hodder & Stoughton. The first book in this series was *The Blitz Girls*.

To hear more from Johanna, follow her on Twitter: @JoBellAuthor

Hope for the Blitz Girls

Book Two in the Blitz Girls Series

JOHANNA BELL

HODDER &
STOUGHTON

First published in Great Britain in 2024 by Hodder & Stoughton Limited
An Hachette UK company

1

A CIP catalogue record for this title is available from the British Library

Paperback ISBN 978 1 399 70879 1
ebook ISBN 978 1 399 70881 4

Typeset in Plantin Light by Manipal Technologies Limited

Printed and bound in Great Britain by Clays Ltd, Elcograf S.p.A.

Hodder & Stoughton policy is to use papers that are natural, renewable and recyclable products and made from wood grown in sustainable forests. The logging and manufacturing processes are expected to conform to the environmental regulations of the country of origin.

Hodder & Stoughton Limited
Carmelite House
50 Victoria Embankment
London EC4Y 0DZ

www.hodder.co.uk

For Eileen/Aunty Lee

This one was always going to be for you.

Hope for the Blitz Girls

Prologue

London, October 1940

Peggy Miller's heart dropped to her stomach when she heard the thundering roar of plane engines in the distance. She checked up and down the street and was relieved to find no more stragglers – she and her fellow air raid warden, Dot Simmonds, had seen everyone who needed to use the public shelter safely there. The rest of the residents on their patch would be hunkering down in Anderson shelters in their gardens, or in their cellars or under-stair cupboards – while a growing number would be taking their chances by simply staying in their own beds.

'They're here already,' Dot shouted over the racket. When searchlights started illuminating the sky above them, highlighting the silver barrage balloons floating high over the city, the women knew for certain that London's nightly visitors were nearly upon them. Peggy grabbed Dot's arm and pulled her behind a low brick wall, where they both threw themselves onto the ground and covered their heads with their hands, braced anxiously, waiting to find out if the bombs were for their sector tonight.

The two women held their breath as the sickening whistle of a bomb falling let rip from above. It was so loud that it was difficult to tell just how close it was going to land. A low rumble followed – it sounded like an incendiary. More whistles came, but the women slowly got to their feet – they could tell from the sound of the planes continuing their journey that they were in the clear – for now. But Peggy and Dot watched in horror as another cluster of the bombs struck a row of houses a few streets over, sparking a mass of flames.

The houses weren't on their patch, but they immediately started running towards them, desperate not only to help whoever might be inside but also to put out the flames before the enemy could use them to guide them back and cause more damage with high explosive – HE – bombs.

When the women reached the terrace, there was already a group of people clutching sand buckets and stirrup pumps tackling the hissing blazes caused by the small devices lodging themselves in the buildings.

'A batch of them landed in my neighbour's house,' a woman shouted urgently, running up to Peggy and Dot. 'She's got kids in there!' They could see the flames through the window – they didn't have long to get the fire under control before the whole house went up and the family perished. Two more wardens arrived – likely the wardens who covered this sector, but there was no time for introductions.

'The bastards dropped a Molotov basket,' the first warden shouted over the noise from the anti-aircraft gunfire. 'At least fifty incendiaries landed on this street, and a few went to the next street along. A family of four lives in there,' he added, pointing at the burning building. The warden was tall and slim, but he slouched down to hide his height. 'Husband's off fighting and the wife squeezes into the cupboard under the stairs with the little ones during raids.' The group looked behind them and saw a messenger – the boy must only have been fifteen or sixteen – sitting on his bike in his Boys' Brigade uniform. Peggy stepped towards him as she rolled up her sleeves.

'We'll tackle the fire ourselves,' she explained. 'If we wait for a crew the house will be ashes by the time they get here. Can you get Control to send out an ambulance?' The boy was already starting to peddle away as she shouted after him: 'And let Victor at the Cook's Ground School post know two of his wardens are here – he can send for us if we're needed on our patch.'

'Thanks,' the tall warden said, smiling, as they all walked briskly towards the burning house.

'No use us sitting around drinking tea and leaving all the hard work to you, just because it's not part of our sector,' Peggy replied. She grabbed a stirrup pump and pointed the hose at the flames as Dot took charge of the pump.

'We'll need someone to keep the water bucket topped up!' Dot bellowed as they entered the house, spraying water into the hallway as they went. Flames were licking the walls, spreading out from the living room where the fire had started.

'We'll finish this – you get them out!' the male warden yelled as he and his colleague slowly made their way into the living room, manoeuvring their own stirrup pump between them, extinguishing the flames.

Peggy and Dot went straight to the stairs, covering their mouths with the sleeves of their overalls. The smoke was so thick they had to feel around for the cupboard while trying as hard as they could not to breathe in too much. Coughing, Dot found the handle and pulled the door open.

A young woman's head whipped up and stared at them, fear in her eyes. Two young children – a boy and a girl, cowered at her feet. As soon as the woman took in Dot's uniform, she gathered the children up and pushed them out of the cupboard.

'Keep low,' Dot ordered, and they all crouched and fled for the front door. Spilling out on to the street, all five of them coughed and spluttered their way from the house. They looked back and could see the fire was smaller now, but it was still burning. Then a familiar face appeared ahead of them, waving her arms frantically in the air, her curly hair bobbing up and down from underneath her tin hat with the movement.

'They sent Viv out,' Peggy said, sounding relieved. The two children were clinging to their mother, who looked ready to pass out. Peggy and Dot guided the family over to their friend, Vivian Howe – Viv to her friends; a paramedic and driver with the London Auxiliary Ambulance Service. Viv led them to her ambulance car, where her usual shift partner, Paul, was waiting.

'I'm terrified about keeping the children in London,' the woman said in between coughs. She took a few deep breaths on Viv's instruction before continuing. 'But they had such a miserable time in the countryside, and nothing was happening here, so I brought them back. Now they're going through this and it's all my fault. I just don't know what to do,' she added, bursting into tears.

The Germans had been bombing London every day – mostly at night – for nearly a month now.

'First of all, you can let us check you three over for smoke inhalation,' Viv said firmly as she and Paul helped the woman and her children into the back of the car. 'I don't want you two going back out there until you've been checked over, either,' she called back to Peggy and Dot. 'There's a flask of tea in the front, help yourselves.'

The two of them huddled together on the kerb, allowing the hot drink to warm their insides. They had quickly cooled down in the early October chill since leaving the burning building.

'Fire's out!' a man's voice bellowed, and the pair of them looked round to see the two male wardens emerging from the house. They staggered into the arms of another pair of waiting paramedics, both coughing violently.

'If anybody's got smoke inhalation, it's those two,' Dot commented. Silence fell between them.

'Everything seems so dark these days,' Peggy whispered, placing her cup on the floor and wrapping her arms around her knees.

'These attacks are relentless,' Dot replied, nodding her head in agreement.

'The dawn is coming. I can see it,' Viv's voice said in response. The two women looked up and saw her standing next to them – neither of them had noticed her approaching. She gestured to them to hand her the flask. 'You just need a little bit of hope to get you through the toughest times,' she added as she poured herself a cup of tea.

I

Dot pulled her jacket tighter across her body as she shivered on her walk home. The early morning air was chilly and foggy. She always felt it more after a busy night on patrol. The moment she stopped rushing around, when the physical labour ceased, and the fires were out, it could almost feel like a normal October morning in London. But then she would turn a corner and walk into a street that was still bustling with urgent activity as rescue workers continued their efforts to haul casualties free of the debris, or firefighters doused smouldering buildings with their hoses. Those people didn't get to slip back into their beds after the all-clear sounded like everybody else.

Dot had spent her fair share of early mornings engrossed in clear-up efforts, so she was grateful she hadn't been needed for any longer at the bomb site after Viv had checked her and Peggy over. The poor family they'd rescued from the fire had gone to stay with the woman's sister a few roads along. The rescue workers had told her she was lucky – the smoke damage was contained to the living room and hallway, so they wouldn't be homeless. But they had advised staying elsewhere if possible until the smoke had had time to clear. The woman was also lucky she had family nearby – the rest centres were overrun these days and people whose homes had been completely wiped out were understandably taking priority.

After helping the woman, who they discovered was called Sarah, and her children to her sister's house, Dot and Peggy had walked over to the public shelter of their sector – in the crypt at the Catholic Church of the Most Holy Redeemer, in Upper Cheyne Row. There, they had helped their colleagues look after those needing shelter until the all-clear had sounded. The shelter was back to full capacity now following swift repairs when it was struck by a bomb on Dot's first night as a warden three weeks before. They had worried people would stop using the place – nearly a hundred people had perished in the blast, including one of their own wardens. But it seemed the people of London understood they were taking their chances wherever they chose to sit out the raids – you were safer in a public or an Anderson shelter than you were on the street, of course, but neither was a guarantee of survival. A lot of people, worn down by the constant bombardments, were staying in their own beds while the bombs rained down around them – especially the older generation who found it difficult to get themselves up and out when the sirens went off in the middle of the night, and then couldn't get comfortable in a shelter. After the intense daylight attacks early on, the Luftwaffe had shifted their energies to mostly night-time raids lasting up to twelve hours. It seemed that part of the Nazis' strategy was sleep deprivation. Daytime raids, when they came, were mostly ignored now, unless the threat was on your doorstep. Londoners were determined to live their lives as normally as they could despite Hitler's best efforts. Mixed in with their fear was relief that the poison gas attacks everybody seemed to have been expecting hadn't materialised.

At the crypt last night, Dot and Peggy had assisted those who needed help back to their homes – all of them relieved to find they were still standing after another night of bombing. After that, the pair of them had gone back to their post at the school to fill out reports before going their separate ways.

Wandering past a group of people digging through a huge pile of rubble, Dot felt a pang of guilt; she always did. But she had done more than enough during this raid, and she was in desperate need of some rest. She would never walk by if it looked as if her fellow volunteers urgently needed her help – she had stopped many times on her way home to assist those in serious need. But Dot let out a sigh of relief when she made it to Viv's flat without any obstacles this morning.

She'd been staying with Viv since walking out on her husband, Tommy, and his battle-axe of a mother, two weeks before. Although, as it had turned out, Beryl wasn't quite the monster she had led Dot to believe she was. After speaking with her mother-in-law, Dot had discovered that Beryl had only been so mean to her during their time living together because, in her own strange way, she had been trying to protect her. Beryl knew her son was capable of awful things, and as much as she put up with him because he was her flesh and blood, she had been desperate to drive a wedge between him and Dot to make Dot leave – for her own good. Beryl couldn't bring herself to betray her son by being honest with Dot and warning her to leave him for her own safety, so she had bullied her instead. She'd hoped Dot would get so fed up with her she wouldn't be able to stand it.

While Dot could understand why Beryl had done what she'd done to a certain degree, she wasn't sure she was ready to forgive her yet. Beryl had apologised, and she'd even thrown Tommy out after seeing him strike Dot on the night she walked out. But Tommy was off fighting with the Royal Engineers again now, and Dot wasn't sure Beryl was strong enough to turn him away if he came home again, cap in hand. Maybe the two women could repair their relationship – but it would all depend on whether Beryl stood firm against Tommy when he inevitably came crawling back begging for forgiveness. Bullies like him always did. Dot had no idea what she was going to do with her life next, but the one thing she was certain of was that she would never go back to him. She knew that she was going to have to face her husband again – either when he was next on leave or once the war was finally over. But the thought terrified Dot so much that she couldn't really bear to confront it. She just wanted Tommy to go away and leave her to live her life in peace, but she wasn't foolish enough to believe he would do that. Besides, they would have to discuss a divorce before she could cut him out of her life for good. Her heart dropped at the thought. She was trying to come to terms with the fact that divorce was their only option. She felt a sense of shame at the idea – would she ever get another chance at happiness if other men viewed her as 'damaged goods'? But what choice did she have? She knew a lot of women stayed in unhappy marriages to avoid the stigma of being a divorcee. That wasn't for her. Dot knew that she deserved more than the way Tommy had treated her – she just needed to be brave enough to see this through.

Making her way into Viv's bedroom and getting undressed, Dot experienced the familiar anxiety she had started feeling whenever she thought about Tommy or her future. Viv had told Dot she was welcome to stay with her and her flatmate Jilly for as long as she needed. As lovely as it was to be living with two such wonderful women, especially given what she had put up with at home over the last few years, she was becoming ever more aware that she needed a home of her own, and to be able to support herself. Walking out on Tommy had been a bold move and she was proud that she'd had the strength to do it. But now she'd licked her wounds and enjoyed some respite, it really was time she stood on her own two feet. She couldn't live off Viv's generosity forever.

Dot crept to the bathroom to have a wash, conscious of not disturbing Jilly's precious final hour or so of sleep between the end of the raid and getting up for work at the rest centre she volunteered at. Dot normally slept on the sofa, but when Viv was away she let her use her bed. Viv had gone straight from the Danvers Street Ambulance Station at the end of her shift to visit her sweetheart William in Sussex this morning, so Dot was looking forward to sleeping in her friend's bed as soon as she had cleaned off the smoke and rubble from the previous evening. That was another reason she needed a place of her own – a permanent bed to sleep in.

Turning the tap on, Dot laughed quietly to herself when she remembered Beryl inviting her to move back in with her now Tommy was out of the picture. Dot would rather take her chances sleeping on the streets than live under the same roof as her again. Especially when she didn't trust Beryl not to let her son back in at the first opportunity.

Dot had no family to turn to – she'd lost her mother when she was just a teenager, and her father had passed away a few months after her wedding to Tommy. An only child, just like both of her parents, she was the only Allen left now. She might have changed her name to Simmonds when she'd married Tommy – but she would always be an Allen in her heart. In moments like this she always felt grateful for her friendships with Peggy and Viv. The three of them might not have known each other for long, having met around the time the bombings started, but they had grown extremely close, and those two women were the nearest thing she had to family now.

Slipping into Viv's bed in her clean nightgown, Dot took a moment to think about her mother and father and how much she missed them both. On the one hand, she felt relieved that they weren't here to suffer through this war, and she also would have hated for them to bear witness to what she had gone through with Tommy. Her father had been completely charmed and besotted by the man – just as Dot had been, and she knew he would have been heartbroken to discover he had encouraged his only daughter into the arms of such a monster.

But on the other hand, it would've been so good to have the pair of them by her side while she dealt with everything that life was throwing at her right now. And she could have moved home with them. Dot's mother had always been such a comfort to her when she was facing tough times growing up, and her father had done an amazing job at taking on that responsibility after her death. She knew a lot of men struggled with emotions and feelings, but her father had always been able to embrace a softer side, and they had been closer for it. Dot realised now that she had been so consumed by dealing with life with Tommy and Beryl since her father's death that she hadn't fully appreciated just how much she missed him and her mother.

She thought back to happier times with them both as she started drifting off to sleep. The three of them had been so content together when Dot was growing up. She wondered if she would ever get the chance to build a happy family and experience that joy and love again. It was one of the things she hoped for most in her new life.

2

Vivian leaned forward in the driver's seat and concentrated hard on the road in front of her. She didn't normally see many other vehicles during her early morning drives to visit her sweetheart William, which was a relief as she found it difficult to navigate the roads with the dipped headlights that blackout rules stipulated.

She was thankful she had her own transport; her flatmate Jilly West came from a very wealthy family – their fathers had attended boarding school together and were now in politics together. When Jilly and Viv had moved into the family's weekend home in London just over a year ago, Jilly's father had insisted that his daughter take possession of his beloved SS Jaguar 100. A lot of cars had been requisitioned and repurposed to be used as ambulances – much like Viv's own ambulance vehicle. But Mr West was wealthy, and he had friends in high places, so his car had been left alone.

He wanted Jilly and Viv to be able to get away from the city as quickly as possible if the need ever arose. Of course, the car had sat parked on the street outside their apartment for months; non-essential car journeys were discouraged. Viv and Jilly walked or took public transport everywhere anyway, and they were both determined to stay in London to do their bit for as long as possible. But Jilly had insisted Viv use the car to go and visit William when he'd been injured in a plane crash a month ago. When Viv revealed that William had no family to look out for him during his recovery, Jilly had given her permission to take the vehicle to see him whenever she had the opportunity. Viv hadn't known much about William's upbringing before, but during long hours talking at his bedside he'd revealed his parents had died in a car accident when he was a child. His only surviving relative was an uncle who had shipped him off to boarding school to avoid having to care for him and the two of them hadn't had any contact for years.

Viv hadn't thought she'd be able to make many journeys to the hospital, seeing as fuel was being rationed. But Jilly's father had a secret stash of gasoline being kept at a nearby garage, which he'd gradually stowed away in the months leading up to the outbreak of war. Viv hadn't been surprised at the news – both their fathers had always been very resourceful. And she hadn't been pulled over and told off by anybody for taking to the road yet, so she planned on continuing until she was forced to stop. However, she felt a pang of guilt every time she got behind the wheel at the fact she wasn't donating the fuel to somebody more needy, or using the car to travel home and see her parents in Surrey. But William had completely stolen her heart and she was desperate to be by his side as much as possible while he recovered. Viv had written to her mother to tell her all about her sweetheart, and her mother had encouraged her to be by his side whenever she could while he was in hospital. Her father's job had kept him at home, so Viv took comfort in the fact her mother wasn't there alone, and she had promised to take William to visit them as soon as he was well enough.

The last time Viv had seen William before his fighter jet had been shot down, she had foolishly turned down his marriage proposal. She'd regretted it instantly, but there were things about her that he didn't know, and Viv had been worried he would see her differently if he did – maybe even wholly reject her. While there wasn't much chance of William finding out her secret any other way, she didn't feel it was fair to keep it from him if they were to take holy vows of marriage. In her mind, as her husband, he would need to know that she'd had an affair with a married man and then lost the resulting illegitimate baby after he'd abandoned her. How was she supposed to give herself fully to William if he didn't know and accept the real her?

When William had gone quiet on Viv after she refused his proposal, she'd assumed she had ruined things between them by knocking his pride. How ironic, she'd thought, that she'd lost him anyway. But then his friend and fellow RAF squadron member Johnny had tracked her down and revealed William was missing in action after his plane had been shot down while trying to protect the skies over southern England from the Luftwaffe. Shortly after, Johnny had visited again to tell her William had been found but that he was in a bad way.

Peggy and Dot had rallied round and accompanied Viv on the angst-filled journey to Sussex, where William was being treated at the Queen Victoria Hospital in East Grinstead. She'd already shared her past with the two women – a rare moment of vulnerability for somebody as guarded as Viv. Her friends had been supportive, convincing her that William would love her no matter what she'd been through before meeting him. Most importantly, they had assured her that she was wrong to feel ashamed of herself for being swept away by the married man who'd broken her heart.

Johnny had driven them all to Sussex that first time – he was able to stop off at the hospital on the way to the RAF base in Tangmere. The first time seeing William had been difficult. The right side of his face had been badly burned in the crash, and he'd still been covered in bandages. Viv had longed to hold his face in her hands and kiss it all better, but he was in so much pain she'd been too scared to touch him. He also had burns down the right side of his body, and his right leg had been crushed. The poor man had been trapped in the wreckage for hours before finally managing to haul himself free despite the pain. He'd crawled to a secluded farmhouse, dragging his bad leg, and then sought refuge with the kind family living there.

The women in the family had cared for William for a few days despite his repeated pleas for them to contact the military to report his location and get him transferred to a hospital. They'd insisted on keeping him there and he'd been too weak to do anything about it. Eventually, they had realised he needed more medical assistance than they could provide. William had later confessed to Viv that he got the impression the mother and her daughters were treating him as a replacement for the son they had lost at the start of the war. They'd even slipped up a few times and called him by the wrong name. William had felt sorry for the family, but it had been a huge relief when they'd finally taken him to a hospital. It turned out they'd got him there just in time. When he was transferred to the Queen Victoria, they'd discovered gangrene in one of his toes, which they'd had to amputate. Viv had expected William to be upset about the loss, but he'd been surprisingly upbeat.

'It could have been a lot worse,' he'd whispered. 'If it had been left any longer it would have spread, and I could have lost my foot or even my whole leg. I'm going to need rehab to help me start walking again anyway, so they can help me get used to walking without my toe while they're at it. It will be a good party trick,' he'd added, and she'd seen the hint of a smile emerging from the left side of his face before he'd grimaced in pain and looked away.

Viv hadn't stayed long on her first visit; William was still very weak, and the doctors were concerned about the length of time his burns had gone without proper treatment. But he had definitely brightened on her arrival, and she'd enjoyed the feel of her hand in his once more. She had taken the train back to London with Dot and Peggy – Johnny had had to report back to duty after dropping them at the hospital. She'd fought back tears for the whole journey; Vivian Howe wasn't the kind of woman who showed her emotions in public. But, back at her apartment, where Peggy had been bedding down at the time along with Dot after a bomb had hit her boarding house, Viv had felt comfortable enough with her friends to let it all out. She had already known she wanted to marry William. She'd known it from the moment she had turned down his proposal. She wished her shame at her past hadn't forced her to push him away. Almost losing him had cemented her desire to be his wife, and she found she couldn't stop the tears. She hated the Germans for what they had done to him, and for what they continued to do to the whole country and the men trying to defend it.

Viv had driven to see William as often as she could manage. The drive only took an hour or so in the early hours of the morning. She would creep into William's ward while he slept and fall asleep sitting in the chair beside him – her head rested on his chest and her hand on top of his. She was always apprehensive about driving over after a night shift and arriving outside of visiting hours but, so far, the nurses had turned a blind eye. They liked the servicemen to have visitors as often as possible because it boosted morale, and Viv wondered if they bent the rules for her more than they would have done for another visitor given her role as an ambulance driver.

She was always amazed at her ability to doze while sitting on the chair next to William's bed. One thing a lot of Londoners had developed during the recent nightly attacks was an ability to fall asleep just about anywhere, and in any position, such was their level of exhaustion. The Germans had been relentless in their efforts since the first big onslaught back in early September – the night most people now referred to as 'Black Saturday'. The raids had continued every single day since – there hadn't been one 24-hour period without at least one alert.

Viv had once been so tired that she'd fallen asleep on the bathroom floor while getting ready for bed. The chair next to William's hospital bed was a luxury in her eyes. When William woke, they would spend precious time catching up and getting to know each other better before she had to rush off again in order to get back to London for her next shift. Viv knew she was head over heels for William the first time she'd slept in the chair next to his bed; she had never before gone to such great lengths to be able to spend just a few hours dozing next to somebody. She still couldn't quite believe that her life now revolved around these trips and her shifts as a London County Council ambulance driver. Before William's crash, she had used dancing at London clubs as a way of taking her mind off the scary state of the world and the things she witnessed on duty. Now, all she needed was some time by his side in order to reset and feel ready to get back out and face raids and their aftermath again.

Today's visit was different. Viv had the day off so she would be able to finally spend some proper time with William. She was full of anticipation as she parked up at the hospital and made her way along the dark, quiet corridors, making sure not to make any noise and wake any of the other patients.

The Queen Victoria Hospital was full of airmen who had been badly burned, just like William. It was one of four specialist Emergency Medical Service units established across the country to deal with burns casualties. Extra wooden army huts had been built there ahead of the breakout of the war, in anticipation of the large numbers of patients. There were three new wards on the site: Ward One was for dental and jaw injuries; Ward Two housed women and children who had been injured during air raids or had inherited conditions the London hospitals didn't have capacity to deal with; and Ward Three – where William was – was reserved for officers and the most severely injured service personnel. Plastic surgeon Archibald McIndoe had arrived from New Zealand the previous September, and Viv had heard how excited the medical world was about his pioneering techniques even before William had been injured. She was relieved now William had ended up in such good hands.

Viv had enjoyed a brief conversation with Dr McIndoe on her previous visit, where he'd been delighted to learn she was a member of the London Auxiliary Ambulance Service. Dr McIndoe was giving the patients saline baths to encourage the healing of their burns.

'I've realised that the men who crash into water are healing faster, so this seemed like the best way to help speed up the healing process,' he'd told her. He'd cautiously asked if Viv would like to wash William's face with a saline solution when his bandages were eventually taken off for redressing. She had been eager to do anything she could to help her sweetheart and agreed to try when she next came for a visit.

'I don't normally ask loved ones to do things like this. The sight of damaged skin can be too much for some. But, given your position—'

'Unfortunately, I'm used to seeing a lot worse,' Viv cut in so he wouldn't have to finish.

When Viv reached William's bed, she settled herself in her usual chair and started to doze off. When the familiar morning noises from the ward roused her, she looked up to see William staring down at her, the left side of his mouth raised up ever so slightly – the best he could do by way of a smile. But she could tell by the way his good eye sparkled that he was happy to see her. They hadn't talked about it, but Viv knew there must be a chance he could lose the sight in his damaged eye. She pushed the thought from her mind and rallied for William – he needed her to be positive.

'I don't have to rush off today. Which is lucky because Dr McIndoe asked me to wash your face before they put fresh bandages on.' She felt William's body stiffen.

'No,' he whispered.

'Why?' she asked, confused.

'No,' he said again, louder and firmer this time, which would have taken a lot for him to manage due to his injuries, the tightness of his skin as it healed, and the bandages around a lot of his face. He turned his head away from her and closed his undamaged eye.

'Darling, I want to help,' Viv whispered, taking his hand in hers, but he pulled back. His rejection felt like a stab to her heart.

'I don't want you to see it.'

Viv could barely hear William now; he was mumbling so quietly. She stood up and ran her fingers through what was left of his hair. He flinched when she first touched him, but then she felt him relax into it as she massaged her fingers around the side of his head. She leaned over to lay her head on the pillow next to his.

'I love you,' she whispered into his ear.

'You shouldn't have to see it,' he replied, his quiet voice breaking. Tears filled Viv's eyes as she realised what the problem was. William was ashamed of his injuries, and he was scared of Viv seeing the full extent of them. She saw a tear escape from his good eye, and she quickly kissed it away. 'You deserve better than a man covered in scars, laid up in hospital. They don't even know if I'll be able to walk properly again after this, let alone what my face will look like.' She'd suspected he'd been putting on a brave front so far. Now she knew she'd been right.

Viv's heart broke for William. She knew all too well what it was like to be ashamed of yourself and to fear the rejection of others. It was just what she felt about her affair. She was desperate to say something to him to make him feel better and help him understand that he had nothing to feel ashamed of. If she confessed her secret to him now, would it make him feel easier about his own insecurities? Could they cancel out each other's shame? How good she would feel to get it off her chest and have it all out in the open. And if he did reject her afterwards, then at least she would know once and for all, and she could get to work on healing her broken heart.

Viv's legs suddenly wobbled at the thought of revealing it all to William. This was it. She didn't want it hanging over them any longer. She could help William by putting herself at risk. She opened her mouth, but then she froze. She just couldn't bring herself to do it. William's shame was different to hers – his injuries were sustained in the course of a brave act. Her shame stemmed from something completely different – how could she ever think they could be compared? She was too much of a coward to confess to him here and now.

'None of that matters to me,' Viv said instead. She lifted her head and walked round to the other side of the bed, so William was forced to look into her eyes. 'I love you,' she almost shouted. The men in the surrounding beds were quietening down and starting to look over at them now but Viv didn't care.

'Shhhh,' William urged her, his eye darting around the room. A tiny giggle escaped his mouth, and Viv breathed a sigh of relief that she had him back on side.

'I'll shout it from the rooftops!' she declared, louder now, as she stood back, raising her arms in the air and spinning around. 'I love you, William Carter! And I will love all your scars!'

A man from a few beds down let out a whooping sound, and suddenly everybody around them was cheering and clapping. Viv was reassured to see the left side of William's mouth upturned in a smile as she moved back towards the bed. He grabbed her hand and squeezed it affectionately.

Once the ward had calmed down again, a nurse arrived with a bowl of saline solution and a sponge.

'We can do it another time,' Viv offered. She didn't want to rush William into anything, but she was also desperate to assure him that she loved him no matter what.

'I don't want to push you away,' he replied. He closed his eye as the nurse gently took the bandages off the right side of his face. He winced now and then, and Viv forced herself not to react as the red, tender, raw flesh was slowly unveiled. That side of his face didn't look like William anymore – it was a mash of flesh and ridges and blisters. Viv forced back a tear when she realised just how much pain William must still be in every day and what he must have gone through, stuck in the wreckage. Once the nurse left them, Viv set about sponging down William's burns with the saline. Despite her tenderness, he recoiled nearly every time the sponge touched him.

'It will get easier,' she told him.

'How bad is it?' he asked.

Viv stopped what she was doing and pulled back so she could look William in the eye. She wanted him to be confident she was telling him the truth and not just saying what she thought he wanted to hear. He still had a patch over his bad eye, so she could only look into his good one.

'I've seen worse,' Viv said casually with a shrug. She tried not to think about all the bodies she had witnessed being pulled from bomb sites over the last few weeks. As bad as William's injuries were, he really was one of the lucky ones. He closed his eye again as Viv got back to the job in hand, and he winced less and less as he got used to the feel of what she was doing. As she worked, Viv thought back to William's initial shame, and what he'd said about her deserving better. She hated that he felt that way, and she hoped she had managed to convince him he was wrong.

If only he knew the truth about her past, maybe he wouldn't feel so strongly that he didn't deserve her love. Viv felt guilty for not having had the strength to tell him everything in that moment. Her confession might even have made him feel better about his own worries. She was more in love with William than ever, and she knew she couldn't keep her past from him if they were going to move forward together. But she was just so frightened he would reject her because of that one foolish mistake. All she could do was hope that she could find the confidence to be honest with him one day soon, and that he would be strong enough to see past her previous failures.

3

Walking past the remains of her old boarding house, Peggy felt grief sweep over her. She had lost so many friends when the house had been hit by a bomb two weeks before. She hadn't even really had time to process what had happened – she seemed to be either working her volunteer role as an air raid warden, sleeping it off, or checking in on the refugees from Austria that she was responsible for. When she did get a bit of downtime, she liked to spend it with Viv and Dot if she could. Her two friends understood exactly what she was going through, and she found it easy to switch off and pretend none of it was real when she was with them.

Peggy knew she should probably try and take some time to deal with her losses, but she feared that if she stopped to confront them now then she might not ever come back from it – it would take over her whole being, swamping her and pulling her into a black hole she would never be able to climb out of. Every time she inched a bit closer – like right now – she quickly pulled herself back and forced the feelings bubbling to the surface back down as far as they would go. But she knew that one day they would boil over.

It wasn't just the friends she had lost when the boarding house was bombed – it was Lilli, too. Peggy had become firm friends with the Austrian refugee when she'd moved into the room next door to her. Poor Lilli had arrived in London with nothing, having lost her parents back home. She'd died when the crypt was struck by a bomb – and she had only gone there to shelter following Peggy's advice. The second Peggy started to think about the guilt she felt over Lilli's death her legs went weak, and she had to grab on to something to stop them from giving way beneath her.

Peggy took a deep breath now and continued shakily past the rubble and remains of her previous home. She had stayed at Viv's apartment for a few nights after Viv and Dot had rescued her and the luckiest of her fellow boarding-house residents from the wreckage. To look at the remains of the building now, she still couldn't believe so many of them had survived. When some rooms had opened up at the building on Royal Hospital Road that housed the refugees she was responsible for, she had moved quickly to secure accommodation for herself and as many of the other survivors as she could. Viv had waved her off with a bag full of her clothes. Viv had been careful to pick the subtlest outfits, which Peggy had noted and was grateful for. There was no way that she could pull off Viv's glam look and she didn't want to look foolish by trying.

She had learned about that the hard way during her school years. There had been a dance at the village hall back home in Petworth, West Sussex, when Peggy was a teenager and, desperate to fit in with the popular girls in her class, she had begged her mother to buy her a new outfit to wear. Peggy had never been a girly girl, and her dress sense had always been very reserved and plain – she liked to blend into the background. But the girls in her class had never really taken to her. They were all into pretty dresses and make-up and she found she didn't have much to say to them and naturally gravitated towards the boys. But once into her teenage years, Peggy felt an urge to be accepted by the girls and thought this dance would be the perfect chance.

Peggy's sister Joan warned her the dress she'd plumped for might be a little too much for the occasion, especially given the fact that their school friends had probably never seen Peggy in a dress before, but Peggy had been adamant it was perfect. She had regretted it as soon as she'd walked into the hall. Nobody said anything to her face, but she could see the group of popular girls she was so eager to be friends with huddled in the corner and whispering to each other, looking back at her every now then and giggling. She had bravely walked up to them to say hello, only for them to collectively give her the cold shoulder. As Peggy had walked to the other side of the hall, she'd heard one of them mutter the word 'mutton' to a chorus of laughter. She had gone straight home and shut herself in her bedroom, where she'd stuffed the dress to the back of her wardrobe and burst into tears. Joan had done her best to comfort Peggy and had tried to reassure her that the girls in her class were just mean and she shouldn't let them put her off dressing in prettier clothes if that's what she wanted to do. But the experience had triggered a complex in Peggy that she couldn't shake off to this day. Though she did own a few dresses now, they were all very plain and she never wore anything that would make her stand out. She certainly never went to dances where she would be expected to dress up. It was the reason she had shied away from joining Viv at her favourite haunt, Café de Paris, despite her friend's repeated invitations.

The rest of Peggy's old boarding-house friends were currently having to make do with clothes donated to the rest centres, but nobody minded – they were alive and nothing else mattered. Most of them were sharing rooms in the new place, but they were just grateful to have a roof over their heads, although they were all very aware of the fact that it might not be for long.

Peggy had ended up sharing a room with Mrs Martin – she had insisted on it, in fact. One of the oldest residents at their previous home, Mrs Martin was a widow following the first war, and she and Peggy had grown rather close since the bombing had started, despite a previous difference of opinion when it came to taking shelter during raids. Mrs Martin had always acted maternally towards Peggy and Lilli, and the younger woman had a lot of respect for her, knowing what she had lived through during the great war and having lost her husband to it. She found herself looking forward to getting back to her room to catch up with Mrs Martin, who always seemed to have a constant supply of tea and sugar despite the fact they were both being rationed.

'Where are you getting it all from?' Peggy had asked one morning when Mrs Martin presented her with her third cup of tea.

'I have my ways,' she'd replied with a wink. Peggy hadn't pushed it any further – she figured she was better off not knowing, but the thought of dear old Mrs Martin dabbling in the black market brought her out in a cold sweat. She looked so innocent with her frail frame, wiry hair and glasses. But she was certainly a feisty lady and, though Peggy was confident she could handle herself should the need arise, it didn't stop her worrying about her dealing with unsavoury characters or getting into trouble with the police. It was incredible what some people would do for a decent cup of tea.

Bedding down at the refugee house also had the added benefit of making it easier for Peggy to look after her charges. Now, instead of quickly dropping in every now and then, she could check on them every day and make sure they had everything they required. She was getting to know them all better, too, now she had more opportunity to sit round the kitchen table with them and just talk, rather than rushing in and doing a welfare check before dashing off again. She was learning more about their lives and needs. Peggy was beginning to realise that she liked to be needed – it was something she had missed since leaving her younger sisters behind in Petworth.

When Peggy made it to her room, she found Mrs Martin sitting in the armchair at the end of her bed, drinking a cup of tea and reading the newspaper. The rest of London was catching up on sleep following the raid before the day started properly, but Mrs Martin never went back to bed after a night in the shelter. To Peggy's relief, her roommate had agreed to use the public shelter at the nearby Royal Hospital since they had moved. People were nice to the refugees there, and the older woman hadn't taken any convincing at all despite her previous reluctance to use public shelters – the bomb at Bramerton Road had made sure of that. Watching her intently reading the news now, Peggy marvelled at Mrs Martin's ability to be so on the ball despite what was a long night with hardly any sleep. Peggy wondered if it was the caffeine from all the tea that she guzzled that kept her so alert. Taking a seat in the armchair at the end of her own bed, Peggy waited while Mrs Martin poured a cup of tea for her – their daily ritual.

'How was it, dear?' Mrs Martin asked once Peggy had warmed her hands on her drink. She closed her eyes and let the steam from the cup rise up and engulf her face before answering.

'It wasn't too bad this time. The only injuries were smoke inhalation.' Peggy winced as pain seared through her throat. She hadn't spoken much since leaving the crypt – she and Dot were normally too tired at the end of a shift to converse, and they often filled in all the report forms in silence back at base before going their separate ways. Theirs was a friendship that didn't need constant conversation, they were just content being in each other's company sometimes, and that was especially so when they were fraught after a raid. Peggy's throat had been sore at the crypt when she'd been speaking to residents taking shelter, but now she had spoken again it felt like she had swallowed broken glass. She thought back to Viv's warning that her symptoms might develop over the next twenty-four hours as a hoarse cough escaped her mouth.

'Including you?' Mrs Martin asked, looking into her eyes with concern. Intrigued, Peggy got out of her chair and checked her face in the mirror. They had a beautiful wooden dressing table at the end of the room that Mrs Martin had insisted on shoehorning in despite Peggy's protests that it left them with absolutely no room to move around in the tiny space. She had no idea where her roommate had acquired it from – they'd lost everything in the bomb blast, after all – but it was clearly very special to the older woman, so Peggy had relented. It wasn't as if she spent a great deal of time in the room, anyway – Mrs Martin was there the most. All Peggy did in there was drink tea and sleep. Peggy started when she caught sight of her reflection. Her face was black with soot and her eyes were red and watery.

'I think I need to clean up,' she whispered, instinctively placing her hand to her throat. She knew that if she went now, the shared bathroom would be free before everybody else started waking up.

'Drink your tea first, dear. It will help your throat and give you some energy to get yourself into the bath.' Peggy smiled at Mrs Martin in the mirror and sat back down again. The hot liquid soothed her throat, and she welcomed a second cup when her friend leaned in to pour it for her. After that, she finally felt able to speak, though only in a whisper. She told Mrs Martin about the incendiary bombs, the house fire and the family they rescued.

'Why didn't you wait for the fire service, dear? You could have been killed running into a burning building.'

'The house would have gone up, and taken the whole row with it, if we'd waited any longer. And we had to get them out before they perished.' Peggy could see that Mrs Martin didn't understand, but she knew in her heart that the woman would have done the same thing, back in her youth, if she had been in the same position. It was different when you were out there, faced with it, knowing there were people who needed help – especially children. Air raid wardens and rescue workers were all constantly putting themselves in danger to try and save others, never stopping to think about the consequences. They were fighting the war, too, only they were fighting it at home.

'Anyway, how were the little ones after all that?'

'Luckily the cupboard under the stairs where they had their shelter is also where their mum stores towels and sheets,' Peggy explained. 'She pushed as many as she could up against the gap under the door when she heard the roar of the flames, so they hadn't been exposed to much smoke when we got there. They'll be fine. The wardens who put the fire out were taken to hospital to be treated for smoke inhalation, though.'

'Those poor little things.' Mrs Martin sighed. 'Imagine having to live through all this at such a young age. I don't understand why so many parents are insisting on keeping their children in London now the bombing has started. I can understand why they brought them home during the phoney war, but surely they should have sent them off again once the attacks started. It's irresponsible to keep them here.' Mrs Martin shook her head. 'Do you know they're calling this the Blitz now?' she added, holding up her copy of the *Daily Express*.

'I'd heard that,' Peggy replied, nodding. 'Short for the German word *Blitzkrieg*, which means *lightning war*. It's certainly appropriate.' They both sat mulling the information over. Peggy could feel herself starting to drift off. She needed to get cleaned up and into bed but she felt the need to defend the mother, Sarah, after what Mrs Martin had said.

'Going back to what you said about the children,' she whispered, 'it's not that simple for some of the families. Elsie and Ted, the kids we rescued, had a terrible time when they were sent out to the countryside when war was declared. The woman they were sent to live with was awful to them. It sounds as if she didn't want any children coming to stay but she was made to put them up. The poor little things were treated like animals. I could see the fear in their eyes when Sarah was telling us about it. Sarah brought them back because we hadn't been attacked then and everybody started to believe it had all been an overreaction. Now, she's torn between sending them off again knowing they might be treated badly or keeping them here where they face the danger of the enemy.'

'Well, I can understand her dilemma,' Mrs Martin replied, 'but she must be able to see that the danger at home is a lot worse than a bit of a battle-axe giving them a hard time out in the countryside. I know what I'd rather put up with. Does she want to keep them happy or keep them alive?' They both fell silent as Mrs Martin's words sank in. Then she sighed. 'It's a shame the little loves couldn't have been placed with somebody like your mother.' She went back to reading her newspaper and Peggy knew the conversation was over. Mrs Martin had given her an idea, though. As she considered it, she felt herself nodding off again, and she found that she didn't have the energy to pull herself up and run a bath. The thought of giving a bit of hope to an anxious mother, and safety to her innocent children, saw a sense of peace sweeping over Peggy, and before long she was sleeping so soundly in the armchair that she didn't even stir when Mrs Martin placed a blanket over her.

4

Dot woke up later that day with an awful headache. She normally slept so much better in Viv's bed, but today she didn't feel rested at all, and her throat was unbearably sore. Realising her symptoms must be due to the smoke exposure, she got up slowly and ran a hot bath, hoping the steam might help her feel better. It normally did the trick. She was due on duty again in a few hours and she didn't want to clock in feeling under the weather – she needed to be in tip-top shape to help keep everybody safe. Viv would normally be back by now and she could ask her for medical advice – her training had been more in-depth than Dot's basic first-aid training for the ARP. But Viv wasn't working tonight so she was staying at the hospital to spend more time with William.

Dot's throat was still hoarse after her bath, her head still pounding as she made her way to the school to report for duty. She laughed to herself when she thought back to the time she'd had tonsillitis. She'd been working on the reception at her father's garage, and there had been no question of her presenting for work when she was so poorly. It hadn't been that long ago, but things had changed so much since then; here she was now, dragging herself to the school despite suffering the effects of smoke inhalation. She hadn't even considered not turning up for her shift. There were people volunteering with far worse ailments, such was the spirit of London under attack.

At her ARP base, at Cook's Ground School, Dot smiled when she spotted Bill in the canteen. She had been so worried about the reaction of the male wardens to another female volunteer when Peggy had encouraged her to sign up to do her bit, but Bill had been warm and welcoming towards her from the start. In fact, all her colleagues had – apart from Stan. Now that Stan had been kicked out following the discovery he'd been stealing from corpses and looting bomb sites, they had a good team at their post. Their senior warden Victor hadn't told anybody else why Stan had been dismissed. Stan was married to Victor's sister, and Victor wanted to save her the shame of people knowing what her husband had been up to. As far as Dot knew, Victor hadn't even told his sister what had happened.

Dot and Peggy were the only other wardens who knew the truth. They had been happy to keep Stan's crimes to themselves and were just relieved to see the back of him. Dot also feared that morale would be affected if the other wardens found out the truth. Nobody had seemed bothered when he'd stopped turning up for duty. It appeared that their colleagues had despised Stan just as much as the two women had done. Dot had been worried when Stan's replacement, Donald, had first arrived. His chubby physique, round belly and deep, booming laugh had immediately brought his predecessor to mind. But, thankfully, as soon as they'd started talking, she'd realised Donald was the complete opposite of the big bully Stan. Where Stan had seemed threatened by his female colleagues and went out of his way to put them down and intimidate them, Donald was impressed by the work Dot and Peggy were doing alongside the men. She knew that he worked at the docks with Bill and that he'd been umming and aahing over signing up to the ARP since the raids had started. He had finally decided to join the ranks after hearing from Bill that they were a warden down following Stan's unexpected departure.

Dot didn't know much more about her new colleague, but she was keen to get to know him, so was pleased to see him sitting next to Bill in the canteen. She checked the time – they still had twenty minutes until their shift started. That was more than enough time for a cup of tea and a natter.

'Ah, Dot – just in time,' Bill said as she approached them.

'Evening, Bill,' she replied. He got to his feet and pulled a chair out for her. She smiled her thanks as she sat down, taking in the warmth behind his eyes as he held eye contact. She hadn't spent a lot of time with Bill, but he was somebody who seemed to put everybody at ease. His rough hands from his work at the docks and weather-beaten skin were in stark contrast to his gentle persona.

'I was just getting the teas in,' he explained before walking off towards the kitchen.

'I hear you were busy last night,' Donald said to Dot.

'It wasn't too bad. Only one rescue – it was quite the fire, though. My throat's still suffering,' Dot replied quietly, rubbing the area. As Donald started talking about a big fire that he'd helped put out a few nights previously, Dot noticed the huge bags under his eyes. They made his eyes look tiny and sunken. The poor man looked exhausted. His chubby cheeks and double chin wobbled when he spoke. She wondered if he had a wife at home to look after him. Suddenly, Bill appeared with three steaming mugs of tea. Dot started. She'd been so engrossed in Donald's story that she had quite forgotten where she was.

'Is he boring you with all his stories from the first war?' Bill asked, winking at Donald cheekily. Bill must have been in his forties, and he looked younger than Donald by around twenty years. Dot found herself wondering if Bill had fought for the country the first time around, too.

'I hadn't quite got on to that,' Donald boomed. 'The poor girl has only just sat down. I was easing her in with a tale about that fire the other night.'

'Donald is quite the storyteller,' Bill explained light-heartedly.

'I was learning a lot,' Dot replied. 'I was so enthralled that I almost forgot where I was!'

'Don't inflate his ego,' Bill said, laughing as he gave the older man a friendly jab with his elbow.

As the three of them talked more, Dot heard that Donald had lost his wife to cancer a few years previously, and his grandchildren had been evacuated when war was declared. His daughter, who lived in north London, had almost brought the kids back when attacks had failed to materialise, but he had convinced her to keep them in the countryside a little longer and she was now relieved that she'd listened to her father. His son-in-law had signed up to defend the country two weeks after the war had started. Dot took a deep breath and finished her tea as Donald started reminiscing about his time in the Army. He was certainly a talker. She didn't think she had ever picked up so much about a person in the time it took to drink a cup of tea.

'So, young lady, what about you? Do you have a man who's off fighting Fritz?'

Dot instinctively opened her mouth to answer, then found that she didn't know what to say. It was two weeks since she'd walked out on Tommy, and only Beryl, Viv and

Peggy knew what she'd done. She hadn't had to tell anybody else about the new situation she found herself in yet, and she wasn't sure where to start.

'I did,' she said quietly.

'Oh, you poor love,' Donald cried.

Bill looked horrified. 'I had no idea, Dot. I'm so sorry,' he stuttered.

'No, no. He's not dead,' she replied, waving her hands frantically. She immediately regretted the action, realising it would be easier all-round if she just told everybody her husband had died in action. Could she take it back, and pretend she was a widow? No. There was a good chance Tommy would be back at some point – her body gave an involuntary shudder at the thought. Lying never got anybody anywhere. However, as comfortable as these two men made her feel, Dot certainly didn't feel like she should be sharing her marriage woes with them.

'It's a little . . . complicated,' she replied carefully.

'You don't need to explain yourself to us,' Bill said, jumping in. He looked concerned for her, and the thought that he cared warmed her heart a little.

'It's okay. I was married but I had to leave recently. I don't want to bore you with the details. But I do need to find a way to support myself soon. I'm staying with a friend, but I can't keep living off her charity.' Dot paused as the men digested what she had told them. She hoped she hadn't made them feel awkward with her honesty. 'I don't suppose they're taking on female workers at the docks?' she joked, trying to lighten the mood. Bill and Donald laughed, and Dot felt relief at the sight of their smiling, sympathetic faces.

'That might not work out for you, but you should talk to Victor if you need to start making some money,' Bill said.

'Victor?' Dot asked.

'He's got some full-time warden roles available.' Dot stared at him blankly. 'They come with a salary. Most of us already have full-time jobs so we volunteer part-time. It would be perfect for you, though, if you need to start supporting yourself. You're already such an asset to the sector, I'm confident Victor would jump at the chance to have you on duty more often.' Dot could feel herself blushing. She wasn't used to compliments – especially about her work, and especially coming from men. 'I'm not sure how much the pay is, but it'll be better than nothing – and you're here most of the time anyway!'

'I'll have a think about it. Thank you, Bill,' Dot replied. She wasn't sure she was up to full-time patrolling, but she was hardly in a position to be picky. And Bill was right – it would certainly be more practical than trying to work a separate job around her volunteering. Despite her reservations, she could feel excitement building. This could be exactly what she needed to get herself on her feet and on her way to starting her new Tommy-free life properly.

5

Peggy arrived at the school with an agenda.

'I want to visit Sarah and her children,' she informed Dot, who she'd found sitting in the canteen with Bill and the new warden, Donald.

'The woman from the fire last night?' Dot asked.

'Well done for getting them all out safely,' Bill chipped in, and Peggy smiled her thanks before answering Dot.

'Yes. I've had an idea about how I might be able to help the children. Elsie and Ted, I think their names were?'

'Yes, that's right. Shall we head off now, then? We can do our usual rounds and then hopefully we'll have time to track her down at her sister's house before the Jerries arrive.' Dot got to her feet, and they waved goodbye to Bill and Donald before checking in with their senior warden – Victor – and heading out to make sure everybody on their patch was adhering to the blackout regulations. They would also need to make a list of everybody's shelter plans for the evening. On the way, Dot told Peggy that Bill had suggested she apply to become a full-time warden.

'That's a brilliant idea!' Peggy exclaimed. 'I can't believe I didn't think of it myself. I know you're keen to get yourself back on your feet and gain some independence, and Victor would certainly benefit from having you on duty more often.' She rubbed the back of her neck, which was sore after her long sleep in the armchair. Peggy still couldn't believe she had slept there all morning and most of the afternoon. Mrs Martin had nudged her awake around the time she normally went downstairs for an early supper and to talk with the refugees in the house. She came round to the sounds of pots and pans clanging and cupboards closing. Which reminded her, she must make a note of all their requests to put forward at the next Committee of Women meeting. The group met regularly to discuss the needs of the refugees they were taking care of in the city. Most of them had adopted several houses each and become godmothers to the refugees living in them. Peggy had only taken on one because of her warden duties. Lilli had been her unofficial interpreter when she'd first started, and she was reminded of her loss every time she struggled through a conversation with one of her charges. But they were all getting a lot better at English, and she always managed to muddle through. One of the younger men – Ralf – had started helping out as his English improved, which Peggy was grateful for. She'd give anything to have Lilli back, though.

'Peggy?'

'Huh?' Peggy swung her head round to look at Dot, who was staring at her expectantly. She'd drifted off into her own little world, thinking about how much she missed Lilli. 'Sorry, what did you say?'

'I didn't think you were listening,' Dot replied lightly. A lot of people would have been offended by Peggy's lapse in attention, but her friend was so easy-going and understanding.

'I was just saying that I'm not sure I'm up to the job.'

'The warden job?' Dot nodded her head. 'But you're already doing it.'

'I know, but this is full-time, and I'd be getting paid.'

'So?'

'So, I don't know if I'm good enough for that.'

'Of course you are! Look at everything you've done so far! Not only have you rescued countless people and saved many, many lives, but you've managed to bring down a criminal.'

'Well, that was a joint effort,' Dot replied quietly, looking bashful.

'You caught Stan in the act and then you did everything you could to make sure Victor knew the truth. You even managed to get your god-awful mother-in-law to lend us a hand. After everything she put you through, you went to her for help because you knew it would save other people the misery and heartache Stan was causing with his crimes. You put that before your own feelings. I think if there's anyone who deserves to be paid for their dedication to helping others, then it's you, Dorothy Simmonds.'

Dot stopped walking suddenly, so Peggy paused too. The early evening light was just beginning to fade, but she could see her friend's eyes were watering.

'Thank you,' Dot whispered, before throwing her arms around Peggy.

'You don't need to thank me,' Peggy replied, returning the hug. 'I'm just speaking the truth.'

They ended their embrace and continued on their rounds. 'The pay for women is £2 3s 6d a week. I think men get £3 5s. That would be life-changing for you, Dot.'

'I could rent my own room,' she pondered out loud, before she knocked on a door. The light that had been escaping from under the front door vanished and they continued on their way.

'Lights out!' Peggy hollered when they approached a house that still had a glimmer of light shining through from under the living-room curtains. She banged on the window when they reached the property, and the light quickly disappeared.

'Sorry!' a little voice shouted from inside.

'Don't mention it, Mrs Adams,' she replied, rolling her eyes dramatically. The woman never turned her light out until they prompted her. Peggy was starting to wonder if she just enjoyed the regular interaction. 'I wish I could do this full-time,' Peggy said.

'Why don't you apply too?' Dot suggested, suddenly sounding chirpier. 'One of the reasons I'm feeling anxious about it is because I won't have you by my side for every patrol. We make such a good team and I'm worried I won't be able to do it without you.'

'Oh, if only I had the time,' Peggy sighed wistfully. 'I'm already neglecting the refugees; I was supposed to take some of the younger ones out this afternoon to help them look for work, but I slept through. And I missed the last committee meeting so they're all desperate for clothes and a whole host of other things I can't remember.' She shook her head. She was disappointed in herself for letting them down. They had all gone through so much and then they'd arrived here to bombings and danger, and the person who was supposed to be looking after them had taken her eye off the ball. 'As volunteer wardens, we're supposed to be on duty three nights a week, but I just can't stay away when the Germans are coming for the city so aggressively. I'll probably end up patrolling with you most of the time, anyway.'

'But then you should get paid for that.'

'Oh, I don't need the money. I've got my family supporting me. I don't think there are many full-time roles available and I wouldn't dream of taking the chance away from you. Please, apply. I'll never forgive you if you don't take this opportunity.'

'Okay, okay. I'll talk to Victor when we clock off later,' Dot said quietly. Peggy could tell she still felt nervous, but she also knew this would be a good thing for her friend. Dot had already grown so much as a person since signing up – taking on a full-time role and getting paid for what she was doing would only make her stronger. It would also make her less likely to fall for Tommy's charms again when he came back into the picture. They hadn't spoken about it yet, but Peggy knew from her aunty's experience that men like Tommy weren't likely to just disappear quietly. She had watched her aunty go back to her husband countless times after he'd beaten her black and blue. She'd only managed to get away for good when Peggy's father had stepped in and saved her the day her husband went too far and almost killed her. Peggy didn't want that for Dot so she had to do everything she could to make sure Dot was in the best possible position – financially as well as emotionally - to send him away when he inevitably came crawling back begging for her forgiveness.

It was completely dark by the time they tracked down Sarah at her sister's house. She opened the door cautiously, with Elsie gripping on to her leg.

'She was clingy after coming back from the countryside, but last night has made her even worse,' Sarah explained as she showed them into the living room. 'My sister works at one of the factories, so it's just me and the children here for the night.' Ted was playing with some wooden figures, pretending they were shooting at each other and fighting. 'He thinks it's all very exciting and he's in awe of the soldiers like his Daddy,' Sarah told them. 'The two of them couldn't be more different in how they feel about what's happening.'

'How old are they?' Peggy asked. They looked to be similar ages to her own young siblings.

'Ted is five and Elsie here is six,' she replied.

Elsie had curled up on Sarah's lap and stared out at Peggy and Dot with wide eyes. She looked exactly like her mother. They both had blond hair, blue eyes and a splattering of freckles on their cheeks, which Peggy could just about make out in the candlelight. Even their narrow noses appeared to be made from the same mould. Ted, on the other hand, had darker and thicker hair, and his eyes were blue, although he shared the same nose as his mother and sister.

'They're close in age to my younger sisters,' Peggy said, smiling as she pictured Lucy, Martha and Annie running around in the garden at home.

'Were your siblings evacuated?' Sarah asked. Her voice wobbled as she asked the question and Peggy could tell she was still struggling to know what to do for the best for her children.

'They already live in the countryside – our family home is in West Sussex,' Peggy explained. 'That's why we're here.' Sarah looked confused and her daughter suddenly burrowed her head further into her lap, clinging on to her mother even tighter. It was as if she could sense what was coming. 'I'd need to check with my mother first, but I can't see that it would be an issue – she loves having a house full of little ones and I know she would never turn down a child who needed help.' She paused for breath and noticed that Sarah was holding on to Elsie more tightly now. 'If you would feel comfortable with Elsie and Ted going to stay with my mother, then I can write to her as soon as my shift is over and ask her to take them in.' Relief flooded the other woman's face, and a tear ran down her cheek. 'My mother is so much fun,' Peggy was addressing the children now, who both looked apprehensive. 'Our house is so big that you can get lost in it, which makes it perfect for long afternoons playing hide and seek. I've got three younger sisters who are the kindest little girls you ever will meet, and there are a couple of older children staying with them at the moment – they're from London, too.'

'But it sounds as if she has a houseful already,' Sarah whispered, sounding defeated.

'Before war was declared, she also had me and my sister Joan there along with the little ones, as well as our two brothers, so she is positively rattling around in the house at the moment! In fact, she's two short of a full house. Honestly, there would be more than enough room for these two – and still room left over for more.'

'I . . . I don't know what to say. I was talking to my sister earlier about what to do, and I told her how kind you both had been last night. I thought at the time that it would be wonderful to have someone like you to send Elsie and Ted to – someone who I know would treat them properly and who I know they'd be happy with.'

'Well, I'm often told I'm a younger version of my mother,' Peggy replied, smiling. 'And I certainly get my compassion from her.'

Suddenly, Elsie burst into tears. 'I don't want to leave you again, Mama,' she wailed before burrowing her head into Sarah's bosom and sobbing loudly. Peggy looked over at

Ted, but he was still playing with his toys and seemed oblivious to his sister's upset.

'I know, but it will be different this time. I need you to be safe,' Sarah whispered into the little girl's ear. 'I can't keep you safe here. We were lucky last night. Next time we might not be.'

Elsie raised her head. 'But you'll still be here!' she shouted through tears. 'What if the Germans kill you!'

Ted's head whipped around, then. 'The Germans won't kill Mummy. Daddy is killing them all!' he cried, making more gun noises and waving his wooden figures around.

Peggy got up and sat herself down next to Sarah. She stroked Elsie's hair in the same way she had stroked her sister Lucy's hair as she'd sobbed before Peggy left for London at the start of the war. For a moment she was transported back to that moment and a wave of sadness swept over her. Peggy missed her family so much. She embraced the emotions briefly before switching her focus back to the family in front of her.

'Your mummy will be better able to protect herself from the bombs if she doesn't have to protect you and your brother, too,' she whispered gently. Elsie's sobbing stopped and she did a big sniff, but her head stayed buried in her mother's chest 'Once you're safe in the countryside, Mummy can go and live in one of the shelters if she wants to.' Peggy knew she shouldn't be lying to a child, but she didn't think this one small fib would do any harm. Elsie looked up at her mother, who nodded at her, smiling. Peggy knew she was putting on a brave face to reassure her daughter. Sarah knew as well as Peggy did that there was a high chance she would be dead by the time her children came back to London. But that was why it was so important they got to safety. The last thing any mother wanted was for her children to die with her when she could have kept them alive even if apart.

Peggy wondered if she would be able to be as strong as Sarah if she ever had children of her own. She couldn't imagine how difficult it would be to send them away knowing you might die before ever seeing them again. 'When you're a mum you will do anything to protect your children,' her own mother had told her once, and Peggy believed it now more than ever.

'Thank you so much,' Sarah whispered over Elsie's head as the youngster continued crying. 'I was terrified of sending them back knowing they might be treated badly again, but I knew they couldn't stay here. I thought I could keep them safe with me, but last night has shown me I was wrong. If your mother will have them, I'd be so relieved.'

'I'll write to her as soon as I get back to my room, and when I hear back, I'll arrange to take Elsie and Ted to her myself. It won't take them long to settle in, and I can promise you they'll be cared for and happy with my family.'

When the sirens started wailing a few hours later, Peggy felt a new sense of hope. The prospect of helping Sarah and her children had given her spirits a much-needed boost. But, as the first rumblings of enemy aircraft approached in the skies above, her good mood evaporated. Sarah had said herself that they might not again be as lucky as they had been the previous night – would she be able to get Elsie and Ted to safety before it was too late? All she could do was keep this hope alive.

6

Viv smiled as she sat opposite Dot and Peggy and brought them up to date on her relationship with William. She wasn't being completely honest – she had left out her angst over not yet revealing her past to him. She didn't see the point in dampening the mood amongst the women with her worries, and she already knew what her friends thought about it all anyway. They would try to reassure her that she had done nothing wrong, and that William would be able to see past it all if he was truly the man for her. They'd discussed it all at length when she had broken down and told them both about her previous affair a few weeks before.

Viv would work it out for herself in the end, and she knew her friends would be there for her if she needed any advice. For now, she wanted to put on a brave face and distract herself from all the worries in her head.

The women had met up at Lyon's Corner House on Coventry Street. It was becoming their regular haunt since Viv had treated Dot and Peggy to afternoon tea there the day after the crypt bomb. It had only been a matter of weeks since that terrible night, but it felt like a lifetime to Viv. So much had happened since: Dot had walked out on Tommy; they'd almost lost Peggy in the boarding house blast; they had gathered the evidence they needed to bring down Stan, and William had been shot down in his plane and then rescued. Alongside all of that, they had struggled through the German's persistent attacks on their city, doing everything they could to protect and help their fellow citizens.

'Are you all right, Viv?' Dot asked suddenly, concern etched on her face. Viv jumped at the sound of her name. She looked over at her friend in surprise. 'Yes. Sorry. I went off into my own little world there.' She paused to take a sip of her orangeade. 'I was just thinking about all the things that have happened since we first met up here.' She turned her attention to her meat patty as Peggy started talking.

'It's certainly been an eventful few weeks,' Peggy said, sighing. 'The Germans have been giving it to us hot and strong.'

Music started up beneath them – there was a band playing downstairs. Viv's feet started tapping involuntarily. She still hadn't made it along to any of her much-loved dances. She used to visit them as an escape – somewhere to dance her woes away. Once she was on the dancefloor, music blaring out around her, all she could focus on was moving her body in time to the beat and having fun. Nothing else mattered in that moment. She even used to pop in for an hour or so before starting a shift – especially if it meant a few snatched moments with William if he had made the journey to London on a night off.

But with all the travelling backwards and forwards to see her sweetheart in hospital, Viv just hadn't had enough time or energy to make it along to one recently. She had tried to convince Dot and Peggy to join her at a dance for one of their catch-ups but the two of them seemed to have fallen in love with Lyon's now, and they always insisted on meeting here. The duo preferred to get together somewhere where they could talk. While Viv could understand that – spending time with them both had taught her that she did benefit from talking over her problems – she still would have preferred to simply dance her cares away.

When she had opened up to Peggy and Dot about her past it had been the first time that she had ever done anything like that and it had brought them closer, but she still wasn't a natural at sharing. Viv wasn't sure why she found it so difficult. It just hadn't been something her family did when she was growing up. She certainly didn't have the close relationship with her mother that she knew Peggy had with hers. A stiff upper lip very much applied to the Howe household. It was one of the reasons she didn't write home very often; when you were keeping all your deepest thoughts and feelings to yourself, there wasn't much else to say. Her letter to her mother about William had been an exception – written when her emotions were heightened following her first visit to him at the hospital.

While Peggy and Dot started talking about a warden who had been injured during a rescue the previous evening, Viv made a mental note to make some time to get along to Café de Paris, her favourite place to bop, as soon as possible. Maybe she would try and make a night of it with Jilly. She hadn't seen her flatmate properly in so long, not to mention Ruth and Emily, who she had met through Jilly.

When the Nippy – a nickname for the servers at Lyon's teashops – came back to their table to ask if they wanted to order any more drinks, Viv was pulled out of her own thoughts again. She went for a cup of Horlicks. She didn't make a habit of drinking it, but she felt like she needed something comforting. Dot and Peggy both ordered more tea. They all watched as the waitress stopped at another table on her way to the kitchen. She leaned over and gave the smartly dressed customer a peck on the cheek. He whispered something into her ear and then gave her bottom a light pat before she continued on her way, giggling like a schoolgirl.

'I've heard it's the best place to pick up a husband at the moment,' Peggy said lightly. 'Mrs Martin read it in the paper. Apparently, every year hundreds of the Nippies marry men they've met while working.' She exhaled and looked around the room. 'Maybe I should give up the volunteering and come and work here.' Peggy laughed after making the comment, but Viv could hear the sadness she was trying to hide. It was time to stop focusing on her own worries and pay some attention to her friend.

'You're not really that desperate to find a husband, are you, Pegs?' she asked gently. 'You're only young – you can't even be twenty-five. You've got plenty of time to settle down and find a man.'

'It's not so much the man, if I'm honest. I've always longed to be a mother.'

'Oh, Peggy. I made that mistake,' Dot said, reaching out to take her hand. 'I was so blinded by my desire to make my own little family that I missed all the signs of Tommy's faults. I rushed into marrying him when I was around your age – I thought nobody else would want me and I'd end up leaving it too late to have children. Look where that got me – I'm back at square one and I've wasted all those years when I could have been out finding the right man.'

Viv felt for her friend. With everything going on with William, she hadn't really thought about the bigger implications of Dot's marriage breakdown. Of course Dot had imagined she'd have children with Tommy – she probably felt like her chance of having a family had been thrown away when she'd left him. Viv thought she had understood how difficult it had been for Dot to leave the marriage, but now she realised that it must have been a lot more difficult than she had first imagined.

'You might be a few years older than Peggy, but you're certainly not too old to find your Mr Right and start a family,' Viv cut in firmly. 'Besides, things are changing, ladies. That's not all we're good for these days – we've got the opportunity to make a difference in other ways and we're doing things our mothers and grandmothers never got the chance to do! So, if we take a little longer to settle down, there's no harm in that, is there?'

'It's okay for you – you've got William,' Peggy replied.

Viv's heart dropped. If only her friends knew how terrified she still was that she would lose him once he learned the truth about her. 'Yes, but I kissed an awful lot of frogs before finding him!' she retorted, trying to use humour to deflect the attention away from herself.

'Well, Tommy was certainly a frog. And that's putting it politely,' Dot said, laughing. 'Besides, I'm focusing on getting my independence back. Viv, I haven't seen you to tell you yet – I'm going to apply to become a full-time warden.'

'That's wonderful news!' Viv exclaimed. 'I think that deserves a toast,' she added, holding up her mug of Horlicks which had arrived while they were all talking, along with two cups of tea. The women toasted with their mugs before falling silent again. Looking over at her friends, Viv could see they were both still thinking about their uncertain futures. 'We just need to make it through the war,' she told them. 'There's hope for all of us at the end of it, I'm certain.' And she did believe it. Maybe it was all the death and destruction around that was dampening her thoughts about William and convincing her things wouldn't work out. She would probably feel more positive when she wasn't surrounded by constant doom and gloom.

'I've just always looked up to my parents and how they are together. I think I assumed that was what I would have, and I guess it feels as though the war has put a hold on it,' Peggy said thoughtfully. 'And, of course, it doesn't help that my favourite book is *Pride and Prejudice*. Every time I read it, it makes me desperate for a Mr Darcy of my own to come and sweep me off my feet. But you're right, Viv, better days are coming. We just need to make it through this. It's silly of me to be thinking about my lack of a love life when people are dying every day.'

'It's okay to want love. You're a hopeless romantic and there's nothing wrong with that. You shouldn't feel guilty about it,' Viv replied sympathetically. Desperate to lighten the mood, she added: 'They'd never give you a job here, anyway. I've heard that they like their Nippies to be able to handle crockery deftly. You broke two mugs during your stay with me – you'd be shown the door within hours!' The three of them broke out in laughter. Dot quickly caught her breath and chipped in: 'They also need to be able to add up, and we've both seen you take an hour to try and work out how to split the bill three ways.' Peggy rolled her eyes and tried to look offended, but she couldn't stop herself from laughing along with her friends.

Their cheery mood was cut short when the familiar wail of the banshee sounded. The three of them looked at each other, shrugged, and continued eating their food. Like many Londoners now, they were ignoring daytime raids unless the threat was nearby. Most people only sought shelter during the day if the Germans chose to drop their bombs in the immediate vicinity. If that happened, then the three of them would be out the door and helping people to shelters at the drop of a hat, but they were happy to stay put for now. The music from the floor below was cranked up a level to drown out the noise of the siren, and only a handful of customers left.

A few minutes after the siren had stopped, the three of them tensed up as they heard the approaching roar of plane engines. The music was still playing, but Viv could sense the apprehension from everybody around them. The Nippies all stopped what they were doing and stood still, and the other customers halted eating and talking. Viv braced herself as the enemy flew overhead, praying that the bombs weren't for this part of London today. The whole room breathed a sigh of relief when the noise passed over them and continued on to another part of the city. Suddenly, the teashop was bustling again, as if nothing had happened. Viv always felt guilty for the relief she felt in this situation; the planes hadn't unloaded here but they would certainly be dropping bombs elsewhere. The fact that she was safe meant there was immense danger unfolding elsewhere.

'So, when are you going to speak to Victor about the full-time position, Dot?' Peggy asked, looking intently at her friend. 'It's been days since we discussed it – I thought you would have had it all tied up by now.'

Viv felt bad that she lived with Dot and was only finding out her exciting news today. They were like ships passing in the night, what with the raids, their differing shifts, and her visits to William. But at least it meant that Dot was getting to use her bed regularly instead of trying to sleep on the sofa.

'I've tried. I promise I'm not putting it off. I know I was hesitant when we first spoke about it, but every time I've tried to talk to Victor, he's been busy – you know what it's like at the school. I'll try again this evening. I'm planning on getting there early and I'll stake out his office until he has time to talk to me if I have to.' She turned to Viv quickly, a look of concern on her face. 'It's been wonderful living with you, Viv, and I truly appreciate everything you're doing for me. But it's time for me to start supporting myself. You do understand, don't you?'

Viv smiled. Dot was always so worried about offending people.

'I understand,' she replied. 'It's only been a few weeks though, Dot. There's really no need for you to rush into renting anywhere just yet. Jilly and I love having you around and you're welcome for as long as you need. I don't want you to feel like you're being rushed and end up in a worse situation than you were before.'

'I'm not sure that's possible,' Dot replied, laughing sadly. 'And don't worry – I know you'd have me for as long as I need. It's just that I feel this urge to dust myself off and start afresh, and this is the first big step. I can't be sleeping on somebody's sofa when Tommy next comes around. I have to show him that I don't need him and I need to believe that myself – that's what will give me the confidence to send him away if he tries to get me back.'

'With any luck his rotten mother will write to him and tell him how well you're doing without him,' Viv said.

'I don't know,' Dot replied, sighing. 'I'd like to believe Beryl when she says she's washed her hands of her son, but I know how manipulative he can be. And a mother's love can withstand so much. That's one of the reasons I turned her down when she offered me my old room back.'

'That and the fact she was wretched to you for the whole time you lived there,' Viv replied.

'There were certainly a number of reasons why it wouldn't have worked. Anyway, speaking of mothers – have you heard back from yours, Peggy?' Peggy shook her head. 'I'm thinking of just taking the children to Petworth tomorrow anyway. The longer they stay in London, the longer they're at risk. I couldn't live with myself if something happened to them before I'd managed to get them to safety. I know my mother and I'm certain she won't turn them away once she knows the situation, even if she doesn't have room for them.'

Viv looked at her friend questioningly. 'Is this another big piece of news that I've missed over the last few days?' she asked. Once Peggy had filled her in on the plan for little Elsie and Ted, Viv knew just what to do. 'I've got the day off tomorrow and I'm off to see William again for a few hours. I'll drive you all to Petworth. Let's say lunchtime, so that we all get a chance to get some sleep after clocking off from whatever delights this evening's inevitable raid brings us.'

'Oh, Viv, I can't ask you to do that – it's at least an hour's drive from East Grinstead, then you'll have to turn around and drive for another hour back to the hospital.'

'I'll be upset if you don't let me do it,' Viv said firmly. 'The children will be frightened enough as it is without having to endure a long train journey. I'm taking you and that's the end of it.' Viv grinned when Peggy relented, on the condition that she stopped in at Peggy's family home for a cup of tea and a rest before driving back to the hospital. Now Viv was looking forward to her visit to William even more than usual. It would be nice to have some company on the journey for once, and she couldn't wait to meet Peggy's mother and sisters.

7

The afternoon raid didn't last long, and the all-clear had sounded by the time the three friends emerged back out on to Coventry Street. Dot and Viv said goodbye to Peggy and then got on a bus back to Viv's flat.

'Jilly's at work at the rest centre, so you could get your head down in her bed before getting ready for your shift later,' Viv offered.

Dot smiled gratefully. She was happy to catch up on sleep whenever she could at the minute, especially if there was a bed on offer.

'I'm proud of you, you know,' Viv added unexpectedly. 'There aren't many people who would be so concerned with getting themselves sorted so soon after what you've been through – especially not with this Blitz raging on daily. You're a stronger woman than you think.'

Dot was taken aback. She had never thought of herself as being strong – far from it after everything she had put up with from Tommy and Beryl.

'Thank you,' she whispered, tears welling in her eyes. She wanted to embrace Viv, it felt like the right thing to do in the moment, but she knew her friend wasn't one for showing affection like that.

'Now, go and get some rest,' Viv added cheerfully. She patted Dot lightly on the back and Dot couldn't help but smile; it wasn't quite a hug, but it would do.

Later that afternoon, feeling refreshed, Dot pulled on her overalls and made her way to the school to clock on for duty. No sooner had she marked her arrival than Peggy grabbed her arm and led her back out of the building.

'I wanted to speak to Victor,' Dot tried to protest, looking back behind her to see if she could spot their senior warden anywhere.

'We'll make sure you get a chance to do that before you go back to Viv's. Right now, we need to get over to the crypt. There's an unexploded bomb at the top of the road. Victor wants us to take over from the wardens on the previous shift and keep people away while the Army tries to move it.'

Dot felt her legs go weak. Out on the street, they passed Bill making his way into the school.

'Are you all right? You look like you've seen a ghost,' he remarked, looking at Dot with concern in his eyes as the pair of women rushed past him. Peggy ignored the comment and Dot held up her hand and gave him a thumbs-up. She had felt the colour drain from her face when Peggy had mentioned the unexploded bomb, but she'd hoped it wasn't so obvious. Why was Peggy acting so excited about this? An unexploded bomb was one of the scariest things that Dot could imagine. It was one thing being out on the streets during raids when you could duck and take shelter from falling missiles, but to go and stand next to one that could explode at any moment – that was truly terrifying.

Turning into Cheyne Row, Dot could see the wardens from the previous shift telling people to leave the area. She wanted to take their very sensible advice herself and go with them. But she was an air raid warden, and this was part of the role. If she wanted to be a full-time warden, then there would likely be more unexploded bombs to guard. Besides, it had become something of a patriotic duty not to show any sign of panic or distress in these kinds of situations. People in nearby houses didn't even evacuate on most occasions. She took a deep breath as they got closer to the scene.

'We're with the next shift – we can take it from here,' Peggy announced confidently.

The two male wardens turned around slowly and looked Dot and Peggy up and down. The taller of the two smirked and turned back away from them.

'It's all right, love. We'll wait for the proper wardens to arrive,' he said, laughing and folding his arms. His colleague looked across at him and chuckled, nodding his head and folding his arms, too, before turning his back on them. Suddenly, Dot's fear of the bomb was replaced with rage at the two men. It was like somebody had flicked a switch on her emotions. She prodded the first warden on the back. 'The only *proper* wardens I see around here are stood right behind you two nincompoops,' she said firmly. The blood rushed back to her face as she spoke. She felt Peggy's eyes on her and knew her friend would be shocked – standing up to men like this was normally her role while Dot stood quietly next to her. She kept her eyes focused on the wardens and mirrored their stance by folding her arms. Nervous energy surged through her body as she watched them both bristle at her retort.

'What did you call us?' the shorter of the two men asked, as they both turned around again to face her and Peggy. He was only a little bit taller than Dot, and he was tubby and looked old enough to be her grandfather.

'Being a man doesn't automatically make you more capable than I am. I've been through all the same training and I'm confident that I've done just as good a job, if not better, than you have.' Dot paused for breath and watched as the man narrowed his eyes at her. She had clearly riled him, but he was struggling with how to respond. 'And I'd hazard a guess that if something goes wrong with that bomb over there,' she added, pointing to the heap of metal that was poking out of the crater it had created, 'then I'm going to be able to get to safety a hell of a lot quicker than someone more than twice my age and three times my size.' She held eye contact with him, hoping that if he lashed out, one of the soldiers working on the bomb might step in to help her. She did her best to look strong and fearless despite the nerves she felt rushing around her body.

'You gonna let 'er talk to yer like that?' his colleague leaned in and asked him in a hushed tone while looking around them – probably to check if anybody was in earshot of the exchange.

The older man huffed and tutted, shaking his head. His hands were at his side now – clenched. 'I've got to get back to file my reports. These two ain't worth my time,' he replied through gritted teeth. He pushed past them, knocking Dot to the side. She'd been braced, though, so he didn't send her flying. The second warden rushed after him, looking confused.

'He's just a cowardly bully,' Dot whispered to herself as she straightened out her overalls.

'And – in answer to your question – she called you *nincompoops*!' Peggy yelled after the pair.

All of Dot's angst escaped from her body in the form of laughter. 'I can't believe I just did that,' she gasped when she'd got her breath back.

'You were amazing,' Peggy gushed. 'I don't know what came over you, but I bloody loved it. Well done!'

'I've been spending too much time with you,' Dot replied, giggling again. They quickly put their professional faces on to advise some passers-by to leave the area. Once the curious pedestrians had dispersed, Peggy looked over at Dot.

'You're going to make a great full-time warden,' she said. 'I can't believe how far you've come in such a short amount of time. You would never have spoken to a man like that when you started volunteering. You were still terrified of your mother-in-law when I first met you!'

'Standing up to Beryl was the first step, I think,' Dot replied, chuckling.

'Then you stuck up for me with Stan,' Peggy added proudly.

'I think those encounters gave me the confidence to finally stand up to Tommy too. And none of that would have happened if I hadn't joined the ARP.' Dot got lost in thought for a moment. She had a lot to thank her new role for – not to mention Peggy, who had encouraged her into it. Her mind wandered back to the encounter with the wardens. 'I probably went a bit over the top with those two, but the way they looked down on us because we're women just got to me. And his remark about us not being proper wardens . . . ' she tailed off, shaking her head. 'All I could think about was Tommy and his view on women and how they should be at home. I saw red.'

'It was no more than they deserved.'

'Do you think they'll say anything to Victor?' Dot suddenly panicked. What if her outburst ruined her chances of getting a full-time warden role?

'Oh, I shouldn't think so! You put them in their place – they'll be too embarrassed to mention anything to anybody else. And if Victor does hear about it then it will only raise you in his estimations. He needs firm wardens who will stand up for themselves and aren't afraid to upset people to keep them safe.'

Dot smiled again, grateful for Peggy's reassurance. They fell quiet and she took in the scene in front of them. The bomb that had dropped into the small green in front of 24 Cheyne Row was huge. It had landed just by the statue of Thomas Carlyle, the nineteenth-century Scottish writer and polymath who had once lived there. Dot only knew that because Peggy had filled her in on the history of the house and the statue when she had done her first patrol. A team of Scottish Royal Engineers was working on the device; they had constructed a pulley above the hole, started to excavate the space around the bomb and given it the nickname Ernestine. Dot felt a little lighter when she heard the name – it made the explosive seem a little less frightening, somehow.

'She's twenty feet down and she weighs around six hundred pounds. It'll take us a few days to get her out,' a soldier said as he walked towards Dot and Peggy. 'People have been coming over to take a look all day. No offence, but you're probably wasting your time standing here trying to keep the area clear. People aren't as frightened of things like this as they used to be – not when the threat of being blown to bits is following them around all day, every day.'

Dot looked around her and could see a small crowd of spectators had already appeared since she and Peggy had shifted their attention to the sapper.

'You've probably got a point,' Peggy replied. 'I expect the residents of the surrounding houses are refusing to budge, too?'

The soldier nodded his head. 'What will be, will be,' he shrugged before he walked back towards his team.

'At least the crypt isn't too close, in case the worst happens. Let's get on with our rounds, then,' Peggy proposed. 'We can send a messenger to let Victor know.'

As they checked on the houses on their patch and made a note of who was at home for the evening and who was planning on going to a public shelter when the sirens started, Peggy filled Dot in on her visit to Sarah and the children.

'I went straight there after leaving the Corner House,' she explained. 'I wanted to give them as much notice as possible, although I'm now wondering if it might have been better to just show up unannounced and whip Elsie and Ted away. That way, they wouldn't have had any time to get upset at the thought of leaving their mother.'

'Was it hard going?' Dot asked. She couldn't even begin to imagine how difficult it would have been to be parted from her mother at such a young age, let alone knowing how much danger she would be leaving her in.

'Elsie is devastated, but Ted thinks it's all one big adventure. Sarah was very calm, but I think she's holding it together for the children. She knows it's for the best, though.'

'Thank goodness she can have confidence that they're going to a good home this time around.'

'I'm so glad we're getting them out of here quickly. I'm ever so grateful to Viv for driving us over tomorrow. I wonder when Jilly's father's extra fuel will run out.'

Dot had forgotten about that. She wondered if Viv realised just how lucky she was to be able to drive and see William whenever she wanted to. Dot hadn't come from money, and she certainly hadn't married into it. Viv was her first friend from such a privileged background, and she was impressed that she had come to London to help with the war effort. One thing this conflict had taught her was that the country was good at pulling together when it was needed, and social hierarchy didn't matter a jot when people were uniting against the Germans. It was refreshing.

It ended up being a relatively quiet night in Chelsea. By the time the enemy planes flew overhead, Peggy, Dot and their fellow wardens had plenty of people settled in the crypt, and between them they could account for all the other residents on their patch. Thankfully, the Germans continued on past them again, and quite a few of the sheltering locals managed to sleep for the duration of the raid. When they got back to the school following the all-clear, it felt strange to Dot not to have any report forms to fill in and send to the control centre.

'I'll walk you to Victor's office before I go,' Peggy offered firmly.

Dot laughed. 'You've got a big day ahead of you – please go home and get to bed. I promise I will not leave this building until I've asked Victor to give me a full-time warden role.'

'Fine. But there'll be trouble if I get back from West Sussex and you're still a part-timer!'

'Off you go,' Dot replied, shooing her friend with her hand.

Peggy passed by Donald on her way out, and he called over to Dot.

'Victor wants to see you in his office, dear!' he announced loudly.

Peggy spun around. 'It's fate!' she shouted, before skipping out on to the street.

But Dot didn't feel as positive as Peggy did about Victor's request to speak to her. He only ever called in wardens when there was a problem. Her heart raced as she tried to work out what she could possibly have done wrong. Then it dropped to her stomach when she recalled her run-in with the wardens from the previous shift. They must have complained about her to Victor. She hung her head on her way to the office. This was not going to be the best time to make her request. Not only was she in trouble with Victor, but she'd have to answer to Peggy when she got back to London to find she was no further forward in her quest for paid work. Dot reached the office and took a deep breath before knocking on the door.

'Is that you, Dot?' Victor's voice called out. She poked her head around the door, and he motioned for her to come in. 'I hear you had a lot to say to a couple of the fellas on the day shift,' Victor said seriously as he looked down at some paperwork on the desk in front of him.

'I'm sorry about that, Victor. I just—'

'Why are you sorry?' Victor glanced up, a look of confusion on his face. Then he started laughing. 'My goodness, Dot, you look terrified! I haven't called you in here to tell you off! Your little exchange isn't even the reason I called you in. I heard about it on the grapevine, and it made me laugh – those two have always had ideas above their station so I was delighted to hear you'd put them in their place. I was also delighted to hear on the grapevine that you're looking for full-time work?'

'I am,' Dot whispered. What was going on? She'd been convinced she was in trouble. Bill must have mentioned their conversation to him.

'Well, I'd be lucky to have you patrolling our sector more often. Especially now I know you can handle yourself so well.' He looked up at her with a cheeky grin on his face, which she couldn't help but return. 'I'm just going over the paperwork now, but I wanted to be certain it was something you wanted?'

'It really is,' she said, trying hard to contain her excitement. What a turnaround! She'd been certain she'd messed it all up, but now Victor was offering her the role before she'd even had to ask!

'I've got a few new recruits lined up who you can show the ropes to. There's not much time for training days anymore.'

'I'd be glad to help,' she replied, beaming from ear to ear. She bounded out of the office, full of excitement and anticipation. This was the start of her new life! She looked up and saw Bill headed towards her. His face lit up.

'You look happy!' he exclaimed.

'Thank you!' Dot cried, and before she realised what she was doing, she'd thrown her arms around Bill and pulled him in for an embrace. She was overcome with gratitude for this kind man, who had clearly gone out of his way to help her. When he returned the gesture, squeezing her gently, Dot suddenly caught herself and stepped back. What was she doing? She didn't know Bill well enough to be showing him such affection, no matter what he'd done for her. Especially seeing as she was still technically a married woman.

'I'm so sorry,' she gushed, staring down at her feet and nervously pushing her hair behind her ear. 'I don't know what came over me there.' She laughed awkwardly. 'I was just talking to Victor, and he offered me the full-time position, and I got the impression that you'd put in a good word because I hadn't even told him I wanted to apply for it yet, and then I saw you and I felt so grateful . . . ' She was rambling now. She winced, embarrassed again. 'You must think me terribly unladylike,' she added sheepishly. Dot looked up to find him smiling down at her, his eyes glistening.

'I rather enjoyed it, if it's not ungentlemanly of me to say so.'

Dot felt her face flush crimson. It *had* felt rather wonderful to be enveloped in his strong arms, even if it was just for a fleeting moment. But she knew Bill was just being kind to save her blushes – he surely must think she was overly emotional and immature.

Dot cleared her throat. 'Well, I must thank you for your assistance. It is very much appreciated,' she said formally. Then she nodded her head and rushed past him, desperate to get out into the fresh air as soon as possible. If she'd stopped to look behind her before leaving, she would have seen Bill standing watching her flee, a big smile on his face.

8

As the car pulled into the driveway at her family home, Peggy breathed a sigh of relief. Poor little Elsie had been heartbroken to leave her mother. Peggy had been prepared for the goodbye to be a tough one, but she hadn't anticipated having to manhandle the child into the car while the little thing clawed at the door like an animal, desperate to escape. Elsie had eventually given in and then sobbed into Peggy's lap for the entire journey. Nothing Peggy said or did could soothe the youngster. Even Ted, who was normally so chipper and seemingly unaffected by anything going on around him, had been silent and subdued the whole way – his toy soldiers sitting neglected in the footwell.

Peggy had sat in the back, between the siblings, so that she could try and comfort Elsie. The little girl had fallen asleep with her head on Peggy's lap about ten minutes before they'd reached Petworth. Peggy had used the period of respite to think about how excited her family would be to see her. It had only been a few weeks since her last visit, and there was no way that her letter would have reached her mother already, so they certainly wouldn't be expecting her. Last time Peggy had been home, it had been because Lucy was concerned for their mother's health. But their mother had shrugged the young girl's concerns off, insisting she was simply suffering severe bouts of indigestion. Peggy had been bereft following Lilli's death and had used the time away from London to seek comfort from her mother. She was looking forward to arriving home on a much more positive note this time. When Viv stopped the engine, Peggy braced herself for Elsie to stir, but she didn't so much as flinch.

'Should we wake her?' Viv asked quietly from the driver's seat. No sooner had she asked the question than Peggy's little sisters had come bustling out of the front door. As they hurtled towards the car, laughing and shouting, Elsie started stirring.

'Is it Peggy?' Lucy shouted as they neared the vehicle. She glanced at Viv in the front, who was waving and laughing, before making her way to the passenger window at the back of the car.

'It is! It's Peggy!' she shrieked. She started banging on the window and jumping up and down, her brown curls bouncing along with her. 'Martha! Annie! Peggy's here!'

The two younger siblings arrived at her side and started jumping up and down next to their sister, desperate to get a look-in. As much as Peggy wanted to get out and scoop them all up into an embrace, she first needed to look after Elsie, who was now sitting up straight and looking outside cautiously. Peggy didn't want to rush her, but she wasn't sure how long she could hold her sisters off. Where was her mother? Viv got out of the car and went round to greet the girls. The three of them instantly calmed down and Peggy could hear Viv introducing herself.

'They're very noisy,' Elsie whispered, rubbing her eyes sleepily.

'I'm sorry they woke you. They're very excited to meet you. Would you like to get out and say hello?' Elsie nodded as a small smile appeared on her face. Peggy was filled with relief. It was the first time she had seen her smile all day. 'How about you, Ted? Do you want to say hello to your new friends?'

'My soldiers do!' he replied eagerly, reaching down to pick up the toys. The girls were so enthralled by Viv that they didn't even notice Peggy, Elsie and Ted getting out of the car.

'Your lips are so red,' Martha was saying in awe, reaching out to touch Viv's lips, which were always decked out in lipstick no matter the occasion – even an air raid.

'Pretty!' little Annie chipped in.

Peggy chuckled to herself. She and her mother were very plain women compared to Viv, and she realised that her sisters had probably never met anybody as glamorous as her friend. Hearing her laughter, the three of them spun around and then threw themselves at their big sister.

'Hello, my little darlings!' she exclaimed, enjoying the feel of them in her arms. 'I've made some new friends who I need you to look after.' As she introduced Elsie and Ted to her sisters, she kept looking back to the house for her mother. It seemed odd to her that her mother had allowed the girls to run out of the house on their own to greet a strange car. The group chatted loudly. Elsie had quickly perked up after learning that she was the same age as Lucy, and that she had a bed big enough for the two of them to share.

'I normally let Annie come in with me when she's had a bad dream, though, so we might have to cuddle up extra tight sometimes!' she was saying now.

Peggy looked over to the house again.

'Is everything all right?' Viv asked her.

Peggy shook her head. Her mother was still nowhere to be seen and she couldn't shake the terrible sense that something was wrong.

'Sarah and Phillip will be home from school soon, and then we can decide where everybody will be sleeping,' Lucy said authoritatively.

'Hang on a minute,' Peggy blustered, distracted from her worries by the statement. 'If Sarah and Phillip are at school, what are you doing at home?' She paused briefly before adding playfully, 'And, more importantly, who put you in charge, little Miss Bossy Boots?'

Lucy giggled cheekily and the rest of the children joined in.

'There are too many children to fit into the school since the kids from London came here,' Lucy explained. 'So, we use the school in the morning and the London lot go in the afternoon. I've finished school for today, silly pants!' She stuck her tongue out at Peggy and wiggled her hips from side to side.

Peggy raised her eyebrows and widened her eyes before reaching down and tickling her sister playfully while she squirmed and squealed. Everybody was giggling and Martha and Annie were begging for a turn when Elsie's voice spoke out above the happy noise.

'Our mummy's name is Sarah. Is that who you mean? Will she be here soon?' she asked hopefully.

Peggy's heart dropped – she had forgotten that one of the evacuees staying with her family was also called Sarah. She stopped tickling Lucy and crouched down in front of Elsie.

'We talked about this, darling. Your mummy needs to stay in London for now, but she'll be coming to visit you soon.'

'Sarah and Phillip's mummy and daddy were here at the weekend,' Lucy said encouragingly.

'Their daddy works in a hospital, so he doesn't have to fight!' Martha declared.

'They told mummy it was lovely and quiet here,' Lucy added proudly. The mention of their mother brought back Peggy's sense of unease. 'Can you take them all round to the garden at the back and let them play while I pop inside and check on my mother?' she asked Viv. 'There's a little gate that will lead you through, to the left of the front door.'

Everybody was wrapped up warm, and it didn't feel as cold as usual for October. Peggy couldn't explain why, but something was telling her to find her mother before letting the children inside. Viv nodded her agreement and ushered the group around the side of the house. Peggy followed and then slipped into the house through the front door.

'Mother!' she called. She was met with silence. She was just debating what room to check first when she heard a muffled groan coming from the kitchen. Blood rushed around her body, making her feel burning hot, as she leapt into action, running towards the room. Looking in, she saw her mother leaning one hand on the countertop, while the other clutched her chest.

'Peggy,' she rasped, turning to face her. Peggy raced to her side. Her mother tried to reach out to her daughter with the hand that had been on the countertop. Without the support, her body gave way. Peggy caught her just as she started falling to the floor.

'You're going to be all right. I'm here now,' she whispered. Remembering her training, she tried to stay as calm as possible. It was a lot harder to do when the casualty was somebody you loved. Gently, she eased her mother on to the kitchen floor, leaning her back up against a cupboard. Then she bent her knees up. She was still clutching her chest, but her groans had been replaced by short, shallow breaths. When Peggy looked into her eyes, she could see they were full of fear. She stared into them and spoke firmly and confidently, hoping it would somehow reassure her mother. 'Keep focusing on your breathing. I'm going to get help.' She couldn't stand to leave her sitting there alone, but she couldn't get her the help she needed without leaving the room.

She ran to the garden and grabbed hold of Viv. 'My mother is in the kitchen,' she whispered urgently in her ear, making sure none of the children heard her. 'Please look after her while I get the doctor.'

'Whatever's happened?' Viv asked.

'I think it's her heart. Please, go – I need you there to do CPR if her heart stops altogether.'

Viv ran to the house without looking back.

'Hey! Where is she going?' Martha shouted.

'She's getting treats!' Peggy lied, thinking on her feet. She really didn't want to leave the children in the garden alone, but she didn't want them to see her mother like that, and her mother needed Viv with her. Dr Brady only lived a few doors down and she would get there and back quicker on her own. As her sisters and Elsie and Ted jumped up and down excitedly, she added, 'Viv won't be able to give you the treats if you go inside and sneak a look while she's preparing them. I need to go and fetch something, but I'll be right back. As long as you all stay here and behave yourselves, you'll get your treats. Does everybody understand?'

'Yes!' they all cried together, grinning at her. She would normally feel terrible lying to youngsters but needs must.

Keeping her mother alive was the priority – she could deal with disgruntled children later. Her legs were shaking as she set off down the street, praying that she would find Dr Brady at home. All she could think about was the look in her mother's eyes before Peggy had left her. When she reached the Bradys' home, she pummelled the door with her fist as hard as she could manage. She'd let panic set in since leaving the house, and it seemed to be giving her power. The door soon swung open to reveal Dr Brady looking angry at the disturbance. But his expression changed to one of concern when he took in the sight of Peggy. Without saying a word, he grabbed his jacket and Gladstone bag and followed her down the garden path. The doctor – in his seventies – was sprightly for his age, and they reached the house together.

'She's in the kitchen,' Peggy said as he let himself in.

His wife, Patricia, was best friends with Peggy's mother and the couple had often enjoyed dinner parties at the house with her parents before the war, so he knew where he was going. Peggy was too terrified to follow him in. If her mother had taken a turn for the worse since her departure, then she wasn't sure that she could cope with seeing her like that. She was still having flashbacks to Lilli's corpse outside the crypt; she didn't want to remember her mother that way too. Her heart pumped so hard she almost felt like she could hear it as she allowed her mind to wander to the worst-case scenario. Tears filled her eyes. She couldn't go back in there – she would only panic and get upset. She would give Viv and Dr Brady the space they needed to treat her together, and she would go and check on the children.

Peggy peered into the garden and saw the five youngsters sitting on the grass, playing with Ted's toys together.

'I bet it's sweeties!' she heard the little boy exclaiming loudly. Her heart dropped as she remembered her little white lie and realised that she wasn't going to get away with the fib. But then she recalled Viv mentioning gum drops she kept in the car; sucking on them kept her awake during her lonely late-night journeys. Peggy went back to the car and had a root around in the glovebox. She smiled with relief when her hand touched a bag of the sweets. There was no question that Viv would be happy for the whole lot to be devoured if it meant keeping the little ones away from what was happening in the kitchen.

The children were delighted to see the bag when Peggy joined them in the garden. As they sat down together and happily sucked on their treats, Peggy knew she should go and check on her mother, but she was still too frightened. What if they hadn't been able to save her? If that was the case, then she decided she would rather live in ignorance for now than know the truth. She was tempted to bundle the children into Viv's car and drive far away – where nobody could ever find her to tell her that her mother was dead. Maybe then it wouldn't be true? She was angry with herself for not frogmarching her mother to Dr Brady when she had last been here. Lucy had known something was wrong; she'd even outlined all the symptoms of somebody struggling with heart problems, but Peggy had been quick to accept her mother's explanation that she was simply suffering severe bouts of indigestion. Peggy should have listened more to her little sister.

Slowly, the back door opened, and Dr Brady and Viv stepped out. Viv walked over. She looked ashen – her red lipstick seemed even brighter against such a pale face. Peggy started shaking.

'She's stable,' she whispered, and Peggy was flooded with relief. 'Go and speak to the doctor, I'll stay with the children.'

Peggy fought back tears as she made her way to Dr Brady. 'Hey! Are those my sweets?' she heard Viv shout, to an eruption of giggles. 'I hope you saved me some!'

Peggy and Dr Brady stepped into the hallway, leaving the laughter behind.

'Your mother is very lucky you were here,' he said.

'Is she all right? Can I see her?' she asked desperately.

'I've given her some painkillers and she's sleeping. I would advise leaving her to rest.'

'Was it her heart?' Peggy asked. 'I should have come to see you when I was here a few weeks ago. Lucy said she'd been struggling, but mother put it down to indigestion and I believed her. I feel so guilty for letting it go. It was obviously an early symptom. Is she going to be all right?'

Dr Brady took his glasses off and cleaned them as he spoke. 'There's no need to go blaming yourself, dear. We all know what your mother's like. Patricia has been trying to offer her help over here for weeks, but she wouldn't hear a word of it. She warned your mother that she would work herself into the ground . . .' he tailed off and sighed as he put his glasses back on, then he looked at her with sympathy in his eyes. 'It was her heart, dear. I do believe that if you hadn't turned up when you did then we would be in a very different situation.' Peggy winced at the thought of her little sisters wandering into the kitchen to find their mother dead on the floor. Thank goodness Viv had insisted on driving her and Sarah's children to Petworth today.

'We managed to get her into bed. She'll need complete bed rest.'

Peggy's mind started racing. How could her mother be on bed rest when she had a house full of children to look after? Especially now Peggy herself had just added two more youngsters to the workload.

'How long for?' she croaked.

'As long as it takes. It appears to have been a mild heart attack, but even so it's likely to leave her weaker in the long term. She certainly won't be bouncing back to normal after this. I'm so very sorry, dear.'

Peggy's head was spinning now. She couldn't go back to London with her mother in this state. Who would look after her? Not to mention the children. As if the doctor had read her mind, he continued, 'I'll be able to pop in and out to check on her and administer medication, and I'm sure Patricia will be able to help out with the children here and there, but she's busy with the WI and she's just started helping out with teaching over at the school—'

'It's all right, I'll be here,' Peggy cut in. She started at the outburst. She'd said that without even thinking. What *was* she thinking? She didn't want to leave London and her role with the ARP. But it was the right thing to do – her family needed her.

'But your mother was only telling me the other day about how well you were getting on with your air raid warden duties. What about Joan? Could she come home to help?'

'I couldn't do that to her. She loves being a land girl. From her letters, it sounds as though it's been ever so good for her.' *And it's my fault our mother is in this situation, because I didn't get her help sooner*, Peggy thought sadly to herself. *Joan shouldn't have to make sacrifices because of my mistakes.*

'Well, I'd still like to check in on your mother regularly, and I don't think you'll be able to keep Patricia away either.'

'You'll both be most welcome anytime,' Peggy smiled. She wished she could ask the doctor to explain what had happened to the children. That was going to have to be her next task and she wasn't sure where to start. Their mother had always been so fun and full of life – they were going to be devastated to see her bedridden and frail. She would have to do her best to nurse her back to health. Seeing the doctor out of the front door, Peggy started compiling a mental list of everything she needed to get sorted in order to stay in Petworth and look after her family.

Her heart felt heavy at the thought of letting down her friends and fellow volunteers in London, not to mention the people she was meant to be keeping safe. She would miss her life there so much – but she couldn't abandon her family when they needed her. Besides, Peggy's mother was a strong woman and Peggy was hopeful that, despite Dr Brady's bleak outlook, this wouldn't be long term.

9

Dot polished off the last bite of her toast and gave a satisfied groan. Viv had returned from West Sussex with a jar of strawberry jam made by the local WI. When the doctor's wife had learned of Peggy's mother being ill, she had gone straight round to the house and cooked sausages and potatoes for everybody before sending Viv off with the jam she had made with her WI friends. Dot had listened to the whole sad tale of their arrival at Peggy's home while she devoured her toast.

'Poor Peggy,' she said sadly, now she had finished eating. 'She'll be heartbroken to be putting her ARP duties on hold. I feel terrible for her – and her mother.'

'She hid it well – she obviously didn't want to upset the children. But yes, there were moments when I could see how distressed she was by all of it,' Viv replied thoughtfully, licking jam off her fingers. 'But Peggy's a good girl – a family girl. She would never leave them in the lurch by coming back to London when they needed her.'

Dot knew Viv had made her own small sacrifice that day – staying on to help Peggy instead of making her planned trip to visit William. Viv had helped Peggy tell the children about their mother and she had done as much as she could to help their friend before heading straight back to London.

She thought about what Peggy was giving up for her family as she contemplated picking up a spoon and eating the jam straight from the jar now their bread had run out. She was taking comfort from the rare sugary hit after hearing such sad news. Peggy's plight brought to mind her own situation. In contrast to her friend, she was on her own now – there was no family for her to look after or to rely on her in an emergency. The thought made her feel lonely – and even more tempted to eat more jam. But then she reminded herself that she had good friends in Viv and Peggy – they had all done so much for each other already. She knew she could rely on the two of them if she needed anything.

'Is she going to let her father know? He might get compassionate leave for something like this. And her brothers?'

'Her mother won't hear a word of it. She made Peggy promise not to tell them anything. She said she would never forgive herself for pulling them away from their war work.'

'But, surely, they should know? It sounds as if she's quite poorly?'

'She was very weak when I went in to see her with Peggy, but as soon as that topic was brought up, she was adamant. She became extremely fierce for a woman who had just been at death's door, and then she fell asleep – almost like the effort of it had worn her out. If I was Peggy, then I wouldn't go against her wishes. I get the impression she's a very proud woman. She will already hate the fact that she's keeping Peggy from her air raid warden role, but there's not a lot that she can do about that. She's in no fit state to be running around after all those children.'

Dot nodded her understanding. This war wasn't just creating casualties of the bombing and fighting – the damage was so much more widespread.

'Peggy has promised me she will write to Joan, though,' Viv added.

Dot was happy to hear that. She knew how close Peggy was to Joan. At nineteen years old, she was the sibling closest in age to Peggy and she often confided in Dot about how much she missed her. She could imagine Peggy's brothers and fathers being understanding when they eventually learned how ill Mrs Miller had been, but Joan would expect her sister to tell her, despite their mother's protestations.

'So, what are we to do to help?' Dot asked.

'Peggy's asked us to keep an eye on Mrs Martin and the refugees for her, and she'll need you to let Victor know that she won't be back for the foreseeable.'

'Of course. He's just taken on some new recruits so at least we won't be a warden down without her. I'll have to write to Peggy to reassure her of that as I know she'll be worried.' She took a sip of tea. 'I'll be in charge of training the new wardens,' she added proudly. She tried to focus on that instead of thinking about her embarrassing encounter with Bill, which is where her mind usually went to when she thought about her new job.

'Oh, the full-time position! Well, of course you got it! Well done, Dot. I'm so happy for you. This calls for a celebration. I'm taking you out dancing as soon as we get the chance – and I won't take no for an answer!'

Dot grinned and nodded her head. It sounded like just what they both needed.

The pair of them visited Mrs Martin later that afternoon to fill her in on Peggy's news.

'Oh, the poor love,' she said sadly. 'And she had been so relieved to find her mother in good health on her last-minute dash to visit her a few weeks ago.' The three of them were sitting in the living room at the boarding house.

'I must say, you're looking well compared to the last time we saw you,' Dot said to the older woman. She shuddered when she thought back to the night Peggy and Mrs Martin's old boarding house in Bramerton Street had been bombed.

'I've found myself a lot happier here, which has been a pleasant surprise. I've been sharing a room with Peggy, of course, and though she's not here an awful lot, I think it's made me realise that I was quite lonely before.'

She paused and seemed to become lost in thought, and Dot wondered if she was worrying that she might become lonely again now that Peggy was back at home. Then she had an idea.

'Peggy's awfully anxious about who will act as godmother to her refugees while she's away.' She shot Viv a warning look and hoped she would understand that she didn't want her to jump in and explain that Peggy had actually asked the two of them to take on the responsibility. She didn't want to ask Mrs Martin outright to do it in case she thought it was too much – but she could put the idea out there and see if she offered to help. Viv smiled knowingly at Dot, and she knew they were on the same page.

'It will be such a shame if they send a stranger along to look after them. They've built such a good rapport with Peggy, and she really understands their needs,' Viv added.

'Oh, I won't hear of it!' Mrs Martin said sharply, sitting up in her chair. 'You tell Peggy that I'll hold the fort here until she can get back. I'm more than capable and, besides, it will give me something to do.'

'That's so kind of you,' Dot replied. The two of them would have done it for Peggy, without question, but they didn't have much spare time between them, and with Mrs Martin feeling isolated it seemed to be a solution that benefited everybody.

'There's one condition,' the older lady added seriously. 'You must come in and see me every now and then.'

'That's a deal,' Dot replied, smiling. She liked Mrs Martin, and she felt a pull towards her which she suspected was down to the lack of an older female role model in her life. Dot noticed a letter on the table between them. It looked to be at least five pages long. She wondered who had written to Mrs Martin; she knew that she'd lost her husband in the first war. Maybe the letter was from one of her daughters or her grandchildren. Then she remembered Peggy mentioning something about one of the grandchildren being on board the SS *City of Benares*, which had been torpedoed by a German U-boat while evacuating children to Canada a few weeks previously. The young woman had been around the same age as Peggy. She desperately tried to search her memory: had Peggy told her that the woman's relative had been one of the lucky survivors? So much had been going on recently, she found that she just couldn't recall either way. Dot looked up and saw Mrs Martin watching her; she felt ashamed at being caught staring at the pile of papers, but the woman's face filled with joy.

'My granddaughter, Mary, has finally made it to Canada,' she said happily.

Dot felt relief flush through her.

'Peggy said she was escorting some of the evacuees?' Viv asked.

'Yes – my husband had family out there so Mary took the opportunity to go and stay with them. She was taking two little boys to stay with them, too. Such an awful business, that torpedo.' Mrs Martin shook her head forlornly and they all fell silent. Dot suspected that Mrs Martin and Viv were, like her, thinking of all the innocent passengers who had died that terrible night. The last newspaper report Dot had seen said fifty-one adult passengers and a hundred and twenty-two crew had died, along with seventy-seven of the ninety children who had been on board. It was funny how specific facts like that stuck to her memory. Maybe it was the shock of the sheer number of people who had perished, especially children, that had made it stay with her.

'My poor Mary was stuck on a lifeboat at sea for more than seven days before being rescued. There were forty-five of them altogether. She was one of just two adult escorts on the lifeboat, and there were six children with them. How they got through it, I don't know. We think we're crammed in at the shelters, and then you hear of something like that. I'll tell you one thing – I'll never complain about the lack of personal space underground again.'

'How on earth did they survive?' Dot asked. She assumed Mary had told her grandmother all about it in her letter, and she found herself thirsty for details.

'A diet of hard biscuits, tinned food, and strictly limited rations of fresh water,' she said, tears in her eyes. 'Another thing I'll never complain about again: rations.' She wiped her eyes and smiled. 'But she is safe and well with family now, and I'm so grateful for that.'

'Speaking of shelters has reminded me of something Peggy wanted me to check with you,' Viv said.

'Yes, dear?'

'She wants to make sure you'll continue going to the public shelter while she's not here.' Viv's tone had become firm and authoritative.

Mrs Martin turned to her and raised her eyebrows. 'You don't need to get bossy with me, young lady,' she answered playfully. 'You can assure Peggy that the Bramerton Street bomb shook me up enough to keep me out of the basement here for life. I would have thought she'd realise that. Fancy her thinking I'd scurry down to the basement as soon as her back was turned!'

Dot and Viv laughed along with her, but Dot could understand why Peggy would be worried. From what her friend had told her about Mrs Martin, she was a determined woman with a strong will, and she had certainly put up a fight against using public shelters before the Bramerton Street bomb.

'Anyway, I shall go and find Ralf now,' Mrs Martin said, 'and he can help me tell the others about Peggy and let them know they're to come to me if they need anything.'

Dot left the boarding house feeling lighter. She was grateful to Mrs Martin for taking on Peggy's godmother role. She was feeling a little bit anxious about her new full-time role now that Peggy wasn't going to be around to accompany her for the majority of the shifts. She sure was going to miss her friend, and she was worried about how Peggy was going to cope looking after a house full of children as well as her poorly mother.

Dot took a deep breath and reminded herself how capable Peggy was – if anybody could handle the new situation that had been thrown at her, it was Peggy. And Dot suddenly felt a determination to do her friend proud. Peggy had put so much faith in her. She had never questioned the fact that Dot was capable of being a full-time warden. It was time for her to focus on doing her absolute best in her new role. She smiled to herself, feeling a sense of pride at the fact that she was getting ready to take the first step towards her new life – one where she supported herself and was no longer forced to rely on anybody else.

10

A week after the ill-fated visit to Petworth, Viv was finishing up after an afternoon shift ahead of getting back on the road to see William. She hadn't managed to get across to see him since missing her planned visit when Mrs Miller had been taken ill, and she had been pining for her sweetheart. Her shifts at the ambulance station had felt harder and harder since she'd returned from Petworth. Some of her colleagues had been injured by shrapnel and debris when an incendiary bomb had landed near them as they tended to victims of an HE bomb. Danvers Street had been low on volunteers as it was, without the numbers dropping further. Thankfully, new recruits were coming forward every day since the Blitz had started, and Viv had put in some extra shifts while a new batch were trained up.

Viv couldn't help but feel sad that it had taken London getting a daily battering for more volunteers to materialise; people who had been blasé and almost mocking of the civil defence volunteers during the phoney war were suddenly clamouring to help defeat the Jerries now. Viv didn't even come from London, yet she had rushed to sign up and do her bit here instead of running away to the safety of her home in the country. The same went for Peggy.

'Better late than never,' Station Officer Spencer muttered to himself when two new drivers arrived for their first evening shift, and Viv found herself nodding along in agreement. She and her partner Paul had just gone inside to fill in the logbook following their afternoon shift. There hadn't been a raid, but they had been sent out to deal with rescue workers who had been injured digging through the rubble from the previous night's attack, trying desperately to reach trapped survivors before it was too late. With the new volunteers easing the burden, the two of them had been given the whole of the following day off.

'I'm off to my local shelter,' Paul declared, picking up a blanket and a pillow from the store cupboard as they passed by it.

'But tonight's raid won't start for hours,' Viv said, confused. She wondered if she had become so accustomed to the siren that she didn't even register it when it sounded now.

'No point in going home to rest, I'll just have to get up and move when the buggers come back again later. I may as well hunker down where I won't get disturbed.' He had a point. Viv had heard of people taking their dinners down to the shelters before the siren even started wailing; Londoners were loath to let Hitler disrupt their lives any more than necessary. 'My neighbours go down there as soon as the father gets home from work; it means they get a good spot, too,' Paul added. 'I plan to tuck myself away in a corner so that nobody need disturb me.'

Viv gave him a thumbs-up as he bounded away. She let out a long breath as she thought about the drive ahead of her. She could really do with getting some sleep herself, but she was keen to get out of London before the nightly visitors arrived. She was apprehensive about arriving at the hospital so early. She had got away with arriving in the small hours so far; it was easy to slip in unchallenged when all the patients were sleeping. Turning up during daylight and expecting to be allowed to stay for the whole night was a very different story. She had no idea if the nurses would be quite so sympathetic of her flouting visiting hours when she was being so obvious about it. If she came across a feisty nurse or matron, then she may well get turfed out at bedtime. She had thought about driving on to see Peggy – even with a full house she knew her friend would make room for her for the night. And she was keen to check in on her and make sure she was coping with everything she had been suddenly burdened with. But she couldn't justify the fuel consumption; Mr West's supply was running low already and having to use public transport was going to make her trips to visit William a lot more difficult and a lot less frequent. Not to mention shorter in length. Viv had a blanket stored in the car, and she was prepared to get what sleep she could laid out across the back seats if it came to that.

The drive was slower than anticipated and it was getting dark when Viv arrived at the Queen Victoria. When she reached William's ward, he was already asleep. She stood at his bedside and examined his face; some of the bandages had been taken off and she could see from the deep markings on his flesh how scarred he would be. It didn't change anything about the way she felt for him. Viv was just about to settle down on the chair next to his bed when she heard footsteps behind her. Her heart dropped when she felt a hand on her shoulder and she held her breath as she waited for somebody to inform her that she would have to leave and return in the morning. All she wanted to do was sleep – she wasn't going to disturb any of the other patients. She turned around slowly and was met with the stern-looking face of a nurse she didn't recognise.

'It's all right, I'll sleep in my car and come back in the morning,' she whispered.

'You'll do no such thing, dear,' the nurse replied firmly. Now Viv was confused. 'You're Viv, I take it?' Viv nodded. 'I've heard about your visits, and I wouldn't dream of throwing you out. He's always brighter after seeing you,' she gestured towards William and smiled. Viv felt relief replace her disappointment. 'I've been looking out for you for the last few days. Dr McIndoe would like to speak with you. I'll take you to his office, and then I'll fetch you a blanket. If you're going to spend the night on a chair, then you can at least be warm.' Viv smiled gratefully and followed the woman out of the ward and along a winding corridor. She couldn't think what Dr McIndoe would want to speak to her about.

'Ah, my handsome pilot's sweetheart,' the doctor called brightly as Viv walked into his office. He was sitting at his desk with a notepad and pen in front of him. His big round glasses were on the table, and he still wore a surgical cap, as if he had just come out of theatre. There was a radio playing in the background and Viv could hear the familiar sound of presenter Bruce Belfrage's voice as he presented the nightly BBC news bulletin.

'Excuse me, I was just making some notes about an operation,' the doctor added. He took off the cap and gestured for Viv to take a seat opposite him before reaching over to turn down the volume on the radio. 'We haven't seen you in a while and I know you must be desperate to get to young Carter, so I won't keep you long,' he said as Viv sat down.

She was about to ask if he had the correct patient in mind, but then she remembered William telling her that Dr McIndoe was so friendly with the RAF patients that he had taken to calling them by their surnames – as they did with each other.

'Is everything all right?' she asked nervously.

'Yes. He's doing brilliantly. Please don't worry about him. But there is just one thing concerning me. It seems that there might have been more damage done to his right eye than we first anticipated.' Viv waited anxiously for the doctor to elaborate as he put his papers to the side and put his glasses on. 'When the time is right – which will hopefully be within the next few weeks – we'll have to operate. We should know then whether we can save the sight in that eye or not.'

Viv's own eyes suddenly stung with tears. 'But . . . the RAF,' she whispered.

'I know, dear. I know,' Dr McIndoe replied sadly.

There was no need to voice it. They both knew that if William lost the sight in one of his eyes, then he wouldn't be able to continue his RAF pilot duties. He'd told her how much it all meant to him the first time they'd met. William would be heartbroken if his time serving for them got cut short.

'We'll do our best, but I'm afraid I can't make any promises.'

'Does he know?'

'He doesn't know. And I think it will be best to keep it that way – if you agree. His facial injuries are already affecting his self-esteem and I don't want a blow like this to knock him even more. I don't think there's any need to worry him when there's a chance that we could still save his sight.'

'I agree. We need to keep him thinking positively,' Viv said confidently. The tears had gone, and she was sitting up straight, trying to show that she could be strong for William.

'If at all possible, then I would like you to be here when he comes out of the surgery. You and his crewmates are the closest thing he has to family, and I know how much your support means to him. I will give you as much notice as I can. I appreciate it might be difficult for you with your ambulance work, but he'll need you by his side if the outcome is not what we're hoping for.'

Viv nodded silently. She would do anything to be there for William. She made to get up, but Dr McIndoe held up his hand.

'There's just one more thing I wanted to discuss with you,' he said, and she sat back down. 'I think Carter's ready for social reintegration. He's had a skin graft on the area around his lips, and it looks much better than it did before although he will still have some scarring. We're going to slowly rebuild the damaged side of his face – there will be a number of reconstructive surgeries needed.' Viv thought back to what she had seen on the right side of William's face just a few minutes before. 'We've had some of the bandages off for a few days now and, so far, he's refused to leave the ward. I need you to build his confidence and help him take the first step – maybe a nice stroll around the gardens in our grounds. He needs to get used to people looking at him, and this is the best place to start – somewhere people are accustomed to seeing these kinds of disfigurements.'

Viv blanched at the word, but quickly recovered herself. 'I have the day off tomorrow, so I can take him out,' she replied. She was thrilled to be able to do something physical to help William, instead of sitting at his bedside simply willing him to heal.

'Good. It's important that we build his self-esteem before I introduce him to the next stage. I've been sending some of the other airmen out into the local town to get used to being in public again and so they can adjust to people's reactions. Some of the residents are being kind enough to let them into their homes. It will be hard for somebody like William, but so important for him in the long term.'

Viv felt a warmth towards Dr McIndoe; he clearly cared a great deal about his patients. No wonder he had such a wonderful reputation.

'I've had a service uniform sent over for him. I send the airmen out in their uniform – I don't like them to feel like convalescents.'

Viv's smile widened. It was an important detail that she wouldn't have thought of.

'I'll get a wheelchair sent to the ward for the morning. He still needs physio on his right leg, so you'll need the chair for your stroll round the gardens. There will be skin grafts on the right side of his body to come, too.' Viv sat in silence as the enormity of everything William had yet to face dawned on her.

'He'll get through this, dear. Especially with you by his side. Anything is possible when you have the love of a good woman, and we can all see how much you love him.'

Viv blushed. She felt proud of the fact her affection for William had been noticed – it meant she must be getting better at showing her feelings. As she got up to leave, Dr McIndoe reached over and turned the volume back up on the radio.

'I'll look forward to hearing about your outing tomorrow,' he said over the sound of the news. She was about to reply when a loud banging noise rang out from the radio. The presenter paused briefly, before continuing on with his roundup.

'Do you think . . . ?' Viv asked in shock. It had sounded distinctly like an explosion – quite possibly inside the broadcasting house.

'They're recording the shows in the basement now so, yes, that could have been a bomb going off at the BBC,' Dr McIndoe replied solemnly.

Viv stood and listened for a few moments more as Bruce Belfrage carried on reading the news, seemingly unfazed.

'Ever the professional,' she said in wonder. 'I'm so proud of London,' she added as she left the office.

11

Dot was dealing cards out between herself and three other wardens around the table when Bill walked into the dining hall. Though the Blitz was now mostly seen as a night bombing campaign, the air raid wardens were still needed on duty during the day just in case. While it brought more opportunity for training and drills, it also meant that Dot had been given many opportunities to scrub up on her card game skills.

She felt her face flush crimson as Bill approached the group, and she did her best to focus on the task in hand so that she didn't have to look up at him. Dot had managed to avoid him since their last encounter when she had thrown herself at him, lost in feelings of joy and gratitude after being told she had the full-time warden position. She shuddered every time she thought about it. Having had a week of day shifts had helped in her desperate need to dodge him; Bill's work at the docks meant he mostly carried out warden duties at night. But when he had turned up early for a night shift one day while she'd still been at the school at the end of an afternoon shift, she had ducked into one of the empty classrooms and hidden in there until it was time to clock off, just to avoid having to face him.

Donald had turned up for duty this afternoon, and Dot had known it was likely Bill would appear to join him. The pair of them tended to work the same shifts at the docks, and Dot knew that Bill liked to help at their post whenever he had the chance. To many people, a day off meant catching up on sleep or seeing friends but to Bill it simply meant warden duties. She often wondered if he ever slept. Dot finished dealing out the cards and she could feel Bill's presence behind her as she picked up her pile and looked through it.

'You've dealt yourself a good hand there,' Bill commented, looking at the cards over her shoulder.

'No helping!' Donald cried out from across the table.

'Don't worry, she doesn't need any help. This one's a dab hand at Black-Out,' Bill replied. He had taken the seat next to Dot and she forced herself to look over at him. She was met with the warmest smile, which she couldn't help but return. Immediately she felt at ease with him again and she felt silly for feeling so anxious about bumping into him. Of course he wouldn't hold her social blunder against her; he was too much of a gentleman to make a big deal out of it or to try and humiliate her further.

'How's the new full-time role going for you?' he asked her quietly as she waited for her turn.

'Really good, thanks. I helped train the new recruits this week. I don't know if you've met them yet?' She gestured to the two men sitting either side of Donald. She had introduced them both to Donald before they'd started the game. Bill shook his head. She took her turn and then looked back to Bill. 'The young chap is Laurie, and the older chap is Frank,' she explained.

'Is Laurie the conchie?' Bill asked in a hushed tone – although not hushed enough.

'Yes, that's me,' Laurie replied loudly and firmly, staring hard at Bill. Everybody fell silent and looked up from their cards. Dot already knew that as a conscientious objector Laurie had come in for a lot of criticism from everybody he met – including his own wife. They had spoken about it during his training and Dot had felt she could relate to his struggles, having had people look down on her for being a female in a 'man's role'. Frank, the other new recruit, in particular, had had a lot to say on the subject during their training, being a first war veteran in his seventies. But Laurie had dealt with his comments and views with grace and the two of them had eventually come to an understanding. They now worked well together. Dot waited nervously for Bill's response. She could understand Laurie being defensive, but she really didn't feel that Bill had been trying to be confrontational when he'd asked her the question.

'I've got no problem with it,' Bill said, holding his hands up. Laurie's face softened. 'I only just made it through the first war myself and if my work at the docks didn't exempt me this time around then I'm not sure if I would have been able to face going back to the frontline myself. I wouldn't wish any of it on my worst enemy.'

Dot took a moment to let the revelation sink in. She'd had no idea that Bill had fought in the first war, though she had wondered. He was the right sort of age, of course, but most of the veterans still in London liked to talk about their experiences at length. She'd known all about Frank's run-ins with the enemy an hour after meeting him, for example. She'd assumed Bill had been a dockworker back then and not been sent to fight. This unexpected news made Dot warm to Bill even more. He didn't feel the need to shout about what he'd already done for the country, he just quietly got on with doing more. Maybe it was the reason he was so keen to spend so many hours volunteering.

'I'm sure you've got your reasons, and you don't need to explain them to me,' Bill added.

Laurie nodded his head in acknowledgement, and the group got back to their game of Black-Out. Once it was over, they started talking amongst themselves. As Dot told Bill about what had happened with Peggy's mother, she found it easy to pretend the inappropriate embrace between them had never happened. She felt foolish for having hidden in a classroom to avoid him days earlier. She should have known that he would be a gentleman about the whole thing.

'It's been strange being on duty without Peggy, but I think I'm doing all right,' she added, trying to sound more confident and upbeat than she felt.

'I know Ted has been impressed with the help you've given him with the training.'

Ted was Victor's deputy. Dot hadn't met him until she'd started the full-time role, and she had been surprised to find he was so young – he was only in his twenties. He'd signed up to fight before war was even declared, but then a training accident had left him unable to serve with the Army. Undeterred, he had gone straight to the civil defence and worked his way up the ranks with determination until he'd been made Victor's deputy. Dot didn't know any details about the training accident – just that Ted had injured his leg, which showed in the slight hobble he walked with. But she couldn't help but think the Army had missed out on having him with them when she had watched him during the air raid warden training.

Bill excused himself to make a round of teas and Dot was pulled away from her thoughts by the mention of looting.

'I heard about that, too,' Frank was saying to Donald as Dot started listening in.

'Did you say there's been looting going on?' she asked. She knew it was a problem everywhere in London, but she hadn't heard of anything out of the norm in their area since

Stan had left. Looting was becoming ever more prevalent all over the city now – hundreds of cases had been reported since the Blitz had started. Criminals knew the police force was stretched with so many officers having gone off to fight, and the raids presented the perfect conditions for them. One gang had managed to carry out a series of jewellery shop robberies in the West End. They didn't even wait for the stores to be hit by bombs to help them gain entry and rummage around; nobody noticed a car smashing into the shopfronts when they were distracted by the sounds of bombs falling and anti-aircraft guns blazing all around.

'Oh, there's all the usual going on round here; shops being cleared out after a raid, and people coming back to their bombed-out homes to find jewellery boxes intact but empty of their most precious jewels,' Frank replied. Dot nodded. There were always going to be opportunistic thieves who did a bit of looting when they spotted an empty wreck of a building.

'But one of my old comrades is based at a post a few sectors over and he said someone has been taking wallets and jewellery from dead bodies,' Frank went on.

Dot's blood ran cold. That sounded just like Stan's modus operandi. But, surely, he wouldn't be back at it after he was lucky to be let off the hook previously? The man would have to be stupid to carry on after such a narrow escape. Dot couldn't help but laugh to herself – of course the most likely culprit was Stan – he was the epitome of stupid.

'There's also a couple of looters using air raid warden uniform as a ruse to get into bombed-out buildings and then clear out all the valuables,' Donald said. 'Makes me sick,' he added, shaking his head.

'Yeah, I heard members of the public have even been helping them load up cars, thinking they're lending a hand to officials who are taking the stuff away to be kept safe,' Frank said.

An image of Stan leaning down and stealing Charles' treasured pocket watch from his body just hours after her fellow warden's life had been cut short by the crypt bomb flashed into Dot's mind. She had hoped that losing his volunteer role as a result of his disgusting actions would be enough to stop him from continuing, but it sounded as if it had simply given him time to hone his skills. She couldn't let him get away with this – she had to do something to stop him.

Dot went to say something to her colleagues but caught herself just in time. What if she was wrong? She didn't have any evidence this was Stan, after all, she was purely working on a hunch. There were hundreds of looters roaming London's streets during and after raids. Just because one of them was doing the same kind of thing as Stan had done, it wasn't proof that Stan was up to no good again. If she voiced her suspicions now and it turned out she was wrong, then Victor would be disappointed in her for letting everybody know about the real reason for Stan's dismissal. She had no reason to want to protect Stan, but his wife – Victor's sister – didn't deserve to suffer. And she knew that some of the men would be quick to label Dot an hysterical woman, jumping to conclusions and trying to get somebody who was mean to her into trouble with no justification. She thought back to Peggy's advice when she had gone to her with her concerns about Stan stealing from corpses after raids in the first place. She'd told her they needed hard evidence before taking the accusation to Victor. So, that was what she needed again now. Dot closed her eyes and wished that Peggy hadn't had to stay in West Sussex, even though she knew it was the right thing for her friend to be doing.

She longed for her support; Peggy would know exactly what to do in this situation.

Dot wondered about asking Viv to help her, but she knew she had a lot on her plate already and she didn't want to pull her away from her visits to William. Viv was such a good person that Dot knew she would sacrifice her own needs in order to help her.

Bill came back to the table with a tray full of teas. Dot felt so comfortable with him, and he had a way of making her feel safe. She wondered whether he might help her investigate. But then she remembered their awkward embrace and shuddered. Bill must already think her over-emotional and foolish – she didn't want to make herself look any worse. No, she would have to find out for certain before speaking to anybody about it.

Dot tried to think of ways to confirm if the looter was Stan until it was time to clock off. And as she made to leave the school, she realised there was only one person she could ask for help – somebody who already knew about what Stan had done before.

Walking up to number 27 Lawrence Street, Dot started feeling nervous. It wasn't that long ago that this house had been her home, and yet it felt like a lifetime since she had thrown Tommy's keys in his face and run away from that life. It felt strange to be knocking on the door instead of walking straight in, but Dot liked the fact that she would be making Beryl get up from her favourite chair to answer the door – a task that she was always too lazy to carry out when Dot had lived here. The two women may have made a kind of peace since Beryl had thrown Tommy out for striking Dot, but that didn't mean Dot didn't still feel a little bit of a mean streak towards the woman who had helped make her life miserable – no matter what her intentions may have been. Dot wondered how clean the place would be now that she wasn't there to carry out all the housework. Then she silently scolded herself for having such cruel thoughts about Beryl, who was technically still her mother-in-law, after all.

When the door swung open, Dot was surprised to find Jim on the other side of it. Jim was Beryl's fancy man and the spiv who had helped prove to Victor that Stan had been stealing from dead bodies while on duty. It was Jim Dot had been hoping to speak to, but she had thought she'd have to ask Beryl to arrange a meeting.

'My dear Dot!' he cried, beaming from ear to ear. 'Please, do come in.' He stepped to the side to let her in, and Dot realised he was holding cleaning rags in his hand. She could smell how pristine the house was and as she looked around it seemed to sparkle even more than it used to after she had given it a good going over.

'Are you . . .?' she asked, gesturing around in the hallway.

'Yes, dear,' Jim replied proudly, holding up the rags. 'Just doing my bit to earn my keep.'

'Bring her in 'ere!' Beryl bellowed from the living room. When they walked in and Dot found Beryl in her favourite chair with her feet up and a cup of tea in her hand, it all became clear. The older woman wasn't picking up the slack and taking care of herself – she had found another fool to run around after her. Only, this fool seemed quite happy about it by the looks of things.

'Your poor mother-in-law was terrified being here all on her own after what happened with you and Tommy, so I've moved in to keep an eye on her and so she has someone to go to the shelter with at night. I can't stand the thought of her being down there all on her own,' Jim explained.

Dot nodded and smiled. Beryl really had landed on her feet here. Dot couldn't help but admire the way she had managed to work this situation to her advantage.

'He likes to look after me,' Beryl said, looking up at Dot with a devilish twinkle in her eye.

At least she has a willing victim, she thought to herself. As Jim bustled about in the kitchen making them tea, Beryl asked Dot about her ARP work and Dot brought her up to date.

'Full time? Well, I've never heard of a female warden being paid – only the men. You must be so proud of yourself,' she said with a genuine look of admiration.

While Jim poured out the tea for them and sat himself down next to Dot, she marvelled at the change in her former nemesis. She wasn't sure what had caused it; it could have been finally being free of Tommy or it could have been falling in love, or perhaps it was down to the two factors together. But something had switched in Beryl, and she seemed to be a much friendlier, warmer person. Maybe, despite the fact the two women had spent so much time together, she had been just as lonely as Dot had been for all those years.

'And have you heard from Tommy?' Dot asked cautiously.

'Oh, he's written to me, expressing all sorts of remorse and begging for my forgiveness, but I got Jim 'ere to burn the letter.'

'I did it straight away,' Jim said proudly. 'Normally I wouldn't encourage a mother to give up on her son, but a good man would never hurt a woman. And if he's capable of that, well, then what might he do to my Beryl? No, I won't abide it.'

Dot smiled seeing Jim acting so protectively, but she feared for the man. She had seen how terrified he had been of Stan when she had convinced Jim to reveal that the warden had been forcing him to buy stolen items he'd lifted from dead bodies. He certainly didn't come across as somebody who could defend himself very well. Tommy was a hulk of a man – a force to be reckoned with. Dot didn't much fancy Jim's chances if Tommy turned up here and found him living in sin with his mother. She saw Jim was wringing his hands nervously now, and she wondered if he was having the same thoughts. But she pushed her musings to one side – that wasn't something that she needed to be worried about anymore. She was free. And the sooner she got out of this house, the better. Just being back here was making her feel anxious that her husband might walk through the door at any minute. She felt nauseous at the thought. But before she could broach the subject of Stan, Beryl started talking again.

'You don't need to spend your earnings on accommodation, dear,' she said, leaning forward in her chair towards Dot. 'I feel terrible thinking of you working so hard and then spending everything on keeping a roof over your head. Your room here will always be available to you. I'd love for you to come back.'

Dot tried to hide the involuntary shudder that her body made at the suggestion. Not only would the threat of Tommy returning loom over her 24/7, but she still felt cautious around Beryl. The woman had been terrible to her for so long. Dot couldn't just forget all that in an instant and trust that her mother-in-law wouldn't go back to her old ways once they were living under the same roof again. And she wasn't entirely convinced that Beryl would turn Tommy away if he came back begging for forgiveness. It was one thing to discard his written pleas but quite another to be strong enough to say no to his face. Despite everything, he was Beryl's son.

'That's very kind. I'll think about it,' Dot replied, before quickly changing the subject and telling them about the looter on the prowl.

'That does sound like Stan,' Jim said, rubbing his chin and looking concerned. 'I haven't heard anything about him being back on the scene, but I'll keep my ear to the ground for you and see what I can find out.'

'Thank you, Jim, I appreciate that,' Dot said, and she got up to leave. Then she stopped dead in her tracks at the sound of a firm knock on the door. She felt the colour drain from her face, then took a deep breath and reminded herself that if Tommy came back then he would walk straight in. It couldn't be him. But her reaction made it clear to her that she definitely wasn't going to move back into the house. She looked around and realised that Jim had already rushed off to answer the door. She heard deep voices and then the door closed. Jim returned moments later looking solemn and holding a telegram in his hand. Dot felt her knees go weak and she sat back down on the sofa. She looked over at Beryl, who had also turned very pale. Was this it? If Tommy had been killed in action, then everything would change. All kinds of conflicting emotions ran through Dot's head – she'd loved the man once, with all her heart. She should be devastated at the thought of him dying. But her first feeling on seeing the telegram had been one of relief.

'He's gone,' Beryl whispered from her chair.

Dot looked over at her again – she had been so lost in thought that she hadn't even noticed Beryl opening the telegram. Dot sat frozen in shock.

'What happened?' Jim asked quietly. Beryl handed him the telegram and as he read it the colour drained from his face. 'He never reported back to his division.' He looked up at Dot and she could see the fear in his eyes. 'Tommy's gone AWOL.'

12

The quiet bustle of the ward woke Viv early the following morning. She forgot where she was for a moment and went to roll over in her bed. The feeling of finding nothing solid underneath her made her jump to a sitting position, as she suddenly remembered.

'Morning, beautiful,' William whispered. Viv smiled and rubbed her eyes sleepily. 'You were out for the count. Whatever's kept you in London must have worn you out.' Viv reached for his hand. His speech was a lot clearer now the bandages had gone from around the right side of his mouth. Whatever Dr McIndoe had done during the surgery had obviously been a success. She felt hopeful for the task he had set her for today. 'Tell me about what's kept you away,' William asked.

Viv obliged, but she left out the part where she had driven her ambulance vehicle – a converted Hudson which she called 'Hudsy' – through a street of burning buildings in order to reach some casualties. She already knew that William worried about her when she was in London, and she didn't want to add to his fears.

'I'm so proud of you,' he whispered, squeezing her hand, and she felt her heart flutter. After breakfast, the nurse from the previous evening – who it turned out was called Deirdre – brought a wheelchair over to William's bedside. As Viv got to her feet, William looked at her cautiously. 'What's going on?' he asked nervously.

'We're going to get some fresh air,' Viv said cheerily. Her heart ached when she saw the fear engulfing him. 'Can you give us a minute, please?' she asked Deirdre, who had been waiting next to the wheelchair.

'Of course, dear.' She smiled. 'I'll be milling about on the ward so just give me a wave when you're ready.'

William shook his head slowly at Viv as Deirdre walked away. 'I'm not leaving,' he whispered. 'Not looking like this. I can't cope with the thought of people seeing me in this state. Everyone will stare at me, and I won't even be able to get away from them,' he added, gesturing at the wheelchair.

'I'm here with you,' Viv replied gently. 'They can stare at the two of us. We'll get through this together. We can get through anything together.'

'It's okay for you, Viv. People stare at you because you're beautiful. But they'll be staring at me because I look so hideous. Then they'll start questioning what somebody like you is doing with a freak like me and I just can't stand it, Viv. I'm sorry but I can't do it.'

'Who cares what anybody thinks?' she asked, taking a step towards him. 'If somebody is willing to judge you for the way you look then they're not worth getting upset about, my love. And, besides, your injuries are there to tell the world that you're a hero who put his life on the line for this country – for their freedom. Anybody with an ounce of sense will know that you are somebody to be respected. And if they don't, well . . . then they will have me to answer to.' Viv thought she spotted a glimmer of a smirk cross William's face briefly. 'What? I'm a force to be reckoned with, I'll have you know,' she said mock-sternly, folding her arms across her chest.

'Oh, I don't doubt it,' he replied lightly. 'I for one wouldn't like to get on the wrong side of you.' But his good cheer didn't last, and Viv felt helpless as she watched his face cloud over again because of whatever thoughts were running around in his mind.

'You can't stay hidden on this ward forever,' she said gently, slowly moving closer to him. 'We need to get you up and about and *living* again. And we can't let what some people *might* think about your war wounds stop us.' As soon as she saw William's face soften again, she ran her fingers through his hair, which was growing back well, and kissed his forehead tenderly. 'Let's do this together,' she whispered as she carefully helped ease him up into a sitting position. Deirdre had clearly been keeping an eye on the situation as she was already making her way back towards them when Viv looked up to try and find her. Together, they assisted William into the wheelchair.

'No racing around like you do in your ambulance,' William joked, although he still sounded anxious.

'I'm a very careful driver, especially when I have such precious cargo.'

'Go on, you two – go and enjoy some quality time together away from these four walls,' Deirdre urged.

Wheeling William through the ward, Viv smiled at all the men waving and smiling encouragingly at them as they went. She knew that William had formed close friendships since arriving. The fact that they were all in similar positions when it came to their injuries and appearance probably bonded them faster than would normally be the case. That and the fact they had all been through similar experiences on the frontline. Viv could understand that it would be easy to become stuck in the safety that the bubble of the ward gave William. She thought back to what she had said to him about how he shouldn't care about what anybody thinks, and she felt guilty for being such a hypocrite. They were words that her friends had used to comfort her when she was worrying about what people would think of her past, but she was still keeping her secret from William because she was afraid of being judged by not just a stranger but the person she loved most.

The thought of keeping things from William reminded her of Dr McIndoe's warning about the sight in his right eye. Viv felt terrible knowing that he was at risk of not only losing half his sight but also his beloved RAF career and she was failing to share that with him. It felt like another big betrayal, even though she had agreed with the surgeon that it was best to hold off divulging the news until they really needed to.

When they reached the gardens, Viv pushed all the worries and fears from her mind and resolved to focus on William – she was here to help him, not feel sorry for herself and worry about her past ruining their future together. Pushing the chair through the gardens, Viv felt relaxed despite the chill in the air. She looked down at William and saw his shoulders slacken. They were surrounded by beauty. Viv felt like she was in a woodland wonderland when she looked around at all the flowers and trees and open space. It seemed to stretch on forever, with various paths in all directions ready to be explored.

'Is it like this where you grew up?' William asked.

Viv smiled. She had just been thinking about her family home in Surrey.

'This place reminds me of our garden at home,' she replied.

William spluttered as if in shock. 'Your garden can't be the size of these grounds, surely?' he exclaimed, trying to crane his neck around to look at her. Viv giggled and stopped pushing the chair so she could sit down on a wall next to William. 'I thought I told you about my father the politician,' she said. She didn't like to tell people about her background because she worried that they would think her spoiled. She had been particularly cautious of saying too much to William since learning of his lonely upbringing, but she was certain that she had told him about her family and the grounds their house enjoyed.

'Yes, I knew he wasn't fighting because he's very important in politics, and I knew that meant your family was likely very wealthy, but I guess I just hadn't realised that you were filthy rich, that's all.'

'We're not filthy rich,' she laughed. 'But we are well off. I don't really talk about it because I want to make my own way in life. People tend to think I'm just a silly socialite when they learn about my father. The fact that I love a good night out dancing doesn't help with that, but people don't seem able to see past it once they know who my father is. I've lived in his shadow all my life, but the war and my ambulance work have given me a chance to step out of it and do my own thing.'

'I think it's amazing that you're staying in London to help when you could be hiding out in luxury in the country. There is no way anybody could label you a silly socialite, Viv.'

'It's not that amazing. There are people doing far more than I am.'

At the sound of gravel crunching, William looked around. Viv looked up and saw two nurses guiding a man in service uniform along the path. His face was red raw and shiny, but it wasn't the horrific burns that made Viv feel bad.

'I was meant to get you into your RAF uniform before taking you out,' she said sadly. 'I'm so sorry I forgot. I was just so excited to get you out in the fresh air.'

'It doesn't matter. I know the doc thinks sending everyone out in uniform will do wonders for our self-esteem, but I think it will take a lot more than that to get me feeling comfortable with how I look again.'

The nurses smiled at the two of them as they passed slowly by, and their patient gave William a courteous nod, but William was too busy watching Viv to notice. Once they had passed, Viv felt William looking at her and turned to face him. 'His face was completely ravaged, and you didn't even flinch. You looked at him as if he wasn't injured at all.'

'How else am I supposed to look at him?' Viv asked, confused.

'It really doesn't bother you? Not one bit?'

'I told you; we're all the same underneath. That poor chap is a person just like you and me. Why would I look at him any differently?'

'You truly are amazing, Vivian Howe,' William said. He leaned forward and put his hand at the back of her head before gently pulling her face towards him and kissing her tenderly on the lips. With the bandages around his mouth now removed, it was their first proper kiss since William's accident.

Viv was relieved she was sitting down, as she felt herself go weak at the knees. She hadn't realised just how much she had been craving intimacy with him until this moment.

She had spent the last few weeks beating herself up over her rebuff of William's marriage proposal before the Blitz had started, and she had found herself desperately clinging on to hope that she hadn't pushed him away for good with the rejection. During her visits to William in the hospital, she had started to allow herself to hope that he might realise she had seen the error of her ways and that she would say 'yes' a million times over if he would only ask her to be his wife again. But then Viv would remember that she was still keeping her past from him, and all her hopes would fade. She felt this familiar mix of emotions as their kiss ended and William pulled away, his good eye shining with happiness as he looked into hers. She wished again that she was brave enough to be honest with him, but then the moment was lost as she panicked at the sight of his red lips.

'What's wrong?' William mumbled, reaching his fingers up to his mouth to feel the area Viv was staring at. He looked down at his fingertips and laughed when he saw the colour that had transferred on to them. 'You and your warpaint,' he chuckled, shaking his head.

Viv laughed along in relief when she realised it was her lipstick. 'I thought I'd ruptured some of your stitches,' she cried.

'I wouldn't have minded for a kiss like that,' William whispered, holding her gaze.

Viv felt herself going weak again, and once more longing for another proposal. Maybe that validation would give her the confidence to share her past with him. But then her doubts took over and the moment was ruined as she quickly looked away from him to rifle around in her bag for her lipstick. As she reapplied the colour, a group of three women walked up the path towards them.

'Turn me around, please,' William whispered urgently. Viv looked up, confused at the tone of his voice. On spotting the women, she raised her hand in greeting. 'Viv, *please*,' William hissed. 'They're staring at me. Please just turn me around.' He was turning his head away from the group as they drew nearer.

'Well, let's give them something to stare at,' Viv whispered back. She got up from the wall she had been sitting on and plonked herself down gently on William's lap – being careful to place her weight on his good leg. He whipped his head round in dismay and she planted a big kiss on his lips before he could protest.

'Oh, yes!' one of the women shouted.

'You give that hero what he deserves!' another yelled enthusiastically, clapping her hands.

Viv pulled away, laughing, and waved at the women.

'Thank you for your service,' the third woman said loudly and sincerely, looking at William fondly as they passed by. He smiled bashfully.

'See, I told you. Everybody is on your side,' Viv said as she gently wiped the lipstick off his mouth with a tissue.

'I love you,' he whispered.

Viv stopped what she was doing and threw her arms around his neck as an overwhelming sense of happiness swept through her body. 'I love you, too,' she whispered into his ear.

'I'm so glad you got me out of that ward for a little while,' William said as Viv held him tight. 'I feel more like myself again already.' There was a moment of silence as they both enjoyed being in each other's arms. 'Everything feels better with you here, Viv.' Viv scrunched up her eyes to try and stop tears from forming. 'If only I could have you by my side permanently to help me through.'

Viv held her breath as she allowed herself once again to hope for another proposal. She was certain that was where his words were taking him, because surely it was clear to William now that he was the only one for her?

'They said I'd find you lovebirds out here,' a familiar voice sang out.

Viv let go of William and quickly finished cleaning up his mouth and got to her feet. She was disappointed at the interruption, but happy when she turned around to see Johnny walking towards them. She knew from William that his friend had been visiting him regularly due to their RAF base being nearby, but she hadn't crossed paths with him at the hospital yet. With William's lack of family, it was a comfort to her knowing that somebody else was looking out for him, too.

'You're looking good!' Johnny exclaimed as he took in William's appearance. 'They've done a great job on those lips. It looked like Viv here was impressed, too,' he teased, as the pair of them squirmed in embarrassment.

Viv had been wondering over the previous weeks if William would find it difficult to be around Johnny – the two of them looked so alike that they were often mistaken for brothers. With his blond hair, blue eyes, and general similarity to her love, even she had been convinced the pair were related when she had first met him. It would have been natural for William to struggle with seeing Johnny while his face was still so damaged. Looking between them now, there was a striking difference in their looks where they had once been so alike. But William was at once relaxed around his friend, and clearly delighted to see him. As the men started catching up, Viv reapplied her lipstick a second time. Then the three of them spent a wonderful couple of hours exploring the grounds, laughing and joking as if they didn't have a care in the world.

As Viv made her way back to London later that afternoon, she thought about how much she had enjoyed her break from the city and the Blitz. It had felt refreshing to pretend they weren't facing such dreadful danger, if only for a short while. But her positive feelings were clouded by her fears for William. Dr McIndoe's words about how he might lose the sight in his eye were ringing in her ears now she had time to herself to think about it all. All she could do was hope that Dr McIndoe would be able to save William's sight. And, at the same time, she allowed herself to hope that she and William would go on to have their happily ever after.

13

Kneeling on the soft earth, Peggy looked round at the children digging holes with her and smiled. She had been back in Petworth for two weeks now, and the eight of them had fallen into a good routine. Lucy had been right when she'd told Peggy she only spent half a day at school; the high number of evacuees in West Sussex had doubled the school population, so they had adopted a double shift system in the county. During the week Lucy went off to school in the morning, and the evacuees stayed at home with her along with Martha and Annie, who were still too young to start full-time education. Phillip and Sarah liked to help Peggy with the cleaning and food prep, but they also helped keep an eye on the younger children when Peggy tended to her mother or nipped into the village to pick up their rations and run other errands. In the afternoons, it was the evacuees' turn to go to school, and Peggy and her sisters often enjoyed a short walk round the village before the little ones went upstairs to spend time with their mother, leaving Peggy to get the dinner ready.

Mrs Miller seemed to be recovering steadily. She was still on bed rest although she had tried to defy Dr Brady's orders several times.

'I'm so bored up here, staring at the same four walls all day and night,' she would moan to Peggy while gesturing around the bedroom. 'And I can't bear the thought of you running this house all on your own.'

Peggy had to admit that she longed for her mother's help – looking after so many children while trying to keep a household running smoothly felt like a never-ending task and she was exhausted. She certainly wasn't keeping the house as clean as her mother's high standards demanded. She sometimes felt that her air raid duties had been easier, especially when Annie was having one of her tantrums. But no matter how much she struggled, she refused to allow her mother downstairs to help. She already felt guilty enough about ignoring the heart issues which had led to her mother being taken ill, no matter how much anybody insisted that she couldn't have known what was to come. And there were only extra children to care for because she had invited them in – not her mother. However, Peggy did agree to let her mother spend time with Annie, Lucy and Martha in the afternoons during the week – on the condition that she had rested all morning. And the girls were under strict orders to sit quietly with their mother in her bedroom and read, sing songs together or tell stories. Martha and Annie still found it difficult sometimes to refrain from high jinks, but Lucy was good at fetching Peggy when they got too energetic, so that she could take them downstairs with her to run off some steam. Mostly, however, the three of them liked to snuggle up in bed with their mother and make up stories or talk about their father and brothers, which gave Peggy precious time to complete chores safe in the knowledge that her mother wasn't exerting herself and putting herself at further risk. Peggy had stood at the door listening in to them as they talked about their memories of family life before the war, and it had warmed her heart to hear them speaking so fondly of the men they all missed so much. She often heard her mother's beautiful voice singing 'Danny Boy' to the girls; the song she had sung to Peggy's brothers before they had gone off to war.

Having spoken to Dr Brady about doing everything she could to help get her mother fighting fit, Peggy was keen to overhaul her mother's diet and make sure she was eating as much fruit and veg as possible. Of course, rationing made that difficult, so she had been pleased to find a large vegetable patch hidden away at the end of the garden.

'I got to work on that as soon as they started the Dig For Victory campaign,' her mother had explained. 'I don't suppose there's much room for it in London, but round here they've been growing all sorts wherever it can be cultivated.'

'Oh, they're getting on board in London, too. There are plenty of allotments around, and I've even seen people putting vegetable patches on top of their Anderson shelters! Imagine nipping out halfway through a raid to pull up some carrots to munch on,' Peggy had replied. Her mother had guffawed at the thought, and Peggy had never been so pleased to see her laughing. 'Some people have been growing veg in their window boxes, although that's often a disaster as any old soul walking past can help themselves – and they do. But people will try and grow their own wherever they can because you can queue for hours at the greengrocers and then they put up the "sold out" sign as soon as you reach the till.' Peggy still couldn't get over all the different things that were being grown by people like herself who'd had no clue about gardening before the war: carrots, beets, parsnips, turnips, swedes, potatoes, peas, pole and bush beans, celery, cabbage, cauliflower, radishes, berries, strawberries, currants and gooseberries – the list was endless. She hadn't had time for it herself in London, but she had found it a welcome chore since she'd arrived home.

Determined to make her mother's meals as healthy as possible, Peggy had turned some of the flower beds in the garden into vegetable patches, too. She had taken instructions from her mother, but it was the children who helped her the most in the end. She had been thrilled to learn that they had all developed green fingers since the Dig For Victory campaign had started. It turned out that they had been roped into helping cultivate all the patches in the village as part of their learning at school. Peggy ended up absorbing a great deal of knowledge from them.

'Did you know that food is just as important a weapon as guns in this war, Peggy?' Ted had yelled when he had burst into the house after his first afternoon at the village school.

Gardening had quickly become an activity that they all enjoyed doing together and now, two weeks since her mother's funny turn, Dr Brady had agreed that she could sit in the garden and watch them all at work. Peggy had helped her down the stairs and set her up on a chair just next to the patch they were working on. She looked up at her mother now, all cosy in the blankets the children had taken great delight in wrapping her up in, and Peggy marvelled at the joy on her face.

'It's just wonderful to get some fresh air,' Mrs Miller said happily, craning her neck up to the sky as if she was basking in the sun on a warm summer's day.

'Even if it is a bit chilly?' Peggy joked.

'Oh, I don't mind. It's making me feel alive,' her mother exclaimed, throwing her gloved hands up in the air.

Peggy giggled. 'That's all well and good, but please don't get too carried away – you're still supposed to be taking it easy.'

Her mother rolled her eyes. 'Waving my arms around is hardly exerting myself. Besides, you'd better get on and pick those mushrooms properly or else I'll be down on my hands and knees doing it for you. It's taking all my will not to get my hands dirty.'

'You'll do no such thing, or else I'll tell Dr Brady and him and Mrs Brady will be round here to march you back to bed before you've even rolled your sleeves up.'

Mrs Miller smiled and winked at her daughter before turning her attention to the children, who were all busy on the next patch along planting cauliflower and peas. They had started chanting *'An hour in the garden is better than an hour in the queue,'* repeating the line they kept hearing on the Dig For Victory radio adverts.

Peggy could see how desperate her mother was to get up and help them, and she felt bad that she wasn't able to get involved. She had always loved gardening and now one of her simplest pleasures had been taken away from her. Peggy knew it must be incredibly frustrating for her mother being so restricted, but she wasn't prepared to take any chances with her health. Besides, she was hopeful that Dr Brady would allow her to start light activities once she had built her strength up a little more. Her mother already looked so much better than she had done on that terrible day – there was a little light behind her eyes again and a bit of colour to her face. Her progress allowed Peggy to hope that she might be able to make it back to London to continue doing her bit before too long.

As she got back to work on the mushrooms, Peggy realised how cathartic the act was, and she hoped more than ever that her mother would be able to start helping her with it soon. The sound of footsteps on the gravel driveway pulled her away from her thoughts.

'Mama and Papa!' Phillip and Sarah cried in unison, leaping to their feet.

'Mummy?' Elsie asked, looking over at Peggy with big, pleading eyes.

'I hope so,' Peggy replied. Parents of the London children came to Petworth every other weekend to visit for the day before returning to the city. Peggy had sent Sarah's details to the parents of Phillip and little Sarah, hoping they would make contact and make the journey together this weekend. As the footsteps grew louder, Peggy could hear voices, and she felt relief when she recognised Sarah's laugh. 'We're in the back garden – there's a gate at the side!' she bellowed, getting to her feet as all the children rushed to the gate.

There was a jumble of bodies, hugging and kissing, as the London children launched themselves at their parents, everybody babbling about what they'd been doing since they'd last seen them and shouting about how much they'd missed each other. Peggy's sisters ran back to her excitedly, obviously swept away with all the emotion in the air. After introductions had been made, the two families agreed to take a walk around the village together and stop somewhere for lunch. Peggy was glad of some respite from being in charge of so many children, though she still had her sisters to look after.

'You need some time to yourself,' her mother said softly as Peggy knelt on the ground to work on another vegetable patch. 'I'll be fine with these three for an hour if you want to have a break.' It was tempting, but Peggy didn't want to take any risks. 'I can lie down on the sofa while they play in the living room,' her mother assured her. 'Lucy is an old head on young shoulders and she's bossy enough to keep the other two in check.'

'I'm not bossy!' Lucy bellowed from the other end of the garden. Peggy was forever fascinated at the fact that young children could hear everything from such a distance – yet if you were standing next to them asking them to do something they appeared to be deaf.

'You are too!' Martha yelled back.

Peggy and her mother laughed together.

'It's all right, Mother. I think it will be nice to have a few hours where it's just us and the girls. And, besides, what am I going to get up to if I venture out on my own? There's hardly anything to do in the village, and all my friends are off doing war work.' Peggy's voice faltered at the end of the sentence – the mention of war work made her pine for what she had left behind in London. Every time the German planes flew over the village on their way to London, Peggy thought of Dot and Viv and crossed her fingers, hoping the ritual would somehow keep them safe during the impending raid. 'Let's get you inside and warmed up, and I'll make some soup for lunch with all this delicious veg,' she declared cheerily to try and cover up her sadness.

Peggy settled her mother on the sofa and her sisters started working on a singing performance to wow them with after lunch. She could hear Lucy and Martha bickering over who was going to sing the lead when there was a knock at the door. 'Probably Dr Brady, come to check you're not scouring the house from top to bottom now you've been allowed out of bed,' Peggy teased, popping her head into the living room on her way to answer the door. She knew her mother had very high standards when it came to cleaning and Peggy had noticed her grimacing at a few mucky spots in the kitchen that she had clearly missed. But Peggy was taken aback when she answered the door to find a dashing young man in RAF uniform standing before her. Peggy was immediately transported back to Viv's flat all those weeks ago, when she had answered the door there to who she had assumed was William, but had turned out to be his friend . . .

'Johnny Warner,' he said now, holding out his hand formally. 'I do hope you don't mind the intrusion, but I bumped into Viv when I was over visiting William. She said you might appreciate some company.'

Peggy couldn't stop herself from laughing nervously and turning crimson as she shook his hand. She thought back to how she had confessed her desperation for love to her friends not so long ago. She knew exactly what Viv was up to. Her exclamation of William's handsomeness when she had first seen a photo of him played out in her mind – and the fact that the two men were so similar in looks would not have been lost on Viv, who was clearly trying to play match-maker here. But Peggy didn't mind; Johnny was wonderful to look at, and although their first meeting had been slightly awkward as they had sat making small talk waiting for Viv to arrive home, she had warmed to him and felt he was a good, reliable sort of man.

'What a lovely surprise,' she said apprehensively. She was suddenly panicking that Johnny had felt obliged to check in on her and wanted to be anywhere else but standing on her doorstep. There were probably many young women falling at his feet, all of whom would be pretty and glamorous like Viv. Peggy looked down at her soil-sodden outfit and felt a flash of embarrassment. She knew from past experience that she couldn't pull off being glamorous or classy, no matter how hard she tried.

'Mama! It's a boy!' Lucy shrieked from where Peggy hadn't seen her watching them in the hallway. Peggy's embarrassment was amplified, and awkwardness was thrown into the mix for good measure. The youngster ran back to the living room giggling and her siblings burst into the hallway to take a look for themselves.

'Is he your boyfriend, Pegs?' Martha asked innocently.

Horrified, Peggy looked back at Johnny, who was smiling at her with raised eyebrows. She quickly grabbed her coat from the stand and stepped out of the house, forcing Johnny backwards along the path. He laughed as he stumbled back.

'Tell mother I've changed my mind and I will go for a walk after all,' she called back to Martha, who was staring at Johnny now in wonderment. Then she quickly stepped back into the house and ran up to Martha. She leaned down to the little girl's ear. 'And he's *not* my boyfriend. You are *not* to repeat that again,' she hissed forcefully, before rushing back out and slamming the door behind her.

Out on the garden path, Peggy slipped her jacket on and straightened herself up, hoping that she didn't appear too flustered.

'Shall we walk?' Johnny asked, lifting his elbow to the side to indicate that he would like to link arms with her. Peggy's tummy flipped as she stepped forward to oblige.

As they got to the end of the garden she cringed and picked up her pace as a chorus of *Peggy's got a boyfriend!* rang out over and over from inside the house.

14

Dot ducked behind a wall as planes loomed in the sky overhead. The Germans were being relentless tonight – this was the second lot to fly over so far. Dot was on her way to visit the site of a reported bomb hitting a row of houses on her sector, having been sent out by Victor when the messenger rushed into the school. She'd been the only warden available; everyone else was already out dealing with other incidents. The first round of planes to visit the city had started dropping bombs almost as soon as the sirens had sounded that evening. She wasn't even sure if Donald and Bill, who had been tasked with getting residents on their sector to the crypt, had managed to complete the job before the first explosions had rung out.

Dot wasn't used to attending bomb sites alone, but she had assured Victor she'd be all right dealing with the situation solo. Now, as she watched a tall figure running ahead of her towards the same road she was headed for, she felt her heart racing and longed to have one of her colleagues by her side. It wasn't the Germans she was afraid of now – it was Tommy.

It had been just over a week since she'd discovered her husband had deserted the Army, and Dot had felt unsettled ever since. She saw his face everywhere she went – he was the man in front of her in the grocery store queue, the footsteps coming up behind her, and the figure walking along the street towards her was always Tommy. Dot no longer felt guilty for the relief she'd felt when she'd thought he was dead because she now realised that, as long as he was alive, she would never feel safe.

As the sound of the German planes faded into the distance without unloading any more explosives, Dot continued on her way. She didn't bother listening out for more planes approaching; the only thing she was keeping a lookout for was the person she had previously spotted, terrified Tommy was going to jump out of the shadows.

Dot had been hopeful at first that there had been a mix-up with the telegram Beryl received and that Tommy was in fact missing in action. He had previously written to Beryl begging for forgiveness, which indicated he had made it back to base. But Beryl had revealed that she hadn't checked the post mark on that letter, and now she came to think of it, she couldn't actually remember seeing one at all. Then Jim had admitted to finding it strange that the envelope had appeared on the doormat seemingly in the middle of the night; it hadn't been there when they'd left for the shelter and then it had been waiting for them on their return in the early hours of the following morning. The post was a little up the spout currently, but they all knew for certain that the postmen weren't out making deliveries during raids.

'He probably pushed it through the letter box himself,' he realised with a shudder before going off to double-lock all the doors and windows. Dot had made her excuses and left, then. If Tommy was in the area, she didn't want to be anywhere near their old home – the place he was most likely to show up at once he decided to reappear.

'He wouldn't dare turn up again around here,' Viv had tried to reassure her when Dot had filled her in. 'He's obviously feeling sheepish, otherwise why would he creep over in the dead of the night to post the letter? He must have been out delivering it during a raid. That certainly doesn't sound like a man who is ready to throw his weight around again.'

Dot had to agree, but she also worried that Tommy would grow angry when he didn't get the reaction he craved from the women in his life. She certainly would have expected him to turn up at the house himself and demand to be let back in, rather than writing ahead to plead for forgiveness. The Tommy she knew would have just sauntered back in and expected everything to be back to normal, including Dot still being his doting wife. He would know that any reply Beryl might send to his letter would never reach him, so what was his plan? Had the letter been an attempt to soften his mother ahead of him returning home? The fact he hadn't shown his face yet worried her more than reassured her. Had he been watching them? Did he know that Dot hadn't returned since the night she left? It all made her feel very anxious about what he might be plotting.

Dot had tried to push her fears aside, but she'd spent the whole week feeling on edge and jumpy. She felt as though she was just waiting for Tommy to make his move and she didn't like the fact that he had all the power. Now, she felt relief when she turned the corner and saw a group of men outside a half-collapsed house, because she felt safe when she was with other people, even if she was out on the streets in the middle of a raid.

'We're all set here, love. There was nobody inside – most of the street still goes to the shelter,' one of the men said as she approached.

'Fast work,' Dot replied. It was normally the role of the air raid warden to assess the situation and find out if there were casualties. 'I can't believe you lot got here before me – I came over as soon as the call came in.'

'Just luck. We were on our way to the shelter ourselves when the bomb hit. My ears are still ringing,' he replied, rubbing at his earlobes and wincing. Dot had assumed they were rescue workers. She was always impressed at how people pitched in to help these days. These men had stayed out on the street with the Germans flying overhead, still unloading bombs on the area, when they could have just carried on to the shelter and left somebody else to pick up the pieces.

'We weren't dawdling,' the man added. 'We left as soon as we heard the sirens. The rest of the street is all families, so they go to the shelters before the nightly visitors arrive, to get the kiddies settled in for a sleep. I might have to start doing that myself from now on.' The men behind him nodded their heads in agreement.

Dot peered along the rest of the houses in the row and saw that the windows in most of them had been blown out by the blast. Then she noticed two figures staggering towards them in the dark. Dot walked quickly in their direction and was soon able to make out that it was a man and a woman. The man was supporting the woman around her waist.

'My wife's fine,' he called out as Dot drew closer. 'But she took a bit of a stumble when the bomb hit,' he continued once she reached them. 'We were at home. We'd decided to finish our dinner before going to a shelter. The blighters don't normally turn up so quickly after the sirens and we only had a few mouthfuls left. They sure took us by surprise tonight.'

Dot thought of the man she'd just spoken to and nodded her head – it seemed the Jerries had caught lots of people out this evening. She wondered again if Bill and Donald had managed to get everybody to the shelter in time.

'Well, let's not hang around here for more bombs,' she said. 'Come on you lot!' she shouted back to the group of men. 'We'll go to the crypt together!'

As the group made their way back along the road, the woman lurched towards her house.

'I've already told you, Edith – we can't go back in! The bombs are still falling and the Germans could circle back at any moment,' her husband snapped.

'Please, just let me get my jewellery box,' she pleaded.

'I'm sorry, but he's right,' Dot said firmly. She'd wasted enough time talking to everybody out on the street, she needed to get them all to the crypt as quickly as possible before any more bombs came down for them. Edith tried to fight back against her husband but winced at the pain in her side and gave in as he guided her away from the door. As they walked, he explained that she had just got up to clear their plates when they heard the planes approaching.

'Then, suddenly, there was the whistle of one falling. We both stared at each other – we were frozen to the spot. We didn't know what to do. It was so loud that we knew it was close, but there wasn't time to do anything. Before I knew it, the house was shaking, the windows were blowing in, and Edith had flown across the room and smacked into one of the cupboards.' Dot looked across at Edith and saw she was still clutching her side as her husband supported her. 'I think it might be a rib or two,' he whispered, 'but I'm trying not to panic her too much.'

'She'll probably need checking over at the hospital or a first-aid post in the morning, but I think we're better off getting her to the shelter now while the Jerries are still circling,' Dot replied. He nodded his head in agreement.

Just then, she heard the sickening drone of plane engines. 'Get down!' she yelled, and they all threw themselves to the ground as bombs whistled down in the distance, drawing nearer. As the noise got closer, Dot braced herself with her hands covering her head and the familiar feel of the pavement on her face. She lifted her head briefly to check everybody was safely on the ground, and she saw Edith grappling with her husband. She could see they were shouting at each other, but she hadn't heard any of it because of all the racket. Realising Edith probably wouldn't be able to bear the pain of throwing herself on the floor with damaged ribs, but that her husband would be attempting to convince her to try, Dot got to her feet and rushed over. The gunfire and bombs were getting closer, and Dot's heart was in her mouth. She didn't have the time or a loud enough voice to explain anything to them. Instead, she just ran at them and bundled them into the nearest doorway. It wouldn't give them a great deal of protection, but it was better than nothing and it was certainly better than standing in the middle of the street as the Germans unleashed hell. Dot saw Edith's face contort in pain as they all slammed against the door. 'Sorry,' she whispered in her ear just before the planes passed over.

The planes dropped a bomb further down the street, near to the spot where they had recently been standing and talking. Shrapnel and debris tore down the road. It just skimmed over the bodies of the men who were lying flat on the ground, and Dot breathed a sigh of relief. Then she looked at Edith again and she could see the realisation on her face: she and her husband would have been wiped out if they'd still been standing in the street.

With the planes moving on, silence fell over them all and the men started slowly getting up and dusting themselves off. They all checked themselves over, as if expecting to find a piece of shrapnel embedded in their bodies. Thankfully, everybody had escaped unscathed.

'Are you all right to run?' Dot asked Edith. Fear had clearly taken over her discomfort as the woman nodded and set off without her husband's support. Everybody followed her lead and Dot was grateful for that; she did not want them out on the street if the Germans came back again.

Once they were safely in the crypt, Dot caught up with Bill and Donald while the others got themselves settled in amongst the crowded space.

'They had a good go at Chelsea tonight and there's been a fair few houses hit, but no major casualties so far,' Donald informed her.

They agreed that the two men would report back to the post to be available for any further incidents, leaving Dot to oversee things at the crypt. Normally she preferred being out and about during raids, but tonight she was happy to be a sitting duck in a shelter. At least with all these people around, Tommy couldn't get to her. When she saw that Edith was asleep, she went to talk to the woman's husband, who finally introduced himself as Alfie.

'Thank you for what you did back there,' he said as Dot settled down on the ground next to him.

'It was nothing. It's hard to know what to do in the moment if someone is panicking and in pain.'

'She's going to kill me for not letting her get that damn jewellery box,' he sighed, rubbing his hands over his grubby face. 'She leaves it on the sideboard in the kitchen so it's ready for her to pick up and take with us whenever we go to a shelter. She can't stand the thought of losing any of it if the house is wrecked.

She's not bothered about the house or anything else inside it – as long as she's got those heirlooms with her then nothing else matters.' He chuckled, then added lightly: 'Even me.'

Dot laughed with him. 'I can understand how she feels about the jewellery,' she said, running her finger over the ring she wore on her right hand – her mother's wedding ring. She wasn't sure what she would do if she ever lost it – it was the last thing connecting her to the most important woman in her life.

'We were so shaken by what had happened,' Alfie said, 'and I was worried about how hurt she was. I just wanted to get us out and to help as quickly as possible. She shouted at me to grab the box, but I was putting all my strength into holding her up and getting her to safety. Surely it was better to save her than the jewellery?'

'I'm sure she'll understand. And you're probably worrying over nothing, anyway. I haven't heard the planes coming back again. I think the Germans have moved on to destroy another part of London.' Alfie seemed to find relief in Dot's words, so she didn't voice the fact that she could picture Stan climbing into their home through one of the blown-out windows and helping himself to Edith's most treasured possessions. 'You'll need to get her to the hospital as soon as the all-clear sounds. Do you want me to go back to your house and get the jewellery box? It's on my way back to the warden's post anyway, and we can keep it safe there until you're able to come and collect it.'

'We'd be so grateful – thank you,' Alfie replied.

Dot smiled back, hoping she would be able to get there before Stan – or whoever it was looting the bombed-out houses.

The all-clear didn't sound for another six hours. When Dot finally emerged from the crypt she blinked into the morning light, upset at the thought of London taking such a battering overnight. She went straight to Edith and Alfie's street. Her heart dropped when she saw most of the front doors on the row of houses wide open. Some of the residents were standing outside, looking dumbfounded. Dot approached a woman in a nightgown, who was holding a shawl around herself and shaking her head with tears in her eyes.

'Is everything okay?' she asked, though she had guessed from the wide-open doors that somebody had entered all the houses through the blown-out windows and then happily let themselves out laden with whatever they'd been able to lay their hands on.

'It's all gone,' the woman whispered between sobs. 'Who would do that? Who would rob us all when we're already going through it? When we've already lost so much?'

Dot knew exactly who would rob them in such circumstances, and she could feel her anger levels rising. She turned on her heel and went to Alfie and Edith's house. After walking in through the open front door, she stopped dead in her tracks. The place was a tip – not because of bomb damage but because it had been ransacked. Not only had the looter stolen from them but they had ripped up floorboards and moved furniture. There was something about it that felt more professional than Stan's approach. His stealing had been opportunistic. This criminal was being more thorough, checking under floorboards; this was somebody who was after more than just a watch here and a ring there. This was somebody who meant business. She'd been so convinced of Stan's guilt, but maybe it wasn't him, after all. Dot was hopeful that whoever was behind the burglary might have been so focused on finding hidden treasure that they'd missed the jewellery box sitting in plain view. But when she looked, the sideboard where Alfie had told her she'd find it was empty.

15

A week after Viv's walk round the grounds with William, she was back at the hospital following another busy night on duty. She had finally reached the end of Mr West's petrol supply the last time she'd refilled the car, and she was upset at the prospect of losing the freedom the vehicle allowed her. Getting the train out to West Sussex was going to seriously restrict the number of trips she could make, as well as how much time she got to spend with William. Having arrived in the early hours exhausted from her night on duty, Viv once again fell into a deep sleep as soon as she sat on the chair next to William's bed and laid her head on the edge of his bed. She woke with a crick in her neck which she was massaging when Deirdre approached her.

'I really do wish we had a spare bed for you, my dear,' she said sympathetically as Viv winced in pain. 'We're full to bursting every day at the moment,' she added with a sigh. 'These poor men. It just seems to be never-ending.'

'I'm just grateful to be able to fall asleep next to William. I don't mind,' Viv replied groggily. 'And I don't normally wake up in pain,' she added as she tentatively rocked her head from side to side to try and ease the ache. 'I must have drifted off in an awkward position, that's all.' Looking around her, she couldn't believe it was time for the patients to get up already – she didn't feel like she'd slept at all.

'He's been doing really well this week,' Deirdre whispered, gesturing at William, who was still asleep. 'He's been round the grounds a few times. I've taken him out with a few of the other servicemen who are up and walking about. Whatever you did with him last week really boosted his confidence.'

Viv smiled and felt a weight lift off her shoulders. She had been so worried about William since her last visit. Their final few hours with Johnny had been fun and William had been in good spirits when she'd left, but her mind had kept wandering back to how he had panicked when the group of women had been walking towards them. Suddenly, Deirdre turned her head to the side and her hand reached to the corner of her eye as she brushed tears away.

'Whatever's the matter?' Viv asked, getting to her feet to put her hand on the older woman's shoulder. As Viv searched her face questioningly, Deirdre took a deep breath and composed herself.

'I'm so sorry, my dear,' she said. She took a step back so that Viv's hand fell away, then she straightened out her uniform and tucked a stray hair behind her ear. 'That was very unprofessional of me. I've had news since I saw you last – my husband is missing in action.' She took another deep breath, closed her eyes, and bit her lip briefly before continuing. 'I'm mostly coping, but every now and then it just gets to me – the not knowing, the not knowing if I'll ever know, and the thought of never seeing him again.' She fought back a sob.

'I'm so sorry.' Viv's heart broke for her.

'I shouldn't be getting upset while I'm at work. I just look at you and your devotion to this man, and I can't help but feel distressed about what I've lost.'

'You haven't lost him. Not yet,' Viv said firmly. She took both Deirdre's hands in her own. 'Look at me,' she urged the nurse until they were holding eye contact. 'You must stay positive. You must believe he will come home. You must believe it. You can't give up on him.' Deirdre sniffed and tears filled her eyes again, but she smiled weakly and nodded her head. 'I thought I'd lost William, but he came back to me. You can't give up hope. If you give up hope, then what do you have left?'

Deirdre smiled. 'He came back to you, and I pray every day my Ronnie will come back to me.'

'He'll do everything in his power to get back to you. Believe me.'

The two women both jumped at the sound of William's voice; neither of them had noticed him waking up. 'I thought about giving up, but the thought of seeing Viv again pushed me on,' he whispered, holding his hand out to her. Viv's heart swelled as she took his hand in hers. 'If he can get back to you, he will. Don't give up on him, Deirdre. And don't grieve for him until you have to.'

'I won't,' she promised firmly.

As William ate his breakfast, sharing his toast with Viv as he always did when she was there, she couldn't stop thinking about poor Deirdre and the anguish she must be going through. One of her colleagues at the ambulance station had a brother missing in action, and she thought about him, too. Then her thoughts inevitably wandered to Dot, who was also suffering, with Tommy being AWOL – though in her instance she didn't want him to come back. But these thoughts made Viv feel lucky in a way; things could have been so terribly different for her, but she'd been given a second chance with William and now she was feeling more determined than ever to make the most of it. The war was teaching Viv that time was of the essence, and she needed to live every day to the full.

'Johnny was here yesterday,' William said, tugging Viv back to the present. 'He seems very taken with your friend Peggy; he wouldn't stop talking about her.' Viv grinned. 'Did you have that in mind when you asked him to check in on her?' he asked. Viv gave him a cheeky wink and popped her last bite of toast in her mouth. William laughed as he waited for her to finish chewing. 'Well?' he pushed as she took a sip of tea.

'Let's just say that I knew he was her type,' Viv said mysteriously. When she'd seen Johnny on her last visit to the hospital, it had seemed like the perfect plan to encourage him to spend some time with Peggy – especially given her friend's recent admission that she was desperate for a man to settle down with. 'I picked up on a bit of an attraction when Johnny visited me in London to tell me about your accident,' she explained, not wanting to give too much away and embarrass her friend. 'It obviously wasn't an appropriate occasion to do any matchmaking, so I bided my time, that's all.'

'Well, I think Johnny is very grateful.'

Their conversation was interrupted by Dr McIndoe doing his daily rounds. After greeting the two of them and carrying out his usual checks, he drew up a chair on the other side of William's bed. Viv's heart started racing as she tried to guess what he wanted.

'It's time to take a look at your damaged eye,' the doctor announced cheerily. He smiled at William as he explained what he planned to do when he got him on the operating table, and Viv found it difficult to worry about what was coming next when Dr McIndoe was being so positive. She remembered her advice to Deirdre and decided to follow it herself by being optimistic about William's surgery. She reminded herself that there was no point in worrying about what would happen if he lost the sight in his eye unless it happened. While there was still a chance that William would see out of his right eye again, she needed to stay upbeat for him.

'But I'll be able to see properly again, won't I?'

Viv looked up and saw the distress on William's face as Dr McIndoe explained that, though he would do his absolute best, there was a chance he wouldn't be able to save the sight in his damaged eye. His light-hearted tone was gone and so was Viv's positive thinking as images of William being medically discharged from the RAF flashed through her mind.

'I know you two don't get much time together, so I'll stop cramping your style now,' the doctor added, suddenly sounding bright again. The shift in attitude gave Viv a jolt, and she tried to nudge herself back to thinking positively once more. Dr McIndoe stood up. 'We've scheduled the surgery for this time next week,' he added, giving Viv a pointed look. She knew he was silently reminding her of their conversation in his office, where he had said he'd like her to be at the hospital when William came round after the operation. She gave him a slight nod while her mind raced, trying to figure out if it was possible. She was on shift the night before. With the car, she would have been able to get to West Sussex in time no matter how late she clocked off in the early hours of the following morning. Viv mentally kicked herself for not saving precious fuel for such an important journey. She would have to make sure she got the first train out of London. She was hopeful she could do it – it was just that it wouldn't be as much of a certainty if she was relying on public transport.

'Let's get you out for some fresh air,' she suggested to William. 'Everything always feels better after a walk.' She waved Deirdre over and asked her to fetch a wheelchair, and in no time at all they were wandering around the gardens again. Viv found a bench and she sat down so William was opposite her.

'I don't know what I'll do if I have to leave the RAF,' William whispered once they were alone again.

Viv grabbed hold of his hand and brought it to her lips to kiss it tenderly.

'You must stay positive,' she said gently, repeating her earlier advice to Deirdre.

Recognition flashed across William's face, and he grinned. 'I woke up to you saying that,' he replied quietly. Then his smile suddenly faded. 'But it's not as simple as staying positive for me, Viv. It's not a case of waiting to see if someone makes it back to me or not. My life doesn't mean anything without the RAF.'

'What about me?' She'd said it before thinking, and immediately wished she could take it back. She'd turned down the chance to be his wife just before his crash – what right did she have to demand any space in his life after the war was over? How could she possibly be upset at the fact he had something more important than her in his world?

'Oh, Viv.' He squeezed her hand and looked at her affectionately.

'Sorry,' she said. 'Just forget I said that – it wasn't fair of me. We need to focus on you and getting you through this.'

'You matter to me, too,' he said. 'And I don't want you to think I don't appreciate everything you've done for me since the crash. I wouldn't have made it this far through my recovery without you.'

'And I'm going to be by your side until you're back to full health,' she promised.

'With you here, I can get through anything,' he declared confidently.

Viv could feel affection pouring out of him. It made her feel so in love with him, and so secure in what they had together. Her usual fears about what William would think when he found out about her past crept into her mind – as they always did whenever she was with him and feeling happy. As her doubts tried yet again to distinguish her warm glow, Viv decided it was time to confront them once and for all. She couldn't go on like this – having her happiness constantly ripped away from her because she was worried about what William might think when he discovered the truth. It was time to find out and deal with the consequences. If he accepted her despite her past, then Viv could finally lift the weight from her shoulders and be free. And if William pushed her away, then at least she would know it was time to give up on her dream of a happily ever after with him before she fell even deeper in love – if it was possible to love him even more than she already did; she wasn't sure it was.

Viv took a deep breath and looked away from William. Having built herself up to tell him everything she was considering backing out – again. She closed her eyes and reminded herself of how heavy the secret had felt all this time, and how it had clouded every single happy moment she had ever enjoyed with him. It was always there in the background. The fear that he would find out and push her away taunted her constantly. Viv had to find out either way, and she didn't feel like she was going to get a better chance than this.

'Where have you gone?' William's voice cut into her internal battle, and she jumped when she felt his fingers gently caressing her cheek. She turned her head back towards him and he leaned forward in his chair, searching her face for the answer she knew she had to give.

'I was just thinking about something I've been meaning to tell you for a long time now,' Viv replied cautiously before pausing to take a deep breath. 'I did something in my past that I'm not proud of, and I've been too scared to tell you about it,' she added.

William sat back in his chair and smiled. 'You don't need to tell me anything, my love. I am devoted to you, and I have been since the day that we met. I love you because of who you are right now, in this moment. I love you because of everything you do, and regardless of anything you might have done before you met me.' Viv felt tears welling in her eyes and wondered once again if William was going to ask her to be his wife. 'But, you see, whatever you did before you met me really doesn't matter – all that matters is the caring, compassionate and beautiful woman who is sitting before me now.'

'Oh, William,' Viv whispered, wiping the tears from her eyes. 'That means so much to me.' She was tempted to go along with what he was saying, and just forget about her impulse to unload her burden. But she knew that if she didn't tell him now then, despite everything he had said, the truth would always hang over her like a noose, waiting to hang her and bring it all to an end.

'I want to spend the rest of my life with you, William.'

He grabbed her hands in his and nodded his agreement.

Viv allowed her heart to swell momentarily before focusing again on what she had to tell him. 'But if we are to do that, then I think it's only fair that you know everything about me. I don't think you can really know me without knowing what I've done. I'm not the perfect woman that you seem to think I am.'

'You're scaring me now, Viv,' he said, laughing nervously.

She braced herself. This was it. She just had to come out and say it.

'I had an affair with a married man and, when I fell pregnant, he left me.' She examined his face for signs of a reaction, but he just looked confused.

'I don't understand, my love. Are you trying to tell me that you're a mother? Because I would love any child of yours as much as I love you.'

'No, I . . . I lost the baby—' Before she could finish the sentence, William had leaned over and pulled her into an embrace.

'My poor darling Viv. I'm so sorry.'

Viv pulled away sharply and held his gaze. 'Did you hear what I said?' she asked. 'I was only pregnant in the first place because I was intimate with a married man. I made love to another woman's husband. And I knew he was married when I did it, but I did it anyway. Do you understand what kind of a woman that makes me? Do you really want to spend the rest of your life with a harlot like me?' She wasn't quite sure what she was doing. William had reacted in a way she would never have dreamed he would – he was only concerned with how losing the baby had affected her, he hadn't even flinched when she had mentioned the affair.

She should be overjoyed but instead she seemed intent on pushing him away.

'You don't need to keep punishing yourself, Viv. I think you've been through enough.' William leaned in again to brush a stray hair away from her face, then he kissed her, and she felt all her worries disappearing. When he gently pulled away, she let out a long breath. 'I can't believe you were worried about telling me that, Viv. I thought you knew that I loved you no matter what.'

'Yes, but it was such an awful thing to do.'

'And I'm sure you've learned your lesson from it. Besides, there were two of you in the relationship, and I would hazard a guess that you were young and impressionable when it happened, seduced by an older man who should have known better. The blame cannot fall on you alone.'

Viv didn't know what to say. This man she had fallen in love with understood her completely and loved her despite her flaws.

'Anyway,' William continued softly, 'I don't believe for a second that you would ever do anything like that again. The Viv that I love wouldn't dream of it.'

'I wouldn't. Not in a million years,' she said firmly, emotions rising inside her, ready to explode out of her body. 'I've beaten myself up over it ever since, and I convinced myself that you'd want nothing more to do with me once you knew the truth.' Tears were running down her cheeks now.

'That's why you never fully let me in,' William said, understanding suddenly sweeping his face. Viv nodded and stared at the ground. 'And why you turned down my marriage proposal?' She nodded again but she couldn't bring herself to look at William. 'You can't deny yourself a happy life because of one mistake in your past, Viv.' She felt his finger tap her chin ever so gently. 'Look at me,' he added softly. She did as he asked, fighting back tears as their eyes met. 'You need to let it go. I love you and none of your past mistakes will change that. You're the woman who has shown me that I can get through whatever life throws at me, and you're the woman who has shown me that she will love me no matter what. How could I possibly reject you because of something you did before you even met me? How would that be fair?'

'I love you so much,' she whispered. William kissed her again and Viv realised she was desperate to build a future with this man – if only he would ask for her hand in marriage one more time.

16

Elsie and Ted squealed in delight as milk shot out of the cow's udders and into a bucket. Peggy's little sisters, who had grown up helping milk their neighbour's animals, were taking the task a little more seriously and were each concentrating on producing the most liquid. Peggy found it funny that the three of them could turn almost anything into a competition. It wasn't any surprise to her, though – she had been exactly the same with their brothers and sister Joan when they had all been younger.

Thinking of Joan made her long for her sister to be here with her, but she quickly dismissed the thought to stop herself from getting upset in front of the children. As much as it pained her, Peggy had decided to honour her mother's wish to keep her poor health from the rest of the family. She had toyed with the idea of telling only Joan – the two of them had always been so close that it felt terrible to be keeping secrets from her. But her sister was enjoying her land work so much and Peggy didn't want her to feel obliged to walk away from it to help. She could cope on her own.

Helping at the farm next door had become Elsie and Ted's favourite thing to do since they had discovered the cows here were the source of the milk that they drank every day. They had both looked at Peggy in bemusement when she had poured milk from a jug on their first morning at the house.

'What's that?' Ted had asked.

'Milk,' Peggy had replied.

'Oh no. Milk comes from a tin,' Elsie had announced, much to the amusement of Martha and Lucy. Annie had giggled, too, though Peggy wasn't sure she had understood – she often just laughed along when her sisters found something funny.

When Peggy had realised that Elsie and Ted had only ever tasted tinned milk, she had taken them all to Mr Grainger's farm round the corner to show them where the drink really came from. The two of them had been astonished, and they were further blown away when Mr Grainger had showed them the pile of eggs his chickens had laid. The eight of them had been making regular visits to help with the animals since. Mr Grainger, muscly and weathered from his many years of farm work, always greeted them with a smile. He often rewarded them with some eggs for their help – though Peggy suspected they hindered rather than aided the old man, and that he could get his work done a lot quicker without their regular 'assistance'.

As the children got on with milking the cows now, Peggy found herself wondering what Johnny would make of the activity. She knew he was a city boy. He had told her he hailed from Birmingham when he'd stopped by to see her. Peggy quickly scolded herself for thinking about him yet again – she couldn't seem to get the man out of her head. It had been just over a week since Johnny's surprise visit and, try as she might, she just couldn't stop thinking about him. Every time something happened, she found herself wondering what he might think of it. She ran through in her mind what she would say to him about certain events and imagined his reaction. Peggy knew she was getting carried away and acting like a lovesick teenager, but she couldn't seem to stop herself. She'd only met him twice – the first time wasn't planned, and he'd given her no reason to think he had turned up to see her in Petworth for any other reason than out of a sense of duty to Viv. She felt embarrassed when she thought about how much she had enjoyed their walk around the village together. He had probably merely endured it, feeling desperate to get back to RAF Tangmere or into London to dance with pretty women at one of the clubs. Peggy didn't expect that he would waste any more time visiting her again, which made her mooning after him seem even more pathetic.

She wondered if she was only pining for him so much because she felt so lonely out here in the countryside. If she told anybody how isolated she felt then she was certain they would laugh at her – she was forever surrounded by company. But she was struggling to keep up with the demands of looking after so many children and keeping such a large house in order. And though her sisters and the other children were good fun to be around, it wasn't the same as having people her own age to talk to. Peggy was finding it difficult being responsible for all of them all of the time. She longed for some adult company and often dreamed of how much easier things would be if Joan was here to help her. She also missed Dot and Viv terribly and constantly felt guilty about leaving her air raid warden role while London was still under attack.

When the children had all had enough of milking the cows, Peggy walked them back to the house, giving them strict orders to wash themselves while she got their tea ready.

They had been at the farm all afternoon and she could tell from the way they were all sniping at each other that they were hungry. It was playful teasing at the moment, but Peggy knew from experience that it wouldn't take long for it to escalate when they were tired and hungry. Turning into their street, Peggy spotted a male figure in the front garden, dressed smartly in what looked like military uniform. Her heart started thumping in her chest and her worst fears raced through her head. Were one of her brothers or her father injured – or worse? She felt sick.

'It's Peggy's boyfriend!' Lucy screeched, breaking away from the group and running at speed towards the man. Peggy had been so busy searching the man's hands for a telegram that she hadn't even looked at his face. Johnny was one of the people she had been hoping more than anything to see again – but he was the one person she had least expected to turn up. Her relief and joy at realising it was him was replaced with embarrassment when she registered what Lucy had just said. The rest of the children were now running along the road towards Johnny, too, and Peggy broke into a run to catch up. When she reached the garden, Lucy was talking at Johnny so quickly it seemed she might run out of breath, and the rest of the children were clambering around him, asking him questions. Peggy made a snap decision not to address Lucy's earlier comment, deciding that ignoring it would be better than drawing more attention to it.

'I'm so sorry about this,' Peggy said. 'Children. Please calm down and give my friend some space,' she added firmly. She couldn't quite believe Johnny had come back to see her so soon and she was worried he'd be put off by all the noise and chattering.

'Don't worry,' Johnny laughed. 'This one was just telling me all about milking cows, and I think this little lad wants to know about flying planes,' he added as he ruffled Ted's hair affectionately. Peggy was relieved. She also felt a burst of affection towards Johnny when she saw how relaxed he was around the rabble she now called her family. 'I hope you don't mind me turning up unannounced. I found myself with the afternoon and evening off and thought it would be nice to see you again.'

Peggy felt herself flushing red. So, Viv hadn't sent him this time – he'd come over of his own accord. Or was he just saying that to be polite? Realising everybody was waiting for her to open the door, she did so and then she herded the children inside.

'Remember it's time to wash up!' she called out after them as they all flew up the stairs. She knew her sisters would be going straight into their mother's room to tell her about their visitor. She turned to Johnny. 'Of course I don't mind. It's wonderful to see you,' she said nervously. Wonderful was an understatement – she was absolutely over the moon. But Peggy reminded herself not to get carried away – he was surely only here again on Viv's orders, despite what he claimed.

'I felt a little silly hanging around on the doorstep, but I couldn't hear the children inside and I didn't want to knock and disturb your mother if she was here on her own.'

'That's so thoughtful of you,' Peggy replied. Just then, they heard a squeal followed by loud laughter from upstairs. Peggy sighed. 'I'll have to round them up.'

Johnny put out his arm to stop her. 'You go and do what you need to do – I'll help them get cleaned up,' he said gently. 'Right!' he shouted, rubbing his hands together and almost bouncing up the stairs. 'Who's going to be the soap monster's first victim?'

Peggy laughed to herself and went into the kitchen to start making corned beef fritters. Giggles and the sound of little feet running up and down the upstairs hallway filled the house. Once the patties were ready to fry, Peggy realised it had fallen silent. She crept tentatively up the stairs and when she reached the top, she could hear Johnny's voice. She followed it to her parents' bedroom. Confused, she peered round the doorway and saw her mother sitting up in bed, with all the children seated on the edge of it, captivated. Stepping into the room, she saw they were all staring at Johnny who was sitting on the chair in the corner of the room.

'Your gentleman friend was just telling us all about how he defends us from the Germans in his plane,' her mother said in awe.

'I thought it had gone quiet.'

'He flies fighter jets and gets the baddies!' Ted shouted, jumping to his feet and putting his arms out to the side, pretending to be a plane. Suddenly all the children were joining in. When Johnny put his arms out and whizzed towards her, Peggy couldn't help but chuckle. Then she did the same.

'All planes ready to fly to the dining table, please!' she announced. They all filed past her, and she went over to the bed to help her mother up.

'Don't worry, I'll take care of this one,' Johnny announced cheekily as he ran round the side of the bed and swept Mrs Miller up in his arms.

'Ooooh!' she cried out before breaking into a big grin.

'She's meant to be taking it easy!' Peggy giggled.

'A little bit of excitement will do her good,' he replied with a wink.

'I do find those stairs a wrench, dear,' Peggy's mother said dramatically as Johnny walked out of the room with her in his arms. He was carrying her with such ease, Peggy couldn't stop thinking about how strong he was.

Johnny stayed for dinner, and he talked to the children for the whole time, never tiring of their endless questions. When everybody was finished, Peggy went to clear the plates, but he jumped up and insisted on doing it. Once he was in the kitchen and the children had gone to put their pyjamas on, Peggy could feel her mother's eyes on her.

'He's just a friend,' Peggy said firmly, anticipating what her mother was going to say.

'He's very charming.'

'Yes, I noticed,' Peggy replied sarcastically, raising her eyebrows.

'Oh, come on, dear. You can't deny your mother a bit of harmless fun at a time like this!'

They both burst into laughter. Peggy could see how much her mother had enjoyed having Johnny to visit. The children had fallen for him, too.

'You should snap him up. A man like that won't stay single for long.'

'He's not interested in somebody like me,' Peggy replied, shaking her head.

'I beg to differ, dear! Why on earth do you think he keeps coming round? I'd like to think he has his eye on me but he's only trying to impress me to get you onside.'

'That's not it at all. He's just a naturally charming chap, and he's only been checking in with us because Viv asked him to. He's one of William's close friends. I'm sure there are a million other things he'd rather be doing.' She paused to take a sip of water. 'So don't go getting yourself carried away with ideas of a son-in-law in the RAF,' she added light-heartedly.

She didn't want her mother to know how disappointed she was that Johnny wasn't interested in her. Peggy couldn't bring herself to admit that she knew he would be looking for a woman who was more glamorous and fun-loving than she was – somebody like Viv. Peggy knew he had been a regular at the London clubs with William before the accident, and she wasn't exactly the kind of girl he could take dancing at Café de Paris. She had tried to fit in with that sort of crowd once before and she wasn't about to put herself through it again. He'd probably end up with one of Viv's friends in the end. But, no matter, she was enjoying getting to know him as a friend and spending time with him, and he had certainly brightened the day for everybody.

When the kitchen noises died down the two women instinctively stopped talking about their guest.

'Peggy, I noticed on the way in that they're playing *Room for Two* at the Regal Cinema in the village,' Johnny said nervously.

She turned around to find him standing in the doorway. His usual charm and confidence seemed to have disappeared. 'Would you care to watch it with me?' Peggy was suddenly lost for words. She opened her mouth to speak but nothing came out.

'She'd love to accompany you, my dear,' her mother said.

'But . . . the children,' Peggy spluttered. 'I need to get them to bed. I can't leave you to do that on your own, Mother.'

'Oh, it doesn't start for a little while, we could walk over once they're all settled,' Johnny offered.

'Nonsense!' Mrs Miller cried. 'You'll give the Bradys a knock on the way and Patricia will come over and help me put the children to bed. They're no bother anyway and I could do it on my own, but I know you'll only fret about me getting up and down the stairs the whole time you're out.'

'Well, that's settled, then,' Johnny said happily, suddenly standing a little straighter again.

'I guess it is,' Peggy replied quietly. She was panicking now, wondering whether Viv had put him up to this, too. But she'd tried to give him a way out and he'd refused to take it. Maybe he was just lonely like her. There was no harm in two friends going to watch a film together.

'Go and get changed, dear,' her mother urged, and Peggy realised sadly that she had nothing suitable for a cinema trip with somebody as smart as Johnny.

17

Dot was filled with apprehension walking along Lawrence Street. It had been a week since Edith's jewellery box had been stolen, and she still felt terrible for the woman. Poor Edith, still in pain from her injuries, had collapsed into Alfie's arms when they'd turned up at the ARP post hoping to pick it up and Dot had explained that she'd been too late to save it. They'd gone to the school straight from the hospital, so she'd then had to warn the couple about the state of their house and the fact they had probably lost a lot more than the jewellery. As Dot had suspected at the time, it turned out that the looter or looters had targeted the whole street. She couldn't stop thinking about the fact they could have been lying in wait, hiding out and watching as she had escorted everybody to the shelter earlier that evening.

The more Dot thought about it, the more certain she was that these robberies were too organised and sophisticated to have been carried out by Stan. She was desperate to track down Edith's jewellery before it was sold on and, whether Stan was the culprit or not, Jim was her only lead right now – her only link to shady back-alley deals and the offloading of stolen goods.

She had wanted to go round and see him and Beryl again since dashing off following the arrival of the telegram, but she'd kept putting it off, consumed with concerns that Tommy was staking out the house and waiting to pounce on her the next time she visited. Or worse, she would knock on the door and Tommy himself would answer. For all of Beryl's assurances that she would send him packing if he turned up, Dot wasn't naïve; she knew Beryl had always doted on Tommy despite his many faults. She'd seen the fear in Beryl's eyes when she'd read that telegram, and Dot also knew how persuasive Tommy could be. And, despite everything, he was still her son. She could never blame the woman for giving him another chance, as much as he might not deserve it. Jim's presence didn't bring Dot any comfort. She'd seen him cower at the sight of Stan, and Stan was as meek as a pussycat compared to Tommy. There was no chance of him stopping Tommy from getting his feet under the table again.

Reports of houses being ransacked while the residents were sheltering had risen over the last few days, so Dot had decided it was time she stopped worrying about herself and did whatever she could do to stop more people from losing their most treasured possessions. Terrified that Tommy would be lurking in the shadows, Dot was on high alert as she approached the front door of her former home. She checked all around her one final time when she got there, and then she put her ear to the door and listened intently for any sign that her husband was inside. Met with silence, she carefully pushed the letter box open and peered through, searching the hallway for his boots. She tried not to think about how strange she must look to her old neighbours. Finally satisfied that the coast was clear, Dot knocked gently on the door. Jim opened it a fraction, glanced through the small gap nervously, then flung it open and beckoned her in, quickly closing it behind her and locking it. He was clearly as frightened of Tommy returning as she was.

'Has he been back?' she asked fretfully.

'No, dear. But we've been jittery all week. My nerves are shot.'

Dot smiled. There was something endearing about Jim's honesty. Beryl was asleep in her chair, so the two of them sat at the table in the dining room to talk.

'She's putting on a brave face, but I know she's struggling. It must be so difficult for her: on the one hand she's worried for her son as he's deserted the Army and he'll be in big trouble, but she's also fearful of his intentions, given how badly things were left between them. And yourself, too.'

'I can't see him turning on Beryl,' Dot replied. And she wasn't just trying to make Jim feel better, she truly meant it. 'All the time we were together, he was fiercely protective of her, even when she was being awful to me.'

'Yes, she has mentioned how hard she made life for you.'

Dot was surprised. Maybe Beryl was genuinely sorry for the way she'd treated her and was eager to make amends. The Beryl she had lived with would never have admitted to such awful behaviour – especially not to the man she had fallen for, who she wanted so desperately to think highly of her.

'I hope you understand that she had good intentions,' Jim said, 'though I appreciate the fact she didn't go about things the right way.'

'It's in the past,' Dot replied. She didn't want to dwell on those wasted years any longer, and she certainly didn't want to stay in this house for a second more than was necessary. 'So, what have you managed to find out about Stan?' she pressed. Despite her doubts, it was the best place to start.

'Well, dear, it's taken me a while to find anything out I'm afraid. I've been trying to get on the straight and narrow since moving in with Beryl. With her love and generosity,' he gestured around him, 'I'm not so desperate that I need to trade with the criminals that I used to. I only carry out honest transactions now, buying straight from the owner of an item.'

Dot raised an eyebrow in response.

'I don't trade with looters or burglars no more,' Jim said firmly. 'I was happy for Beryl to believe I was a pawnbroker bombed out of his shop when we first met, rather than a spiv. But now I've fallen for her good and proper, and she's been so good to me, the least I can do for her is to become the man she fell in love with.' Dot was surprisingly touched by what she was hearing. 'Besides,' Jim added sheepishly, 'I was always a bit scared of the black-market chaps.' Dot smiled. She couldn't help but like Jim. 'I'm pleased you're making more of an honest living,' she replied genuinely.

'I still move in the same circles as some of the spivs. I made some good friends over the years. So, I've done some digging, and I've discovered that there's definitely a new black-market operation in full swing in Chelsea. Whoever's behind it started small, which is why I hadn't twigged that there was anybody new on the scene other than the usual players when we last spoke. Nobody had been talking about it then, but they've become a little more prolific over the last week or so, and they're not taking too kindly to anybody who questions where they get their goods from.'

'They?' Dot asked.

'Yes, there's two of them from what I can gather. They seem to have approached everybody but me with their stolen goods, which makes me suspicious that one of them is

Stan, given our history and my link to you. Also, the fact they're intimidating anyone who questions where they get their hauls from sounds familiar.'

Dot thought back to when she'd first met Jim and he'd shown her the bruises Stan had given him when he'd tried to turn away his business. He'd also tried many times to intimidate herself and Peggy when they'd worked along-side him as air raid wardens – it was his trademark move. Everything was making sense again, now. If Stan had teamed up with somebody else to carry out this spree, that would explain the different methods which had so recently had her doubting his involvement.

'Thank you for looking into it for me, Jim,' Dot said as she got to her feet. Now she had the information she needed she was keen to get out of the house and try and work out the next step to take. She was still pondering the best course of action when she clocked on for duty at Cook's Ground School later that day. Now it seemed likely that one of the looters was indeed Stan, she thought it would probably be best to let Victor know. But the problem was that she still only really had a hunch that it was Stan – she didn't have the hard evidence that she needed to prove it. And how was she going to establish who he was working with? If only Jim had got names for her. But she knew that would be impos-sible – none of his contacts would pass on information like that and it was likely they didn't have it anyway, nobody committing those kinds of crimes was going to be operating under their real name.

Dot didn't want to cause any problems for Victor by tak-ing her assumptions to him before she could prove any-thing. She knew he'd be compelled to confront Stan once he learned there was a chance he was stealing again, and that was sure to raise issues for him within his family. No, she needed to be certain. The only way she'd been sure previously was when she'd caught Stan in the act herself. Knowing how nasty he could be, and aware of the fact he would most certainly be holding a grudge against her now, Dot wasn't keen on the idea of tracking Stan and his accomplice down on her own to check what they were up to.

'It's me and you tonight, Dot,' a friendly voice said, cutting into her thoughts. She turned around and found Bill smiling down at her. She immediately felt at ease. Maybe this was a sign that she should confide in him? He would know what to do. He would probably take Donald with him to track Stan down and get to the bottom of it all. She wasn't as concerned about revealing Stan's past criminal activities now it seemed likely he really was one of the men behind the rise in looting in the area. And, if it turned out that she was wrong, she felt like she could trust Bill to keep the information to himself. Bill had been a complete gentleman about her outburst of affection a few weeks before, when he could have easily run off and told all the other wardens about it and left her a laughing stock.

The two of them headed out together to check on the residents on their patch and make sure the blackout was being adhered to. Bill was telling Dot some tale about a fire at the docks when her attention was grabbed by a group of men piling out of a house across the road. Bill stopped his story and smiled at the men as they walked towards them laughing and joking with each other. He hadn't noticed that Dot had stopped dead in her tracks and was struggling to breathe as panic consumed her.

'Is yer lass all right there?' somebody in the group asked Bill as he moved to the side to let them all pass. Bill turned around to see what the man was pointing at and then he immediately sprinted back to Dot. He firmly placed both his hands on her shoulders and leaned himself forward, so his eyes were level with hers.

'Take deep breaths,' he urged softly as she gasped for air. Dot tried to do as he said, but all she could manage was short, sharp puffs, and the occasional gulp. Terror was racing through her body, her heart was beating faster than it ever had before, and she couldn't seem to get enough air into her lungs.

Bill started taking deep breaths himself so Dot could try and mirror him. 'Don't worry, lads – I've got this,' he called out as the group caught up with them and passed by looking concerned. Dot's eyes wandered across to the men and Bill gently eased her head back so that she was looking at him again. 'Focus on your breathing,' he urged.

Once the men had gone, Dot suddenly felt calm descend over her while she stared into Bill's eyes. Her breaths in and out became longer, until she was breathing deeply and in rhythm with him. When her breathing was finally back to normal, Bill led her over to the kerb and helped her sit down next to him.

'What happened?' he asked. 'You don't have to tell me, but I want to help you,' he quickly added.

'I thought I saw my husband with those men,' she whispered, feeling silly for reacting in such a dramatic way. But she hadn't been able to stop the fear from taking over her body. It had been building ever since she'd learned that Tommy could be back in the area, and when she'd seen the tall man at the back of the group, she'd been convinced it was him. Even in the darkness, she could have sworn she'd spotted the same bend in the nose that her husband had and the swagger as he walked. She waited for Bill to laugh at her or dismiss her distress.

'He must have done some awful things to you,' he replied, shaking his head sadly. He put an arm around Dot's shoulders, and she felt the final residue of panic leaving her body. He didn't think she was over-reacting, despite the fact that he didn't know what had happened with Tommy – just that she'd walked out on him. She took another deep breath and realised that she felt completely safe in Bill's arms. He was like a big brother. Before she realised what she was doing, Dot was telling Bill about how she'd met Tommy and been swept off her feet. She moved on to how he had changed and become controlling over the years, and she confided how awful her relationship with Beryl had been and how unhappy she'd felt before it all came to a head. Dot was amazed at how easy she found it to talk to Bill about these very personal issues, and how comforted he made her feel just by listening.

'When he went for me that night, I knew I had to leave. I was a fool to forgive him the first time. I didn't have anywhere to go, but I just couldn't live like that anymore.'

'You were so brave to do what you did, Dot. I'm incredibly proud of you for getting away from that man. He doesn't deserve somebody like you.' He squeezed her shoulder affectionately and she felt her tummy flip. She knew he was just being kind, but it felt good. She was surprised by how special his support made her feel.

'I just wish I knew why he's gone AWOL, and what he's planning. It's driving me mad, Bill. I see him everywhere and I can't think straight!'

'You gave me a bit of a scare back there; is that the first time you've struggled to breathe like that?'

Dot nodded her head and, as she thought back over what had triggered her reaction, she started chewing on one of her nails. It was a bad habit she had started over the last few days and something she did whenever she started feeling nervous or anxious.

'I was convinced he was with those men. I just froze and panicked. I don't know how I'm going to keep up this job if I keep getting myself in a state like this. I thought I'd be happier once I was free of him, and I was for a time. But he's still managing to make my life a misery and I don't even know for sure if he's in London. He might not even be bothered about having anything to do with me anymore – he could be somewhere else entirely starting a new life!' Finally voicing her fears made Dot overcome with emotion – everything she'd been trying to ignore came pouring out in the form of tears.

Bill pulled her in close to him and rubbed her back comfortingly as she let it all out. 'I'm going to look after you,' he whispered into her ear. Dot pulled away and looked at his face. He looked fiercely protective. She wasn't quite sure what she had done to deserve such kindness from him. She hardly knew him. But it all felt right – she just felt safe when she was with him.

'I'll make sure we work as a pair while Peggy is in the countryside. I don't want you out here on your own until we work out what – if anything – Tommy is up to.'

'But your job at the docks—'

'I'm due some time off, and if it's to come and be on patrol then my boss won't argue.'

'Bill, I can't let you do that. You must need the money.'

'What do I need money for right now?' They both started laughing. 'I've got enough wages saved up to pay my rent and bills. I'm sure Peggy will be back soon. If her mother's anything like she is then she'll be fighting fit again in no time. And if I run out of money, well, we'll think of something.'

Dot didn't know what to say. The relief was overwhelming. She gave up on trying to find the right words and instead she reached her head up and kissed his cheek softly. She wouldn't normally dare do something so brazen, but they were in darkness now, nobody was around, and she felt confident that Bill wouldn't take it the wrong way.

'Thank you,' she whispered.

'Any decent man would do the same. I couldn't live with myself if that brute got hold of you and I could have been there to stop him.' They sat in silence for a few moments. 'Are you all right to get back to our rounds?' Bill asked.

'Actually, there's one more thing I'd like to talk to you about,' Dot confessed. She'd come to realise that Bill was a brilliant confidant, and he would be the perfect person to help her work out what to do about Stan. Besides, she was going to have to tell him about it all if he was going to be with her for all her shifts from now on. Bill nodded his head knowingly as she told him about how she'd seen Stan stealing the pocket watch from their fellow warden Charles following his death when the crypt had been bombed. He listened intently as she told him the rest of the story and explained why she thought Stan was up to his old tricks in the area once again.

'I knew he was a wrong 'un, and I knew something must have gone on for Victor to dismiss his own brother-in-law out of nowhere like that, especially when we were so low on numbers. But I just assumed he'd done something awful to Victor's sister.' He shook his head in disappointment and anger. Dot could just about make out a vein pulsing at his temple in the darkness. She knew Bill had been close to Charles, so it must have made hearing what Stan did even more upsetting. 'I'm so glad it was you who saw him stealing from Charles. A lot of people would have turned a blind eye for an easier life. You would have had more excuse than most, with everything else that was going on, and given that you didn't really know any of us all that well.'

'My conscience would never have let me ignore it.'

'That's what I like about you, Dot. You're such a good and honest person. I could tell that from the moment I met you.'

She was flattered, and not quite sure how to respond. Suddenly Bill appeared flustered.

'Sorry if I've embarrassed you. I tend to speak my mind too much. I'm forever saying things out loud that should be kept in my head. Donald's always telling me off for it.' He turned his head away from her.

'No, don't apologise!' She grabbed his arm so that he looked round at her again. 'It was a very nice thing to say. And I'll never complain about you saying nice things to me.' He smiled at her nervously and she wondered if he thought of her as a little sister or if he felt more than that for her. She was starting to feel confused about her feelings for him. She quickly decided that the best thing to do was change the subject. 'Anyway, back to Stan: I wanted to ask for your help before, but I was worried you'd think I was letting my imagination run away with me. I really do think he's back operating in the area, though.'

Bill looked thoughtful now. 'Obviously I'd heard about the looters and burglaries going on, but I didn't know about what Stan had been up to before, so I didn't make any connections.' He paused for a moment and looked deep in thought. 'One of the lads at the docks mentioned something today about one of his neighbours. He didn't want to go to a shelter last night, so he hunkered down at home – no big deal there, right?'

'Not at all. Lots of people are staying at home instead of going to shelters,' Dot replied. She was intrigued to know where this was leading.

'Right. Well, he made up a bit of a bed under his dining-room table. He figured it might protect him if a bomb struck the house. He was dozing as best he could amidst the noise from the bombs and the planes and the sirens. All of a sudden, he thought he heard glass smashing – and it wasn't the windows breaking from the impact of a bomb or anything like that.' Dot's eyes widened. Bill nodded – he could see she had a good idea what happened next. 'While he was trying to work out what the noise could have been, he heard a load of scuffling and movement from the living room, so he got up and went to investigate. He found two fellas going through all his stuff.'

Dot put her hand over her mouth. She couldn't even begin to imagine how terrified the poor man must have been. 'What happened?' she whispered.

'Well, he was confused at first, because one of them was wearing an ARP uniform. He thought maybe they'd been sent to clear another house and got the wrong place. So, he asked them if they needed any help, and the other one, who was tall and slim, was in Army uniform. It was dark so he couldn't make out much, but he says he definitely had a big, crooked nose. He turned round and just started pummelling this bloke with his fists. Messed him up something rotten. They thought he'd been caught up in a bombing when he made it to hospital.'

Dot gasped and her blood ran cold.

'While it was all going on, the one in the ARP uniform was shouting at the Army one, trying to make him stop, but he cowered in the corner when his companion turned round and threatened him. Then the Army chap gave the ARP fella a good pasting, too.'

Dot opened her mouth and tried to speak, but no words came out. She just stared, open-mouthed at Bill.

'Don't you see, Dot? I didn't make the connection when we were talking about it at the docks, because I didn't know about what Stan had done before. But the fella in the ARP uniform – he described him, and it sounded just like Stan. You're right, Dot – he's at it again, and he's using the uniform to help him gain access to bombed houses so he can help himself to whatever he wants.' Dot hadn't taken in anything Bill had just said. All she could think about was his description of the other burglar – the one who had turned violent. Because the man Bill had described sounded just like Tommy.

18

Peggy smiled all the way into the village. The conversation between herself and Johnny flowed so naturally, and he'd made her laugh so hard that her face ached. He really did have a fantastic sense of humour, which felt so refreshing to Peggy. Having finally decided upon a plain navy-blue dress that she normally wore to special family lunches, she had nipped into her mother's bedroom and taken one of her smart jackets to wear, knowing that she wouldn't mind. A memory of the girls from school glaring at Peggy, whispering and laughing at her for dressing up to try and fit in with them flashed into her mind but she took a deep breath and pushed it away. She would never kid herself that she could ever be as classy as the women Johnny was used to spending time with at places like Café de Paris, but a smart jacket wouldn't make it look like she was trying too hard. Peggy just wanted to look nice for Johnny.

Once Peggy was back downstairs, Mrs Miller had given her daughter a discreet nod of approval and Johnny had declared her 'dashing'. Peggy had tried to hide her delight, reminding herself that Johnny was just there as a friend. But she had never been good at hiding her emotions and her big grin had most certainly given her away. When Johnny had beamed back at her she had instantly looked away, embarrassed.

Now, as they approached the cinema, Peggy could feel eyes on them. She blushed as she wondered what everybody would think of her stepping out with a RAF pilot. She knew how people liked to gossip in this small village, and she suddenly felt anxious. Would they think her foolish for swapping her usual bland clothes for something a little more sophisticated to step out in with Johnny? Possibly sensing Peggy's feelings of unease, Johnny linked his arm with hers, and she was suddenly grinning from ear to ear again, standing taller, and feeling proud to be on his arm. It felt nice to pretend that this handsome and funny chap was as keen on her as she was on him. So what if she would have to explain to everybody afterwards that they were just friends because she wasn't his type of girl?

There was a group of men from the Observer Corps sitting at a post right next to the cinema, watching for aeroplanes. When Johnny went over to talk to them, Peggy thought back to the very first time she had been to this cinema. She had gone with Joan to watch Fred Astaire and Ginger Rogers in *Swing Time*, the week the cinema had opened, back in the summer of 1937. They had since built a café on the side of the building, and when Johnny came back over to her, she suggested they go and have a drink before the film started. Once they were settled in at a table with their drinks, Peggy found herself reminiscing out loud about the times she had been to the cinema with Joan.

'We went whenever there was a new film out. Our brothers always laughed at us – they thought sitting in the dark watching a big screen was cheerless and they had more exciting things to be doing, but we loved the time together, just the two of us.'

'You miss her, don't you?'

'Oh, I miss her so much.' Peggy sighed. Her voice quivered when she spoke and she stared into her drink, desperately trying to force back the tears that were pooling in her eyes.

'Hey, it's all right to miss her.' Johnny reached out and put his hand on her arm. 'It sounds as if the two of you are close, and you've had to go through rather a lot without her. Has she been to visit since your mother fell ill?'

Peggy shook her head and looked into her drink again. 'Please don't think badly of her. The truth is, I haven't told her just how poorly mother has been. Mother was adamant I didn't worry everybody by telling them, so even my father is in the dark. I was going to tell Joan anyway, but then I didn't think it was fair to pull her away from her war duties when I can cope well enough on my own. Don't get me wrong – I'd give anything to have her here with me. I'll admit that I've struggled looking after all the children on my own, and if she was here with me then it would all be so much easier. But I can't do that to her. I won't.'

'It's very noble of you, Peggy. Joan's lucky to have you looking out for her. I think most people would have only thought of themselves and what would make things easier. And, for what it's worth, it seems to me that you're doing a wonderful job with those children.'

Peggy's heart swelled with pride. She felt overcome with emotion as she looked into his eyes. 'Thank you,' she whispered.

'And I know things were dire with your mother when she first fell ill. Viv told me about how serious it was. But you wouldn't know that to look at her now – and that's down to you, Peggy. You've been nursing her as well as looking after those children. And you doing such a good job with the little ones has meant she's had less to worry about and has been able to focus on trying to get better.'

Peggy laughed nervously. She had never been good at taking compliments. 'Now Mother's up and about a little bit and seems to be out of the woods, maybe I could ask Joan to come and visit. It would be so good to see her. And I think Mother would forgive me for sharing her secret as soon as she sees Joan again – she'd be too delighted to be reunited with her to be angry with me, especially now she's not so poorly.' Peggy thought for a moment and allowed herself to get excited at the prospect of seeing her sister again. 'And I think I have things under enough control that Joan wouldn't feel compelled to give up her land work and move home to help me.'

'You should write to her when you get home this evening,' Johnny urged.

'I will,' she replied happily. Peggy suddenly felt lighter. Maybe the burden of keeping things from Joan had been worse than she had realised. Now they were on the subject of families, Peggy asked Johnny about his.

'I was close to my brothers, too,' he said quietly. He coughed to clear his throat and Peggy's heart ached for him.

'What happened to them?' she whispered.

'They were both killed in action on the same day.'

'Your poor mother,' Peggy gasped. Then she reached out and put her hand over Johnny's in an attempt to comfort him.

Peggy couldn't even begin to imagine the pain the poor woman, and Johnny, had gone through. Her pining for Joan suddenly felt very silly.

'Felix and Jack were both based at Tangmere with me and William. Felix was shot down on the same day as William. The three of us were part of a group trying to defend the base from Luftwaffe air raids. Felix destroyed one of the German aircraft, but then his Hurricane was hit. They thought he might have been able to bail out at first but when they found the aircraft wreckage they discovered his body, too.'

'I'm so sorry.' Peggy rubbed his hand.

'I was up in the air with them, but I didn't see him or William going down. I heard about them both over the radio though and had to carry on, knowing I'd probably lost the two of them in one fell swoop. And then the bastard Germans managed to bomb the base in the end. That's when Jack was killed. They got thirteen of us altogether that day. Thankfully William wasn't number fourteen in the end.'

Peggy thought back to when Johnny had visited London to let Viv know William was missing in action. The pain he must have been going through, yet he'd made that journey especially to notify Viv, knowing that she wouldn't have any other way of being informed.

'I didn't want my mother to find out through a telegram. I had to be the one to tell her. Of course, I was given leave straight away, but I stopped off in London on the way home so I could try and find Viv to make sure she knew what had happened. I still can't believe I found her so quickly. I hadn't expected to be able to find her, but I just knew I had to try. I'd seen the way she looked at William and I knew how much they meant to each other. It felt as though Felix and Jack had led me to her.' He laughed and ran his hand through his hair. 'I can't believe I just told you that. You must think I sound so silly, talking about my dead brothers somehow guiding me to your friend in London.'

'No, not at all,' Peggy said firmly.

'Anyway, the fact there was still hope for William helped get me through. The four of us had been so close. We met during our training, and William was like another brother to us by the time of the attack. I don't know if Viv has told you, but he doesn't have any family of his own – we were more than happy to welcome him into ours.' Johnny stopped to clear his throat again before continuing. 'I told Viv I was going back to base when I left London, but I continued on to Birmingham and I got to my mother before the telegrams arrived.' He paused. 'Telling her about Felix and Jack was the hardest thing I've ever had to do – even more difficult than learning that I'd lost them both. But it had to come from me.'

Peggy's heart broke for Johnny and his mother. 'What about your father? Does he know?'

'Oh, he left us when we were young. It's always been my mother and her boys. Now it's just the two of us. Well, we have William, too. She hasn't met him yet but I know they'll get on brilliantly.'

'And your mother let you go back to Tangmere?'

He laughed sadly and shook his head. 'She begged me not to leave. She wanted to write to my superiors asking for me to be released from service. Not that I would have gone along with that, even if they'd agreed. I had to go back and continue the fight for my brothers – they would have done the same for me. And I needed to make sure they found William, whether he was dead or alive. Then, when I got back, I found out the Fleet Air Arm Station at Ford had been dive-bombed by Stukas two days after my brothers had been killed. They wiped out thirty-nine men that time. Even if I'd been contemplating giving it up and going back home to my mother, there would have been no chance after that. I couldn't sit back while my comrades were being targeted.'

'When I met you – when you came to Viv's to tell her William had been found but he was injured – you must have still been so upset about your brothers, yet you never gave a hint of your distress, and you were so kind to Viv.'

Johnny nodded. 'William being found gave me the boost I needed. It was the hope I'd been holding out for. With that to focus on, the pain of losing Felix and Jack was eased a little.'

Peggy squeezed his hand. He'd been so selfless, travelling to London to fetch Viv and take her to William when his own loss was still so raw. 'Viv never mentioned any of this.'

'Viv doesn't know.'

Peggy couldn't hide her confusion.

'Telling William about Felix and Jack was almost as difficult as telling my mother had been, especially when he was in such a state himself and I was so worried about whether he would even make it out of that hospital alive. I thought about keeping it from him, but I knew he was like me in that his anger at the Germans would keep him fighting to get stronger so he could get back in the air and help defeat them. I knew he wouldn't give up when he had the two of them to avenge. But it took it out of me. Talking about them made it all feel more real. So, I asked him not to tell Viv. I didn't want her asking me about them.'

'I'm so sorry, I shouldn't have pried.' Peggy felt terrible for making him talk about something he had tried to keep hidden away to save himself extra pain.

'No, it's okay.' Johnny looked up and fixed eye contact with her. 'With you it feels different. It feels good to talk about them and accept that they've gone. I'd started convincing myself that they'd been sent to a different base and that I'd see them again when the war was over, but I know that all I was doing was prolonging the agony.'

'I'll always listen when you want to talk about them. I'd love to know more about your brothers.' She kept her voice low, staring into his eyes, which were watering slightly now.

'In time, I'll tell you all about my family,' he promised. 'But, for now, we have a movie to watch,' he announced with forced cheerfulness, which Peggy tried to match with a smile as they got up to go and find their seats in the auditorium.

Watching the film, Peggy was mesmerised by the leading lady, Frances Day. She was struck by how effortlessly glamorous the woman was – just like Viv. In fact, with her perfectly coiffed hair and lipstick, she brought to mind an older version of her friend. Of course, she couldn't see the colour of the actress's lipstick because the film was in black and white, but Peggy was certain it would have been bright red just like Viv's always was. Though she was American, Frances Day had been popular in the UK for some time now, and Peggy was surprised she hadn't noticed her similarity to Viv before now.

'I really enjoyed that, although Frances Day always makes me feel inferior on every level,' she said lightly as they walked home arm in arm.

'What do you mean?'

'Oh, she's just so glamorous, don't you think?'

Johnny seemed to be deep in thought for a minute before replying.

'She is very glam, yes. And she's a very attractive woman.' Peggy's heart dropped as they continued on in brief silence. 'If that's what you like,' Johnny added quietly.

Peggy felt her cheeks flush. She was desperate to ask him to elaborate and tell her exactly what he did like, eager to hear him say that it was a woman just like her. But then she scolded herself for getting carried away when Johnny was clearly just trying to be nice to her after she had made a comment which showed that her confidence was low. Peggy didn't want to put him in the awkward position of having to let her down. She changed the subject and once they arrived back at her house, she invited him in for a cup of tea.

'I would love to, but William has his operation in the morning and my sergeant has given me leave to visit him with some of the other lads to try and boost his morale. I don't know when he's going into surgery or how long it will take, so we want to arrive early to make sure we're there when he comes out. I'd best head back and get some rest. I really enjoyed today, though – thank you.'

Peggy blushed. She wished she could get that under control. 'I enjoyed it, too. Do you think Viv will be there tomorrow?'

'I hope so. To be honest, I don't think William's going to be interested in seeing me or any of the other lads. It's Viv who has been getting him through this whole thing.'

'She'll do everything she can to be there, I know it.' Peggy felt an ache for her friend. She wished she could be there to support her.

'Oh, I don't doubt that. It's just that nothing is ever certain anymore.' Johnny looked sad for a moment but then his face brightened, and he was grinning. 'And remember, you have a letter to write before you go to sleep.' Peggy smiled. She was going to write to Joan, but she had decided to continue to keep her in the dark about their mother. She felt stronger somehow after Johnny's visit. His words of praise had boosted her and made her realise that, though she was finding it hard, she was doing just fine here on her own. She didn't want to worry her sister unnecessarily. And Peggy didn't want to be the reason Joan left the Land Army. She would never forgive herself – and their mother wouldn't, either. Johnny was her inspiration; after everything he'd been through losing his brothers, he was still pushing on and doing his bit when nobody would have blamed him for at least taking some time out at home to grieve for them with his mother.

'It's the first thing on my list of chores,' she teased. 'Will you give Viv my love when you see her, please? I miss her and Dot dearly.' She suddenly wished she had been able to plan ahead enough to write Viv a letter that Johnny could pass on to her.

'Of course I will.'

'Hang on!' she cried, suddenly struck by an idea. 'Wait right there. I won't keep you too long, I promise.' Johnny looked confused but happy to do as he was told, so Viv ran into the house and grabbed her writing gear. She quickly scribbled a note to Viv and placed it in an envelope, which she handed to Johnny at the door.

'You want me to give this to Viv if she's there?'

'Please,' Peggy replied, her eyes glistening with excitement. It was only a silly little note, a few lines long, but the thought of surprising Viv and having that brief connection with her was making her feel giddy.

'If she's not there then I'll leave it with William, and he can pass it on when she next visits. If she doesn't make it tomorrow, then I don't imagine it will be too long before she drops by.'

'Thank you.'

There was an awkward silence as they both stared at each other. Peggy knew it was time to say goodbye, but she didn't want their time together to end. She was bursting to ask Johnny when he would be stopping by again, but she didn't want to come across as desperate or needy, and she certainly didn't want to put any pressure on him to spend time with her. She was already anxious that he was only here on Viv's orders. Apart from all that, Peggy knew it was difficult for him to plan ahead as he didn't often get advance warning of when he was needed to fly.

'You have a letter to write, too,' she blurted suddenly, keen to lengthen the time before they had to say goodbye.

Johnny raised his eyebrows in confusion.

'You should write to your mother,' Peggy said gently. 'She will be eager to hear from you regularly.'

His face softened. 'You're right. I'll do it before I go to sleep tonight. And I will think of you lying on your bed and writing your letter.'

If Peggy had blushed previously, then she wasn't sure what she was doing now – probably glowing red like a tomato.

Johnny burst into laughter at the look on her face. 'I'm sorry. That was very ungentlemanly of me,' he said mock-seriously. When he gave her a mischievous wink, she couldn't help but laugh along with him. He really was quite cheeky. But she knew that's all his comment had been – a bit of fun from somebody who couldn't resist being a little bit naughty. When he leaned in and gave her a light kiss on the cheek to say goodbye, she didn't allow herself to read anything into it. But she did hold her hand to her cheek as she lay in bed that night, thinking of him and how much she yearned to see him again.

19

When Paul climbed wearily into the passenger seat next to Viv, he looked ashen. 'They've hit another tube station,' he said.

Viv's heart dropped. That was sure to mean bodies to take to the mortuary, rather than wounded casualties to assist. 'Where?'

'Balham. There hasn't been anything on our patch yet so they're sending whoever they can over to help.'

Viv started the engine and followed the slow line of ambulance vehicles that were trailing out of the station. 'Do you know how bad it is?' she asked.

'Not yet. But if a water main has gone then we'll just have to hope the floodgates hold like they did at Tooting Broadway last week.'

Viv tried to concentrate on what her partner was saying, but all she could think about was William's surgery the following morning. She had been unable to think of anything else all day. As she swerved to avoid a messenger on a bike, she could feel Paul's concerned eyes on her. 'I'm just tired. Sorry about that,' she said stiffly. She was annoyed with herself for letting her angst about William distract her from the task in hand. She hadn't had time to go and see him since Dr McIndoe had told them about William's surgery being booked in, a week before. She couldn't wait to get back to

Sussex in the morning, but she was also anxious about the outcome of the operation. Her fears for William's sight had been weighing heavy on her mind ever since that last visit. And she was concerned about getting there on time now that she was having to rely on public transport. On top of all that, she couldn't stop panicking that William had changed his mind about wanting to marry her.

Viv knew that she was being selfish. William had far more important things to worry about than their relationship, like recovering from the crash and whether he was ever going to be able to see properly again and continue his career with the RAF. But she had found herself constantly replaying in her head all the times she'd thought he was going to propose again. Torturing herself over the reasons why the proposal hadn't materialised had become like a new horrible hobby. Had William wanted to ask her to marry him again, but then changed his mind, fearing she would reject him just like the last time? Or had the thought of asking for her hand in marriage a second time not even crossed his mind? Maybe Viv had wasted her one chance with him.

Viv loved William so much, and she knew that he loved her, too – she could see it in the way he looked at her. She'd always longed to find a man who looked at her the way her father looked at her mother, and she realised she had that now. Viv had caught that look of love on William's face so many times since his accident. Every time she had mentally scorned herself for having turned him down and then willed him to propose again. They had already wasted so much time, and she knew that was her fault. Viv was desperate to make things right and get them back on track. If only she could make William realise that, too.

'Did you hear what I just said, Viv?'

'Huh?' she looked round at Paul, confused.

'Don't worry about it,' he replied.

His tone was light, so she was confident she hadn't upset him. The two of them knew each other well enough not to get offended when one of them was a bit preoccupied. It was to be expected, what with everything they had to deal with. She didn't know anybody who was able to keep a clear head at the moment. If the lack of sleep wasn't bad enough, constantly coming face to face with death and trauma was certain to send even the strongest person over the edge.

Turning a corner, Viv spotted two figures in overalls and tin hats up ahead. It was too dark to tell, but from the outline of the one on the right, she would have put money on it being Dot. She slowed to a crawl and peered over. Seeing that it was indeed her friend, she pulled up next to her and her colleague and instructed Paul to roll his window down.

'Hello! Are you off to Balham?' Dot called out.

'Yes. You?'

Dot nodded in response. 'A messenger just came past and told us they're trying to get as many people over there as possible. We were going to walk, but—'

'Jump in the back,' Viv ordered, knowing what she had been about to ask. The Hudson had had its rear seats pulled out and replaced with basic wooden bunks, blankets and stretchers. The back doors had been removed too. In their place hung a cloth curtain – making it easier to get patients in and out. Viv waited as Dot's colleague helped her into the back. She couldn't make out much in the darkness, but he looked tall and strong, and Dot seemed to be at ease with him. She wondered if it was Bill, who Dot had mentioned a few times recently. The four of them were silent for the remainder of the journey, listening out for aircraft and hoping the Germans weren't planning on returning. Viv knew they would all be preparing themselves for whatever devastation lay ahead. But when she reached Balham, she was forced to pull up behind the row of ambulance cars ahead of her.

'We can't get through any further, they've closed the road off,' one of the drivers ahead shouted back. The group got out of Hudsy and followed the rest of the volunteers along Balham High Road in the direction of the station. Viv and Dot both gasped at the same time when they saw the massive crater the bomb had created in the road. It stretched right across the width of the whole street – and a bus was sticking out of the middle of it. Water was pouring into the crater like a small waterfall. There was a sense of calm in the air despite the dramatic scene in front of them. A crowd of onlookers had already gathered. Viv looked down in dismay at the concrete, rubble and twisted metal which filled the space in the hole around the bus.

'Bomb fell by the doorway of United Dairies,' a fireman explained, coming up from behind them and making Viv jump. 'It collapsed the roof of the connecting underground tunnels, then the number 88 crashed into the crater.'

'Is there a fire down there?' Paul asked.

Viv's heart filled with dread at the thought.

'No, but the bus has burst a water main. I dread to think how many people have drowned down there.' There was a moment of silence as they all took in the horror of what had happened beneath them. 'We're pumping water out so the rescue workers can get in, but it's mixed up with soil and debris so it's a slow process.'

'I thought they had floodgates down there,' Paul said.

The fireman nodded. 'They do, but it sounds as if people rushed to get out as the water came in. Lots of them made it out all right, but from what we can make out there are a fair few who got caught up in the deluge.'

Viv shuddered. She thought she'd seen everything this war had to offer, with fires, collapsed buildings and direct bomb blasts. Being swept away to drown in a tunnel of water and debris didn't bear thinking about.

'Where will we be best off?' Dot's colleague asked.

'I need medics over here!' a warden shouted. The group turned around and saw him running towards them. 'We've just had a load of people out of the tunnel who need checking over, and we're starting to get people off the bus,' he explained.

'Can we help with the rescue effort at the station?' a voice from behind Viv asked. She'd forgotten they had walked over with a group of other volunteers.

'We're good over there. We're just digging for bodies now. I could really do with more hands to check over the survivors and help them on their way. Most of the injuries are minor, so I'll take wardens as well as medics and they can do basic first aid and hand over the more serious casualties to the medics.'

Once they were settled in at the makeshift first-aid post that had been set up, Viv found herself feeling relieved that they hadn't been tasked with assisting the rescue effort underground. Broken bones and scrapes were a light relief in comparison. As she set to work treating the people who were sent her way, she got talking to an elderly woman who had stumbled across to be checked over.

'There's nothing wrong with me, dear, but they won't let me leave until you've made sure. Have they found the stationmaster?'

'I don't know. I haven't seen him,' Viv replied, looking around briefly for somebody in railway uniform.

The woman looked concerned as Viv did her usual checks. 'I don't think he made it out,' she said quietly, shaking her head sadly. 'Him and his whole family always camped out near his office. The way it all came in, they'd have been buried, the lot of them. Such a tragedy. Though, surely it's better to all go together, don't you think, dear? That's what I always say. Nobody wants to be the one left behind.'

'What happened down there?' Viv asked. The woman was clear of any injury, but there was nobody else waiting and she was keen to learn more about what had happened in the tube station. Dot was busy cleaning up a facial wound on a man next to them, but Viv could sense her leaning in to listen to the conversation while she worked.

'We were at the south end of the north-bound platform; that's where me and my neighbours always go to shelter. We heard the bomb, but we didn't feel a blast. But then the lights went out. The watertight doors were closed, but people panicked and hurried to open them. When I heard the rush of water and shingle, I thought we were done for, I really did.' She paused and closed her eyes briefly before continuing. 'It was pitch black, but a man started shouting about how he knew a way out. Of course, we just followed his voice – what other option did we have? We clambered through all sorts of tunnels and eventually made it out. Someone's just told me the chap works for London Transport, so he knows the tunnel network like the back of his hand. We're so lucky we had settled in close to him this evening. I'm not sure we'd have made it out without him. I know there must be many who weren't as lucky as us.' More people had filed over now, so Viv had to send the woman on her way. As she set to work checking over the next patient, who had suffered a knocked head and some grazes in the scramble to get out, she tried not to think about the poor stationmaster and his family being buried under the torrent of water and debris.

As the hours stretched on, a steady stream of casualties trailed through the first-aid post. Viv only treated minor injuries, but almost everybody she spoke to was worried about somebody they knew who didn't seem to have made it out. As night turned into day, she watched on as a ladder was lowered into the crater and the bus passengers were helped out from the back of the vehicle and on to the road. Amazingly, nobody on board had been killed. As the passengers made their way to be helped by the wardens and medics, the bus driver wandered over. He was accompanied by an ambulance worker, and he had a bandage wrapped around the top of his head.

'I just want to make sure everybody is okay before they take me off to hospital,' he explained fretfully. Viv could see he was still shaking as he talked about what had happened. 'I'd felt the bomb blast, but I didn't know where the thing had landed, and I didn't see the crater until we were in it.' Viv listened in intently. She couldn't even begin to imagine how terrible the man must be feeling, though she knew nobody would blame him – it would have been impossible to see the hole in the road in time with the blackout restrictions in place. 'The bus started prancing around like a horse and the next thing I knew I was lying in a shop doorway.'

'You were thrown right out of the bus?' Paul asked.

The man nodded his head grimly. 'They got me straight to a first-aid post – the one over there,' he explained, pointing at the other side of the road. 'They want to take me to hospital for concussion, but they let me wait here until the passengers were off.' He started working his way through the queue of people, shaking their hands and apologising. He was met with warmth and gratitude; nobody was blaming him for the bad luck he had encountered.

'We could do with getting you to hospital on the next run,' the medic he'd come over with said.

'All your passengers look fine to me, but we'll make sure of it before sending them home,' Viv assured the driver.

'Thank you,' he smiled. 'I didn't even realise what had happened until they'd bandaged me up. I went back to my bus, and I thought somebody had moved it at first. But as I got closer, I realised the roof was sticking out of the crater.' He rubbed his neck and shook his head slowly from side to side. Suddenly, Bill was on his feet and gently guiding the man away. 'Come on, mate, let's get you to hospital,' he said as the medic with the driver gave him a grateful look.

By the time Bill had returned, all the bus passengers had been dealt with and no major injuries had been reported. The sun was up now, and the rescue effort at the tube station was fully underway. As Bill and Paul discussed heading over to help with the digging, Viv felt torn. She wanted to stay and help – she wasn't one to abandon her colleagues, especially when they were facing such a grim task. But she knew she had already missed the first train out of London, and she was getting worried she wasn't going to make it to Sussex in time to be waiting for William when he came out of surgery.

'Did you hear me, Viv?' Paul's voice cut into her thoughts, and she immediately felt awful for being too distracted to listen to him yet again.

'I'm sorry, I was somewhere else again. I just don't know what to do for the best.'

Paul and Bill looked at her with confused expressions until Dot cut in.

'Oh, Viv! It's William's surgery today, isn't it?'

'Yes. I don't think I can possibly make it in time, but I have to try. Only, I don't want to leave you all digging out bodies . . .'

'Go!' Paul and Dot shouted at her in unison, as Bill looked on in confusion.

Dot looked over at him and smiled. 'I'll explain later,' she told him.

'We can handle things here,' Paul assured her. 'Everything has calmed down now, and they have more than enough volunteers ready to help with the digging. You won't be leaving us in the lurch. I was going to suggest that you and Dot headed back now anyway.'

'I'll wait for Bill, and we can walk back to the school together,' Dot said quickly, giving Viv a reassuring nod. That was a relief. Dot had filled Viv in on the news about Tommy over the course of the night, and fears for her friends' safety had been one of the things holding her back from rushing to be by William's side.

'I'll make sure she gets home unharmed,' Bill added.

'If you're sure?' Viv asked the three of them cautiously. Her tummy was doing somersaults in anticipation of her race to get to the hospital on time, and she was so desperate to get moving that she was almost bouncing on the spot despite her exhaustion. But she needed to be certain that she wasn't letting anybody down.

'Yes,' Paul replied firmly. 'And you should take Hudsy – you'll be more likely to make it on time.'

'I can't do that!' Viv whispered urgently, looking around them to make sure nobody had heard Paul's wild suggestion.

'It won't be a problem,' he replied. Sensing her apprehension, he moved closer so they could discuss it without being overheard. 'Look, I'll stay here and help for the rest of the day. There are never any daytime raids anymore. If you're unlucky enough to be missing with one of the ambulance cars on the one day the Germans decide to bomb us before nightfall then I'll find a way to cover for you. But I honestly can't see it happening. Take Hudsy, drive like hell to Sussex and be there waiting for William when he comes round from the surgery. Just make sure you're back at base before our shift tonight, so we can get back out in Hudsy when the nightly visitors get here.'

Viv stared at her partner and chewed her lips nervously. This was a big risk to take. She could get into a lot of trouble – she could get Paul into a lot of trouble. Could she really do it?

'Come on, Viv,' Dot urged as she walked over to join the two of them. 'If this war has taught us anything, it's that we need to live life to the fullest because it can be over in the blink of an eye. You almost lost William once. Throw caution to the wind – go and be with him when he needs you most. You've done enough for London for one day.'

Viv was suddenly standing tall. 'I'll be back by nightfall,' she promised, before turning on her heel and running back to Hudsy. Once in the driver's seat she had one important thing to do before starting her journey. She reached down into the side pocket and pulled out her trusted lipstick. After applying it with the aid of the rear-view mirror, she felt ready to get going.

'I'm coming, my love,' she whispered, before turning the car around and driving away from the rubble and destruction behind her with a renewed sense of purpose.

20

When Peggy woke the morning after her trip to the cinema with Johnny, she couldn't stop smiling. She had fallen asleep before even starting her letter to Joan, with the memory of Johnny's lips on her cheek taking over all her thoughts. Even the children moaning about the lumpy porridge she made them for breakfast couldn't dampen her spirits. Once she had sent them all off to get washed and dressed, she got some tea and porridge ready to take to her mother in bed. But when she turned around to leave the kitchen, she was surprised to find her standing in the doorway.

'What are you doing down here?' she asked in a panic. 'Is everything all right? How did you get down here?'

'I'm capable of walking down the stairs, dear.' Her mother sighed, pulling out a chair and sitting herself down at the table. She seemed slightly out of breath, but quickly recovered and looked up at Peggy with a triumphant smile. Peggy placed the breakfast down in front of her mother and joined her at the table.

'Dr Brady was very clear on how important rest is for your recovery,' she said gently. Her mother was prodding the porridge with her spoon. 'Before you say anything about the porridge, I know full well that it's lumpy, but it tastes just fine.'

Mrs Miller laughed to herself before eating a mouthful. 'Very good, dear,' she said, nodding her head. 'Now, how did your date go with that lovely young man?'

'It wasn't a date, Mother,' Peggy replied sternly. 'It was two friends watching a film together. And you're not getting away with it that easily – why are you coming down the stairs on your own at this hour when you should be resting?'

'Peggy, I can't stay up there all morning. Honestly, I'm going out of my mind! I can rest just as easily on the sofa. And it will mean the little ones can sit and read with me while you pop into the village. It will give Phillip and Sarah a break from watching them.'

Peggy took a moment to think. It didn't seem like the worst idea. She had been feeling bad about leaving the older evacuees in charge of the younger ones along with her smallest sisters in the mornings, while she ran errands and did her chores. It would be nice to send them out to play for a few hours, and it would also be enjoyable to have her mother downstairs with her for once.

'You must promise to sit still,' she said firmly. 'You're still on bed rest, only you're doing it on the sofa. No getting up and trying to help me with the housework.' Her mother narrowed her eyes playfully at her. 'No matter how badly I might be doing it!' Peggy added lightly.

'I promise, I promise,' Mrs Miller cried, holding her hands up in defeat. 'But you don't have to be so delicate with the duster—'

'Mother! I'll send you back up to your bedroom,' Peggy threatened mock-sternly as she wagged a finger teasingly at her.

'Sorry. I'll go back to eating my lumpy porridge. That will keep me quiet.' They both burst into laughter, then.

Peggy looked at her mother as they giggled together, and she felt overcome with affection. She had come so close to losing her. An image of her mother clinging to the worktop and gasping for breath flashed into her mind and she did her best to swat it away. It did no good to dwell on the past and what might have been. She reminded herself to focus on the present and making the most of each day. Her mother's scare along with everything she had witnessed in London had certainly taught her the importance of that.

'That was a good try, but you didn't manage to distract me enough to forget to demand more details about last night,' Mrs Miller said when she had finished eating her porridge. She pushed her bowl to the middle of the table and took her mug in her hand. 'That wasn't actually that bad,' she added, nodding to the empty bowl. Peggy rolled her eyes at her mother's cheekiness.

'There's not much to tell, really. We *are* just friends.'

'But you would like it to be more?'

'Oh, Mother. He's just perfect.' Peggy blushed and looked away in embarrassment. Where had that come from? She couldn't believe she had just blurted it out like that. That kiss had really put her head in a spin.

'It's okay to like him,' her mother said sympathetically. 'For what it's worth, I think he likes you, too.'

'I already told you he's not interested in someone like me.'

'Yes, but I still think you're wrong. I've seen the way he looks at you. Come on, dear, what's holding you back?'

Peggy bit her lip. She'd held back from revealing her true feelings to her mother the night before, but maybe it was time to be vulnerable. Her mother had always been great at helping her and Joan overcome personal issues when they were growing up. She'd never had the worry of boy trouble; her problems had been mostly to do with silly quarrels between her and Joan or their friends. But, still, it had always felt good to talk things over with her and she had always dished out sound advice.

'I just don't think I'm his type,' Peggy admitted sadly.

'And what exactly do you mean by that?'

Peggy was finding it difficult to admit that she didn't feel good enough for Johnny. It was one thing to think it in her head, but to say it out loud would mean sharing her deepest insecurities.

'You've seen Viv,' she muttered, and she looked up to see understanding dawning on her mother's face.

'He's not with Viv, dear. And if he wanted a woman like Viv then he would be out pursuing a woman like Viv instead of spending time with you here.'

'But you haven't been to the London clubs and seen the women he must meet when he's out. Glam, sophisticated, upper-class *ladies*, just like Viv. I'm just a silly girl from the country who has to borrow clothes from her mother to even look passable for a trip to the cinema.' She thought back to all the times Viv had tried to convince her to join her for an evening at Café de Paris and cringed at the pathetic excuses she had made to avoid it. Peggy knew from experience that she would stick out like a sore thumb somewhere like that. She had learned a long time ago that she didn't belong in that kind of setting.

Mrs Miller sat up straight and her tone turned sharp. 'I won't have you putting yourself down like that, Peggy. You're just as good as any of those women and a man like Johnny would be just as lucky to have you as any of them.' Peggy tutted and shook her head. She knew her mother was just telling her what she was required to say as a parent.

'Don't you tut at me, young lady. You may be grown up and responsible – you might even be looking after *me* at the moment. But I am still your mother and I know a hell of a lot more than you do about men and their ways.'

'Sorry,' Peggy muttered, feeling ten years old again. Her good mood from the night before had completely vanished.

Her mother's tone softened again. 'You don't need fancy clothes and make-up to prove anything to anybody, least of all Johnny. That's all on the outside – it doesn't change what's on the inside. That's what matters.'

Peggy wasn't convinced, but she wasn't about to try and persuade her mother. This was embarrassing enough as it was without having to explain further why she didn't feel good enough for the man she had taken a shine to. It was all right for her mother. Though she never spent any time on her looks and rarely got dressed up in fancy clothes, she had turned heads with her effortless beauty wherever she went for as long as Peggy could remember, while Peggy herself always seemed to fade into the background. Peggy's father was as besotted with his wife now as he had been the day they'd met. Her plain style was certainly proof that not all men were interested in well-dressed glamour-pusses. But Peggy was certain the man she was interested in wanted somebody with a bit more spark than she could muster. Because it wasn't just about the clothes and make-up; women like Viv carried themselves a certain way – they had an air of confidence that Peggy had never been able to match.

'Honestly, Peggy. Just because he's with the Millionaire's Mob, doesn't mean to say he's only interested in women with wealthy backgrounds. I thought you knew better than to make assumptions like that.'

'What?' Peggy asked, confused. 'Millionaire's Mob? What are you talking about, Mother?'

'Oh,' she replied sheepishly. 'I thought that's why you seem convinced he's after somebody rich.'

'It's got nothing to do with money, though I suppose being wealthy comes hand in hand with being glam. But I would like to know what this Millionaire's Mob is, please.'

Her mother sighed. 'When he introduced himself to me, Johnny mentioned that he was with 601 Squadron over at Tangmere.'

'Yes,' Peggy said, nodding. She was still none the wiser. She thought back to when Johnny had met her mother properly and remembered she had been in the kitchen getting dinner ready when he had gone upstairs to help with the children – and then ended up sitting with them all in her mother's bedroom. So, she hadn't been there to hear their introductions – not that his mention of 601 Squadron would have meant anything to her.

'Well, 601 Squadron is known as the Millionaire's Mob. They're an auxiliary squadron made up of elite young men – the crème de la crème of London society. They were put together by Lord Grosvenor.'

'Well, no wonder they all hang out at Café de Paris,' Peggy said. She groaned and held her head in her hands as it dawned on her. 'I was worried about him being attracted to women who are more glamorous than I am when I thought he was just a normal chap. But the fact he's probably filthy rich makes him even more out of my league!' Then she had a realisation. She looked up again. 'Hang on. You said London's crème de la crème. Johnny's from Birmingham? And his mother raised him and his two brothers on her own, which gave me the impression he'd had quite a humble upbringing.'

'Well, yes – they were originally a group of upper-class men from London with their own planes when they were set up, and that's where the nickname came from. But, what with the Battle of Britain going on like it has, their number has been somewhat depleted. Other pilots have been drafted in to take the places of the dead men, so it's not such a fancy squadron as it was originally. They'll be slightly more diverse by now, I'm sure. But the nickname still stands.'

Peggy thought for a moment. This was just more proof that Johnny wouldn't be interested in getting romantically involved with her. Even if he wasn't one of the wealthy squadron members – which seemed likely given what she knew about him – he would still be used to keeping company with people with money and class, people who were nothing like her.

'What does your sister think about all this?' her mother asked.

'I haven't mentioned him to Joan.'

'Why ever not? You two tell each other everything. I would have thought she'd be the first person you'd turn to for advice on a matter like this.'

'I . . . well, I haven't written to her since leaving London.'

'That explains it! I had a letter from her yesterday and she was asking after you. I didn't get a chance to mention it to you before Johnny arrived, and I didn't want to dampen your spirits while he was here. She's been worried sick about you, Peggy. She must have been writing to you in London and panicking when she didn't hear back.'

'You didn't want me to tell her you were ill, and I didn't know how to explain the fact I'd left London to come and stay here. I've never lied to her, and I just couldn't bring myself to do it.'

'Oh, darling, I'm so sorry. Why didn't you tell me? If I knew it was causing you such anguish, then I would never have asked you to keep it from her.'

'It's okay. I didn't want to worry her either or make her feel like she should come back to help, so it wasn't just you who was keeping me from writing to Joan. But now that you're getting better, I was planning on getting back in touch with her. I feel terrible that she's been writing me letters which have gone unanswered.'

'You must write to her today. Promise me?'

'I promise.'

'And you can always get around the fact you're here by saying I needed help with all the children. We have so many now that it would be believable!'

'That's a good idea.' Peggy replied, smiling again. She couldn't believe she hadn't thought of that herself. She had really missed her contact with Joan, and it could have been avoided. She didn't really need to lie to her – just omit a small detail.

'I'm long overdue to write to her, too, so I'll mention you've come back for the same reason. Letters arriving from both of us at the same time should cheer her up and make up for all the worry.'

'I'll get the girls to draw her some pictures,' Peggy suggested.

Her mother nodded in agreement. 'And make sure you mention this worry you have about Johnny. I'd be interested to know her thoughts on it.' Peggy suddenly felt glum again.

'Even if you are convinced that he's not interested in you, what have you got to lose by dropping him some subtle hints and seeing how he reacts?'

Peggy thought back to how close she had come to asking Johnny to elaborate on what he found attractive in a woman when they had been talking about the film the previous night and she shuddered. She certainly wasn't brave enough to start dropping serious hints.

'If I write to Joan for advice today then will you promise to stop going on about him?' Peggy asked.

Her mother sighed. 'I'll try my best. Just remember that these are dangerous times. That young man is putting his life on the line on a regular basis. Every time he gets in a plane, there's a good chance he won't be getting out of it alive.'

Peggy thought about how Johnny's brothers had been killed. She knew that fighter pilots and their crews were getting shot down all the time, but she had tried not to think about the danger Johnny was in whenever he was on duty – or even just at his base.

'If you really like him, which I think you do, then you need to think about the fact that time isn't necessarily on your side. Please think about doing something about it before it's too late.'

Peggy still didn't know Johnny all that well at all, but the thought of losing him brought tears to her eyes. Despite that, she still wasn't sure if she could bring herself to admit her feelings to him without being certain that he felt the same way.

'I promise I'll ask Joan what she thinks I should do,' Peggy assured her mother, hopeful that would buy her at least a week or so before she was pestered about it again. Then she went upstairs to chase the children who, by the sounds of it, had finished getting dressed and were now bouncing on the beds. After shooing them all downstairs, Peggy followed the children into the living room and found Mrs Miller on the sofa with a pack of cards on her lap.

'Mother! You're meant to be reading quietly with them,' Peggy scolded, but her mother batted her away.

'Mummy! Are we playing games?' Martha squealed excitedly. Peggy went to step in, but she stopped when she saw Elsie's face light up. The little girl's blonde hair bobbed up and down as she bounced towards Mrs Miller, and she placed her arms around her in the gentlest of embraces. Peggy marvelled at the fact that somebody so young could be so understanding and careful when it came to a grown-up's health. She had noticed Elsie and her mother growing closer over the last few weeks. After struggling with being away from her own mother initially, Elsie had started slowly gravitating towards Mrs Miller during the small amount of time they spent together. Peggy had realised the youngster seemed to feel a pull towards her mother – shyly loitering near her whenever she sat in the garden with them all, and then gradually starting to talk to her in particular. Elsie was quiet around Peggy and the other children, in contrast. Peggy had tried to make her feel as welcome as possible, yet Elsie had spoken more to her mother in the short periods they had spent together recently than she had to Peggy the whole time they had been here. She felt sad that the youngster hadn't felt at ease enough to open up to her, especially after she had seemed comforted by Peggy on the journey from London. But Peggy had enjoyed watching her come out of her shell around her mother. She didn't want to deny Elsie this time with Mrs Miller when they were forming such a wonderful bond – one that the youngster clearly needed. So, Peggy bit her tongue and left them to play cards with Ted, Martha and Annie while she saw Lucy off to school.

She had to admit that a game of Snap was hardly going to set her mother's heart racing dangerously fast, but Peggy still felt a little wary; she wasn't one to defy doctor's orders.

'Can we go and help at the farm?' Sarah asked eagerly with Phillip at her side, while Peggy washed up the breakfast dishes.

'I should think Mr Grainger would be happy to see you both,' Peggy replied. She smiled as the siblings dashed from the room and straight out of the house. They really did deserve a break from helping her look after the little ones. When she was finished, Peggy popped her head into the living room and was happy to find the card games were over and her mother was now quietly reading a story to the children. Reassured that Mrs Miller wasn't exerting herself too much, Peggy went up to her bedroom to fetch her writing set so she could finally pen a letter to Joan. Her chores would just have to wait.

21

The sun was fully in the sky by the time Viv finally made it out of London. It had been a slow and torturous drive so far, blighted by diversions caused by collapsed buildings and debris. So far, her worries had been put on hold by her quest to get out of the city. Now, as the open road stretched out in front of her, her mind started to focus and process everything. She still couldn't believe she was driving Hudsy out of London – she was taking such a risk! But whatever punishment she might face on her return would be worth suffering if it meant she got to be there for William when he needed her.

Viv couldn't help but feel bad for leaving Dot when she was in such an awful situation. She'd been shocked when her friend had filled her in on her suspicions that Tommy was back in London and in cahoots with Stan, using the former warden's uniform to get them into bomb sites so they could rob the dead or homeless occupants. That really was the lowest of the low. But it was the fact that Tommy was almost certainly back in London which made Viv's blood run the coldest, and she had been able to tell from the way Dot's voice shook that she was terrified he was planning on coming after her. Why else would he be secretly back in the city where his wife had left him, and his mother had thrown him out of the family home? There was nothing for him in London. After fleeing the Army, he could have gone anywhere to start afresh. Why return to London when it was being heavily bombed, and it was probably the most dangerous place in the country to be right now? Not to mention the fact that it was the city he was known in and therefore he was most at risk of being spotted and reported for desertion while being there, even if he was lying low. Viv wondered what could possibly be so important in the area that it was worth taking those risks for. There was the prospect of looting, of course, but other cities were being targeted and offered that opportunity to immoral characters, too. He could easily have gone anywhere else to steal from the vulnerable, but he'd had to choose London. Then there was the fact that he had seemingly teamed up with the one other person who had a vendetta against poor Dot. Viv sighed to herself when she thought of her friend. Dot didn't deserve any of this. If Viv hadn't been on such an important mission, she would have considered turning Hudsy around and going back into London to track Tommy down herself. She wasn't sure what she would do when she found him, but she was just so desperate to put an end to the misery he was inflicting on Dot, even after she'd had the courage to finally leave him. It just didn't seem fair. The anger she was feeling was coming out in Dot's driving; she looked around her and was pleased to see she was making good time on her journey but then she started suddenly and eased her foot from the gas pedal when she realised that she had been speeding a little dangerously while rage consumed her. She knew Paul had told her to drive like hell to Sussex, but she wasn't sure he had meant for her to go *that* fast.

Back at a comfortable, safer speed, Viv tried to push thoughts of Tommy from her mind. She didn't want to risk everything because of him. She was just relieved that Bill was with Dot now and that he had promised to get her home safely. She wouldn't have been able to leave without that assurance. Even though she had only met him properly for the first time the night before, she had seen him in action at bomb sites over the previous weeks and there was no doubt in her mind that he was the perfect person to look after Dot while Tommy was sniffing around and getting up to no good. Not only did Bill come across as kind and compassionate, but he was a strapping man who could clearly look after himself. And she had sensed an air of protectiveness emanating from him whenever he spoke about Dot or interacted with her.

The thought of Tommy trying to harm Dot had Viv gripping the steering wheel too tight, but she caught herself before her foot started pressing down on the gas too hard again. She reminded herself that Dot was safe with Bill, so there was no reason for her to keep fretting about it. Besides, it was daylight now, and even Tommy wouldn't be silly enough to try anything while the sun was up, if coming after Dot was on his agenda. Viv would be back in London by dark and they could come up with a schedule to ensure Dot was never left on her own. Dot had mentioned something about Bill taking some time off from his job at the docks to make sure he could be on duty with her until either Peggy came back to the city or Tommy was caught. The thought of Dot's ex-husband facing a court martial brought a smile to her face.

Pulling into the hospital grounds, Viv turned her attention back to William. Though Tommy wasn't the most pleasant person to think about, at least thoughts about him had distracted her from worrying about her sweetheart. It was almost ten o'clock now, but Viv had no idea if William would be out of surgery yet. She parked up and quickly made her way to Ward Three. She panicked when she saw men in uniform standing around William's bed. Instinctively, she ran along the remainder of the corridor, anxious to find out what had happened and why they were all there but William wasn't. Her mind instantly flew to the worst-case scenario, and she suppressed a sob. One of the men turned around and when she saw that it was Johnny, she launched herself at him.

'What's happened? Where is he? Where's William?' she cried urgently.

'It's all right, Viv.' Johnny had his hands on her shoulders, and he took a step back so she could see his face. 'William's out of surgery,' he said gently, holding eye contact with her. She felt her heart rate slow down and now it was tears of relief instead of fear prickling her eyes. 'They've got him in a recovery room until he comes round, then they'll check his eyesight before fetching us. It sounds like it all went well, though. They think they've saved his sight.' Viv sobbed into her hands. The other servicemen were standing awkwardly next to them now.

'Come on, lads,' Johnny said. 'We'll give Viv a moment to recover and go and get some drinks from the canteen. We'll check in on William in a little while – this lady is the first person he'll want to see when he comes round anyway.'

'And you!' Viv cried, looking up at him earnestly. 'I'm not sending you away, Johnny. You're like a brother to him. He'll want us both there with him, I'm sure of it.'

He smiled gratefully. 'Thank you, Viv.' Then he directed his attention to his colleagues again. 'You guys go head to the canteen, and I'll come and fetch you when William is ready.' They nodded and shuffled off. 'They're all quite young,' he explained quietly. 'I don't think they know what to do around women, let alone one who is crying.'

Viv laughed and pulled out her compact to check her make-up hadn't smudged.

The wait for William to wake up was agonising. Johnny had managed to see William before he went into the operating theatre, and he assured Viv that he'd been in good spirits, which had lifted her own. Viv was gasping for a cup of tea, but neither of them wanted to leave William's bed in case a nurse came to fetch them while they were gone. Eventually Deirdre arrived to do her rounds.

'I didn't realise you'd made it, my dear. He'll be over the moon you managed to get here. Have you been here long?' she asked Viv.

'It feels like hours,' she replied, sighing.

Johnny laughed. 'It really hasn't been long at all,' he said, looking up at the clock on the wall.

'You must be exhausted, my dear. Have you come straight from being on duty?'

Viv nodded and as she did her head felt heavy. She quickly gave it a shake and did some rapid blinking to try and wake herself up.

'I've got to be back in London by nightfall because I'm due back on shift.' She didn't want to admit that she had Hudsy with her and faced leaving her colleagues and residents on her patch without vital transport and supplies if she wasn't back in time for the next raid.

'Lie yourself down on William's bed, you silly thing! He doesn't need it right now, and this one here will give you a nudge when William's ready.' She pointed at Johnny, who shook his head.

'I've already tried, Deirdre, but she won't hear a word of it.'

'He'll be awake soon,' Viv told them both firmly. 'I don't want to waste precious time waking up and feeling groggy when he calls for us.' Viv wasn't going to have long to spend with him and she didn't want to miss a second. Johnny looked at Deirdre and shrugged as if to say 'what can you do?' and the nurse shook her head and laughed.

'Suit yourself, my dear.'

'A cup of tea would be much appreciated, though,' Viv said sweetly, hoping she wasn't pushing her luck.

'Being tired doesn't stop you being cheeky, then?' Deirdre replied, raising her eyebrows playfully. 'You're in luck – they're bringing round elevenses for the patients shortly. Tell them I said you could have a cup each.' She made to leave but Viv grabbed her arm gently. 'Is there any news on Ronnie?' she asked softly.

Deirdre's face fell and she sat down heavily on the bed. Viv had noticed that, though she had been her fun and friendly self, she didn't have her usual spark and her eyes looked somehow sad – like she was putting on a front. It had reminded her of how the nurse had looked the day she told Viv and William about her husband being missing in action. Deirdre patted the space on the bed next to her. Viv had been standing up ever since arriving, worried that if she sat down she might fall asleep. But there was clearly something weighing heavily on Deirdre, who had become a friend and always looked after her during her fleeting visits to the hospital, so she obliged.

'I'll go and fetch those teas,' Johnny announced, pointing at the porter who had just entered the ward with a refreshment trolley. Viv smiled. He had obviously picked up on the fact Deirdre had some bad news to share. Viv hoped it wasn't the worst kind of news. The thoughtful action reminded Viv of what a lovely chap Johnny was. She made a mental note to make sure she asked how his visit to Peggy had gone before she left the hospital. Viv had been so busy and preoccupied by her worries for William recently that she had almost forgotten she'd asked him to check in on her friend. Her tummy fizzed with excitement when she remembered William mentioning that Johnny was quite taken with Peggy, and she wondered if her subtle attempt at matchmaking had worked. When Deirdre started talking, Viv felt bad for thinking about something so trivial when the woman sitting next to her was obviously struggling with something important.

'I've had some news, but I'm afraid it's not good,' the older woman began, going on to explain that her husband had been with a bomber crew targeting the Germans when their plane had gone missing. Viv instinctively took hold of her hand. 'One of his crew made it back to the UK in the end.' Her bottom lip wobbled, and she stopped to take a deep breath.

'Take your time,' Viv said gently. She took Deirdre's hand in her own and waited for her to continue.

'They managed to carry out their operation – they unloaded the bombs on the target, and they were on the return journey. The plane would have made it back, only they had the Luftwaffe on their tail, and they were shot down.'

Viv knew this didn't sound good, but she needed to try and stay positive for Deirdre. 'They evacuated?' she asked hopefully.

Deirdre nodded. 'The man who made it back, he scrambled away into undergrowth as soon as he reached the ground to keep himself hidden in case the Germans were looking for them. He said he only realised Ronnie was nearby when the lights from a vehicle came round the corner – that's when he saw him lying in the middle of the road. Ronnie must have been out cold otherwise he would have got himself under cover, too.'

Johnny came back over and handed both women a cup of tea and then took a seat on the chair next to the bed. Viv noticed he didn't have a cup himself and must have given his to Deirdre. She wondered if it was good for Johnny to be listening to this. She knew as a fighter pilot his duties were different to that of Bomber Command crews, but he still faced the same danger when it came to being shot down from the sky by the enemy. Viv liked to protect herself in a bubble of blissful ignorance whenever she wasn't on duty, choosing not to think about the threats she would be exposed to on her next call-out.

'Their wireless operator was already dead – he'd been struck by shrapnel while they were still in the air,' Deirdre continued. Viv was certain she saw Johnny's hand twitch slightly. 'The Germans had the rest of their crew in the truck. The crewman in the undergrowth had to sit and watch as two of the Germans got out and poked and prodded Ronnie.' She stopped abruptly, squeezing her eyes shut as if trying to force the mental image of that scene out of her head. Deirdre let out a long breath. 'They seemed to signal that they had found a pulse, then they hauled him into the truck with the others and drove away. So, I guess my best hope is that they've captured him, but are they humane enough to fix him up before throwing him into a prisoner of war camp?'

Viv didn't know what to say. She knew that the Geneva Convention rules, which were meant to protect POWs, weren't always followed. 'At least he didn't die in the crash,' she said weakly. 'So you still have some hope.'

'I'm sure he would rather have died in the crash than have to surrender to those bastards and follow their orders until this wretched war is over,' Johnny snapped. He looked up suddenly, regret written all over his face. 'I'm so sorry,' he whispered.

'Don't worry, my dear,' Deirdre replied soothingly. She smiled sadly. 'Ronnie would feel the same way as you. That's what makes this even more difficult. He'll be alive somewhere over there, but he'll most likely be in pain and he'll be wishing he was dead. I just can't bear to think of him suffering.'

'Then you mustn't,' Viv said firmly.

'I know. I know,' Deirdre replied meekly. 'It's just so hard.'

'I understand that. But you have enough here to keep you busy and distracted. You've got to keep going and you've got to stay strong. Ronnie will need you to be there for him when he gets back.'

'How did you find out all that detail?' Johnny asked. 'If you don't mind me asking?'

Viv was grateful for the change in direction. It was all very well her telling Deirdre she had to stay positive, but she felt like a hypocrite seeing as she hadn't stopped fretting about William over the last twenty-four hours – and he was safely back on home ground and in caring hands.

'Of course not, my dear.' Deirdre sat up straighter now and wiped her eyes quickly.

'It's just, I thought the official correspondence would have simply stated he was believed to be a prisoner of war?'

'And it did. His crew mate wrote me a letter. After he saw Ronnie and the others being driven away, he lay low for a while before taking a chance and walking off in search of help. He managed to stumble across members of MI9, who knew operations were going on that night in the area and were out searching for survivors. The first thing he did when he got back to Britain and had his debrief was write to me. He feels terrible.'

'Why?' Viv asked.

'He's convinced he should have spotted Ronnie sooner and dragged him to safety.'

'Then they would have caught him, too,' Johnny said.

'Exactly. That's what I told him. I wrote straight back to him and said there was nothing he could have done. I know he's a good man – or else he wouldn't have written to me to explain what happened. I told him I'm just grateful one of them managed to get away. At least me and the families of the other airmen can stop wondering if our men are dead or alive.'

'I'm glad you wrote back to him,' Johnny said quietly.

'Of course, my dear,' Deirdre replied. Then, she got to her feet and with a forced cheerfulness, she added: 'Now, like you said, I have enough to do here to keep my mind occupied. I shall go and check on your young man.'

'Thank you,' Viv said. 'And, Deirdre, I'm glad you haven't been left wondering about Ronnie. To know he's alive must be a relief, despite the circumstances.'

Deirdre simply smiled and bowed her head before walking off along the ward. Viv wanted to ask Johnny if he'd meant what he'd said about Ronnie preferring to be dead than captured by the enemy. He must feel that way. But she didn't know him well enough to pry like that. She wasn't even sure she would ask William that – but she was afraid it was how he felt, too. She decided to try and brighten the mood.

'So, I wanted to thank you for dropping in on Peggy,' she said perkily. Johnny turned to face her and his whole demeanour changed. He looked like a different man – one who was happy and cheerful instead of one who had just been reminded of the dangers of his duties.

'Yes!' he exclaimed, standing up to search in his jacket pocket. Viv watched him curiously. 'She gave me this to pass on to you,' he said excitedly. Just the mention of Peggy had made him come alive. Viv didn't need to enquire any further – it was clear that he was smitten with her friend. She took the envelope from his hand and ripped it open, eager to have some news from Peggy.

Dearest Viv,

I miss you all so much but I'm confident we will be reunited soon.

I trust you are looking after Mrs Martin for me, as well as Dot. I hope you are finding time to look after yourself, too.

I hope everything goes well with William's surgery. I'm thinking of you both and I just know you will get your happily ever after!

All my love,

Peggy

Viv held the piece of paper to her chest and beamed from ear to ear. It was a short note and it had obviously been scribbled in a hurry, but it felt wonderful to have that link to Peggy after what felt like so long apart. She was pulled back to reality when she heard Deirdre calling her name from the other side of the ward. She looked up and saw the nurse standing at the open door.

'He's awake, and he's asking for you both,' she said happily.

Johnny got up and made to walk towards Deirdre, but Viv grabbed his arm and pulled him back.

'Not so fast,' she said, hopping from one leg to the other in nervous anticipation as she searched in her handbag for her compact. Once she'd found it, she opened it up and placed it in his hand before lifting his arm up so she could see her reflection in the mirror. 'Just there. Now, don't move,' she ordered as she rummaged in her pocket. It was his turn to look confused now. But understanding dawned on his face when she pulled out her lipstick. Johnny laughed as she applied it and quickly adjusted her hair. 'Now, we go,' she declared confidently before grabbing the mirror back from him and running off ahead towards Deirdre.

Butterflies danced in Viv's belly as she followed the nurse along the corridor with Johnny just behind her. She found that she had Peggy's words ringing in her ears about getting her happily ever after, and she hoped with all her heart that her friend was right about that.

22

In the end, Bill escorted Dot back to Cook's Ground School soon after Viv had left. Dot had been keen to stay and help with the aftermath of the tube bombing and bus crash for as long as possible, but Bill had put his foot down, insisting that she looked in desperate need of rest. It had felt nice to have him looking out for her, but Dot had found herself feeling self-conscious about her looks given the fact he had noticed she was so tired. As they wandered through London's battered streets together, she kept her head down, not wanting the early risers to catch a glimpse of her looking so dreadful. They spent most of the journey in a companiable silence, and Dot wondered why she was so bothered about her appearance in front of Bill.

She had been so shocked when he'd described the man operating with who they now believed to be Stan that she hadn't immediately told him that she suspected the thug in question was Tommy. But when she had been reunited with Viv at Balham it had all come pouring out. Thankfully, Bill had been within earshot, so she hadn't had to repeat it all. He'd been shocked but the news had made him seem even more determined to protect her.

Dot thought back now to what Bill had said about the two burglars – with the taller one intimidating and threatening the man in the ARP uniform, who was likely to be Stan.

If she was correct in her suspicions, then it would seem that Stan the bully had finally met his match. She smiled to herself, remembering Peggy's words about bullies always getting their comeuppance in the end. She'd thought that Stan had got his when he'd lost his role as a warden, but now it seemed he was getting a little more. She could only hope that it would be Tommy's turn next.

When they got to the school and went to Victor's office to fill out the usual end-of-shift forms, they found Ted sitting at the desk with Victor asleep on a makeshift bed in the corner. His snores echoed around the room. Victor often slept at the base between raids because he found it difficult to get any rest at home during the day. Apparently, his wife was a bit of a chatterbox who insisted on sharing the latest gossip from the shelter with him no matter how much he protested. Dot had never understood why he didn't set himself up in one of the classrooms where he was less likely to be disturbed, but Peggy had told her that he liked to be on hand in case he was needed for anything urgent. And she supposed wardens coming in and out of the room was probably less disruptive than a spouse rabbiting on in your face.

'We'll take these and fill them in over in the canteen,' Bill whispered to Ted, picking up the relevant forms and nodding his head in Victor's direction. Ted gave him a thumbs-up and then they all froze as Victor's snoring stopped abruptly. He muttered to himself and rubbed his eyes before rolling over and starting to snore again. There was a collective sigh of relief. Nobody wanted to be the one responsible for waking somebody up at a time when sleep was so precious.

'Did you make it over to Balham?' Ted asked quietly.

'Yes. The messenger found us,' Bill replied. 'They're still digging for bodies over there, though. It sounds as if they'll be recovering them for weeks yet.' Dot closed her eyes against the thought of it. She hated the fact that so many people had perished in such a way. It was a terrible way to go. And she knew that being stuck down there didn't affect somebody who was already dead, but it just seemed like one final indignity to have to wait for somebody to dig you out so you could be identified and buried in the proper way. Dot hoped that when her time came, she would be shipped off to the morgue without delay. She quickly grimaced at the fact she was thinking in that way. Before the war she had never really thought about dying, even after losing both her parents, let alone come up with preferences on how she might go and how her body would be disposed of. Now that dealing with death was a daily occurrence, as routine to her as her morning porridge, it had become the norm. She couldn't remember when the switch had happened, but she was hoping that death would become alien to her once again and soon, when this awful war was over.

'Are you all right, Dot?'

She looked up, startled. Victor's snoring had stopped, and the room was silent. 'You were in your own little world, there,' Ted said softly.

'Sorry about that,' she replied, giving her head a quick shake, as if that would throw the bad thoughts out of her mind. 'I'm just a little tired.' If she had been with Viv or Peggy then she would have confided everything that was running around in her head. But she didn't want to come across as weak in front of Ted and Bill. She needed her male colleagues to know that she was just as capable of dealing with all of this as they were. Plus, Dot was already relying on Bill to protect her from Tommy when she didn't even know for certain that he was nearby. She didn't want him to think she was any weaker than she must already appear to be, even if she felt it.

Bill placed a protective hand on Dot's shoulder. 'It was a busy night and I'm done-in, too,' he said. Dot's heart swelled at the way he had instinctively jumped in to support her. 'We'll fill these in and then both go and get some rest.'

'Good idea. Take care, you two,' Ted said a little too loudly before realising his slip-up. Wincing, he peered round at Victor, who stirred and grunted, turned over, and immediately started snoring again. 'Aah, that's more like it. Order is restored,' Ted joked.

When Dot and Bill walked into the canteen, Frank and Laurie were sitting at a table playing cards. They had gone from working well together despite their initial clash to becoming unexpectedly close friends. Frank had even been for breakfast with Laurie and his wife a few times and managed to convince her to go easy on her husband for being a conchie by telling her about all his heroic acts as a warden.

'Busy day shift?' Bill joked.

'We're more than happy to have quiet days while the nights are so busy,' Laurie replied, looking up from his cards. 'In fact, I was just about to make a round of tea – can I tempt the two of you?'

'Most definitely,' Dot and Bill replied together. They looked at each other and laughed before sitting down at the table. Laurie placed his cards face down on the table and went into the kitchen.

'Are you just back from Balham?' Frank asked. He placed his cards down in front of him and sat back in his chair.

The two of them nodded. 'Bad over there, was it? I'd have thought the death toll will be high?'

'They're still going but I don't think it will be as bad as they first thought,' Bill replied. 'There was a rail worker down there – right place, right time – he led a load of passengers out through the tunnels. If it wasn't for him then I'm sure it would have been a lot worse. It was a long night, though, with casualties trickling out slowly.'

Frank nodded his understanding and didn't ask any more questions. He would have understood how much the pair of them were craving sleep.

Dot started filling in her incident sheet. She saw a movement out of the corner of her eye and glanced up in time to spot Frank leaning over and slowly lifting up Laurie's cards one by one. He must have sensed her eyes on him as he lifted the final card up because he suddenly looked over at her. She lifted an eyebrow and grinned.

He smiled back and put his finger to his lips. 'You wouldn't tell on an old codger like me, would you, Dot?' he whispered as he carefully sat back down on his chair.

'I can't see anything to talk about here,' she replied, getting back to her paperwork with a smirk on her face. Bill had kept his eyes firmly on his form the whole time. When Laurie came back with the tea, it was a matter of seconds before Frank claimed victory by triumphantly throwing his cards down on the table and cheering.

'How do you keep getting me like that?' Laurie groaned. He caught Dot's eye and winked at her as Frank celebrated his victory, oblivious. So, Laurie knew what his opponent was up to, then, but he was playing along and letting him get away with it. Dot felt a stab of affection for the younger man.

'My guess is that Laurie is getting sent off to make tea rather a lot at the moment,' Bill joked as Dot walked with him back to the office so they could hand in their forms.

'It's kind of him to humour Frank,' Dot replied. 'Especially when he makes such a song and dance out of winning.'

Their laughter was suddenly cut short as they neared the office. Dot could hear sobbing coming from the room. At first, she panicked that they might have lost a warden last night, but then she remembered it had been so quiet in their sector that the messengers had diverted everybody over to Balham to help there, where there had been no rescue team injuries. When they reached the office doorway, they peered in cautiously. Dot could see Victor sitting upright on his makeshift bed looking dazed and confused while a woman stood in front of the desk bawling her eyes out. Ted was standing at the other side of the desk looking uncomfortable as he glanced back and forth constantly between Victor and the mystery woman, as if he was waiting for one of them to say something or take some action. With the woman obviously too distressed to talk and Victor clearly still trying to wake up and remember where and who he was, Dot walked straight up to the woman and guided her gently to one of the chairs at the edge of the room.

'There, there,' she soothed. 'Whatever it is, we'll work it out together.' Her desperate need for rest had vanished now she was faced with somebody who clearly needed help and wasn't getting any from the useless men in the room. She was very fond of Victor and Ted, but goodness were they hopeless when it came to anything involving emotion.

'Ted, why don't you go and make this poor woman a cup of tea,' Bill suggested. Dot smiled to herself. At least there was one man in the room with some compassion. Ted bustled out, still looking uncomfortable, just as Victor finally bounced into life. He threw off his covers and got to his feet.

'Sorry about that. I was in such a deep sleep, and I thought the crying was part of my dream. It took me a moment there to get my bearings.' He paused and gave his eyes another rub. 'What are you doing here, Ginny, and whatever is the matter?' He walked over to the woman who was now sitting on a chair but still inconsolable. So, Victor knew this woman. Dot wondered if it was his wife. She hoped she didn't have bad news for Victor.

'This is my sister, Ginny,' Victor explained, addressing Dot and Bill. Understanding dawned on Dot and she looked over at Bill who looked as if he was just having the same realisation. 'Yes, yes – my sister who is married to Stan,' Victor confirmed to them both.

Ginny didn't look up, but it seemed she was getting herself into a worse state as her breathing was becoming erratic.

'Try taking deep breaths,' Dot suggested, remembering how Bill had helped her during her terrifying episode when she had panicked that she'd seen Tommy. Dot knelt down in front of her and started taking deep breaths herself, hoping it would encourage her to follow suit. Eventually, Ginny did. Bill and Victor remained silent as Dot and Ginny's breathing gradually came into sync. Once she had finally calmed down, Victor's sister stood up and threw herself at him, encasing him in her arms. She was a large woman and she seemed to swamp her slight brother. Dot's mind was transported back to Victor struggling to restrain Stan in this same room when he had gone for Jim over the pocket watch revelation. She had wondered then if Victor's sister was slender like him or ungainly like her husband, and now she knew.

'I'm so sorry, but I didn't know where else to go,' she declared into his shoulder.

A muffled 'it's okay' emerged from the embrace.

'Do you want to tell us what the matter is? Maybe we can try and help?' Dot suggested carefully, hoping Ginny might let Victor go before he started struggling to breathe. As she'd hoped, Ginny stepped away from her brother and he shot Dot a grateful look while composing himself.

Ginny slumped back into the chair and sighed. 'It's Stan,' she said, her voice quivering.

'What's he done now?' Victor said, instantly angry. His hands bunched into fists.

'Oh, stop!' she snapped, throwing her brother a reprimanding look. 'You've always thought the worst of him and even now – when he hasn't done anything wrong – you're convinced he has!'

Dot watched Victor and could see that he was swallowing back the words he longed to say. It must have been awful for him to witness his sister falling for such a brute while he was powerless to stop her. Dot had always admired the fact Victor had kept Stan's stealing from everybody else in order to protect his sister. He must have been desperate to shout 'I told you so!' and revel in the fact he'd been right about his brother-in-law, yet he'd chosen to spare Ginny's feelings. But now Dot was starting to wonder if the truth was going to have to come out – like it always did sooner or later. Her heart started racing as she recognised that news about Stan would most probably involve Tommy, too.

'Can you please tell us what's happened?' Dot asked, trying to keep the nervous edge out of her voice.

'That's just it! I don't know!' Ginny cried, starting to sob again. 'Stan didn't come home from his shift last night.'

'His shift?' Victor asked cautiously.

'His shift!' she repeated, sounding frustrated and staring hard at him.

'What shift?' Victor replied, his confusion clear in his voice.

'His warden shift – here!' Ginny snapped. 'Stan hasn't come home, and I thought I'd find him here but he's not here, is he? So, where is my husband? What's happened to him? Is he buried under a collapsed building somewhere? I knew all this do-gooding would get him in the end!' She was looking between the three of them, and they all looked from one to the other nervously because it was now clear that something bad must have happened to Stan, and that his wife had no idea that he'd been dismissed from the ARP.

23

Once Peggy had finished her letter to Joan, she felt lighter. It seemed that keeping everything from her sister really had been weighing on her. She stuck to what she'd agreed with her mother, telling Joan that she'd moved back home to help look after an influx of evacuees but explaining that she was hoping to get back to London as soon as possible. No lies there – just an omission. She mentioned Johnny in passing but she didn't bring up her fears that her growing romantic feelings were not reciprocated. She wanted to see what Joan's reaction to the new man on the horizon was before she revealed all her insecurities. Going over it with their mother had felt like enough for now.

When Lucy came home from school, they all sat down together for lunch.

'When Patricia visited, she mentioned a WI meeting being held this afternoon,' Mrs Miller mentioned once all the children had stopped gabbing and were quietly eating their food. Peggy looked up at her mother warily. 'I thought I might pop over,' she added casually before taking another mouthful of food. When Peggy raised her eyebrows in reaction to her mother's suggestion, the older woman started desperately trying to convince her. 'It's not far to walk and it would be so good to see everybody again. I wouldn't stay for the whole meeting – I'll just show my face and let everybody know I'm getting on all right and then come straight home. They'll all be wondering where I've got to by now. And you could even escort me over, to make sure I don't stay too long—'

'I don't think it's a good idea,' Peggy cut her mother off mid-sentence. She already felt like they were pushing it by having her mother off bed rest, but she didn't want to get into a big discussion about it in front of the children for fear of worrying them. Her mother had probably counted on that and hoped Peggy would relent to avoid upsetting anybody. But Peggy's warden work had made her more assertive than she used to be, and she wasn't about to back down on this.

'But Dr Brady has signed it off,' her mother pleaded.

'Has he?' Peggy was surprised. Dr Brady had been very careful to keep her updated on everything to do with her mother's health, but he certainly hadn't mentioned a WI meeting to her. That felt like it would be a big deal worthy of discussion and planning.

'Yes! He said fresh air was going to be good for my recovery. Remember?'

'He did say that,' Lucy chipped in, full of authority.

Peggy gave her little sister a sideways glance and huffed to herself before replying to her mother.

'That was when we were talking about getting you out in the garden to sit and watch us tending to the vegetable patches. That's a far cry from walking all the way over to the village hall and joining in with a busy meeting.' Watching her mother's face drop, Peggy felt terrible. She understood how difficult the last few weeks must have been for her, and she could appreciate how frustrating it must be to be stuck at home when she was starting to feel fitter and healthier.

But Peggy truly didn't think this was worth the risk. Not when they had come so far.

'Why don't I talk to Dr Brady about it tomorrow?' Peggy suggested.

Her mother shrugged and pushed the food around on her plate, reminding Peggy of a petulant child. Neither of them had asked for this reversal of their roles and she wished they could go back to how it used to be.

'I wrote my letter to Joan this morning,' Peggy said cheerfully, trying to steer the conversation back to a place where her mother was in the adult role, advising her daughter on matters of the heart. As uncomfortable as sharing her insecurities had been, it had felt nice to talk to her mother openly about how she was feeling that morning. And Peggy was only realising now how much she had missed being in the child role after the time she had spent looking after her mother and all the children. But Mrs Miller just smiled weakly and gave her a small nod.

'Is everybody finished?' Peggy asked loudly over the chatter that had started up amongst all the children. That was normally a clear indicator that they were done with their food. After getting a nod from everybody, she asked Sarah and Phillip to clear the plates and excused the others, instructing Ted and Elsie to get their school things together ready for their afternoon lessons. Phillip and Sarah had started walking the two younger evacuees to school, which meant that Peggy didn't need to rush to get everybody ready to walk over together.

'I'm feeling rather tired after being downstairs all morning, actually,' Mrs Miller said as children shot off in all directions. 'I'm going to go for a lie-down.'

'That's a good idea,' Peggy replied. She was relieved her mother had given up on the WI meeting. 'Do you need help getting up the stairs?'

'No, thank you. I'll be fine.' Mrs Miller got to her feet and seemed to be deep in thought for a moment. 'I know the girls normally like to come up to my room when the others are at school in the afternoon, but I think I'd better rest after my busy morning.'

Peggy nodded her agreement. She knew her sisters would be disappointed, but at least Martha and Annie had spent some extra time with their mother this morning. And Peggy would be able to divert their attention to drawing pictures to send off to Joan along with her letter. Then they could all walk into the village together to post everything and they would probably run into the others on their way home from school. Making the plan in her head reminded Peggy that her mother had wanted to send a letter to Joan at the same time.

'I'll pop up later to get your letter so I can post it along with mine,' she called out as her mother reached the stairs.

Mrs Miller turned round looking panicked, but she seemed to quickly gather herself. 'I don't think I'll be finished in time,' she replied. 'You go ahead and post yours and I'll let you know when I'm done. She'll have enough excitement getting your news through – mine can wait another day or so.' She turned back towards the staircase before stopping suddenly and turning back to face her daughter. 'Can you make sure the girls do their drawings on the kitchen table, please? I don't want any accidental marks on the furniture. Oh, and don't worry about bringing me up any refreshments. I feel ready to sleep and I'd rather not be disturbed.'

That was odd. Mrs Miller normally complained that Peggy didn't send enough food and drink up to her during the day. Peggy watched her mother slowly move up the stairs and breathed a sigh of relief that she had seen sense. The poor woman was worn out after a morning playing cards and reading on the sofa. Peggy didn't understand how her mother had imagined she was going to make it to the village hall, let alone sit through the WI get-together. Peggy was tempted to forget the idea altogether, but she would mention it to Dr Brady when she next saw him. She knew her mother well enough to know that, though she might have admitted defeat today, she would keep on about this until she got her way, and there was no doubt in Peggy's mind that Mrs Miller would bring it up with the doctor herself to check she had asked him. But she was confident that he would be on Peggy's side on the matter, and they could agree that it would be something to work towards once Mrs Miller was stronger. Maybe they could even have one of the next meetings at the house. Peggy smiled at the idea. That would satisfy her mother's need to be *doing* something, and she would get the chance to socialise properly again. It would even save her having to travel to the villagc hall. Maybe she could ask Mrs Brady to organise a handful of the women to visit along with her the next time she came over to spend time with her mother. They could have tea and do some knitting. She knew they were working on new patterns for service socks for the Army.

Peggy felt a rush of excitement at the thought of helping her mother get involved again without pushing her too much. They were going to have to tread carefully to ensure she didn't set herself back after doing so well with her recovery.

Peggy set the girls up in the kitchen with their drawing things and sat with them in the hopes her presence would diffuse any of the usual arguments over who got to use which colour. Annie opted for her go-to drawing of a potato man, which Peggy knew would make Joan giggle. Martha was slightly more adventurous with a scene from the garden, and Lucy set to work on what appeared to be a picture of a man. As she coloured it in, it became apparent it was a man in unform.

'Who are you drawing?' Peggy asked her, expecting it to be one of their brothers or their father.

'That's your boyfriend,' Lucy replied, straight-faced. Then all three girls burst into laughter.

Peggy tried to keep a straight face too, but she couldn't stop herself from laughing along with them. She wasn't even upset at Lucy calling Johnny her boyfriend – it was just lovely to see them finding pleasure in something so silly. Besides, the more she reacted to things like this, the more they would tease – she had been exactly the same with Joan when they were growing up.

'He's just a friend,' she replied, trying to keep the edge out of her voice and sound relaxed about it. She didn't want them calling Johnny her boyfriend the next time he visited. If he even visited again. Maybe now he had taken her out for the evening he would consider his favour to Viv completed. Though she hoped that when he passed on her note to her friend, Viv would insist he hand-deliver her reply. Peggy was certain she could count on her for that. She wasn't ready to let their friendship fade yet, even if Johnny was only being nice to her because Viv had asked him to. A bang from the hallway made Peggy jump. It had sounded like a door slamming.

'What was that?' Martha asked, looking up, alarmed.

'I'm not sure,' Peggy replied, getting to her feet. 'You three wait there – I'll go and check.' She laughed to herself as she pictured her mother, bored already, trying to creep around the house unnoticed and failing miserably by accidentally making lots of noise. But when she checked all the downstairs rooms, there was no sign of her mother. The noise had definitely come from the bottom floor of the house, so she supposed a door must have blown shut in the wind.

When she got back to the girls, they were already arguing over colours. After calming everybody down, she enjoyed the peace and quiet as they concentrated on putting the finishing touches to their artwork. Once it was all completed, along with a note from Lucy on her picture to explain that the pilot she had drawn was Peggy's boyfriend, they all got ready to walk to the Post Office.

Peggy sneaked Lucy's drawing out of the envelope and added a correction to her message while she was distracted putting her jacket on and helping the others with theirs. Peggy paused at the bottom of the stairs before ushering the girls out of the door. She was desperate to check on her mother, but she had been very clear that she wasn't to be disturbed. Peggy didn't like to go out without making sure she had everything she needed, but she reminded herself that she should respect her mother's wishes; Peggy was already in her bad books for refusing her permission to go to the WI meeting – she didn't want to make matters worse.

Peggy and her sisters ran into their house guests on their way back from school after posting Joan's letter and pictures. The eight of them stopped off at the farm on the way home, so when they got back it was all hands on deck to get dinner prepared before they all became too hungry. As she started on the vegetables, Peggy considered going upstairs to check on her mother. But the house had been quiet on their return, and she was still feeling wary of bothering her, so she decided to wait until the food was ready. When she was about to serve up, she called Lucy to go and fetch their mother.

'She's not there,' the youngster said some minutes later, bursting into the dining room looking flushed. She must have run downstairs in a panic after finding the main bedroom empty. Peggy panicked at first, but then she thought logically about it and realised her mother was probably in the bathroom. All the meals had been served up by now and the children were waiting patiently at the table. And now that the house was still and quiet, there was no sign of any movement from upstairs.

'You lot get started – I'll go upstairs and check what she's up to,' Peggy said. She hadn't even made it out of the door before the sound of cutlery hitting plates rang out. Peggy knocked tentatively on the bathroom door and waited but there was no reply. She edged it slowly open – the room was empty. She went back across the hall to the main bedroom in case they had just missed each other, but her mother definitely wasn't in there, either. Peggy started checking all the bedrooms. There was absolutely no reason for her mother to be in any of them, but Peggy wasn't sure what else to do. The rising sense of panic she was now experiencing grew each time she walked into a room to find it empty.

'Mother!' she yelled when she got to the top of the stairs. 'Mother! Dinner's ready!' Her heart raced as she flew down the stairs, trying to push out of her mind the thoughts of her mother collapsed in a corner of a room, hidden from view. She checked each and every room downstairs, continually shouting, but there was still no sign of the woman. By now, the children had come out of the dining room to see what all the noise was about.

'Has anybody seen her?' she asked them desperately.

Sarah had her arms around Martha and Annie, comforting them. The sight of her sisters looking scared snapped Peggy out of her panic. 'Sorry, everybody,' she said, trying to keep her voice calm and steady. 'There's nothing to worry about. I just . . . I can't find Mother. I mean, I'm sure she's fine. She probably just popped out. Though I don't know what for . . .'

'I'll check in the garden,' Phillip offered.

Peggy racked her brain, trying to work out where her mother could possibly have gone and why. Then her stomach lurched at a memory. The banging noise earlier that afternoon. Could that have been Mrs Miller leaving the house? Was that why she hadn't wanted Peggy to disturb her – because if Peggy had gone to her room then she would have discovered it empty after she had sneaked out of the house like a rebellious teenager? Peggy huffed and shook her head. She should have known something was up when her mother relented on the WI idea so quickly. Peggy couldn't believe she had fallen for the oldest trick in the book. Well, she wasn't going to let her mother get away with it.

'Sarah, can you help get the little ones ready for bed, please?' she asked the confused girl as calmly as she could manage as she grabbed her jacket and started putting it on.

'Yes, but, where are you going?' she replied anxiously.

'I'm off to the village hall to bring my wayward mother home,' Peggy declared loudly.

24

'It worked!' William exclaimed as soon as Viv walked into the room. She heard a cheer from Johnny just behind her and she clapped her hands in glee. 'Well, aren't you just a vision? You're even more beautiful through two eyes,' William added.

Viv rushed straight up to his bed and threw her arms around him. He held her close. She took a moment to drink in the sensation; despite the fact William was laid up and recovering from surgery, she felt completely safe in his arms. When Viv finally pulled away from the embrace, she studied William's eye, gently pushing his hair away from his face to get a better look. His hair had started growing back so quickly.

'I'm so happy to see you! And I'm so relieved they managed to save your sight,' she said through tears. William's eye and the skin around it still looked sore, but he didn't seem to be in any discomfort.

'Not as happy as I am to *see* you,' he joked. He grabbed Viv's hand and pulled it to his mouth to give it a kiss.

'All right, you two. You sure know how to make a man feel awkward, huh?' Johnny called out.

Viv blushed. She had forgotten poor Johnny was in the room with them. But when she looked over at him, he was smiling playfully.

'Listen, mate, I'm so pleased for you,' he added warmly. He walked up to the other side of the bed and rubbed William's shoulder affectionately. 'The other lads are still here, but you were asleep a little longer than we anticipated. We need to get back to base before the chief puts us on jankers for being late to report for duty. I'll leave you to catch up with Viv and I'll bring everyone back another day.'

'Thanks for checking in,' William replied. 'And you can let the rest of the squadron know I'll be back soon! I've just got to get my leg sorted and perfect walking without my big toe and then I'll be up in the air again shooting those damn Jerries down!'

'That's the spirit,' Johnny shouted. 'I'll see you soon,' he added happily before leaving Viv and William on their own in the room.

Viv sat down heavily in the chair next to the bed. Her heart had dropped at William's mention of taking to the skies again. Her elation at his quickening recovery had been replaced by fears for his safety. She'd always known there was a real possibility he would return to the RAF, of course, and it was something she had even longed for because that would indicate a full recovery. It had crushed Viv's soul to think of him being discharged due to his injuries. But she had grown used to William being at the hospital, and the peace of mind that afforded her. Once he was serving again, he would be away from this bubble of safety. Viv had been worried about him before, but now her feelings for him had grown so much stronger, and she had come so close to losing him, she felt as if the constant angst would be unbearable.

'What's the matter, my darling?' William asked.

Viv suddenly snapped out of her stupor. 'I'm so sorry. I don't want to bring you down on such a happy day,' she replied, forcing a smile.

'You're worried about me getting back out there, aren't you?'

Viv's gaze switched to the floor in response to William's question. 'I know I'm being selfish. It's just that I've got used to you being here and being . . . well, *safe*. I know you'll be happier back out there helping hold back the Nazis but—'

'It's what I *must* do. It's driving me crazy sitting around here all day every day while they keep killing innocent people. Women and children, Viv. Women and children!'

'Don't you think I know that? I've seen it all first hand. I've seen the tiny hands sticking out of the rubble and I've comforted the women who have had to watch the children they gave birth to die in front of their eyes in the most brutal way.' Viv normally did well not to let the things she'd seen on duty affect her, but tears were pouring down her face now as thousands of images of pain and destruction flashed through her mind.

William reached out and took hold of her hand. 'Then you'll understand why I need to do everything within my power to help stop the brutes responsible. If I can prevent even one of those planes from getting to their target, I'll save lives. I've got to do it, even if I lose my own life in the process.' Viv heaved out a sob at the mention of William dying. 'I don't want to lose you,' she wept, shaking her head. She'd never been one to lose control like this, but she found that she couldn't stop herself from unravelling in front of this man.

'I don't want to lose you either, Viv,' William said gently, rubbing her hand. 'That's another reason for me to protect the skies – every plane that gets to London is another threat to you. Especially when you're out there in the thick of it instead of keeping yourself safe in a shelter. And the worst thing is that while I'm still recovering, I'm stuck here with nothing to distract me from the thoughts of it and no way to do anything to stop the enemy.' He sighed and ran his fingers through his hair before taking hold of her hand again. 'Don't you think I spend all day every day terrified of what might happen to you? You're everything to me. I've never loved anybody the way I love you, Viv. You've ignited something in me.'

William shuffled around to get himself sitting up straighter and Viv's heart started racing. Her tears stopped as anticipation, hope and excitement took over – was he building up to another proposal? It would certainly be the perfect moment. *Come on, William*, she willed him in her head. *I want this more than anything. Just ask me one more time and I promise I'll say yes!*

He held eye contact with her, and she held her breath in expectation. 'I don't know what I'd do if anything happened to you, Viv. But I'd never ask you to stop putting yourself at risk to help others, because I know that you need to do everything that you can – just like me. And I'd rather die taking out one of their planes if it meant the bombs didn't make it to you in London.'

'I love you,' she blurted. She couldn't help it. She was so overcome with her feelings for him.

'I love you, too,' he replied softly. Then he leaned forward to wipe away the tears that were still trickling down her cheeks. 'Now, what do I have to do to get a cup of tea around here?' he asked, his tone suddenly light and cheeky. 'I'm gasping!' he joked.

Viv's hopes were instantly dashed. 'I'll go and fetch you a cup,' she whispered. As she got up and walked out of the room, Viv felt as though she was in a daze. Out in the corridor she threw her back against the wall, leaned her head back, and put her hands over her eyes. Dropping her hands back down to her sides, the note from Peggy slipped out of her pocket and on to the floor. She reached down to pick it up, and her friend's words of encouragement glared up at her from the page:

I just know you will get your happily ever after!

Without warning, Dot's voice was joining in with Peggy in Viv's head. It was as if the two of them were standing in front of her, egging her on:

If this war has taught us anything, it's that we need to live life to the fullest because it can be over in the blink of an eye. You almost lost William once. Throw caution to the wind – go and be with him when he needs you most.

Maybe she *should* throw caution to the wind – and throw all respectability out of the window! An idea had popped into Viv's head. Her tummy flipped as she considered the possibility. Could she really do it? She was suddenly terrified, but she knew it was now or never. She would never have the courage again and Dot was right, this could all be over in the blink of an eye. That was reason enough to demand what she wanted and to hell with the consequences! Viv's heart raced as it worked overtime pumping blood quickly around her body while she stomped back towards William's room. She was really going to do this. She stopped at the closed door, nerves suddenly taking over. Then she took a deep breath, swiftly topped up her lipstick and burst through the door with renewed confidence.

Both William and Deirdre looked up in surprise at her arrival. The nurse looked as though she was doing some routine checks. But Viv wasn't going to be stopped now she had her heart set on what she needed to do next. If she faltered, she might lose her nerve and never get it back again.

'Where's my tea?' William asked, laughing nervously, as Viv walked up to him full of determination.

Deirdre stopped what she was doing and cautiously took a step back.

'Are you all right, my love? You look . . . different?' William added quietly.

'William Carter.' She took another deep breath and told herself she could do this. 'Turning down your marriage proposal was one of the most – no, it was *the* most foolish thing I've ever done. I've regretted it every day since. Many times a day, in fact.' William looked embarrassed and Viv felt a stab of shame for the hurt he must have gone through since that evening, convinced that she didn't want to be his wife. 'I've been desperate for you to ask me again, but I realise that I might have blown my only chance. Well, if you won't ask me again then I'm just going to have to take the bull by the horns and ask you myself.' She heard a gasp from the corner of the room but tried to ignore the fact that Deirdre was still here. At least she would have somebody to console her if William turned her down.

'I would love nothing more than for you to do that,' William said as a big grin spread across his face.

Viv exhaled heavily and started laughing in relief. There was an encouraging cough from Deirdre in the corner, and she looked at William again and realised that he was looking up at her expectantly now.

'Oh, erm, I suppose I'd better ask you, then,' she whispered, flustered. William nodded his head encouragingly and Deirdre let out a little squeal before whispering an apology.

'Sorry, I just . . . I don't think I'd made it that far in my head,' Viv added nervously. 'Okay, here goes.'

'Will you marry me?' they both said loudly at the same time.

'Yes!' they shouted together.

Viv threw her arms around William, who was laughing along with her. She was so lost in the moment that she didn't even hear Deirdre cheering and clapping behind them. Viv stood back from the embrace when she heard the door flying open, and she just caught sight of the back of Deirdre's head as the woman sprinted down the corridor shouting 'They're getting married!' to a chorus of cheers and clapping.

25

Ginny was pacing backwards and forwards in the office, clearly trying to process the news her brother had just given her about her husband. The poor woman had had no idea that Stan had been dismissed from his warden duties. It turned out that Victor hadn't seen his sister since letting Stan go. He'd avoided going round to visit her, as he hadn't fancied an awkward run-in with his brother-in-law. He had just learned that if he'd called round to their house, he would have discovered that Stan had been regularly donning his uniform and heading out under the pretence of warden duties. If Stan's constant lying about his whereabouts hadn't been a big enough kick in the teeth for Ginny, Victor had then revealed that he'd been forced to let Stan go after learning that he'd been stealing valuables from dead bodies.

'I don't believe you,' she muttered, shaking her head. 'There must have been some mistake. My Stan wouldn't do that.'

'Ginny, one of the other wardens saw him lifting a pocket watch from our dead colleague shortly after he was blown to bits in the crypt. And then we got confirmation from the spiv he sold it on to.'

Dot breathed a sigh of relief and silently thanked Victor for not bringing her into it by revealing that it had been her who'd caught Stan red-handed and then presented all the evidence to him. She knew she'd done the right thing, but emotions were running high, and Ginny was obviously under Stan's spell; Dot didn't want to end up bearing the brunt of her anger.

'I still think there must have been some mistake,' Ginny replied firmly. She stopped pacing and looked hard at Victor. 'You've always thought the worst of him. You never stop to give him a chance – there could be an innocent explanation!'

Dot prayed Victor wouldn't turn to her to back him up.

'He dropped himself in it when I confronted him about it and then . . .' There was a pause as Victor rubbed his brow. It looked as though he was grappling with something, trying to find the right words. Ginny tapped her foot impatiently. 'Your eternity ring,' he said finally, sounding defeated.

'What?' she brought her hand up to look at the sparkling ring on her finger. 'What about it?' she pressed nervously.

Victor exhaled heavily. 'I thought you would have recognised it when he gave it to you. But you were probably in denial. I didn't want to believe it either but, in the end, it was the only explanation.'

'Victor. You're not making any sense,' Ginny snapped. 'Stan got this for me for our wedding anniversary. He'd been saving up for ages. Why would I recognise it?'

'Because it was Carol's,' Victor replied quietly.

Ginny's head snapped back at the mention of her friend. Carol and her husband Jack had died during one of the first bombings, and Stan had been there to help pull their bodies out of the rubble.

'No,' she whispered, running her finger over the diamond. 'No, no! It's *similar* to Carol's – that's why Stan picked it out.

He bought it for me just after she and Jack died. He thought if I had a ring like hers then it would bring me some comfort. He's thoughtful like that. You need to stop this right now, Victor! How could you even say something like that to me? You know how close Stan and I were to Carol and Jack.' She was shaking her head and pacing again.

'He was there when they died, wasn't he?' Victor asked firmly. He seemed determined to make his sister see sense now. 'He pulled them out of the rubble, Ginny. And then a few days later you had a shiny new eternity ring identical to Carol's and you've been besotted with him for so long now that you drink in his lies, desperate to believe he's a good man and not the wretched pig I knew he was all along. The wretched pig that, deep down, you know he is, too!' Ginny's mouth gaped open, and she stared at Victor in shock.

He took a deep breath and spoke with less anger this time. 'I wanted to tell you, but I didn't know for certain. Then, when I was given evidence of his crimes, I confronted him about Carol's ring. Stan confirmed it himself, Ginny.' She was shaking her head, tears trickling down her cheeks.

'I'm sorry I didn't tell you. I knew the truth would break your heart, so I told him I'd keep it to myself if he left the wardens and the spiv who had reported him to me alone. I was worried he would go after them looking for revenge.'

Ginny sat down again and let out a big sob.

'I toyed with the idea of telling you anyway, but everything seemed to calm down after that and I thought maybe I'd given Stan the shock he needed to get back on the straight and narrow.'

'How could he do this to me? And to Carol? What kind of a man steals from a dead woman, let alone someone who was supposed to have been his friend? And then gives the stolen jewellery to his wife? I've been such a fool!'

'You were in love. We're desperate to see the best in the person we've fallen for, and it's easy to overlook the bad when we're so deeply in love with them,' Dot offered quietly. She had never been able to understand how somebody awful like Stan had a wife, but she now realised that if anybody should be able to get their head around it, then it was her. She had been fooled herself and had spent years adoring Tommy before finally seeing clearly and recognising that he had been manipulating her all along. Dot knew now that Tommy didn't deserve her love and devotion, but she had needed a big wake-up call to get to this position.

'I hate to cut in,' Bill said. He stepped forward cautiously. 'But, the thing is, Stan was dismissed a couple of weeks ago now. When you arrived, it seemed as though you thought Stan was still turning up for his shifts here all that time?'

'Yes, that's one of the reasons why all of this is so difficult to comprehend. I've been waving him off with his flask of tea and sandwiches nearly every day as usual. He hasn't mentioned anything about being dismissed.'

'And he's been wearing his uniform?' Bill asked.

Ginny nodded. 'So, what the bloody hell has he been up to?' she exclaimed suddenly.

'I think I might have an idea,' Dot said nervously. She didn't want to leave it up to Bill to explain. She felt bad enough that she hadn't had a chance to warn Victor that she had shared the details of Stan's crimes and dismissal with Bill when their boss had wanted to keep it quiet. It was best that their theory about Stan and Tommy working together came from her. And it was time for her to reveal it; everybody was looking at her expectantly.

'We don't know for sure,' she started.

'Oh, come on, dear – just spit it out!' Ginny snapped, getting to her feet. Victor shot her a reprimanding look, and she threw her hands up in defeat, sitting back down heavily. 'Sorry. In your own time. I'm just keen to find out where my good-for-nothing husband is so I can wring his neck for pulling the wool over my eyes all this time.'

Dot smiled nervously. She wasn't sure who Stan should be fearing the most right now – her husband or his own wife. She found herself feeling quite anxious for her nemesis. Because, if his disappearance wasn't down to Tommy turning on him again and he showed up any time soon, then he might be facing an even bigger threat from Ginny when she got hold of him.

'Well, we've heard that there's a looter operating locally, and he's wearing a warden uniform to help him gain access unchallenged to bombed-out buildings.'

'Son-of-a—' Victor roared, shaking his head. Bill put a hand on his shoulder to rein him in and stop him from exploding on the spot. 'I never got around to getting his uniform back off him. I wanted to wait for things to settle down and then I was going to try and talk to him about it when Ginny wasn't around. But we've been so busy. Do you think he's been wearing it to help him steal more?'

'Like I say, we don't know for certain, but the description of the warden in question does sound very much like Stan.'

'Just when I thought he couldn't get any worse,' Victor said angrily.

'I'm afraid there's more,' Dot said quickly before Victor or Ginny had a chance to start ranting again. 'It's a bit of a long story, but . . . ' She glanced over at Bill who gave her an encouraging look, which gave her the confidence to continue. 'My husband. He's . . . well, we're not on the best of terms, let's put it that way. He's not a very nice man, as it turns out. Anyway, you don't need to know the details, but what you do need to know is that he went AWOL from his regiment around the same time that Stan was kicked out of the ARP. And the looter using a warden uniform to gain access to bomb sites – it appears that he's teamed up with somebody else. And that person sounds worryingly like my husband.'

'By all accounts, it sounds as if – providing we're correct in these assumptions, of course – well, it sounds as though Dot's husband might be getting a bit aggressive in the course of their misdemeanours,' Bill added.

'If we're right and they're working together, then the story we've heard is that Tommy – my husband – turned on Stan recently and gave him quite a battering during the course of one of their robberies,' Dot continued.

'He came home a few days ago covered in grazes and bruises,' Ginny said slowly. Dot could see everything falling into place by the look on her face. 'He told me he'd been injured by shrapnel during a raid,' she added, shaking her head sadly.

'It's got to be the two of them working together,' Dot said. 'I'm certain now.'

'Oh, goodness,' Ginny exclaimed. She threw her hands over her mouth. 'Now Stan's missing – do you think your husband might have something to do with it? Might he have hurt him?'

'That's what I'm worried about,' Dot replied gravely.

'Where could they be? What do you think he's done to him?' Ginny demanded, getting to her feet and walking towards Dot.

Bill had placed himself between the two women before Dot had even had a chance to react. Then Victor grabbed hold of his sister's shoulders and guided her around to the other side of his desk.

'I'm . . . I'm sorry,' Dot stuttered. 'I wish I could help. But I'm so scared of Tommy that I've been doing my best to stay away from him so I've no idea where he could be.' Bill placed a reassuring arm around her shoulder. 'I honestly have no idea where either of them could be hiding.'

'We'll find them,' Bill said confidently.

Dot's head was spinning. She had despised Stan since the day she'd met him – he'd done nothing but taunt and threaten her. But now she found herself in a situation where she was fearful for his safety, and she felt responsible because it was her husband who was the threat. Dot couldn't help but feel responsible if Tommy had caused harm to Stan.

Just then, the office door bounced open, and Ted walked in with a tray of teas.

'There we go,' said Bill calmly. 'Let's all sit down with our tea, and we can figure this out. We just need to come up with a plan of action.'

'You took your time, didn't you?' Victor asked his deputy.

'Yeah, sorry about that, boss. I got chatting to one of the messengers in the kitchen. He's just back from Balham.'

'I'll bet they're still digging out bodies,' Bill said grimly.

'Well, yes, they are. But they've also found another in one of the houses near the station.'

'I didn't realise the blast had taken out any houses,' Bill replied.

'That's just the thing,' Ted replied. He sat down and took a sip from his mug. 'This fella wasn't collateral from a bomb blast. Poor chap was discovered face down with his head caved in on the dining-room floor. The family who lives in the house had spent the raid in their Anderson shelter. They found him when they went back inside after the all-clear sounded this morning. He was surrounded by all their jewellery and a wodge of cash they kept hidden under a mattress.'

Dot felt her knees go weak and when she looked over at Ginny, she noticed the colour had drained from the woman's face too.

'Looks like this one's a murder,' Ted added eagerly, completely oblivious to the change in atmosphere around him.

'Stan,' Dot and Ginny both gasped in horror.

26

Sarah ushered the children back into the dining room to finish their dinner while Peggy put her shoes on.

'I shouldn't be long,' she called behind her, stomping to the door. Peggy was angry and upset with her mother for tricking her, as well as being furious with her for taking such a risk with her health. What had she been thinking, walking all the way into the village on her own? She flung open the door, and then froze at the sight in front of her. Dr Brady's car was parked at the end of the drive. Fear consumed Peggy. She ran on shaky legs towards the vehicle, searching for her mother and hoping with everything she had that she would find her sitting up happily in the passenger seat and chatting to the doctor. Dr Brady stepped out of the car just as Peggy reached it.

'It's all right, she's going to be fine,' he said reassuringly, holding out his hands to slow down her approach. Peggy couldn't see anybody in the front of the car, so she peered into the back and saw her mother laid across the seats, her head resting on Mrs Brady's lap. She looked restless and pale, and Mrs Brady was stroking her head like she was a child in the midst of a nightmare. 'I've given her something to help her rest and she should settle soon. She needs to sleep it off,' Dr Brady explained gravely.

'Sleep what off?' Peggy asked him, backing away from the window. She didn't want her mother to catch sight of her and grow distressed. 'What happened?'

'She turned up at a WI meeting and had another funny turn.'

Peggy threw her head back and groaned. All their hard work, and she had thrown it all away for a WI meeting. Her mother had been doing so well. Peggy had even allowed herself to hope that she might be able to return to London soon.

'Well, what did you think would happen, sending her off into the village on her own like that? I thought we'd agreed to bed rest until I confirmed otherwise. The furthest she should have been going was into your garden. I thought you understood how important that was.' The doctor's tone had changed now, and Peggy felt compelled to defend herself.

'I didn't send her off,' she replied. 'She sneaked out of the house like a cocksure teenager when I refused to give her permission to go to the WI meeting. I was on my way to fetch her back as soon as I realised what she was up to – that's where I was headed when you pulled up.'

'You hadn't noticed she was missing before then?'

Peggy flushed with shame. 'Well, no.' If Peggy had felt bad before then she felt terrible now as she looked up at the doctor's raised eyebrows. She switched her gaze down to the floor and picked at her fingernails. She knew that she should have gone to check on her mother the moment she heard that door banging. If she had, Peggy could have gone after her mother and stopped her before she pushed herself too far. 'She was resting in bed this afternoon and I didn't want to disturb her—'

'Don't worry. I've known your mother long enough to recognise that she's a strong-headed woman who rarely stops until she gets her own way. I'm surprised you've managed to keep her contained for this long, to be honest.' Peggy managed a weak smile of relief. 'But this can't happen again,' Dr Brady added firmly.

Peggy nodded sombrely. 'I know. I let my guard down.' She hung her head. Maybe she wasn't coping as well as she'd thought she was.

'Perhaps it's time to accept some help. You're looking after rather a lot of people on your own. I'm surprised your sister hasn't come back to support you in all of this.'

'No,' Peggy shook her head. 'I was a little distracted today, that's all. But I've been coping just fine up until now and I won't lose my focus like that again. I don't want Joan to have to give up her land work.'

Peggy knew exactly where she had gone wrong. Her silly fantasies about Johnny had diverted her attention. He'd taken over all her thoughts when he wasn't even interested in her romantically. She needed to stop acting like a lovesick schoolgirl and put all her efforts in to looking after her mother and the children. All Peggy had to do was shut off her emotions, throw herself into life at home, and stop getting swept up in daydreams about a handsome pilot who was simply being kind because he was based nearby and because their mutual – persuasive – friend had asked him to. She still hardly knew Johnny – she'd only met him a handful of times. Peggy had been foolish to let ideas of romance with him take over and cloud her judgement.

'You were doing well up until this setback,' Dr Brady commented kindly. 'And, like I said, I know your mother well enough to believe she did this behind your back.' He paused and looked over at the car. 'She had a lucky escape today. It was a good job I popped in to drop off some wool that Patricia had forgotten just before she collapsed,' he added. Peggy winced at the image of her mother flopping helplessly to the floor in front of all her friends. 'I think this will have scared her into understanding that, though my orders might leave her "dying of boredom" as she often tells me – at least they won't *actually* lead to her dying.' The doctor had meant the comment light-heartedly, but it had made Peggy feel sick. 'But you still must make sure you keep a closer eye on her. We don't want her getting carried away again as soon as she starts feeling signs of improvement.' He paused to think for a moment. 'Let's keep her on complete bed rest for a few days and then I'll reassess. Do you think you can manage that?'

'I can.' Peggy would lock her mother in her bedroom if she had to. But she was confident this incident would have shocked her mother into following the doctor's orders. For a little while, at least.

In the end, Phillip told the other children that he'd found Mrs Miller in the garden getting some fresh air and, along with Sarah, he'd kept the younger children in the dining room while Peggy helped Dr and Mrs Brady get her mother upstairs and back into bed. Peggy didn't want any of them upset at the sight of Mrs Miller being brought in like that and she certainly didn't want them to know that she had suffered a setback.

Whatever Dr Brady had given Mrs Miller to help her sleep had kicked in by then, so Mrs Brady and Peggy had taken a shoulder each while Dr Brady had supported her back and legs. Thankfully, Mrs Brady was around ten years younger than her husband, so together with the doctor's good strength for his age and Peggy's youth, they had managed the task with relative ease.

With her mother safely in bed and sleeping off her ordeal, Peggy went in to see each of the children to tuck them in and say goodnight. She apologised for having assumed the worst of her mother, laughing with them about the fact she had jumped to the conclusion that she had sneaked out of the house without telling her.

Once she was on her own downstairs, Peggy couldn't keep back the tears that had been threatening to pour out of her ever since she had seen her mother looking so pale and vulnerable on the back seat of Dr Brady's car. She wanted to scream at the woman for being so foolish and selfish and for putting herself in so much danger. But, at the same time, Peggy was desperate to wrap her arms around her mother and tell her how much she loved her. She also felt sad and frustrated that this blip would delay her return to London. Her mother had been getting stronger and stronger by the day – if she had just been able to hold out a little longer, then they could have eased her back into normal life and Peggy could have returned to doing her bit for the ARP. Now they were back where they had been when her mother had first fallen ill.

Then Peggy felt guilty for the fact she was so desperate to leave when her mother was so unwell. And, to top it all off, she was also battling the added guilt for allowing her feelings for Johnny and her angst about whether she was good enough for him distract her from her duties at home. Peggy was so consumed by the tidal wave of emotions washing over her, that she didn't hear the door creaking open. She jumped when she felt little arms wrapping themselves around her.

'Don't cry, Pegs,' Lucy whispered into her big sister's ear. The show of affection was too much for Peggy and she found the tears escaped her eyes even more quickly as she was overwhelmed by love for the little girl. But she quickly pulled herself together and put on a brave front for the youngster.

'I'm sorry, darling. I was just having a moment. But everything is fine and there's nothing for you to worry about.'

'Apart from the Germans,' Lucy replied.

She had been deadly serious, but Peggy couldn't help but laugh. 'Yes. You're absolutely right,' she said, smiling. 'But as long as you're here with me then you'll be safe.'

'If we're safe then why are you sad?'

'I miss London, that's all.'

'But why do you miss London? Elsie says it's scary there since the war started. She doesn't want her mummy to be there. And I don't want you to be there either.'

How could she explain it to an innocent six year old who just wanted everyone she loved to be safe? 'I just want to do my bit to help keep people there alive, that's all. I saved Elsie and Ted and their mummy when their house was struck during a raid. I want to help more people.'

'But don't we have enough of our family helping already? There's Lee and Jamie, and Daddy. Even Joan is doing something. And now Mummy is poorly. Can we please just keep you away from danger?'

Peggy's heart ached for her little sister. She should have realised how anxious Lucy must feel with so many of the adults she loved involved in the war effort and their mother being ill. She had assumed her little sisters were too young to understand just how much danger the country – and most of their family – was in. But she should have known not to underestimate Lucy. Lucy had always been wise beyond her years. She'd proved that when she'd written to Peggy with her fears for their mother's health.

'It might be dangerous in London, but it's important to me to do my bit, too,' she said gently.

'But you *are* doing your bit,' Lucy argued.

Peggy laughed and shook her head. 'It's not the same,' she whispered.

'It's not the same, Pegs, but it's just as important. Elsie and Ted might have been killed in London by now if you hadn't brought them here, and we would have all been split up without you. Goodness knows what would have happened to Mummy. You don't need to be in danger to be doing your duty.' Peggy realised that Lucy had a point. 'How did you get to be so clever?' she asked her, playfully tapping Lucy on the nose. 'Now, let's get you to bed. You have school in the morning.'

After tucking Lucy in for the second time that evening, Peggy went to bed herself. The drama of the afternoon had left her exhausted. As she ran through it all in her head once more, she resolved to stop wasting her time and energy obsessing over Johnny and put everything she had into doing her bit in Petworth.

27

Sitting at the back of the bus with Bill, Dot's head felt as though it would never stop spinning. So many theories and possibilities were running through her mind, but all the ones she kept coming back to involved Tommy. Would he flee for good now that he'd murdered Stan? Or would he decide he had nothing to lose and stay in London to come after her? Her heel tapped the floor repeatedly and her knee jigged up and down as she chewed her nail and stared out of the window. Dot wasn't sure which option she preferred. Obviously, she didn't like the idea of Tommy hunting her down and exacting revenge for leaving him, but she certainly didn't want to have to spend the rest of her life looking over her shoulder, never knowing where or when he might turn up. She jumped when Bill placed a hand firmly on her knee to stop it jumping up and down.

'It's going to be all right,' he said gently.

She stopped chewing her nail and spread her hand out in front of her to inspect her fingers. Every nail was chewed down to the quick. They looked so sore, but she hadn't registered any pain. Dot had always been so proud of her long, strong nails. But the last few weeks had seen her develop a habit of nervously biting and chewing them.

'You'll be chewing your fingers off next if you're not careful,' Bill joked. Dot smiled weakly at him. 'I guess it could be worse. I could have taken up smoking to help me cope,' she replied. Dot had friends who said smoking helped ease their angst, but she hated the smell of cigarette smoke and shuddered at the thought of smelling like an ashtray. She folded her arms to stop herself from chewing any more fingernails, and then she turned back to the window and stared out at the passing scenery. The roads had already been cleared following the previous night's attacks, and people were picking their way over rubble and collapsed buildings to go about their day as best as they could. Dot loved London for refusing to give in.

'Will we have to go back and tell Ginny once we've identified Stan's body?' she asked. 'Only, I don't know that I'll be able to face her.'

'We don't know it's definitely Stan,' Bill replied.

'Oh, come on. We know it's him. Ginny knows it, too. That's why she passed out when Ted told us about the body.'

The poor woman had still been out cold when Bill and Dot had volunteered to go to the house in Balham to identify Stan and pass on their suspicions about Tommy to the police. Victor had stayed behind to care for his sister and comfort her when she came round.

'Well, I know you won't be keen to see her again, especially with news that Tommy could be behind this, but I think the school might be the best base for us at the moment.' Dot looked at him quizzically. 'Think about it. If the body really is Stan, and Tommy has murdered him, then we don't know what he might be planning next. If he's been in the area all this time, then he probably knows you're staying with Viv. I was thinking about taking you back to mine to hunker down, but there's always people at the school so there's less chance of Tommy getting in unnoticed and we'll have backup if he tries anything.'

'What about Viv and Jilly?' Dot wasn't about to leave them behind to face Tommy on their own.

'We'll need to get a message to them. I haven't thought it all through properly yet. But I certainly don't like the idea of either of them being at home if Tommy turns up looking for you. We might need to convince them to hide out at the school with us. Or I'm sure they have other friends who could put them up for a night or two until things die down.' Dot nodded her head, trying not to panic. 'I can't see him being on the run for long once he's got the police as well as the military on his tail,' Bill added. 'Let's just get to Balham and confirm the dead guy is Stan before we do anything else.'

Dot sighed and turned to stare out of the window again, watching the ever-changing backdrop of London passing by. She felt as though they might never reach Balham, and the steady rhythm of the bus started lulling her head up and down. The next thing Dot knew she was being gently nudged awake.

'Dot, Dot,' came Bill's voice in her ear. 'It's time to wake up. We need to get off at the next stop.'

She jolted upright, embarrassed to see she had fallen asleep with her head resting on Bill's shoulder. She wiped a trail of dribble from her mouth and hoped he hadn't noticed. 'Why did you let me sleep?' she hissed urgently, suddenly alert and straightening out her jacket.

'You needed it,' Bill replied gently. 'Now, come on,' he added as he got to his feet and held out his hand to help her up. 'We've got a grim task ahead of us.'

They were still pumping water out of the tube station when Dot and Bill arrived in Balham. There was a lot of shouting and gesturing going on as a group of men, including Peggy's partner, Paul, set about hauling the bus out of the crater.

'It's got to be that house down there,' Bill said.

Dot followed his line of sight and spotted a policeman standing outside a terraced house. There was no sign of any bomb damage to any of the properties in the row. They walked over and introduced themselves.

'We think we might know who the victim is,' Bill offered.

'Ah, now, that would be jolly helpful. You see, he's got no ID on him so we're a bit stuck.'

'What about his warden badge?' Dot asked.

'He's not one of your lot, love,' the officer replied before wandering into the house to fetch his sergeant. Doubt started creeping in as they waited on the doorstep. As far as they knew, Stan had been using his ARP uniform to gain access to the properties he was stealing from. And his accomplice had been wearing military uniform when Bill's contact had come across them, which was one of the reasons Dot had feared it was Tommy. If the dead man wasn't in a uniform, then maybe this was nothing to do with Stan after all, and another looter had met a sticky end? The officer came back and waved them into the house.

'Do you want me to do it?' Bill asked Dot.

'I've seen enough dead bodies by now,' she replied, trying to keep her voice light to hide how anxious she was feeling. But when Dot walked into the living room and saw the man lying dead on the floor, there was nothing she could do to disguise her horror. Her breath caught in her throat as she started struggling for air, just like when she'd thought she'd seen Tommy in the street the night before. Only this time she *had* seen Tommy.

Bill quickly guided Dot out on to the street and set about trying to calm her down by encouraging her to take deep breaths again.

'It's all right. It wasn't Stan,' he soothed. But the relief on his face vanished when Dot looked up into his eyes. It must have been clear from her reaction to the body and the way she was looking at him now, eyes full of fear and confusion, who the dead man was. He may not have been in his uniform any longer – she didn't recognise the clothes he'd been wearing – but Dot was certain without a doubt it was her husband lying lifeless on that floor. She prayed that Bill understood that, because she didn't want to have to say it out loud.

'Oh,' Bill whispered, looking back into the hallway and then quickly turning back to face Dot again. 'Was that? Was that . . . *Tommy*?'

Dot simply nodded. She was focusing on her breathing and trying hard not to lose control again. Flashes of the man she had once loved so dearly, lifeless on the floor, a pool of blood at his head, kept flooding her mind. Tommy was dead. Her husband. The man she had fallen head over heels in love with. The man who had turned into a monster so subtly that it had taken her years to realise. The man who had made her life a misery, who'd hit her and made her feel that being on the streets would be happier for her than being with him. Dot had felt guilty for the relief she'd felt when she'd thought he'd been killed in action, but now that she knew he definitely was dead, she didn't know how she was supposed to feel. The shock of seeing him lying on the floor like that was all she could think about.

Once her breathing was regular again, Bill went to let the police officers know who their murder victim was.

'What do you think happened?' Dot asked him when he returned to her outside on the street. 'I was convinced we were going to find Stan dead in that house.' She paused to take another deep breath. 'I can't quite believe it. That's it. It's over. Tommy's gone.'

'The police are on the lookout for Stan now, so hopefully we'll find out soon.'

Dot's heart started racing again. 'They're looking for Stan? You don't seriously think Stan could have done this?' It seemed impossible to her. 'You saw the size of Tommy. And you heard for yourself how he overpowered Stan during their robbery the other night.'

'I don't see what other explanation there is,' Bill offered. 'They were clearly working together, and this certainly looks like a robbery gone wrong. Add to the mix that Stan is missing . . .' He paused and rubbed his chin, deep in thought. 'Maybe it wasn't Stan. I do agree that under any other circumstances he wouldn't be my immediate number one suspect. But when you take all the facts into consideration then it makes some sense.'

Dot started chewing what was left of her thumbnail. She wasn't convinced. Yes, Stan was a bully who liked to throw his weight around, but she had only ever seen him do that with people weaker than himself. She couldn't imagine him being brave enough to take on somebody like Tommy, let alone come out of it the victor.

'No matter whether Stan did this or not, he's still going to be the best person for the police to speak to,' Bill added. 'If he is innocent, then he's likely to know what actually happened in that house. I can't think of another reason for him to disappear the very night that Tommy turns up dead.' Dot stopped chewing her nail and nodded her agreement. 'Speaking of which, we should probably get back to the school and put Ginny out of her misery. Stan will wish he had been the dead body once she catches up with him.' Bill started to laugh and then caught himself. 'Goodness, I'm sorry, Dot – that was a really insensitive thing to say given your situation.'

'Don't apologise,' she replied. 'Ginny is a force to be reckoned with, and I hope she gets to Stan before the police do.' She took a moment to try and make sense of all the feelings that were running around in her head. 'Bill?' she asked cautiously.

'Yes, Dot.'

'Would you think terribly of me if I told you that I don't know how I'm supposed to be feeling right now? I mean, my husband is dead. I should be devastated. But—' Dot stopped, unsure whether she should admit her true feelings. She really liked Bill and she didn't want to taint how he thought of her. But she felt so comfortable when she was talking to him, it almost felt natural to share everything, totally honestly. The same way she would say anything to Viv and Peggy without question.

'It's okay, Dot. You can confide in me. I promise that nothing you're feeling about what has just happened would make me think any less of you.' Dot folded her arms and looked back along the hallway into the house where Tommy had died.

'Are you confused because you feel relief that it's Tommy in there and not Stan?' Bill asked carefully.

Dot visibly relaxed and found herself crying. She was overwhelmed by everything that had happened over the last few hours, and by the fact that Bill understood her so well.

'It's okay to feel like that,' he said. 'After everything that man put you through, and the fear he had you living in recently. You're a good woman, Dot, so I know that you will also be sad about his death, and that you'll grieve him. But you are allowed to feel relief. You're allowed to feel whatever you feel, no matter what it is.'

Dot cried harder. It felt good to let it out, even if they were standing in the middle of the street.

'I think we better get you a cup of tea before we head back to the school to break the news to Ginny. She's going to be out for blood when she realises Stan is still out there somewhere.'

Dot smiled and let Bill guide her to a nearby café. She was halfway through her cup of tea when it suddenly hit her.

'Beryl!' she gasped, looking up at Bill in horror. 'My mother-in-law,' she explained quickly, getting to her feet and gathering up her things.

'Wait, where are you going? What do you mean?' he asked, holding out his arm to try and slow her down.

'The police will be on their way to tell her about Tommy. I can't let her find out like that. I've got to get to her before they do.' She raced out of the door with Bill at her heels.

'Looks like we're doing another trek through London,' he muttered.

Dot stopped outside the café and turned to face him. 'You don't need to worry about me,' she said. 'Tommy's gone. He can't hurt me anymore.'

'Yes, but Stan is still out there and—'

'And you need to tell his wife and Victor,' Dot said, cutting Bill off. 'Stan's no threat to me, even if he did kill Tommy. He'll be off licking his wounds somewhere and hiding from the police if he had anything to do with this. He might even be injured himself. Please. I need to get to Beryl before the police. And Ginny needs to know her husband isn't dead.

It makes sense for us to split up.' Dot felt terrible pushing Bill away like this after everything he'd done for her, but it seemed logical for them to do these things separately.

'Right, wait there,' he instructed, holding out his hand in a 'stop' gesture.

'I need to get moving,' Dot panicked. 'I can't get the tube from here and I don't know where along the line it will be running from. The bus is unbearably slow!' She was desperate to get going now and angry that her own confused thoughts about Tommy's death had stopped her from realising she needed to get to Beryl as quickly as possible. It was important that she broke the news to her and spared her having to learn that her only son was dead from a police officer.

'I might be able to get you there quicker, just give me two minutes,' Bill pleaded. 'It's Lawrence Street, isn't it?'

Dot nodded. Bill must have remembered where she'd been going the night they had bumped into each other. She closed her eyes against the memory of that evening – that was where it had all gone wrong. What would have happened if she hadn't bumped into Bill on her way home that night? It had been the sight of her walking along the street – as innocent as it was – with another man that had riled Tommy up. Maybe if she hadn't been wearing lipstick when he'd confronted her about it then he wouldn't have been quite so angry. Those two circumstances triggered the chain of events that had led them to where they were now – with Dot fending for herself, Beryl living happily with Jim, and Tommy dead. Did Dot want any of that to be different? She was saved from answering the question when Bill bounded back out of the café with a scruffy looking man in tow.

'This is Fred,' Bill explained. 'He's one of the chaps I work with at the docks. I spotted him in the café when we first arrived – he came over to help with the clean-up at the station.'

'That's great,' Dot replied. She was jumping from foot to foot now, anxious to get on her way. She was getting frustrated with Bill for wasting time like this. What was he playing at?

'He also drives a taxi,' Bill added pointedly.

'Oh!' Dot exclaimed.

'Come on, love, I'll get you home as quick as I can,' Fred said. He started walking off towards a line of parked cars.

'Thank you, Bill,' Dot said gratefully, grabbing hold of his hand. 'For everything,' she added, giving it a quick squeeze.

'I'll see you soon,' he replied as he waved her off.

Fred tried to strike up a conversation on the journey but quickly gave up when he was met with one-word answers from his passenger. Dot stared out of the window, trying to decide how she was going to break the news to Beryl. There was going to be no easy way to do it and she was dreading it, but she felt strongly that she needed to be the one to say the words.

When Fred's car pulled into Lawrence Street, Dot was hopeful that she'd made it to Beryl before the police. The road was quiet and there was no sign of any activity outside the house she used to call her home. She still didn't know what she was going to say. She thanked Fred, who assured her Bill had already given him cash to cover the fare, and then she stood outside the front door for a few minutes, trying to work up the courage to knock and deliver the news that was going to break her mother-in-law's heart. Because, no matter what had happened with Tommy recently and how Beryl had been feeling about her son, the fact remained that he *was* her son.

After taking a deep breath, Dot finally knocked on the door. She cleared her throat as she heard footsteps approaching along the hallway. But when the door opened, she knew she was too late. There was a policeman standing in front of her, and she could see Beryl at the end of the hallway, in a heap on the floor and quietly sobbing into another officer's arms.

28

When Viv pulled cautiously into the yard at Danvers Street Ambulance Station, she felt an aching in her jaw and her cheeks. She laughed to herself when she realised that her face was tender from smiling so much. She hadn't stopped grinning the whole way from West Sussex back to London. In fact, she hadn't stopped smiling since the moment of her joint proposal with William. Her heart fluttered as she replayed the moment in her head for about the hundredth time.

When Deirdre had run off down the corridor cheering and celebrating and spreading their news, Viv and William had continued to enjoy their emotional embrace. The excited nurse had returned about five minutes later and placed a small box on the bedside table.

'I assume you'll be needing this,' she'd said, grinning conspiratorially at William. And once she had left again, William had presented Viv with a beautiful diamond ring. It turned out that his grandmother had left her engagement ring to him when she'd died some years before. He'd been obsessed with the sparkly jewel as a child and boasted to anybody who complimented it that it would one day belong to his wife, who he claimed would be just as beautiful as his grandmother.

'And now I've found her,' he'd whispered, slipping the ring on to Viv's finger. He'd been keeping the ring in his locker at Tangmere, along with a letter for Viv, which he'd written the day after she'd turned down his proposal. Johnny had been instructed to pass them both on to her if anything happened to him in the skies. 'This ring was always meant for you, and I wanted you to have it even if I wasn't here anymore,' he explained. 'Johnny nearly gave it to you along with the letter when I was MIA,' he added, laughing to himself. 'Thankfully he decided to hold out hope for my safe return a little while longer.'

'So . . . you had always intended to propose again?' Viv asked him cautiously.

'Of course! That's why I asked Johnny to bring the ring to me here as soon as I arrived. Deirdre has been keeping it safe for me. She's been on tenterhooks every time you visit.'

Viv had giggled at that. 'No wonder she was always so attentive. She wanted to have the ring ready as soon as you asked me to marry you again.' William nodded. 'But then I jumped in and beat you to it.'

'Well, not quite – I think we ended up doing it together. I'm sorry for making you wait.'

'Why *did* you wait so long? I've given you enough hints.' With the reassurance that he was still sweet on her, Viv had felt the confidence to press him.

'I wanted to be certain.' William had broken eye contact then and turned his head to look at the wall. 'And I also wanted to wait until I was fully recovered. You deserve a man who can look after you and not one who needs caring for.'

'I'm sorry for forcing you into it before you were ready, but you need to know that I would marry you no matter what – you could need round-the-clock care, and I would still jump at the chance to be your wife!'

'You don't need to apologise,' William replied, grabbing hold of her hand and gazing into her eyes again. 'You've made me realise that's the case. And that makes you even more beautiful to me – inside and out. My grandmother would be proud to see her ring on your finger.'

Viv had started to weep tears of joy at that point, but the moment had been cut short by an influx of well-wishers. They hadn't had a second on their own again until Viv had realised that she needed to leave to get back to London in time for her shift.

Now, parking up Hudsy, she checked the clock and saw she'd made good time; she'd be able to put her head down for an hour or so before clocking on. She checked the fuel gauge and felt a stab of guilt. Though not taking Hudsy to West Sussex might have drastically changed the outcome of the visit, she couldn't help but regret the fact she had used up precious fuel on the trip. She resolved to ask Jilly to contact her father to find out if he had an extra stash anywhere that she could bring in to top up some of the ambulance cars.

Before going inside, Viv rubbed her ring finger. Staring down at the empty space on it, she envisioned the mesmerising diamond sparkling on it as it had done just a couple of hours before. She had taken her engagement ring off before leaving the hospital, agreeing with William that he would continue to keep it safe until it was appropriate for her to wear it permanently. The thought of anything happening to her during a raid was bad enough, but she couldn't run the risk of some wretched thief like Stan or Tommy patting down her lifeless body and stealing her most treasured possession – her link to William. And, if she did happen to die before they had a chance to marry, she didn't want William to have to go through the pain of losing the ring as well as his fiancée. Viv had thought about taking the ring home with her and hiding it away in her flat, but she was also terrified of losing the heirloom if the building took a hit. As if the risk of it being destroyed by bombs wasn't enough, there was then the possibility of it being stolen from the rubble. They had decided it was safer to leave it behind. Deirdre had agreed to continue looking after it until William was discharged, at which point he would take it with him back to Tangmere and store it in his locker again.

Viv wanted Dot, Peggy and Jilly to be the first people in London to know her exciting news, and the fact she wasn't wearing the engagement ring would help her keep it to herself until she could tell them. She realised she might not be able to hold off telling everybody until a letter had reached Peggy with the update, but she could certainly ensure that she shared it with Dot and Jilly together, and before anybody else here. If Jilly's father had an extra fuel stash, then maybe there was some way she could drive over and visit Peggy to deliver the news in person. No matter how she ended up doing it, she felt giddy at the thought of her friends' reactions, and she couldn't wait to see them all.

William had promised to hold off telling Johnny, too, to avoid him passing on the news to Peggy before Viv had a chance to reveal it. She wasn't sure if Deirdre would be able to stop herself from shouting about it whenever William next had visitors, but she hoped she'd be able to contain herself. And Viv was going to write a letter to her parents to tell them her happy news as soon as she had the chance. Though they weren't big on sharing feelings, she was confident that her mother would be happy for her and that her father would find William to be an agreeable son-in-law.

Viv went inside and hung her overcoat and tin hat up in the cloakroom, before walking through the relaxation area, where the crew on the current shift were reading, playing cards, and knitting while a radio blared in the background. When Viv had first started her volunteer work here, the room had been pretty sparse, save for a few tables and chairs donated by members of the public. But the crews had reclaimed all sorts of pieces of furniture from bomb sites since then, with the proper permission, and it was now quite a cosy place to gather while waiting for the sirens.

She spotted Paul in the corner, asleep in an armchair with a book splayed out across his chest. She hoped he hadn't stayed on at Balham for too much longer that morning in order to cover for her. Viv waved a greeting to her other colleagues and made her way through to the dugout: a concrete-topped shelter built into a corner of the wooden building, which had been lined with sandbags and filled with camp beds and stretchers for crew members to sleep on. They had also recently squeezed in some inflatable mattresses, given the long hours volunteers were working. It was roughly segregated, with women at one end and men at the other. Viv crept in as quietly as she could and settled herself on one of the empty stretchers laid out on the concrete floor – the only available space left to rest. She longed for her own comfortable bed, but she didn't want to waste time travelling home and returning again. She thought once more of William, and the next thing she knew, she was waking up to the noise of the sirens.

'The blighters are early tonight,' somebody groaned from the other side of the room. Viv rubbed her eyes and took a moment to enjoy the fact that her fiancé was safe in a hospital bed in West Sussex. She was dreading his return to the RAF and knowing that William would already be in the sky trying to keep the German planes at bay every time there was an air raid warning. She would constantly have to deal with the fact that he might already be dead by the time the enemy reached London. After splashing her face with some cold water in the bathroom and applying her lipstick, Viv went outside and found Paul checking over Hudsy.

'Well done for getting him back in one piece,' he joked. 'I've restocked the supplies and he's ready to go again. How is William?'

Viv was bursting to share their good news, but she stopped herself. She would feel terrible if Dot heard it from somebody else. Instead, she updated Paul on William's condition and the success of the surgery before asking how he got on at Balham.

'I stayed on for another few hours and helped get the bus out of the crater, and then I came back here to get some rest.'

'I saw. The book Jimmy loaned you is obviously still keeping you gripped,' she teased.

He rolled his eyes at her playfully and they went inside to wait for the call-outs to start coming in. When they were sent to a direct hit on a house nearby, Viv was reminded of her decision to keep her engagement ring safe away from London. Arriving at the scene, her first thought was that there could be no survivors. The house was nothing but a smoking shell and there were pieces of furniture spread across the road in amongst piles of rubble and bricks. She tended to some of the neighbours who had been injured, and one of them told her about the family from the house that was hit. There was a young woman living there with her mother, who was helping her look after her two children. The youngsters' father was off fighting in the war, and their mother was heavily pregnant with her third child. Viv's heart dropped when she heard that. She looked across at the remains of the house and wondered how anybody could make it out alive. She looked away again as a man emerged from the site carrying a small, lifeless body.

'They normally go to the communal shelter. I'm not sure why they didn't make it tonight,' the woman added as Viv bandaged her shoulder for her. She wondered if the neighbour was still in shock from the blast because she didn't even flinch, despite how much pain she must have been in. 'It just goes to show how one wrong decision can have such a big impact,' the woman added, shaking her head and staring at the destruction in front of them. 'I always felt better staying at home. I find the public shelters so uncomfortable and smelly. If it's my time to go then I'd rather go in comfort. But now I'm not so sure.'

Just as Viv was moving on to the next casualty, there was shouting from the far end of the bomb site and Paul came running towards her.

'Come with me!' he cried as he got nearer. 'We need a stretcher!'

'Can you finish up with this lady?' she asked the medic who was working alongside her. 'The wound above her eye is going to need some cleaning up but apart from that she hasn't got any serious injuries.'

'Sure,' the medic replied. 'I'll hold the fort here.'

There weren't many people to get through as the majority of the neighbours had been in public shelters. Viv jumped to her feet and ran over to Hudsy to help Paul get out a stretcher.

'They've just found a pregnant woman,' he explained as they ran back to the fallen house carrying the stretcher between them.

'Is she still—?' Viv asked.

'Just about,' Paul replied breathlessly. 'She was underneath a dining table which protected her when the ceiling and chimney fell on top of it.'

'What about the children? And the grandmother?' Viv asked as they waited at the roadside. The rescue workers were doing their best to get to the woman, but she was trapped in the space under the table by the bricks and rubble that had landed around it.

'One of the children is dead – they found him first.'

Viv thought back to the body she had seen being carried away. She'd hoped she might have been proved wrong and that there would have been something that could have been done to save the poor little thing.

'The other kid and the grandmother are still unaccounted for. Apparently, they tried to get into the communal shelter tonight, but it was full.'

Viv's mind wandered and she pictured what might have happened if there had been space there for the family tonight. She imagined the mother, exhausted, and devastated at the loss of their home, rubbing her baby bump and expressing relief and gratitude that neither she, her children nor her mother had been inside it when it had been destroyed. Instead, the woman now faced coming to terms with the fact she had lost at least one of her children, if not both, as well as her mother. And goodness knew if her unborn baby would make it through the trauma. Viv hoped against all hope that it would survive.

'Quiet!' one of the rescue workers yelled, and everybody around them fell silent. Viv watched as one of the men shone his torch in amongst the mound of rubble where the woman was trapped. He put his ear up to a small opening.

'She's just felt the baby moving,' he announced, his voice full of relief. There was a round of applause, but he swiftly held his arm up to silence everybody again. He put his ear back to the hole and listened intently. Everybody around them waited with bated breath. The man brought his head back up and then looked around desperately. 'Can anybody see an armchair?' he asked loudly. He got up and carefully picked his way around the debris. 'Her youngest son was sitting in an armchair when the bomb hit,' he added with urgency. Suddenly, everybody was trawling the site for signs of the chair.

Viv spotted what looked to be the arm of a chair up against the remains of the wall. 'Over there!' she shouted.

A group of rescue workers started carefully pulling away everything that had landed around the armchair. A beam from the ceiling was balancing on the top and had hidden the rest of the chair from sight.

'I think he's under there!' one of them yelled.

'Let's go and get another stretcher,' Viv suggested. She was hopeful they would end up taking mother and son to hospital together. At least they could make that journey before coming back to pick up the rest of the family to take to the morgue. When they got back, the pregnant woman was being gently eased out from under the table. They had just managed to get her on to a stretcher when one of the men who had been working on digging her son out came over. He knelt down next to her.

'We found him. He'll need checking over, but I think he's going to be all right,' he told her.

She grabbed hold of her bump and starting crying. 'I kept telling him to get off the chair and go to my mother and his brother under the stairs,' she explained between sobs.

'Well, it looks as if the armchair was blown over when the bomb hit,' he replied. 'It protected him when the ceiling and chimney collapsed, just like the table protected you. You're both very lucky.'

'What about his big brother, and my mother?' she whispered fearfully. 'They were in the cupboard under the stairs. There wasn't enough room for us all in there.'

The man looked up at Viv anxiously.

'They're still looking,' Viv lied, thinking what a good job it was that the woman's younger son hadn't listened to her orders to join the two of them. 'Now, let's get you and baby into the ambulance, and we can check you over while we're waiting for your youngest to join us. We'll let you know as soon as there's any news on the others.' She went round to pick up the stretcher from the head end, being careful to manoeuvre the woman so that she didn't catch sight of the flattened mound where the stairs had once stood. When they had the woman comfortably lying in the back of Hudsy and had ascertained that, amazingly, everything seemed to be fine with her and the baby, the mother started getting agitated and panicking about her oldest son and her mother.

'Let me go and look for them,' she pleaded, trying to sit herself up.

Paul gently eased her back down again, explaining that she needed to get to the hospital for a thorough check over and that any more stress would be bad for the baby.

'We need to get her away from here before she gets herself in too much of a state,' Viv said quietly. 'I'll go and check how they're getting on.' When she reached the group of men trying to dig the boy out from under the armchair, she noticed that Bill was helping them. She automatically searched for Dot at his side and panicked when she didn't see her friend. She rushed over to him.

'Where's Dot?' she demanded. 'You said you'd look after her!'

'Woah, hold on, she's fine,' Bill replied gently, holding out both hands defensively.

'You're not supposed to leave her side while Tommy's on the prowl,' she hissed, not caring about the other men who had stopped what they were doing to stare at her.

'Tommy's no longer a threat to her, Viv,' Bill replied calmly.

'Oh.' Her shoulders relaxed and she let out a long breath. 'Sorry. I panicked when I saw you without her.' Bill smiled and nodded his understanding. 'Thank goodness they finally caught up with him,' Viv added. Bill told the other men to carry on without him and walked out of earshot, inviting Viv to follow him.

'He's dead, Viv.' Her head started spinning. That wasn't what she had been expecting to hear. Bill told her everything that had happened while she had been at the hospital with William. 'A friend of mine drove Dot over to her mother-in-law's shortly after we saw the body. She wanted to be the one to tell her.'

'Of course,' Viv replied quietly. She was still trying to take it all in herself. But she would have to process it later because there was a young boy to reunite with his mother, first.

'Right, let's get back to digging,' she declared, rolling her sleeves up and walking back towards the rescue team with purpose.

29

Peggy did well not to think about Johnny the day after her mother's great escape and funny turn. She had been too angry with her mother to talk to her about her escapade the previous day, but she had kept herself busy fussing around her and making sure that the children were too distracted to realise that anything was wrong. Peggy was so swept up that she didn't get a chance to do any of her usual obsessing. Fearing Mrs Miller would be too weak to entertain Martha, Lucy and Annie in her bedroom while the evacuees were at school in the afternoon and Peggy got on with her chores as usual, she took her sisters into the garden to help her pick vegetables for the dinner, which they then helped her prepare. It meant the task took three times as long as it normally did, but the girls enjoyed it so much that they didn't question the break in their routine or even ask to see Mrs Miller.

However, when Peggy fell into bed that evening and closed her eyes, the handsome pilot was the first thing that popped into her head. Annoyed, she dug out her favourite book, *Pride and Prejudice*, and started reading. But when she got to the bottom of the first page, she realised that she had no idea what she had just read. She sat up and composed herself, vowing to fully focus on the pages in front of her. But when she started reading about Mr Darcy he materialised as Johnny in the scene she had painted in her head.

Throwing the book down in frustration, she realised that she should have known better. *Pride and Prejudice* had always been her go-to book to lift her spirits, but only because she liked to fantasise about having her own similar romantic love story. It really wasn't a good choice when she was trying to forget about the man that she had taken a fancy to. Peggy decided to write to her brothers instead. She hadn't received any letters from them for quite some time. It wasn't unusual for them – they were both bad at writing home. But Peggy wanted them to know that she was thinking of them and that she was proud of them; things she knew she didn't tell them or her father enough. By the end of the letter her eyes were drooping. She signed off and then let the paper and pen slide to the floor, happy that she was drifting off with a head clear of her unrequited love.

The following morning, after Lucy had left for school, Sarah and Phillip agreed to take the rest of the children over to the farm. Peggy had decided she was ready to talk to her mother about the WI incident, so she was grateful to have the house free of little ears.

Mrs Miller looked brighter when Peggy took her morning tea and porridge into her. 'Bed rest has served you well, then?' she asked sarcastically.

'The silent treatment is over, then?' her mother shot straight back in an identical tone, raising an eyebrow at her daughter. 'That's a shame as I was rather enjoying the peace and quiet.'

They held eye contact with serious expressions on their faces for less than a minute before Peggy's lip began to quiver and her face softened. Her mother did the same and then they were both laughing.

'I can never stay angry with you for long,' Peggy said, shaking her head in resignation. She sighed and sat down on the edge of the bed. 'I came in here ready to give you a big lecture about listening to Dr Brady and doing as you are told.' Her mother took hold of her hand and fluttered her eyelashes at her dramatically. 'All right, you don't have to overdo it,' Peggy said, giggling.

'I *am* sorry,' her mother replied softly, looking genuine now. 'I gave myself a bit of a fright. And I realise that I probably scared you, too. I accept that I need to take this a little more seriously from now on.'

'I really wish you would. You were doing so well and now you've set yourself back. Not to mention the fact that you could have ended up in real bother if Dr Brady hadn't been in the right place at the right time.'

Mrs Miller hung her head, looking sheepish.

'What were you thinking?' Peggy pushed. 'I wasn't just scared, Mother – I was terrified when I realised you were missing.'

'I don't think I *was* thinking, darling. And that's the honest truth. I didn't set out to worry anybody or to put myself in danger. I truly thought I'd be fine to go for a little walk and see my friends.'

'I know you thought that, but I'd told you no and Dr Brady hadn't signed it off. You might think you know better than me because you're my mother, but I was only following the doctor's orders – and you should be doing the same because you certainly don't know better than him.'

'I thought he was just being overprotective because he knows how angry your father will be when he finds out I was ill and that nobody told him. It's in his interests to make sure I recover and nobody in the village realises how poorly I've been. I felt so perky all of a sudden, and I was so fed up with being confined to the house!'

Peggy's heart dropped at the mention of her father. She had thought there wouldn't be any need to worry him with news of her mother's ill health and that she'd be back to her old self by the next time he came home on leave. But this setback had made her question whether he needed to be informed sooner rather than later. Besides, the whole WI group had witnessed her mother collapsing and being rushed away by the local doctor, so her health was going to be the talk of Petworth for a while.

'You need to listen to Dr Brady from now on, or else I'll have no choice but to write to Father and tell him what's been going on.'

'Peggy, no,' her mother pleaded, using both hands to hold on to hers now. 'He's got enough to worry about without adding me to the list.'

'Exactly. And I was happy to keep him in the dark while you were recovering well, but if you continue to pull silly stunts like this then I *will* tell him.'

'I thought you said you weren't going to lecture me,' her mother replied sullenly.

'Yes, but I think you needed it,' Peggy replied firmly.

'I've learned my lesson, okay? And I promise to take it easier from now on. I won't even come down the stairs unless your lovely chap arrives to sweep me down them in his arms again.' Her mother's eyes glinted and her face lit up as she talked about Johnny, but Peggy had prepared herself for this.

'I'm afraid you'll be up here a rather long time, then,' she said resolutely.

'Oh no, what's happened?' her mother asked, her face full of concern.

'Nothing. That's just the point. He's not interested in me like that, and I've embarrassed myself by getting carried away with thoughts of something developing with a man who is simply showing me kindness.'

'I don't think—'

'That's the end of it, Mother. I won't hear another word of it. You only managed to sneak out of the house for so long unnoticed because I've been distracted over the last couple of weeks. It stops now. I'm fully committed and focused on doing my bit in Petworth.' There was silence between them, and Peggy felt confident that would be the last mention of Johnny from her mother.

'Goodness, you are very assertive today, darling,' Mrs Miller commented cheekily.

Peggy couldn't help but laugh again. 'Let's just get you better and get this blasted war over with. Then I can moon over men out of my league as much as I want to!' Peggy joked.

'Johnny's not out of your league,' her mother muttered. Peggy threw her a stern look. 'But that sounds like a good plan,' Mrs Miller added quickly.

'Good,' Peggy replied, feeling positive. 'Now, eat your breakfast and get some more rest. Then if you're a good girl I might let the little horrors up for some cuddles this afternoon.'

Peggy left the room with a renewed sense of purpose, and she spent the rest of the day pushing all thoughts of Johnny away every time they tried to sneak into her head. In fact, she managed to keep it up for another couple of days, until there was an unexpected knock at the front door one afternoon while she was preparing dinner. Peggy's heart raced; the evacuees were at school and her sisters were upstairs reading with her mother. Dr Brady had visited with Patricia that morning to do some checks on her mother. She couldn't think of anybody else who would be calling round unannounced apart from Johnny. She forgot herself for a moment and rushed excitedly out of the kitchen towards the front door, before remembering that she was meant to be ignoring her feelings for him and focusing on her mother and the children. Peggy stopped in her tracks and took a moment to compose herself. Then she walked carefully and calmly back into the kitchen. It had only been a light knock – he was probably worried about disturbing her mother. But that meant she and the girls probably wouldn't have heard it. Maybe he would go away if Peggy ignored him? She really wasn't sure she had the willpower to turn him away herself, knowing that her knees would go weak as soon as she saw his face smiling at her. The best way forward would be to let him think nobody was home. He would go back to Tangmere, his duty done by calling by. He would be able to tell Viv he'd tried and would probably feel relieved he hadn't had to spend any more time with her.

Peggy was just getting back to chopping carrots when a louder knock at the door made her jump in the air. Suddenly, all three of her sisters were running down the stairs at speed. Peggy ran out into the hallway to try and stop them, but they were shouting and laughing so loudly that there was no way Johnny – or whoever it was at the door – wouldn't have heard them.

'Open the door, Peggy!' Martha cried.

'It's the pilot! He's got flowers!' Annie bellowed as they jumped up and down at the bottom of the stairs. Peggy walked towards them with a quizzical look on her face.

'We saw him out of Mummy's window!' Martha explained.

Peggy rolled her eyes and shook her head. So much for hoping he would go away quietly. But then she had another thought: why was he bringing her flowers? Peggy's heart skipped a beat at the thought of him declaring his undying love for her on the doorstep and putting to rest all her fears. How romantic! Maybe she had been premature in assuming Johnny wasn't interested in her? She tried to hide her excitement as she opened the door, not quite believing the fact that Johnny had arrived to prove he did like her after all, just as she had resolved to move on from him – that had been a close call! When Peggy saw his smiling face, she had to stop herself from throwing herself into his arms.

'I hope you don't mind me calling round again so soon,' Johnny said, smiling. Peggy stared expectantly at the flowers. 'I picked these on the way,' he explained, following her gaze. 'I thought they might brighten things up for your mother in her bedroom.' Peggy's face fell before she had a chance to hide her reaction. 'Oh, erm, I would have preferred to buy her a proper bunch, but flowers are very hard to come by at the moment. I thought these looked pretty special though,' he added apologetically.

Peggy quickly composed herself, grateful that he had mistaken her downcast response for something other than rejection. Of course the flowers weren't for her! What had she been thinking? Any time she was tempted to start mooning over Johnny, she needed to remind herself of this feeling of disappointment – because this was what it would always be like if

Peggy continued any sort of friendship with him, always hoping for something more and building her hopes up only to have them cruelly dashed when she realised once again that he just wasn't interested in her in that way. When she looked at Johnny again, he was clearly waiting for her to say something.

'That was very thoughtful of you. She loves wild flowers,' Peggy replied carefully.

'Are you coming in, Johnny?' Martha asked. 'Can we be aeroplanes again?'

Her sisters were bouncing up and down behind her. She turned to shush them and then found Johnny staring at her eagerly when she turned back to face him. She really didn't want to send him away, but she knew it was for the best. 'Why don't you girls take the flowers up to Mother?' she suggested. 'I'll bring a vase up shortly.'

They squealed and Johnny handed the bunch over to Lucy who took great care in carrying them up the stairs as her younger sisters trailed behind her. Peggy scolded herself in her head again for thinking he would have turned up with flowers for her.

'How is your mother?' Johnny asked.

'Not great,' Peggy replied quietly. She looked over her shoulder to make sure her sisters were out of earshot and then she stepped over the threshold and pulled the door to behind her. 'She's had another funny turn and she's back on bed rest.'

Johnny's face fell. 'I'm so sorry to hear that. Is there anything I can do?'

'No. No, that won't be necessary, thank you. You don't need to worry yourself about us, we're just fine.'

'Does she need some company to lift her spirits?' he added cheekily. Peggy laughed nervously. 'No. She really needs to rest. I'm afraid we rather underestimated the gravity of her condition, and this has been quite the wake-up call.'

'I can come in and spend some time with the children if you need a break?'

Peggy sighed and shifted her weight from one foot to the other. Why wasn't he getting the hint? He was making this so difficult. Peggy wanted nothing more than to spend time with him, but she knew it would mean more to her than it would to him. She would only be torturing herself, prolonging the inevitable pain of rejection. Why couldn't Johnny see that she was trying to give him a way out, to release him from his duties so he could go and pick wild flowers for a girl who was better suited to him?

'That really won't be necessary. I can cope just fine, thank you, if I concentrate on the task at hand,' she replied rather more stiffly than she had intended.

Johnny looked taken aback but he quickly recovered and gave her one of his striking smiles. 'It feels like I might have come at a bad time. I'll leave you to it and come back as soon as I can and—'

'Please – don't worry yourself about us,' Peggy cut in sharply. His face fell but she pressed on. She needed to do this to preserve her feelings. She had to stop hurting herself by spending time with him and building her expectations. 'I don't really have the time for visitors. You can let Viv know that you stopped by to check on me and that I'm getting on just fine. I'm sure you have much more exciting things to be doing with your precious time off and I would hate to keep you from them.'

'Oh, I wasn't . . . I mean, I haven't been coming round just because Viv—' Johnny started to say.

'I'd better go and check on my mother in case the girls have worn her out with their excitement,' Peggy said, cutting over him. 'It was good to see you. Thank you for her flowers. But I really must be getting on.' She stepped back into the house and her heart ached as she took in Johnny's face – open-mouthed in shock, just staring at her, while she gently closed the door.

It's for the best, it's for the best, it's for the best, she repeated in her head over and over again as she stood, pressed up against the door with her eyes closed, full of regret.

Mrs Miller didn't mention the flowers or the visit, and she must have primed Peggy's sisters because they didn't say another word about Johnny when she went upstairs with a vase and helped them arrange the blooms. Her mother did, however, give Peggy a concerned look, which Peggy returned with a warning stare, making it clear that she did not want to talk about any of it. She busied herself with chores and fun activities for the children over the next few days, pushing any thoughts of Johnny out of her mind as soon as they tried to creep in. And as the days moved on and he didn't return, Peggy tried her best to convince herself that she was glad about it.

30

When Viv's shift ended, she wondered if she should stop by at Beryl's on her way home to check in on Dot. After a lot of internal debate, she decided against it. She didn't want to intrude upon the women's grief and, besides, she was confident that Dot would come and see her when she was ready. On her way back through the ruined streets of London, she marvelled at the little boy who had been saved by an armchair; his mucking around on it and ignoring his mother's pleas to go to the cupboard under the stairs had saved his life. Viv couldn't imagine how his mother would have felt if he had followed her orders and joined his brother and grandmother, only to perish along with them. She had only been trying to keep him safe. It just went to show that no matter how hard you tried to protect those you love, ultimately, your lives were in the hands of fate. There really was no 'safest' place to hide out while the Germans were attacking, and everyone was just taking their chances together.

As soon as Viv walked through the door at home, Jilly came rushing up to her. Viv had been looking forward to sharing her engagement news with Jilly and Dot as soon as she could get them both together, but the thought didn't even cross her mind now, as she prepared to update her roommate on Dot's situation.

'There's something wrong with Dot,' Jilly whispered urgently, motioning to the living room. 'She got back about an hour ago and she's been sat on the sofa, staring into space, ever since. I can't get a word out of her.'

Viv felt a rush of affection at the thought of her friend coming back to her when she was in such turmoil. It meant a lot to Viv that Dot was turning to her in her hour of need. She just hoped that she would be able to offer her some comfort. Viv had never known anybody who had been widowed before and she wasn't quite sure what the best approach would be, especially given the unusual circumstances. If she were in Dot's shoes, she imagined she would have felt relief that Tommy wasn't able to do her any more harm. But the two of them had been married – she had been deeply in love with the man for a number of years. Just because she had finally realised that she deserved better than the awful way he treated her, didn't mean to say that she wouldn't be upset that he was dead. Viv understood that her friend would likely be feeling a mix of emotions that she would find tricky to navigate. Viv quickly told Jilly what had happened to Tommy.

'Oh no, poor Dot,' she gasped. 'I mean, I know she left him and everything, but—'

'I know,' Viv cut in. 'I've been thinking about how I would feel in this situation and all I can be certain of is that she must be feeling upset and confused. I know Dot went to see her mother-in-law when she found out. I think maybe now she's come away the shock might have kicked in. I'll go and see to her. You get some sleep.'

'Thanks. It was busy at the rest centre last night and I'm exhausted, but I didn't like to leave Dot on her own like that. I just sat with her when she didn't respond to me and hoped you'd be back soon.'

Jilly went straight to her bedroom and Viv found herself a little envious. She was exhausted, too. But she was willing to do whatever Dot needed to help her through this.

'Morning,' she said cautiously as she walked into the living room.

Dot's eyes were red from crying, her face was pale, and she was sitting with her arms crossed over her body, as if she was hugging herself. She didn't respond or look up when Viv spoke, or even when Viv sat down next to her.

'Have you heard?' Dot asked the question so quietly that Viv almost didn't pick it up. She was still staring straight ahead. A single tear ran down her cheek.

'Yes. I ran into Bill.' Dot nodded her head knowingly. They sat in silence for a few minutes while Viv tried to think of the best thing to say. In the end, she decided that maybe it was best not to say anything, but instead to simply be there for her friend. 'You don't need to talk about it. How about we just go and get some sleep? You can come in with me. I don't like the thought of you lying down out here all on your own.'

'I am very tired,' Dot whispered in reply.

'I'm not surprised. It doesn't sound as though you've slept since before the Balham bomb. I've only had a couple of hours since then myself. Let's get to bed and we can talk when you're ready. I think some sleep will help you make some sense of everything you're feeling.' She carefully led Dot to her bedroom. Dot was still in so much of a daze that Viv had to help her out of her uniform. As soon as they lay down next to each other in bed, Dot rolled over to face away from Viv. Within minutes her breathing had become slower and heavier, and Viv allowed herself to fall asleep safe in the knowledge that her friend was finally doing the same.

The sun was going down when Viv stirred awake. She didn't normally sleep through the whole day, but she had certainly had a lot of rest to catch up on. She rubbed her eyes and rolled over to find the rest of the bed empty. Sitting up, she wondered how she had managed to sleep through Dot getting up and leaving. But then her friend walked into the room, dressed in her ARP uniform, and carrying two cups of tea.

'You're not seriously going in this evening?' Viv asked her, gathering the bed sheets around her to shield her from the nip in the air. Dot smiled at her as she handed Viv one of the cups and sat down on the bed. Viv was pleased to see her friend's face had a bit of colour back. She still looked tired – but everybody looked tired these days.

'What else would you have me do, Viv?' Dot asked her lightly. 'I'd rather be out doing something useful when the Germans come than stuck in a shelter with nothing to do but think. Besides, Tommy didn't want me to be an air raid warden. If I don't go in then, even in death, he'll be controlling me.'

'I just . . . how are you feeling?'

'I feel a little bit like my right arm has been cut off.' Dot sighed and took a sip of her tea. 'And although my arm had always been a vital part of my body and had helped me live a happy life for a long time, in recent years it had become infected. It had been sore, and it was causing me a lot of pain and stress.'

Viv was gasping for her tea, but she was listening so intently that she found she couldn't pull her eyes away from Dot to focus on drinking.

'So, although I'm sad to have lost my arm, I know that, in the long run, I'm better off without it. Does that make sense?'

Viv nodded and finally sated her thirst with a quick sip of her drink. 'That makes perfect sense,' she replied.

'Thanks for looking after me this morning. I'd been scared to go to sleep in case I dreamt of Tommy. Every time I closed my eyes, I saw his body. But I felt safe as soon as I was lying next to you. I don't think I've slept that well in weeks.'

Viv placed a hand on Dot's shoulder in a show of support as Dot ran her through everything that had led up to her expecting to identify Stan's body and discovering the dead man was in fact Tommy. 'I went straight round to Beryl's. We held each other for hours while we cried and tried to make sense of how we were feeling. When the sirens went off, we took our chances in the Anderson shelter; neither of us could face anybody at the crypt. Then we had the fright of our lives when Jim burst in halfway through the raid. The two of them have got into the habit of going for fancy dinners at hotels and then spending raids in their bunkers.' Viv raised her eyebrows in surprise. 'I know,' Dot laughed. 'I was intrigued too, given Jim's dodgy financial circumstances. But it turns out that he's been getting custom from some of the management at these hotels, so they let him in on the cheap to keep him quiet.'

'Nice work if you can get it,' Viv joked.

'Anyway, Beryl had been meant to meet Jim at one of their regular haunts but then obviously the news of Tommy and my arrival put her in a spin – she completely forgot. He was so worried about her that he ran all the way back to her house at the height of the attack.'

Viv let out a long breath and shook her head. 'It must be love,' she commented.

'Poor chap – I thought he was going to keel over when he bounded in. There was sweat pouring off his face and he looked like he'd seen a ghost. I'm not sure he's run like that for years. It was a bit of a distraction from Tommy, of course, but then we had to explain everything to him. I'm afraid I was in a bit of a stupor by the time I got back here.'

'Did the sleep help you make sense of it?' Viv asked carefully. 'Of the way you're feeling?'

'No.' Dot laughed sadly and shook her head. 'I didn't tell Beryl this, but the first thing I felt when I saw Tommy's body was relief.' She broke eye contact and sat staring into her half-drunk cup of tea. 'I was glad he was dead, Viv. Just like I'd been relieved when I thought the telegram Beryl was sent was notifying her of his death. Does that make me a terrible person? Because I feel like a terrible person.'

'Of course it doesn't,' Viv replied quickly, rubbing Dot's shoulder reassuringly. 'Tommy hurt you. And you were frightened that he wanted to hurt you even more. It would be natural to feel relief that the threat of him has completely gone forever.'

Dot sighed again. 'And then there's the fact that even though I felt that initial relief, and I'm thankful I don't have to keep looking over my shoulder in case he's lurking in the shadows, I also feel sad that he's gone. How can I mourn a monster? But it's like I'm grieving the man I originally fell in love with, even though Tommy wasn't that man anymore. That man died a long time ago. I'm so confused, Viv.'

'It will take time,' Viv replied. She didn't know what else to say. 'I don't think there's any right or wrong way to feel in this situation, so I don't feel like I can give you any advice. But I'm here. You can talk to me about it whenever you need to. Or we can just sit together and drink tea.'

'I know,' Dot said. 'Do you know what was really odd?' she asked. Viv raised her eyebrows inquisitively. 'It felt right to be with Beryl yesterday. I've been getting on with her much better since leaving Tommy. Once I realised that she'd stuck up for me and thrown him out, and Beryl explained why she'd treated me the way she had, we've had a better relationship. Now I feel as if Tommy's death might have even brought us closer together. He was the only thing stopping us from bonding. All those years I pined for a mother figure, and she was right there. But it's like she couldn't be released until Tommy was gone.'

'Maybe that will be one good thing to come out of this.'

'Maybe,' Dot replied thoughtfully. 'Anyway, I'm so sorry; I can't believe I didn't ask after William.' She turned to look at Viv, now. 'How did his surgery go?'

'There's no need to apologise. You weren't in any fit state to have a conversation last night,' Viv replied sympathetically. She so wanted to share her news with Dot, but it just didn't feel right to expect her to celebrate their engagement when she was going through such a difficult time. It could wait until things had settled down. 'It was a success!' she declared happily.

'Oh, thank goodness,' Dot replied. 'You must be so relieved.'

'I am,' Viv said. It felt strange to be holding back something so big from everybody, but she was certain it was the right thing to do. She got up to have a wash and Dot left to check in on Beryl before she made her way to clock in at the school.

The next few days were busy with raids and the two women hardly saw each other. When they did, they fell into bed together and slept peacefully. Viv felt comforted by having Dot lying next to her. They didn't talk much before dropping off every day; neither keen on reliving the horrors they had witnessed on duty. But Dot did reveal that there was still no news on Stan's whereabouts, despite Ginny's quest to round him up and punish him for everything he had put her through. His disgruntled wife was apparently making a nuisance of herself at the police station, berating officers for not dedicating more time to their manhunt. There was still no hard evidence that Stan was responsible for Tommy's death, but as the days passed with no news on his whereabouts, it seemed more and more likely that he had been involved. Bill was still looking out for Dot, just to be on the safe side, which had put Viv at ease.

Viv woke up early one afternoon and found she couldn't settle again. Dot was working a day shift and so Viv was in bed alone. It had only been a week since Tommy's death, but she had quickly become used to having her friend by her side as she slept. Viv wondered if she was struggling now because Dot wasn't there. Having Dot fill the empty space beside her had been comforting and now she had the bed back to herself she felt vulnerable. Every time she tried to get back to sleep, thoughts of William being shot at in his plane flashed into her mind. Now the Battle of Britain was over, she had no idea what his future with the RAF looked like. There was talk of fighter squadrons going on the offensive over occupied Europe, and Viv couldn't get the image of William captured by the enemy out of her mind this particular afternoon. She sat up and replayed the proposal in her head, to try and drown out the scary thoughts with happy memories. But then William being jovial about getting back to Tangmere invaded the scene and Viv had to stop. Everything came back to her fear of losing him.

Viv got up, remembering the note from Peggy that Johnny had given her on the day of William's surgery. She had been so swept up in the excitement of their engagement, and then on her return to London preoccupied by her volunteer work and the news of Tommy's death, that she had forgotten all about it until now. She decided that reading over the short message would make her smile. Viv felt a rush as she thought about how excited her friend was going to be to learn that her confidence in her 'happily ever after' had not been misplaced. Viv had kept the engagement to herself for so long now that it almost felt as though it hadn't happened at all. But she had determined over the last few days that she would wait to share the news until she was back with Peggy, Dot and Jilly together – so that she could reveal it to them at the same time. She didn't want to tell one without the others, and so it could wait.

While reading over Peggy's note again cheered Viv for a moment, it then had the opposite effect, as she re-read the line about Mrs Martin and was reminded of her promise to the older lady to visit her regularly in Peggy's absence. Viv hadn't made it over to the boarding house once since Peggy had left London, and she was certain that Dot hadn't managed to visit either. Accepting that further sleep before her next shift was no longer a possibility, Viv got out of bed and got herself ready to pay Peggy's roommate a visit.

31

Dot sat in the canteen at Cook's Ground School with Bill and Laurie, eating toast and drinking water. It had been a long day shift and she couldn't face any more tea. The three of them had been drafted in to help clear rubble and search for survivors at a bomb site when they had first clocked on, relieving the wardens from the night shift. Once everybody had been accounted for and the residents who had returned from shelters to find their homes destroyed diverted to rest centres, they had settled in at their base to wait for the Germans to return. Dot hoped they would attack early so she could get caught up in extra duties instead of waiting for the next raid in an empty apartment and then sheltering with strangers. Viv and Jilly would both be volunteering this evening, and she didn't like the thought of being alone with her thoughts.

Bill had been brilliant since the discovery of Tommy's body. Despite not having had any sleep himself, he had returned to the school to update Victor and Ginny and deal with the fallout from Stan's furious but relieved wife while Dot visited Beryl. He'd then made sure he was on duty with Dot for every single shift that she had, despite the fact that Tommy was no longer a threat.

'I promised to look after you until this is all over, and I will be true to my word,' he'd told her when Dot had argued there was no need for him to forgo work at the docks on her behalf. 'I don't mean to frighten you, but we don't know for certain that it was Stan who killed Tommy. He could have been caught up in any number of things that ended in his murder. I don't want to take any chances while his killer is still out there.'

Dot hadn't been worried. She was now convinced that Stan was responsible for her husband's brutal end – the only thing she couldn't get her head around was how he had managed to overpower Tommy.

When the night shift started rolling in, Dot had an idea. She would stop in and see Beryl instead of going back to Viv's on her own. She hadn't managed to spend much time with her mother-in-law since Tommy's death, and she was keen to know how Beryl was getting on now the dust had settled a little. If she was meeting Jim at one of their hotels that evening, then maybe they would let her tag along. Dot had always envied Viv for her ability to 'dance her troubles away' and now she found that she fancied giving it a go herself. When Bill got up to walk her home, she told him of her plan.

'Suits me – Beryl's house is even nearer to home for me, so I'll escort you there,' he said, smiling.

'I'll take Victor my newspaper before we go,' Dot said. 'I'll meet you out the front.' She walked along the main corridor towards Victor's office, tossing the rolled-up newspaper from hand to hand. She was looking forward to switching off tonight and maybe even enjoying herself.

'Here you go, boss,' she called cheerfully as she opened the door to his office, holding out the newspaper. But she froze when she saw who was sitting behind the desk. It wasn't Victor – it was Stan. Stan looked just as shocked as

Dot felt. Realising she was still holding the paper aloft in mid-air, Dot dropped it to the floor and closed her gaping mouth. Quickly looking behind her for someone to come to her aid, she realised she was on her own and she had no idea what to do.

Dot was face to face with the man she was convinced had murdered her husband. But she had such mixed emotions about Tommy's death that she wasn't sure whether she should be angry with Stan or grateful to him. And Dot had become so certain over the last week that Stan would never show his face around here again that she wasn't prepared for this in the slightest. As they stared silently at each other, Dot reminded herself that, no matter what Tommy had done to anybody else, he hadn't deserved to die the way he had done – and if Stan was responsible then that made him a murderer. She gulped as she realised that she probably had good reason be afraid of the man sitting in front of her.

'I'm so sorry,' Stan croaked, making to stand up.

Dot held out her hands instinctively. 'No,' she said firmly. 'You stay right where you are.'

Stan slumped back in the chair, defeated. Taking in his appearance, Dot noticed that the bully she had once known didn't seem to be present anymore; the man was a shadow of his former self. His face was covered in fading bruises and stubble, and his filthy warden uniform was ripped in places. He also looked weak. She wondered where he had been hiding out all this time and whether Tommy had been responsible for his bruises and ripped clothes.

'What happened?' she asked him carefully. There didn't seem any point in checking that he was Tommy's murderer – that much was now clearer than it had already been to her.

'You have to understand,' Stan begged. 'He wasn't a good man.'

Dot scoffed. 'Don't you think I know that?' she answered. 'I was married to him – I know what he was capable of. That doesn't mean it was okay to bludgeon him to death.' As Dot spoke, her early memories of Tommy came flooding back. Tears pricked her eyes. 'Nobody deserves that.'

'He was planning on hurting you,' Stan pleaded. 'And it wasn't like that – I promise. I didn't mean to kill him! You've got to believe me. I don't have that in me!'

Dot took a few steps into the office now. She wasn't frightened of Stan, even after what he'd done. She could see how killing Tommy had affected him; it was as she had always suspected – he was a bully who liked to run his mouth off but only ever picked on people weaker than himself. So, what *had* happened with Tommy? Stan certainly wasn't any match for the soldier – that was why everybody had been so quick to assume that he would be the one to turn up dead. Dot needed to get to the bottom of this before somebody else found Stan here and he was hauled off by the police. She knew she needed to get answers from Stan right now, because it could well be her only chance.

'So, tell me what happened,' Dot said. She slowly took a seat opposite Stan, keeping the desk between them as a barrier. 'I believe you when you say he wanted to hurt me. I'd discovered he was back in London, and I had a good idea that he was robbing corpses and houses with you.' She looked away from Stan in disgust before continuing. 'I didn't think he'd let me walk away from the marriage without a fight.' Just then Dot heard footsteps running down the corridor. She turned around just as Victor and Bill swept into the room. Dot stood up and walked towards them.

'It's all right, we're just talking,' she said calmly, hoping to reassure them both that she didn't feel like she was in any danger.

'I'm sorry, Dot,' Victor spluttered. 'I didn't want you to have to see him. I left him here waiting while I ran to fetch somebody to man the phones while I took him to the police station. He wants to hand himself in.' He turned his head towards his brother-in-law now and his tone switched from apologetic to angry as he glared at him. 'He wasn't supposed to be talking to anybody. Least of all you.'

'When I ran into Victor and he told me Stan was in his office, I realised you were headed straight for him,' Bill added. He put a protective arm around Dot's shoulder.

'I'm fine, Bill. Honestly,' Dot said lightly. 'He hasn't moved from that chair.'

'Right, well, we'll get him off to the police station now. Laurie will be here in a few minutes to man the office,' Victor said. As he and Bill made to walk round to the other side of the desk, Dot pulled them both back.

'No, please!' she yelled. 'I need to know what happened. He was just about to tell me. Please just let Stan tell me, and then you can take him.'

'Are you sure you want to know?' Bill asked quietly.

'I *need* to know,' she replied. They both nodded and took a few steps back towards the doorway, and Dot sat back down opposite her husband's killer.

'I met Tommy when I was offloading some items in a pub,' Stan started.

'Selling things you'd ripped from the dead bodies of innocent people,' Victor cut in scornfully. Dot turned around and gave her boss a warning glare. When she turned back to Stan, he was staring shamefully into his lap.

'I'm not proud of anything I've done,' he said quietly. 'But Ginny likes the finer things in life, and I was finding it hard to keep her happy. I guess I got desperate and when I did it the first time, I swore I'd never do it again. But it was so easy – when people die in the attacks, people seem to just assume that their belongings get destroyed.' Dot could see Victor and Bill shaking their heads out of the corner of her eye. 'It was *too* easy. And I didn't think I was doing any harm. Not really. Then it became a bit of an addiction, I suppose.' There was a scoff from behind her and Dot turned around with another stern look. She didn't want Stan to change his mind about telling her the truth.

Victor held up both his hands apologetically. 'I'll go and chase up Laurie,' he muttered before leaving the doorway.

'So, as I was saying, I met Tommy in the pub. It was soon after I'd come across you asleep in one of the classrooms.' Dot blushed. She didn't like the thought of Bill knowing how desperate and pathetic she'd been after leaving Tommy. She nodded her head at Stan to invite him to continue. 'He saw my uniform and started asking about you. I wasn't your biggest fan at that point, I'll admit. You'd just got me turfed out of here.' Dot coughed dramatically. 'All right, all right – I'd got myself chucked out. But I was angry with you, and I blamed you, even though it was all down to me.' Dot nodded again, this time in agreement. 'We had a drink together. We had a few drinks. Tommy told me he was meant to be back with his regiment, but he'd stuck around because he wanted to teach you a lesson.' Dot's blood ran cold. 'I was angry and bitter, and I wanted revenge, too.'

'What were you planning?' Dot asked, though she wasn't sure she wanted to know the answer.

'We never got that far,' Stan admitted. 'We were too drunk to come up with any sort of plan. After one too many whiskies, I ended up confessing what I'd done to get kicked out of the ARP, and how I saw that as your fault. I showed Tommy some of the loot I had on me. He was impressed. And he said he would need some cash to pay for accommodation and such, seeing as his mother had thrown him out of his home.' Stan looked up at Dot now. 'He blamed you for that, too,' he added.

'Oh, I'm sure he did,' she muttered disdainfully.

'Tommy said he also needed cash to pay for whatever he had planned for you, but I swear he never told me what he was going to do.' He took a deep breath. 'Anyway, I told him I was going to have to jack it all in now that I didn't have my volunteer role anymore. People round here would know I wasn't on the books and ask questions if I started sniffing round the dead bodies. That's when Tommy suggested we could use my uniform to gain access to bombed-out houses. He was still in uniform, too, and he said nobody ever questioned anything he did when he was wearing it because it garnered so much respect – so, together we would make a great team. We just had to wait until the rescue teams had cleared off and then we could go and help ourselves, and nobody would ask any questions because of our uniforms.'

'So, where did it all go wrong?' Dot asked.

'Well, he got greedy. We struck lucky at some bomb sites, but we had to dig through a lot of rubble at most of them before we got to anything worth taking. With so many people homeless, many were going back to houses that had only been damaged a little bit, so the places with easy pickings were occupied again by the time we got there. Tommy started making me break into houses with him during raids.

Only, sometimes the occupants weren't at shelters – they were at home. We made it out unseen the first few times, but there was this one guy who caught us at it—'

'And Tommy roughed you up in front of him,' Bill cut in, gesturing to Stan's bruises. Stan nodded.

'I didn't want to do anymore after that. It was getting too risky, and I was the one who was going to get into the most trouble because it was my uniform that was tricking people into thinking we were carrying out official duties. Tommy stopped wearing his uniform after the run-in with that chap because he realised he would be easier to identify and track down, but he forced me to keep wearing mine. Every time I tried to refuse to do anything he demanded, he would beat me up or threaten me. Tommy wouldn't take no for an answer.'

Dot watched as Stan's mouth quivered while he recounted his story. It seemed impossible to her that this was the same man who had stood in this very room intimidating Jim just weeks earlier, after having forced him to buy his wares using violence and pressure. How the tables had turned. She almost laughed at the irony of it all.

'Then, when we were in that last house—' Stan stopped abruptly and closed his eyes on the memory. He took a deep breath. 'That night. There was so much going on at Balham Station. Tommy was adamant that he wanted to target houses just down the road. I thought it was a stupid idea. I was worried one of the rescue workers would recognise me, or we'd be in a house when the occupant came home. But he pulled a knife on me. He said he just needed to do one more job and then he'd have enough cash to take care of you.'

Dot swallowed anxiously and she felt suddenly nauseous. She'd been so close to whatever Tommy had planned for her.

'We burgled the house he'd targeted. He went straight for that house and as soon as we were in, he made a beeline for the bedroom and pulled a box of jewellery out from under the bed and cash from under the mattress. Someone must have told him it was there. I remember thinking how happy he must have been that Balham Station took a hit because it gave him an excuse and cover to get into that house. But I was just relieved it was all over.' He paused and rubbed his hand over his head a few times. 'Only it wasn't over. We got downstairs and Tommy said we were going to go out the back door and through the garden and over the fence to the next house. I protested – saying he'd told me it would be one last job. I don't know what came over me to stand up to him like that. It had only ever got me beatings previously. I knew he could overpower me – he was stronger than me and more skilled in combat and he'd already battered me a fair few times. I think maybe I'd been so close to getting away, and he'd pushed me for so long, that something inside of me just snapped.'

'I know the feeling,' Dot said quietly, thinking about what it had taken for her to finally stand up to Tommy after all the years of bullying. Something had snapped inside of her, too.

'I regretted it immediately. I knew from experience that I was no match for him. I knew what was coming and I knew there was no point in fighting back. So, when Tommy turned around and lunged for me, I jumped backwards, putting my arms up so my hands were protecting my face. As I jumped back, my foot flew up and it must have caught him somehow. I'm not really sure what happened to be honest, but one minute he was coming at me, then my foot connected with something and then he flew backwards. There was a crack as the back of his head hit the bottom of the fireplace. He struck it with such force that he bounced off it and rolled over to land on his front. I expected him to get straight back up and come for me again, but as soon as I saw he wasn't making any effort to move I took my chance to get the hell out of there before he came round. I was so panicked that I didn't even pick up any of the loot. I didn't realise he was badly hurt, let alone dead.'

Dot shook her head slowly. Tommy's head hadn't been caved in during a brutal assault as everybody had assumed by the damage to his skull. His death had been a complete accident; a fluke that had ended up saving Stan as well as her, because goodness knows what would have happened to them both if Tommy had made it out of that house alive that night.

'When did you realise that you'd killed him?' Dot asked.

Stan shuddered when she asked the question. 'I've only just found out. I've spent the last week hiding in tube station shelters, trying to keep as many people around me as possible because I thought Tommy would be out there gunning for me. I came straight here to see Victor as soon as I heard Tommy was dead.'

'You really are pathetic,' Dot said scornfully as she got up off the chair. She walked over to Bill. 'I've heard enough,' she declared. 'Now let's go and get Victor because I want to go with him to hand this pathetic excuse for a man into the police.'

32

Viv smiled when the door to the boarding house on Royal Hospital Road opened and she was greeted by Ralf. The refugee had become a familiar face at bomb sites over previous weeks. He was always keen to help the rescue teams with the heavy lifting and he asked after Peggy every time Viv bumped into him. She was never able to give him any news, but she appreciated his kindness in checking in. Today, however, she was happy to be able to tell him that she had heard from Peggy and that she seemed happy in the countryside with her family. Ralf led Viv through the hallway and into the dining room, where around ten people were diligently working on making surgical dressings. Viv had been expecting a quiet catch-up with Mrs Martin and she was surprised to walk into such a hub of activity.

'Hello, dear. It's so lovely to see you,' Mrs Martin exclaimed joyfully. She got up from her spot at the head of the table and made her way over to Viv.

'I'm sorry I haven't been round sooner,' Viv replied guiltily. 'But it looks like you've been keeping busy!'

Mrs Martin grinned happily and led Viv to the kitchen. She directed her to sit at the table while she made them tea. It was quieter in here, and Viv took a moment to enjoy the calm while Mrs Martin worked away.

'So, tell me, dear. What news do you have to tell me? What have you been up to since I saw you last?'

'I got engaged!' Viv declared excitedly. The words had come out of her mouth before she'd had a chance to stop them. She hadn't planned on telling Mrs Martin – especially not before telling her friends. But she had spent so long bursting to tell people and censoring herself that it seemed she wasn't able to keep it in any longer.

Mrs Martin spun around to face her and clapped her hands in glee. 'Why, that's wonderful news!' she cried.

Viv blushed and laughed nervously. 'I'm so sorry. I didn't actually mean to tell you that,' she blustered. 'I haven't even told Dot or Peggy yet.'

'Why ever not, dear?' Mrs Martin asked. Then she held up a finger. 'Hang on. Let me get this sorted and you can tell me over tea,' she added. The older woman put the teapot, mugs and milk on the table. Then she got down on her hands and knees and rummaged around in the back of a cupboard before pulling out a pot full of sugar. 'For special occasions,' she declared proudly. Viv stared at the pot in wonderment. She hadn't seen that much sugar in a long time. But she didn't get a chance to ask about how her host had come across it because Mrs Martin was already demanding information from her.

'First, you must tell me about your man and the proposal,' she instructed. 'Then I need to know why you have kept it from your closest friends.'

Viv told Mrs Martin about how she had met William and detailed their courtship, right up until their joint proposal the week before. She was normally such a reserved person, and she wasn't quite sure why she was giving a woman she hardly knew so much detail about her relationship. But Viv felt comfortable, so she went with it. She wondered briefly if previously confiding in Dot and Peggy had opened up the floodgates for her emotionally.

'Well, that is just the most beautiful love story,' Mrs Martin announced. Her eyes appeared moist, and Viv wondered if she was thinking about the husband she had loved and lost. 'I assume you will be setting a date to get married as soon as possible. You'll want to get it done before he goes back to the RAF.' Viv stared at Mrs Martin in silence. 'Don't tell me you haven't got that far, surely? Time is of the essence!'

'I know. I just . . . it all happened so quickly and then I had to get back to London. We didn't get a chance to talk about making any arrangements. I don't even know if he wants to get married while the war is still on.'

'Of course he does. But I'm sure you'll be visiting him again soon, so you can start making plans then. Oh, how exciting!' Mrs Martin clapped her hands again. 'If you need somebody to help with your dress then you know where I am,' she added, nodding towards the dining room. 'I'm a dab hand with a needle and I've got lots of willing volunteers under this roof. We could rustle something up for you in no time.'

Viv hadn't even thought about what she would wear to marry William. But the offer came as a relief because, now she did think about it, she realised a wedding dress was going to be hard to come by in the current climate.

'Thank you,' Viv replied gratefully. 'I might just take you up on that offer.'

'I would be honoured to help. I enjoy making the surgical dressings for the first-aid posts, and we know they're being used because one of my friends has recognised my writing on the labels. But it would be wonderful to have a bigger, more personal project to tackle.' Mrs Martin looked wistfully into the distance and Viv wondered if she was thinking about her husband again. Suddenly, her host snapped back to attention. 'Now, you must tell me why you haven't told Peggy or Dot your wonderful news yet,' she said with urgency. 'You'll need to get that sorted soon, dear.'

Once Viv had brought Mrs Martin up to date on Dot's circumstances, the older lady sighed sadly. 'That poor girl. I can quite understand why you haven't told her your happy tidings yet. But while you worry it might be insensitive to share it with her while she's going through such a tough time – have you considered the fact that something so positive happening to one of her closest friends might be a welcome boost and a distraction?'

'Hmmm . . . maybe,' Viv replied. She still wasn't sure.

'Well, we will work it out. But in the meantime, I'm afraid I have another problem for you to deal with.'

Viv watched Mrs Martin quizzically as she shuffled out of the room. She hoped this wasn't going to be anything too taxing as she already felt a little overwhelmed. Mrs Martin returned a few minutes later clutching an envelope. As she handed it to Viv, she could see the writing was big and sprawling, like a child's.

'It's from one of Peggy's little sisters,' Mrs Martin explained as Viv pulled the letter out of the envelope. She remembered the bigger one – Lucy – writing to Peggy to voice her concerns over their mother's health and wondered what had been so important the girl had felt the need to inform Mrs Martin about it. She assumed the youngster had the address from writing to her sister here, and Peggy would undoubtedly have told her family all about her kind roommate.

'I haven't heard much from Peggy myself, and what she has written to me has been brief,' Mrs Martin explained. 'She didn't sound like herself. I was worried that she wasn't happy, but I put it down to being so busy. But now her sister has confirmed it and I just don't know what I can do to help.'

Viv felt sad as she read Lucy's short letter – she was asking if Mrs Martin could arrange for Peggy's friends to visit them in Petworth to cheer her sister up because she was struggling with being away from London.

'I hadn't realised she wasn't happy,' Viv said when she'd finished reading. 'I haven't heard much from her myself, but I just assumed she was busy. I'd asked a friend to check in on her and it sounded as if they were getting on well. He hasn't mentioned her being low, and he even passed me a note from her recently. She sounded happy then. I wonder what's gone wrong.' Viv felt terrible that Peggy was feeling so down and that she hadn't even realised.

'I don't know, dear. But I do know that Peggy's birthday is coming up. Maybe we can think of something to do to mark that and lift her spirits at the same time. It sounds as if Dot could do with a bit of a boost, too.'

Viv closed her eyes and thought for a moment. Then she suddenly snapped them open and looked at Mrs Martin with a big grin on her face.

'What? What is it, dear?' Mrs Martin asked excitedly, tapping her fingers on the table in anticipation. It was as if Viv's delight was contagious.

'I've got the perfect plan,' Viv announced confidently. 'And it's going to solve all our problems in one go. But I'm going to need your help to organise it.' Viv smiled to herself as Mrs Martin rushed back to the cooker to prepare a fresh pot of tea to aid them through putting together their plan of action. She couldn't wait to get started.

33

Peggy smacked her lips in delight as she wolfed down the chocolate cake Patricia had made for her birthday. Dr Brady and his wife had visited that morning to deliver the creation and wish Peggy a good day as well as checking her mother over. Mrs Miller had come on in leaps and bounds in the few weeks since her WI meeting disaster and had started coming downstairs to spend time with everybody – though she was strictly still under house arrest. To Peggy's relief, her mother hadn't let the swift recovery go to her head or developed ideas above her station again. She seemed to understand the need to continue taking things slowly despite the fact she was feeling fitter and healthier, and she appeared determined not to set herself back again by insisting she could do more than the doctor had signed off.

The Bradys had been their only visitors for Peggy's birthday so far, and she wasn't expecting anybody else. She was more than content to sit and eat cake with her mother, sisters and the evacuees who felt so like family now. She hadn't wanted a fuss for her birthday, and she was pleased that her wishes had been honoured. Peggy tried not to think about what she would be doing if she was in London today. As she looked around at everybody now, happily tucking into their cake, she felt bad for feeling such a pull back towards the city. But London was still suffering terribly at the hands of the Nazis, and she was desperate to do more to help.

The Germans had ramped up their assaults on other cities, now, and it just seemed like the horror of this war would never end. Birmingham had been hit three times in a matter of days, and Coventry had suffered a huge hammering around a week before. Peggy had caught something on the radio this morning about Bristol having been struck worse than ever the night before, but she had turned the news off when she'd heard the children coming down the stairs.

Christmas was only a month away now, and Peggy found herself wondering if her father and brothers would get any leave over the festive season. Her mother wouldn't be able to hide her poor health from them once they were back home. Maybe her father would come up with a way of getting Mrs Miller the support she needed to help look after the children while she recovered. Peggy had been tempted a few times over recent weeks to write to her father herself and tell him what was happening, but she had found that she wasn't able to go through with it. No matter how desperate Peggy was to get back to London, her mother and her sisters needed her, and she couldn't bring herself to betray her mother like that. When Mrs Miller suggested the final slice of cake should go to Patricia, Peggy agreed and wrapped it up ready for one of the children to deliver. But her mother insisted Peggy do it and threatened to go herself when she tried to protest. Grudgingly, Peggy put on her boots and wrapped up against the cold as best as she could, pulling on the jumper her mother had knitted her for her birthday before her thickest coat. She glanced at the vase of wild flowers on the side; the children had picked them for her this morning, but the thoughtful gift had only upset her because it reminded her of Johnny and how disappointed she had felt when he had visited last.

'Can I bring this broom in now?' Peggy shouted as she was stepping outside. She had noticed it next to the doorstep when she'd let Dr and Mrs Brady in that morning.

'No, no, no – leave that there!' her mother bellowed frantically.

Peggy rolled her eyes and shook her head before heading on her way. She was hoping to be back home within ten minutes, but when Patricia invited her inside, she felt as though she couldn't say no. Before she knew it, her mother's friend was making them cups of tea and rambling on about all sorts. It was unnerving, as Patricia wasn't normally very chatty. She was also surprised that Patricia was happy for her to leave her mother home alone with all the children for so long, though Peggy knew Phillip and Sarah would be keeping everybody in line. When Peggy finally got away, it was starting to get dark despite the fact it was only four o'clock in the afternoon. Peggy folded her arms against the cold and walked quickly, knowing she would need to go straight to the kitchen to start preparing dinner now she had been delayed. But when she walked up the path to the front door, she noticed that the house was in complete darkness. Anxiously, she hurried to the door and stepped inside, at which point the lights burst on, blinding her, and she was met with a sea of faces and a chorus of '*Surprise!*'

Once over the shock, Peggy looked round at everybody cheering and clapping, and her heart swelled. She didn't know who to go to first. There was Dot and Viv, and next to her a handsome man with scars on one side of his face who was holding a walking stick. She assumed he must be William by his likeness to Johnny and from her memory of Viv's photograph of the pilot. Despite the damage to his face, he still resembled his friend. Mrs Martin was there, too. And then Viv spotted Joan. *Joan!* She ran at full speed into her sister's open arms and spun her around as the room filled with chatter and laughter.

'I can't believe you're here!' Peggy cried after finally pulling away to take all of her in. Joan was slimmer than she'd been the last time they'd been together – but then so was everybody at the moment. But she looked strong. 'The land work has been good for you!' Peggy cried happily.

'Oh, Pegs, I love it. But I've missed you all terribly! And, of course I'm here – I couldn't miss your birthday!' Then Joan looked around at their mother, who had sidled up next to them. 'We need to discuss what we're going to do about this one,' Joan said conspiratorially. 'I already knew something was up from the tone of the letters the pair of you were sending me, so when Viv got in touch, I wasn't surprised to learn that Mother had been taken ill and you'd both been keeping it from me.' Peggy's face dropped. 'Don't worry – Mother's explained. I understand the reasoning, but you really should have let me decide. I'm not going to leave you to handle all this on your own anymore.'

Peggy smiled and breathed a sigh of relief. Then something occurred to her. 'Hang on, *Viv* wrote to you?' she asked.

'I certainly did,' her friend declared as she joined them. While Peggy listened to Viv's story of coming up with the idea with Mrs Martin and desperately writing to everybody, hoping the unreliable postal service would be kind to them, she noticed Johnny talking to William in the corner and looking over awkwardly. Her heart fluttered. What was he doing here? She'd been so cold to him all those weeks ago and had heard nothing from him since. Then it hit her – if Viv had organised this then of course she would have invited Johnny. And Peggy knew how difficult he found it to say no to Viv. She would have to tell her friend to give up on her matchmaking efforts.

Viv explained now how Mrs Martin had known where to send their letter for Joan because Peggy had mentioned where she was doing her land work so many times. They had invited her to meet them at the village hall that afternoon if the letter reached her in time. They had also written to Mrs Miller, who they'd instructed to leave a broom on the doorstep to signal that she had received their letter and that she was in on the plan. When they arrived and spotted the broom, they'd huddled together round the corner, shivering, until they'd spotted Peggy huffing out of the house. That's when they had hurried inside to set up.

'We knew we were risking the wrath of your mother by telling Joan about her health scare,' Viv added. Peggy noticed her friend giving her mother a cheeky sideways glance, which was met with a playful scowl, 'but Mrs Martin was prepared to take the blame.'

'And when I got my letter from Viv, I realised it was high time that I was honest with everybody,' Mrs Miller chimed in. 'It was wrong of me to burden you with all this and I'm sorry. When I read about Lucy's letter, it broke my heart.'

'Wait, *Lucy's* letter?' Peggy exclaimed.

Mrs Martin handed it to her, and she read it with tears in her eyes. 'She's becoming quite the scribe,' she remarked when she was finished.

Viv finished the story by explaining that Mrs Martin had managed to source them some fuel so that Viv could drive them across in Mr West's car. She had also promised to get hold of more to donate to the ambulance cars at Viv's station. Peggy was just wondering whether she should voice her concerns over her elderly friend's black-market dealings when her mother cut in.

'Joan wants to help, Peggy, and we'll get this figured out together,' she said.

Before Peggy had a chance to protest, William limped over.

'It's wonderful to finally meet you, William,' Peggy said happily. Though she'd accompanied Viv to the hospital along with Dot on that first visit after William's reappearance, the two of them had waited outside while Viv had reunited with him. 'I take it your surgery was a success?' she asked hopefully. 'I imagine you can't wait to get back to Café de Paris with Johnny,' she joked once he'd filled her in on his eye and his physio progress.

'Johnny? Heavens, no!' he replied, laughing.

'But, I thought—'

'Johnny's only ever been there with me a few times – and only because I dragged him there!' She noticed now how William was a lot better spoken than his pilot double, and he seemed to have the well-to-do air about him that Viv gave off effortlessly, even when she was in dirty overalls. 'I managed to get him there to meet Viv and then once or twice after that, but it's really not his scene!'

'Really?'

'Oh yeah. He'd much rather go to the flicks or hang out in a quiet corner of a quaint pub with a book, the boring so-and-so,' William replied, laughing. 'He might be part of the Millionaire's Mob, but he couldn't be further from the stereotype if he tried,' he added in a quieter voice. 'Some of them own their own planes, for goodness' sake, but we only ended up there because they were desperate for pilots, not because of money.'

Peggy's heart dropped and she looked over at Johnny. He didn't appear to be his usual cheeky self and she had a feeling that was her fault. Had she been wrong to judge him as she had done, and assume he would only be interested in glamorous women who came from wealth? Maybe he had been happy spending time with her and hadn't ever longed to be on a dance floor in the city instead. She shamefully recalled judging Viv for her love of the London high life the first time they had met, and she felt a pang of regret and sorrow. Once Peggy had taken the time to get to know Viv properly, she had realised that her first impressions of the glamorous ambulance driver had been wrong – Viv was as down to earth as herself. Why had she made such wild assumptions about Johnny? She should have known better, but she also realised that her insecurities triggered by her teenage experience had probably clouded her thoughts.

William started talking to Joan, and Viv pulled Peggy in close.

'What happened between you and Johnny?' Viv whispered. 'I know something's gone on because when I saw him after William's surgery, he was all smiles at the mention of your name. Then I bumped into him at the hospital again when I was telling William about the plans for today and I had to practically force him to come along. I think he only agreed in the end because William needed a lift to get here.'

But Peggy didn't get a chance to reply because William called Viv to the front of the room and tapped a spoon against a glass to silence everyone. Peggy groaned inwardly at the thought of having to give a thank-you speech or having them all sing happy birthday to her.

'We wanted to get you all together to celebrate Peggy's birthday and give our friend a bit of a boost,' Viv announced to nods of approval. Peggy cringed and felt her cheeks flush red. She felt a presence next to her and turned to see Dot smiling at her. Peggy hadn't even had a chance to say hello to her yet. Dot grabbed her hand and squeezed it while Viv continued. 'And we also thought it would be a great opportunity to share some good news with you all; I'm delighted to tell you that William and I are engaged!' There was a collective gasp of shock and then everybody started cheering and shouting.

'Did you know?' Peggy asked Dot, but she could see from her friend's face that she'd had no idea. Peggy peered across at Johnny, who looked just as surprised as everybody else. That explained why Viv had insisted on him coming even when he'd tried to protest. The only person who didn't seem fazed by the news was Mrs Martin. Peggy laughed to herself. Trust Mrs Martin to be embroiled in the plan.

'Tell us everything!' Dot cried as Viv bounded over and threw her arms around them both.

When she'd finished, Dot looked confused. 'But William's surgery was weeks ago,' she said. 'I can't believe you didn't tell me before.'

'I wanted to wait until I could tell you both together and, besides, the timing wasn't right, Dot – you were grieving. It didn't feel right to start celebrating my happy ending when you were going through that.'

'Grieving?' Peggy asked in a panic, wondering who had died since she'd last had an update from London.

'This is going to need a drink,' Viv declared, and she rushed off to get them all glasses of something strong while Dot started telling Peggy what had happened with Tommy and Stan. Peggy was startled. What a turn of events. She'd missed so much.

'I'm so sorry I couldn't be there to help you,' she whispered before taking a sip of the drink Viv had brought over and placed in her willing hand.

'You were needed here,' Dot replied, her voice full of understanding. 'And Bill and Viv have looked after me brilliantly, as well as Jilly.'

'Does Jilly know about the engagement?' Peggy asked.

'No,' Viv replied. 'I wanted her to come along today but she couldn't get away from the rest centre. Things are hectic. I'll tell her as soon as I'm back in London.'

'I'm so glad you got your happily ever after,' Peggy said, beaming at her friend. 'I knew you two were made for each other.'

'When are you going to get married?' Dot asked.

'Well, I have something to ask the two of you first,' Viv said excitedly. 'Will you be my bridesmaids? Along with Jilly, of course.' Peggy and Dot both cried out *yes* at the same time, and the three of them jumped up and down with big grins on their faces. 'As for the wedding, time is of the essence; we don't know where William will be posted now the Battle of Britain is over. The squadron could be going on the offensive, so we want to set a date as soon as possible.'

Peggy felt sick at the news, and she automatically searched out Johnny. Watching him playing games with her sisters, her heart ached. She'd been too overwhelmed by everything to realise until now, but, seeing him again had brought back to the surface all the feelings she'd tried to deny. Now she felt a deep fear of losing him. His job suddenly felt more dangerous, even though it had been very much so before. Peggy thought back to what William had said about Johnny and wondered if her assumption that he wasn't interested in somebody like her was correct. If he wasn't in the habit of hanging out with the rich set as she'd thought he was, then she might have made a big mistake in pushing him away. She realised it was probably the alcohol talking – Viv had topped up her glass at least twice while they'd all been catching up. But Peggy felt an urgent need to apologise to Johnny for being so brash with him and she was even building up the courage to tell him how she really felt. Surely, after all her agonising, it was time to put this to rest once and for all – whether she was humiliated or came out of it with a smile on her face. She might not get another chance and it wasn't like she was going to be bumping into him all the time. If Johnny rejected her then Peggy would just have to make it through the rest of this party, which would be easy enough with so many other people to talk to and more drink on hand. Then she would simply avoid him at the wedding. After that, she wouldn't have to worry about bumping into him again.

Suddenly full of confidence and feeling buoyed by Viv's story of speaking up about what she wanted from her relationship with William, Peggy gulped down the last of her drink and asked Viv to refill her glass. Then she walked over to Johnny with purpose.

'I'm sorry to have intruded on your party. Viv was insistent that I come, and you know what she can be like,' Johnny said awkwardly.

Peggy had been just about to talk but his words knocked the wind out of her sail. She found herself bristling at the thought of him being here when he didn't want to be – just like all the previous times he'd been here.

'Yes, yes, I do. She's very hard to say no to. But I guess you knew that seeing as she's forced you to spend so much time with me already.'

'No, Peggy – that's not what I meant.' He sighed and shook his head sadly. 'I knew that was what had upset you last time I was here. Goodness, I'm so foolish. I should have come back to explain when you weren't so busy, but you were so cold with me that day. I wondered if I'd done something else to offend you and I didn't want to make matters worse by turning up when you clearly didn't want me around.'

'I wanted you around,' she blurted, 'I was just conscious of the fact you were only here because Viv asked you to babysit me. I wanted you to be here because you liked me the same way I like you.' The words had come out of her mouth before she'd had a chance to censor them. She silently cursed the alcohol.

Johnny's face softened. 'I think I do like you the way you like me,' he replied gently. 'I thought I'd made it obvious, but I'm not the best at things like that.' Peggy's head was spinning. 'I did come and see you the first time because Viv asked me to check in on you. But I only agreed to do that because I'd been really taken by you when I met you at her apartment in London. Obviously, they were strange circumstances, so I jumped at the chance to get to see you again in a more relaxed setting. I was sad when I learned what had happened to your mother, but also secretly delighted that you were going to be so close to the base.' Peggy could feel herself blushing. She could also feel her mother and Joan's eyes boring into her, so she turned her body to the side slightly so they couldn't see her face. 'And then I just wanted to see more and more of you. I've loved spending time with you and getting to know you. I honestly have no idea what I did to make you doubt that.'

'It wasn't you,' she confessed. Peggy couldn't believe she was doing this, but Johnny had been honest with her after she had been so rude to him – the least she owed him was an explanation for her rotten behaviour. 'I convinced myself you wouldn't be interested in me because I'm not fancy or glamorous enough for you,' she admitted quietly as she played with her nails and stared at her hands.

Johnny spluttered. 'What on earth gave you that impression?' he exclaimed. 'Actually, it doesn't matter. All that matters is that I really like you, Peggy. That's all you need to know. And now you've told me that you like me, too, shall we just wipe the slate clean and start afresh?'

'Yes please!' Peggy exclaimed, smiling broadly, and trying to ignore the sound of her mother and Joan squealing excitedly from somewhere nearby. She wanted to join in with their squealing – she was desperate to, but she managed to contain herself. Peggy put her drink down on the side, deciding she would keep a clear head for the rest of the night so that she could replay this conversation in her head in bed later. She couldn't quite believe that after starting this birthday thinking it would be nothing to write home about, it had turned into one of her best ever – maybe *the* best ever. When she turned back towards him, Johnny leaned down and gently kissed her on the cheek. Her knees went weak, but the moment was spoiled by somebody tapping Peggy on the shoulder. She turned around and found Viv.

'I think you need to see this,' Viv said seriously.

Peggy's heart dropped. It was only right that something would go wrong to undo all the happiness she was feeling, she thought to herself as she left Johnny and followed Viv into the kitchen. But when she got to the doorway, Peggy watched in wonder as Mrs Martin gave her mother a full-blown lecture about how she needed to take better care of herself and accept the fact she needed looking after. If anybody else had spoken to Mrs Miller in this way, the woman would have given them a piece of her mind. But she was listening intently and nodding along to everything the older woman said to her. Joan was sitting at the table with them and when she spotted Viv and Peggy in the doorway, she got up discreetly and went to join them. Pulling Peggy gently into the hall, she whispered to her.

'This woman is amazing, and Mother seems to think she's the oracle when it comes to health. It's a shame we can't have somebody like her around to keep Mother in line, really. Honestly, I've never seen her so obedient. She wouldn't be sneaking out under *her* watch.' Joan sighed wistfully and turned to continue observing the two women. Peggy felt Viv perk up behind her. Then her friend was pushing past her and Joan to get into the kitchen. Mrs Miller and Mrs Martin stopped talking and looked up at Viv when she entered, and Viv leaned down to whisper in Mrs Martin's ear.

'Now, that's a wonderful idea, dear!' she exclaimed, clapping her hands together in delight. 'But we'll have to make sure I'm welcome,' she added carefully, eyeing Mrs Miller.

'I just wondered if you'd be interested in having Mrs Martin here to stay for a little while,' Viv offered cautiously. 'The two of you seem to get along just swell, and I know Mrs Martin is feeling lonely in London.'

'Plus, I'm rather good at keeping errant children in check,' the older lady added confidently. Peggy and Joan exchanged a look. They all knew it wasn't the children who needed keeping in line, but better to let their mother think that it was. Peggy felt nerves rushing through her body. If her mother agreed to this then she would be free to get back to London and her volunteer work, and Joan wouldn't have to take any time away from her land work.

'And Peggy would go back to London?' Mrs Miller asked.

'Well, we certainly wouldn't need her here,' Mrs Martin replied.

Peggy grabbed Joan's hand in anticipation.

'I think it's the perfect solution,' their mother said happily. She looked over at Peggy and smiled.

'Thank you,' Peggy whispered through tears. 'Thank you, Mrs Martin, for agreeing to look after everybody here so I can get back to doing my bit. Thank you, Mother, for agreeing. And thank you, Viv, for coming up with such a good idea – and for the party!'

'Speaking of which,' Viv declared with a glint in her eye, 'I've been trying to get you and Dot to Café de Paris for so long, but if I can't get you there then I will have to bring it to you!' She rushed into the living room and Peggy could hear her putting a record on. When they followed her in, she was already teaching the children and Dot to jitterbug while Johnny and William watched on in amusement. Viv waved them over and Joan and Mrs Martin happily joined in too.

'I'll look after Mother,' Peggy mouthed.

'I don't need—' her mother started, but Peggy gave her a look and she abruptly stopped. They stood next to William and Johnny, and Johnny put his arm around Peggy's shoulders.

'Are you not dancing?' she asked him, eyebrows raised quizzically.

'William here needs looking after,' he replied with a devilish grin. Peggy was delighted to see his cheekiness had returned, and she couldn't believe that he was more like her than she'd realised – using his friend as an excuse to get out of the dancing just as she was using her mother. Watching her friends and family dancing around and having so much fun together, stood next to the man she was falling for and who she now knew liked her, too, Peggy felt like the happiest woman alive. They'd all been through such dark days. She knew there were many more ahead, but she decided to put to the back of her mind the danger a good number of them were going to be facing once this gathering was over. For now, she would enjoy being with everybody, and feeling full of happiness and hope.

'You know, these two really would be fine here if we wanted to join in,' she suggested to Johnny playfully. He shushed her quietly and, with a glint in his eyes as he stared into her own, he leaned in for their first proper kiss.

Lyon's Teashop

I loved reading through this sample menu from a Lyon's teashop in 1942 and deciding what Viv, Dot and Peggy would have ordered.

I think I would have plumped for a hot apple turnover and a cup of tea!

Thank you to the author of the blog, Andy Gryce, for publishing it, along with a great deal of useful information about the chain.

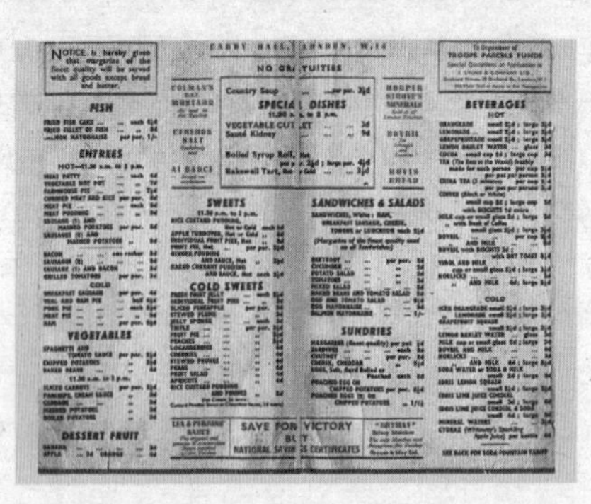

NOTICE is hereby given that margarine of the finest quality will be served with all goods except bread and butter.

NO GRATUITIES

FISH

ENTREES

COLD

VEGETABLES

DESSERT FRUIT

Country Soup

SPECIAL DISHES

VEGETABLE CUTLET

Sauté Kidney

Boiled Syrup Roll, Hot

Bakewell Tart, Hot or Cold

SWEETS

COLD SWEETS

SANDWICHES & SALADS

SUNDRIES

BEVERAGES

HOT

COLD

SAVE FOR VICTORY

BUY

NATIONAL SAVINGS CERTIFICATES

New Treatments for Burns Victims

I was keen to include mention of saline baths that McIndoe introduced for burns victims. It is said he devised the treatment plan after noting the faster healing rates of pilots who had landed in the sea.

While researching, I came across a photo of a patient reclined in a saline bath, reading a papcr, drinking warm milk and smoking a cigarette while nursing staff work busily around him. I love how relaxed the patient looked while being being treated for something so horrific.

You can find the photo here: https://historicengland.org.uk/images-books/photos/item/MED01/01/1338

SS City of Benares

I wanted to touch upon the tragedy of the torpedoed SS City of Benares after reading about it during my research. It was such a devastating loss, made even harder by the fact that there had been so many children on board fleeing to safety.

I found it incredible that forty-five passengers had survived for seven days at sea in a lifeboat, rationing hard biscuits, tinned food, and a small amount of fresh water each.

You can find a photo of the SS City of Benares and find out more about the tragedy here: https://www.bbc.co.uk/news/uk-england-merseyside-11332108

Passing the Time During an Air Raid

I was happy to discover that some enterprising soul created a card game called BLACK OUT! during the dark days of The Blitz.

So, I thought it would be fun to have Dot and her colleagues playing the game while they were on duty and waiting for air raids.

BLACK OUT! contained forty-six cards divided into six series of cards: Silhouettes, Black-Out Views, Black Out, Your Light's Showing, Black-Out Fashions and Searchlights.

The instructions on the box read: 'The amusing topical card game BLACK-OUT! The Game to cheer you up EVERYBODY'S PLAYING IT!'

You can find pictures of all the playing cards here: https://www.iwm.org.uk/collections/item/object/30084189

Balham Tube Station

I was shocked when I learned about the Balham Tube Station disaster.

The horror of what happened that night was brought home when I saw photos of the tunnels at the station filled with rubble and debris.

Whenever I read about other incidents in London, my mind kept going back to the people trapped in those tunnels; people who had gone down there to keep safe.

The photo of the bus sticking out of the bomb crater took my breath away, and my mind also kept wandering back to that, so I wanted to share it with you.

Acknowledgements

It's always tricky to know where to start with this bit – I often find it harder to write than the book! But I feel like a good place to begin is with you, the reader. So, thank you reader, for buying/borrowing/downloading my book. I really hope you enjoyed it.

Thank you to my wonderful agent, Kate Burke at Blake Friedmann, and to all the team at the agency.

Also, huge thanks must go to everybody at Hodder & Stoughton, but especially Olivia Barber, Amy Batley, Jo Dickinson and Cara Chimirri. With a special thanks to Kay Gale for her beady eye on the copyedit.

I'd also like to once again express gratitude to Naomi Clifford and Frances Faviell. Just like when I was writing *The Blitz Girls*, their books: *Under Fire and A Chelsea Concerto* provided invaluable insights into life for women volunteers in London during World War 2. I also relied heavily upon Chris McNab's *The Blitz Operations Manual*, so heartfelt thanks to him, too.

Love and thanks always to my supportive husband, Mark, and to our daughters Emma and Georgia. Also, to our dog Boris – walks with you always ease my writer's block.

I also owe a great deal to the readers who spread the word about my books and those who champion me on social media (you know who you are), as well as anybody who leaves a review anywhere. Those reviews mean the world to me, and they are so important to authors – so I thank you all from the bottom of my heart for taking the time to support me in such a valuable way.

And, finally, to Eileen/Aunty Lee; this one was always going to be for you, but I took for granted that you would be here to see it. You were meant to outlive us all! Thank you for stopping people in supermarkets to tell them about my books. I'll see you in another place.